Christmas
for the
Halfpenny
Orphans

CATHY SHARP

HARPER

Harper
An imprint of HarperCollins*Publishers*
The News Building,
1 London Bridge Street,
London SE1 9GF

A Paperback Original 2016

1

www.harpercollins.co.uk

A catalogue record for this book
is available from the British Library

ISBN: 978-0-00-811850-1

Typeset in Sabon LT Std by Palimpsest Book Production Ltd,
Falkirk, Stirlingshire

Printed and bound in Great Britain by
Clays Ltd, St Ives plc

MIX

Paper from

For my husband with love.
You make it possible!

ONE

'Wait until I catch you, you little bitch!' The man's voice struck terror into the hearts of the two small girls hiding under the stairs. 'I'll tan your hide, Sarah, you see if I don't.'

Samantha squeezed her twin sister's hand reassuringly but didn't say a word; Pa had sharp ears and even the slightest sound might give their whereabouts away. She hardly dared breathe as she heard the sounds of doors being opened and slammed shut as their father searched for them. Tears were trickling silently down Sarah's face when Samantha touched her cheek. Both of them knew that if Pa found them they would be beaten, but Sarah would bear the brunt of it, because Pa hated her. He blamed her for causing their mother's death, as she'd been born last and it had taken so long that Ma had been exhausted and died soon after.

Neither of the girls had known their mother, but Pa said she was a saint and, when drunk, accused Sarah of murdering her. Samantha had come quickly and the parents had been gazing fondly on their daughter when Jenni May was gripped with terrible pain once more and this time it had gone on for hours, ending with Sarah's birth and Jenni lying in an exhausted fever from which she never recovered.

When the girls were younger, a woman had come in every day to take care of them and to cook Pa's meals. She was a pretty woman, sharp when addressing the twins, especially Sarah, and quick with her hand, but whenever their father was around she was all sweetness and light, and he was taken in by her every word. When she said Sarah was awkward, stubborn and rebellious, Pa agreed that she must be kept in check, but he left the chastising to Melanie.

Although he had drinking bouts every so often, he'd been content enough whilst Melanie looked after the house and everyone had expected they would marry one day, but the previous year, a few days before the twins' tenth birthday, there had been a fierce quarrel and Melanie had left them, vowing never to return and swearing that Ernie May was an impossible man. She said he'd taken advantage of her good nature and she wouldn't put up with it a minute longer – declaring that only she would have had the patience to take care of brats like his, and that she would have no more of it. After that, Pa's temper had grown worse and worse and he'd taken against his daughters, particularly Sarah. It was Sarah who had caused all his troubles, because she had killed her sainted mother. He wished she'd died at birth and wanted only to be free of his responsibility towards the twins.

Samantha knew all this, because Aunt Jane had told her when she visited a week previously. Their aunt was a tall thin woman with a sharp face and a hard mouth, though her eyes sometimes told of something more inside her, something she kept a tight rein on. Samantha had asked her why Pa hated them so, and her aunt told her in a harsh voice that felt to Samantha like the lash of a whip. Sarah had merely stared at Aunt Jane, taking very little in as always. It wasn't that she didn't understand anything, as Pa and Aunt Jane thought, but she was slow at putting things together in her mind and she couldn't form the words properly unless Samantha told her how.

'You should have been an only child,' Aunt Jane had told Samantha. 'The other one caused all the trouble by killing your mother. My brother adored his wife and they longed for a child, even though Jenni was always fragile. The doctors told her she ought not to have children, because of her weak heart, but she wouldn't listen – and Ernie could refuse her nothing. All would have been well had that idiot not taken so long to come and killed poor Jenni.'

'But that wasn't Sarah's fault,' Samantha said, feeling protective of her sister. 'Mummy wouldn't have blamed her.' In Samantha's mind her mother was a beautiful angel, and sometimes when Sarah was weeping and Samantha was hurting with her twin's pain, she'd felt the presence of someone warm and loving and believed it was her mummy. Sometimes, she felt that their mother was close by, caressing them, and she thought Sarah sensed it too.

'Jenni was as soft as butter over kids and I dare say she'd have loved her,' Aunt Jane said, a bitter twist to her mouth, 'but she's gone and Ernie has never been the same since. He drinks because he can't bear it that she's gone and he hates Sarah.'

'It isn't fair,' Samantha said. 'Sarah doesn't mean to break things but she's clumsy and it just happens . . .'

'Well, I've told you why your pa drinks and I've made my offer,' Aunt Jane said in her blunt manner. 'Your pa doesn't want either of you and he's made up his mind to go away to work at sea – and that means you'll be on your own. I'll take you in, Samantha, and gladly – but I won't have her. She should be in a proper home where they take care of girls like that . . . I could ask at St Saviour's. I hear Sister Beatrice is a good woman, even though she's a nun and I can't abide them as a rule . . .'

Samantha had looked at her beautiful sister and wondered how her aunt could speak so coldly of her beloved twin, who was so innocent and lovely. Her soft fair hair framed perfect features and her wide blue eyes were soft, slightly vacant and dreamy, but her smile was like sunshine, the light coming from her sometimes so bright that it made her twin blink with its radiance. Samantha knew that although twins, they weren't exactly alike; her hair was a darker blonde, her eyes more grey than blue, and they could clash with storm clouds when she was angry – or that's what Melanie had told her when Samantha flew into a temper to protect her sister.

Why did her aunt want to put Sarah in a home? It wrenched at Samantha's heart to think of being separated from the twin she loved and she vowed that she would do anything to keep them together, but she wouldn't tell her aunt that; she'd only get angry and tell her she was a fool.

'There's nothing wrong with Sarah, except that she's

slow sometimes,' Samantha said, facing up to her aunt. 'I'm nearly eleven now. I've been helping Sarah to wash and dress, and making supper and breakfast for us all since Melanie left – and I can look after us both. I shan't go anywhere that Sarah isn't welcome.'

'Suit yourself then,' her aunt said, pulling on neat grey gloves. She was dressed all in grey without a touch of colour, and Samantha knew her house was dull and dark, much like her. If she'd gone there without Sarah there would be no sunshine left in her world. She loved Sarah with all her heart and she was never going to abandon her, no matter what anyone said. 'The offer is there, but I shan't run after you – and I won't take her. The best place for her is a mental asylum . . .'

Samantha hadn't answered her – she was too upset and angry. Why could no one see that her twin was the dearest, sweetest girl ever? Willing and obedient, she did everything Samantha told her and she never screamed defiance or did anything naughty – and it certainly wasn't her fault that she'd broken Pa's favourite pipe.

Despite his unkindness and careless brutality, Sarah adored her father and she often picked up his slippers or a discarded jacket, nursing the object in her arms and crooning a song that no one else understood. Samantha had tried to make out the words but, although tuneful and pretty, the song's meaning was unclear.

Earlier that evening, while Samantha prepared Pa's tea so it would be ready for him when he came home, Sarah had helped by laying the table in the big kitchen, as she'd been shown. When Samantha came through from the back scullery with a pot of hot potatoes, she'd seen that her twin had taken down Pa's pipe rack from the shelf and was stroking one of the pipes. Samantha had immediately been anxious, because the delicate long-handled clay pipe was one of Pa's favourites.

'Put that down, Sarah, and help me with the dishes,' she said.

The sound of her voice had jerked Sarah out of the dream she'd been in, her fingers snapping the long thin stem of the pipe.

'Oh, Sarah,' she cried, distressed, knowing what it would mean. 'What have you done?'

Sarah had dissolved into tears and before either of them realised it, Pa had come in and was staring at the broken pipe.

'You little devil!' he said and lunged at Sarah, swiping her across the face with his fist. He was a big man and strong; the force of the blow knocked the fragile girl off her feet and sent her crashing into the oak dresser, causing a china teapot to tumble from the shelf and break into pieces on the floor. 'Now what have you done? Child of Satan, that's what you are!' Pa roared at her. 'That belonged to your sainted mother. I'll kill you. I've had enough of your wickedness—'

Sarah stared at him in horror and then ran from the room before he could hit her again.

'Pa, she didn't mean to do it!' Samantha said, throwing herself between them. She was still holding the pot of hot potatoes and when Pa caught hold of her, he burned his hand on the pot. 'It was an accident . . . Oh, Pa, I'm sorry . . . I didn't mean to burn you.'

Pa thrust her away but instead of going after Sarah, he picked up his jacket and went out of the kitchen, pausing at the door to glance back at Samantha. 'If I find you still here when I get back, I'll kill the pair of you,' he threatened before storming out.

Samantha had placed the cooking pot on the floor near the range to keep warm and then gone in search of her sister. She'd found her under the bed in their room and it had taken several minutes to coax her out.

'Sarah didn't mean to . . .' she sobbed in Samantha's arms. 'Pa's cross with Sarah?'

'Yes, Pa is cross,' Samantha said and hugged her. 'But he'll go down the pub and have a few drinks and forget about it. Come to the kitchen and have some supper. We'll put Pa's in the range to keep warm for him.'

It had taken Samantha ages to bring her sister downstairs and even then she ate only a few mouthfuls of the food. Sarah had left her sitting on the lumpy sofa in the kitchen while she washed the pots in the scullery. After the kitchen was tidy she took her sister upstairs and put her to bed. Pa had threatened things before when he was angry, but then he would get over it and perhaps bring them a packet of chips home for their tea the next day.

Only this time he hadn't got over his temper.

Samantha had woken to the sound of her twin's screams, something she'd heard so seldom that she knew Sarah must be terrified. As her eyes accustomed themselves to the light, which came from a lamp in the hall, she saw Sarah lying on the floor and Pa standing over her, kicking her as if she were a piece of filth he'd found in the gutter, his savagery beyond anything Samantha had ever seen.

Without stopping to think, Samantha seized the chamber pot and flung the contents over her father.

Some of the wee went into his face and must have stung his eyes for he was temporarily blinded and screamed out in a mixture of pain and frustration.

'You hellcat, you've blinded me!' he cried, stumbling towards her, his hands flailing to grab hold of her.

Samantha pulled her twin to her feet and propelled her along the landing and down the stairs, seeking refuge in the large cupboard under the stairs. She pushed Sarah right to the end and crawled after her, shoving some empty cardboard boxes in front of them in an effort to conceal their whereabouts if Pa looked inside.

'I know you're in here,' Pa's voice was suddenly very close and the stair cupboard door was jerked open, the light from his torch waving about. It touched on Sarah's face but she must have been hidden from him as seconds later, he swore and slammed the door shut again. 'I'm not coming back – do you hear?' his tone was loud, penetrating the door and reaching Samantha. She trembled as he went on, 'You can starve before I come back, do you understand me? You're to go to your aunt, Samantha – and that Child of Satan can go to the devil for all I care . . .'

Samantha held her breath as the minutes ticked by. The noise had died down and the house was quiet. Pa must have gone to sleep by now, surely. Yet she dared not risk coming out until he'd left for work. Putting her arms around Sarah, she held her close as they both shivered in their nightclothes. Only when the house had been silent for what seemed like hours did Samantha risk venturing into the hall in search of a coat to keep them warm.

It was very dark and she had to feel her way along the

8

walls, frightened of making a noise and bringing Pa down on them again, but the house seemed unnaturally quiet. She took her own coat and Sarah's from the old wooden hallstand and carried them into the cupboard. At least they were safe here and perhaps when Pa came back tomorrow, he would be sorry for his show of temper. He was always worse when he'd been drinking and Samantha couldn't believe he'd really meant to kill either of them.

In the morning the girls were stiff, cold and hungry when they crept out. The black marble clock on the kitchen mantle said it was past six o'clock. Pa went to work at six every morning so unless he'd overslept he must have gone, though Samantha had been awake ages and she'd heard nothing. The range hadn't been made up and it was cold in the kitchen, but the one in the scullery was still warm. Samantha stoked it up and added the coal and the wood her father had bought in the previous day.

She was hungry and looked in the pantry, but discovered that the half loaf of bread left from their meal the previous day was missing, as were the cold sausages and the cheese that had been on the pantry shelves. Pa must have taken them for his dinner at work. All Samantha could find was some stale cake she'd made earlier that week; there was enough to cut each of them a slice and, she discovered, there was sufficient tea left to make a brew, though only a drop of milk and no sugar.

It would be weak tea but it would warm them through a bit, she thought, as she carried the meagre breakfast through to the kitchen. Sarah was staring at the kitchen shelf, a look of dismay on her face.

'Pa's pipes gone,' she said. Her gaze travelled round the kitchen, the look of fear and puzzlement growing. 'Tankard and coat gone . . . Pa gone . . .'

'No!' Samantha cried as the fear struck her too. 'He couldn't have gone . . . He's coming back; he must be . . .'

Looking around the room, she saw that the few treasures that had stood on the dresser shelves, like their mother's tea caddy and a pair of silver berry spoons, had gone. All that was left was an assortment of china that didn't match and a brass tin, where pins and bits were stored.

She put down the tray she'd been carrying and ran from the kitchen and up the stairs, flinging open the door of her father's room. He wouldn't have deserted them . . . surely he wouldn't. Pa wasn't really a bad man; it was only that he missed their mother and got drunk sometimes.

As soon as she looked round the room, Samantha knew that it was true. Her father had few possessions he treasured and only a couple of extra shirts and his best suit, which he wore only for funerals or weddings. The cupboard had been left open, as if he'd torn everything from its place in a hurry, and his brushes and shaving things had also gone from the washstand.

The truth hit Samantha like a drenching of cold water. Their father had abandoned them, as Aunt Jane had said he would. He might have told Samantha of his plans had Sarah not broken his favourite pipe, but instead he'd gone down the pub to get roaring drunk and then he'd tried to kill Sarah.

Yes, he really had meant to do it, perhaps because

he knew Aunt Jane wouldn't take her. Perhaps he'd thought it better for everyone if Sarah were dead?

Samantha couldn't believe what her thoughts were telling her. No, Pa wouldn't do this, he wouldn't attack his daughter and then go off leaving them both to starve . . . But he had. She sat down on the bed, feeling empty, drained. What was she going to do now?

Samantha knew there was no money in the house. Her father never gave her a penny. He paid the rent and brought home the supplies they needed – and he'd taken everything they had of value. She looked about the room, knowing that the contents wouldn't fetch more than a few pence from the rag-and-bone man. There were still a few things in the scullery and kitchen, things that had belonged to their mother. Sarah had broken the best china pot, but there might be some copper pans and a few silver spoons in the drawer. She would have to go through every room and take whatever items she could find to the scrapyard later. Samantha was frightened of Alf, the man who ran the scrapyard, but she couldn't think of any other way to get money to buy food. After that, she wasn't sure what to do. She knew they wouldn't be able to stay here: the rent was due on Saturday and Pa wouldn't be around to pay it.

Samantha ran her hands over her sides, her body aching in the same places that her father's blows had rained down on her twin. She didn't know why she always felt her sister's pain, she just did. That realisation brought her out of her shock and she got up off the bed, knowing she had to go downstairs and see what she could do to help. Poor Sarah must be hurting all over – she already bore the scars of more than one

11

beating and last night's attack had been the most vicious of them all.

What people didn't understand was that Samantha and her twin lived for each other. Each felt the other's pain and sorrow as if it were her own. That was why Samantha couldn't do as her father ordered and go to Aunt Jane. She'd made it clear she would send Sarah to a place where Samantha knew she would be unhappy. They would never see each other – and that would break both their hearts.

When Samantha walked into the kitchen she found Sarah nursing the clay pipe she'd broken the previous evening, which Pa hadn't bothered to pick up from the floor. Tears were trickling down her cheeks and Samantha knew that her twin understood Pa had gone, even if she couldn't grasp what that meant for the two of them. They were all alone in the world now, with no one to turn to, no one who would take them both in.

Well, there was nothing else for it: they would just have to look after each other. As soon as she'd got her sister fed and dressed, Samantha would go to the scrapyard and sell everything of value, and then she would set about finding somewhere they could stay. There were plenty of houses that were standing empty after having been bombed-out in the war. Tramps and homeless people slept in them, and so could she and Sarah – just for a while, just until she could decide what to do . . .

'Put that pipe in your pocket and come and eat your cake,' she said, wrapping an arm around her sister. 'We'll be all right, Sarah love. I'll take care of you now.'

Sarah's smile was loving and trusting as she looked at her. 'Samantha take care of me,' she repeated, and sat down at the table to eat her cake and drink the tea that was now cold.

TWO

'Well, here's to you, Sally,' Angela Morton lifted her wineglass to the young woman who had been such a friend to her at St Saviour's and was now leaving her job to take up her training to become a nurse. 'I'm sure we all wish you the very best in your new life – and you must promise you will come and see us when you can.'

'Yes, of course I shall,' Sally promised. Angela noticed the girl's blush as everyone drank the toast and then crowded round her, friends hugging and kissing her and telling her how much she would be missed.

It was true that the young carer would be missed, as much by Angela as any of them, but she knew in her heart it was for the best. To stay on at the children's home would have brought back too many memories of the man who had filled the children's ward with laughter when he visited the hospital as a volunteer, the man Sally had hoped to marry until he lost his life in a car accident.

Hearing the phone shrilling, Angela left the staff room where the small party was taking place and ran upstairs

14

to answer it in Sister's office. It stopped as she reached it and she frowned, wondering if it had been business or perhaps Mark Adderbury . . . but he would more likely have used the extension in her office had he wanted to speak to her.

A sigh left her lips. It had been a while since Mark had bothered to get in touch, though he'd continued to call in at the home occasionally in a professional capacity. He still nodded and spoke in passing, but his special smile had been conspicuous by its absence. Angela had always thought of Mark as one of her closest friends; when she'd been overwhelmed by grief after her husband of a few months was killed in the war, Mark had been the one who helped her get through it. For a while she'd believed their friendship might develop into something more – but that was before Staff Nurse Carole Clarke came on the scene.

Eager to ensnare a rich husband, the attractive young nurse had made a play for Mark. He'd been flattered at first and they'd gone on a couple of dates, but when he tried to break up with her she told him she was pregnant. Mark had done the honourable thing and proposed. Although she thought he was making a terrible mistake, Angela had felt it wasn't her place to intervene. But when she caught Carole tampering with records in an effort to discredit Sister Beatrice, and found out that she had lied about being pregnant, Angela had no choice but to get involved. Appalled by his fiancée's duplicity, Mark had ended their engagement. Carole had stormed out, saving Sister Beatrice the trouble of dismissing her, but her departure hadn't healed the rift that had opened between Angela and Mark. If anything, he was more distant. It was as though his initial shock over his former fiancée's behaviour had turned to embarrassment and now he couldn't bear to face Angela.

In the staff room, Sally's colleagues were still saying their farewells, but Angela was in no mood to return to the party. Instead she carried on down the stairs, meeting Sister as she reached the hall below.

'Ah, Angela,' Sister Beatrice said. 'I was just on my way up to see you. I've been speaking to Constable Sallis. It appears they've found a couple of young girls in an abandoned house. They're in a weakened state apparently. He asked if we would take them in while inquiries are made. Naturally, I said yes.'

'Poor darlings,' Angela said. 'How old are they?'

'He was rather vague,' the nun said and shook her head. 'He thinks about eleven, but he isn't sure about the younger one.'

'Ah, well, I'm sure we can fit them in somewhere in the new wing. We have so much more room now that we're able to move in there.'

'Yes, thank goodness. Mark Adderbury telephoned me earlier. He suggested we have a small party here for the staff to celebrate the opening of the new wing. He thinks it would be a good idea to ask the Bishop to open it for us. Naturally, I agreed, though I do not particularly see the need myself . . .' She waved her hand in dismissal. 'But if the Board think we should . . .'

Angela noticed the faint sigh. Sister Beatrice was looking pale and tired. A few months previously she had been attacked by an unfortunate and disturbed boy named Terry and though it didn't seem possible that she would still be affected by a minor injury, it was clear she was no longer the forthright and energetic Sister Beatrice of old.

'Is anything the matter, Sister? Are you quite well?'

'Why do you ask? I'm perfectly all right. What nonsense.' Sister Beatrice walked off; evidently annoyed that Angela should express concern. She prided herself that she was never ill and routinely shrugged off colds that would send lesser mortals to their beds. Angela shook her head and made her way to the kitchens.

The cook, Muriel, was complaining to Nan, who was trying to placate her but without much success. 'How I'm supposed to manage with that wretched girl late again I don't know,' Muriel said. 'She was away two days last week – and she knows there's a mountain of work to do today if I'm to bake as well as make jam from those lovely plums and apples we've been given. I can make a pudding with some of them, but most of the plums are too ripe for eating.'

'I expect that's why they gave us such a lot,' Nan said.

The comment made Angela smile. As head carer, Nan had no idea how much badgering went on behind the scenes to keep St Saviour's kitchens supplied. Angela thought the stallholders at Spitalfields' wholesale fruit market must be sick of the sight of her, but she'd asked them not to throw their surplus out if it was still useable.

'It might be too ripe for you to sell on, Bert,' she'd told her favourite wholesaler the previous morning. 'But we can always use it for jams and puddings.'

'Anythin' for you, me darlin',' Bert had said, making her an extravagant bow and kissing her hand. He was

17

in his sixties if he was a day, but handsome, with strong grey hair and harsh features that belied his soft heart. 'I'll scrounge some boxes of fruit for your orphans, love, don't you worry.'

In the months since she'd come to the East End of London as the Administrator for St Saviour's, she'd learned to love the warm-hearted men who worked the fruit and vegetable wholesale market. They'd made several generous donations of fruit and vegetables, and she wasn't going to allow their generosity to go to waste, despite a girl being late for work.

'I'm sure Nancy will give you a hand with the fruit, Muriel, and you know how the children love your jam.' Angela smiled at her. 'I'll have a word with Kelly when she comes in, if you like – perhaps I can find out why she is late so often.'

'We're so short-handed these days. I really miss that Alice Cobb; she was always ready to help out in an emergency,' Muriel sighed as she chopped and peeled.

'Alice stayed on as long as she could after she married that nice young soldier, but she's a mother now and it's too soon for her to come back to work,' Angela reminded her.

'She had her baby in June, and a lovely little thing she is too. Alice has been talking about coming in for a few hours when she's ready.' Nan saw Alice often, now that she'd taken the girl under her wing, and kept them up to date with her news.

'If you need any help with washing up, I could give you a hand,' Angela offered. 'And I'll take the trays up to the nurses if you like.'

'Nurse Wendy usually comes down for hers at about

ten . . .' Muriel glanced at the clock. 'I've got the washing up from breakfast, and then I'll need a hand if I'm going to get my baking done and that wretched jam – so if you could possibly ask Nancy to come down, please, Angela.'

'I'll give you a hand with the washing up,' Nan said. 'I've got linen to change today, but Jean will manage without me for a while. I shall miss Sally though.'

'Yes, we'll all miss her, but you have Tilly Tegg to take her place, and she seems very willing,' Angela said. 'Yes, you do need to get your preserves done, Muriel; it will soon be time to think about Christmas again . . .'

'Don't talk about that yet,' Muriel begged. 'I'll soon have to start thinking about making cakes and puddings for Christmas. Thank goodness we've got some dried fruit on the shelves this year. Three years ago I had to make them with carrots and prunes to bulk the mixture out and they didn't taste the same.'

'Well it's still only September,' Angela said. 'So there's time yet. I'll make a tray of tea and take it up for myself, if you don't mind.'

'No, certainly not, you get on and do what you want,' Muriel said, making Angela smile as she remembered how fussy Muriel had been when she first arrived at St Saviour's.

Angela left the kitchen with her tray and met Nancy in the hall. Terry's sister had settled well into her new role at St Saviour's, even though Angela knew she worried about her young brother in the special clinic Mark Adderbury had found for him. Terry was better than he had been, but still not mentally stable enough to be allowed out yet.

Nancy willingly agreed to help with the jam making,

and went into the kitchen. Angela pressed for the lift to come down from the next floor. She was lost in thought as it whirred up to her office floor. As she got out and walked past the sick and isolation wards, she saw Mark come out. He stopped, smiled hesitantly as he saw her, and then took the tray from her. Angela went on ahead and opened her office door. Mark brought the tray in and deposited it on her desk. She offered him some tea, but he shook his head.

'Mustn't stop long,' he said. 'I was thinking I should telephone or come and see you, soon. How are you, Angela?'

'Very well, Mark – but how are you? I haven't seen you to talk properly since . . . oh, after the concert we had at Easter. I understand you were away at a conference over the summer?'

'Yes, amongst other things. I always seem to be in a hurry these days.'

'Well, it's nice to see you . . .'

'Actually, the concert was one of the things I wanted to talk to you about, Angela. Everyone was so pleased with that, and it raised much more than the price of the tickets in donations. I was thinking perhaps we might have a Christmas concert this year . . .'

'How funny, so was I!' Angela said, a laugh escaping her. 'I know it's too early to be thinking of it yet. Muriel was quite alarmed when I mentioned Christmas – she's having staff problems.'

'I expect you have plenty of them here.'

'It isn't easy to find reliable staff. And now we've lost one of our best girls – Sally Rush is leaving to take up nursing.'

'How is she these days?' Mark said frowning. 'It was a terrible shock losing Andrew Markham that way . . . he was a brilliant man, both as a surgeon and with those marvellous books of his.'

'Yes, the children still love them. Nancy told me that some of them ask her why there are no new books.'

'Nancy seems to be doing well here.'

'She's learning a lot, assisting Muriel and helping with the younger children, but naturally she can't forget poor Terry and what happened. She visits her brother occasionally, but . . .'

'Terry's breakdown was traumatic for everyone.' Mark seemed intent as he looked at her. 'And you, Angela? I never seem to find you around these days. You work terribly long hours. You should make time for some fun.'

'Well, I do, when I can,' Angela said, 'but I have other charity work nowadays – meetings I go to in the evenings. I'm only working here this evening because I have to finish a report on—'

'Not too busy to go for a drink later, I hope?' He looked at her and Angela was unsure what she could see in his eyes. 'We really ought to talk . . .'

'Oh . . .' Angela hesitated and then inclined her head. 'I should be finished by eight – if you want to meet somewhere?'

'I'll pick you up then and we'll have supper at that pub by the river – we went there once before, if you remember?'

'Yes, thank you,' she agreed. 'I shall be ready by eight and I'll come down to the hall. It will be nice spending time with you again, Mark.'

21

'Yes, I've missed our time together,' he said. 'I'll look forward to this evening.'

'Yes, me too,' she said, giving him a smile as she watched him leave. It was time she started work on that report, yet she lingered for a moment, thinking about Mark and the way he'd always been there for her until Carole came between them.

As she put a sheet of paper into her typewriter, Angela's thoughts turned to Kelly, the girl Muriel had complained about so bitterly. She was a pretty dark-haired girl and bright, always friendly when Angela saw her – so why was she proving so very unreliable?

'Oh, Mammy,' Kelly Mason said, looking at her mother as she sat slumped in her wooden rocking chair by the kitchen fire. The kitchen looked as if a bomb had hit it, and needed a really good clean. 'Why didn't you tell me if you were feeling ill again? I would have done all this last night. I can't stop now or I'll be late again and Nan . . . I mean Mrs Burrows, told me that she will have to let me go if I keep having time off.'

'You get off then, my love,' her mother sighed. 'Make me a cup of tea first and then I'll get up and see to the bairns.'

Kelly saw the weariness in her mother's face and sighed inwardly, knowing that she couldn't desert her mother when she was like this; getting the younger children ready for school would be too much for her. When Mammy started to tremble and took her tea with unsteady hands, Kelly knew there was nothing she could do but stay for another hour or so to see to the children before she left for her work at St Saviour's.

Running upstairs to pull her siblings from their beds, Kelly was thinking about her job at the children's home. She loved working there, even though she was only employed in the kitchens as a skivvy, washing up, scrubbing and helping Cook by peeling mounds of potatoes and chopping cabbage or scraping carrots. Sometimes, Kelly thought she would throw up if she saw another carrot covered in mud, because they had to be scrubbed under the tap in the scullery before she could peel them; she hated the ones with wormholes, especially if there was still something inside, and Cook was so fussy about her food. If she found one speck of dirt in the cabbage she made Kelly's life a misery.

Her sister and brothers squealed as she yanked the covers off them and then physically ejected them from bed; they were lazy devils and did little or nothing to help Mammy, even though Cate was old enough at nine to help with the simple chores.

'Get up and wash now,' Kelly said crossly, 'or you'll get no breakfast. I've got to get to work and I can't wait about for you. Mammy isn't well this morning so you can do the washing up before you go to school.'

'There's no school today 'cos there's a hole in the roof and we wus told not to go in,' her brother Michael complained bitterly. 'I ain't goin' ter get up yet, our Kelly. You're mean to get on at us like you do.'

'Well, you may have a day off but I don't,' Kelly said. 'I'm not telling you again. There'll be toast and dripping and a cup of milk for you downstairs. I'm leaving as soon as I've washed up the supper things – and if I find Mammy worse tonight because you didn't help her, Cate, you'll feel the back of my hand.'

'I'll help Mammy,' Robbie said. He was only five but more serious than the others and she knew he tried but he couldn't do much other than set the table or fetch things from the shop.

'Thank you, Robbie love,' Kelly said. 'Make the others help her too and make sure she doesn't do too much. I've got to hurry or I might lose my job.' She didn't earn much but even a few shillings extra helped to pay the rent and make sure there was coal for the fire.

She took Bethy from her cot and into the bathroom, washing her face and changing her nappy. Bethy was nearly three and still in nappies; it seemed she wouldn't learn to use the potty or perhaps Mammy was too tired to train her into it as she had the others. She'd never really been well since the birth of her youngest child.

Kelly ran back downstairs, knowing that her younger sister would get up even if Michael did not. In the kitchen she settled Bethy in her high chair with a piece of bread and strawberry jam; toast was too hard for the little girl and she liked to suck on her bread until it was soft and she could swallow it without having to chew. Kelly wasn't sure if the child was backward or simply lazy, like most of her family seemed to be. She herself seemed to take after her Irish grandmother who had brought up a family of twelve and never stopped working until she dropped down dead in her mid-fifties of a heart attack.

Almost an hour later, Kelly had fed the baby, brought a semblance of order to the kitchen and abandoned her brothers and sister to their quarrel over who should do what, as she grabbed her shabby coat and left the house. She saw a bus coming that would take her close to

Halfpenny Street and ran to catch it, sighing with relief as the cheery conductor collected her fare. At least she was on her way to work and perhaps Nan would let her off as she was only a bit late . . .

THREE

Angela popped out at lunchtime to pick up some shopping, taking it back to her flat before returning to Halfpenny Street. In the heart of Spitalfields, the street was typical of others in the neighbourhood with its rundown houses and shabby commercial properties. St Saviour's had started life as a grand Georgian house with gardens at the rear and three floors plus attics above, but it had long ago lost its air of grandeur. People of all nationalities lived and worked in the surrounding streets, which had once formed part of the prosperous silk district, populated first by émigré Huguenots. In later years many Jewish syna-gogues and businesses had taken the silk merchants' place, and they in turn had moved on as a variety of new, much poorer inhabitants flooded in. Even on a lovely September day, the street looked grimy and most of the buildings were dilapidated, but what had for a time been the old fever hospital was now a place of hope for the children who lived there. The window frames and doors had recently been painted and it looked more cheerful now that the attic windows were no longer boarded up, the roof space having been turned into two large offices.

On her return, Angela met Staff Nurse Michelle coming downstairs with a tray of dirty cups and plates as she entered the hall, and stopped to speak to her.

'Is Muriel still behind? I think Nan gave her a hand earlier as Kelly Mason was late again . . .'

'Kelly is having a bad time at home,' Michelle said with a sympathetic look on her pretty face. She was a striking girl with midnight black hair and a pearly complexion. 'Have a word with her before you think of sacking her, Angela. She isn't lazy. I think it's just that her mother can't manage without her help.'

'Give me the tray, Michelle. I know you have better things to do upstairs.'

Angela carried the tray through to the kitchen and discovered Kelly talking with one of the newer carers, Tilly. They were sitting at a table drinking tea and seemed intent on their talk until she entered, but their conversation died and she fancied Kelly looked a bit apprehensive.

'Don't let me interrupt you,' she said. 'I came in the hope of a cup of tea.'

'I'll get you one, Miss Angela,' Kelly said. 'I'm taking my lunch break, miss, and we were only talkin' about Ireland. Tilly was telling me her auntie married a man from Derry.'

'Yes, you're Irish, aren't you?'

'Only on me mam's side,' Kelly said. 'Me dad is English; London bred and born. I was tellin' Tilly how me mam's been ill all year and I've been lookin' after her as much as I could—' The girl broke off, a look of anguish in her eyes. Angela understood instantly, because Michelle had warned her. It explained Kelly's lateness and constant days off. 'Only in me spare time, though . . .'

'Yes, I see,' Angela said. 'Has your mother had the doctor, Kelly? Do you know why she's so poorly?'

'He wouldn't come to us, miss,' Kelly said. 'We live in a slum down near the Docks. Dad hoped Hitler would do us a favour and blow the cottage up, but it's still standin' and the council say we're a long way down the list – but it's damp see and Mam suffers from a heart condition. She feels the cold somethin' awful – and I think I take after her; it's why I'm always gettin' a chill.'

'Well, we shall have to see what we can do to help your mam,' Angela said. 'Would your family move into a better place if one were offered, Kelly?'

'Oh yes, miss,' Kelly's face lit up. 'Me dad would do anythin' to make her well again.'

'I'll speak to some people I know,' Angela said. 'I'm helping a Church charity to provide deserving cases with decent housing they can afford. We don't have enough houses for everyone and there's always a long waiting list but . . . it would help if we had a doctor's report . . .'

'The doctor won't come to our house; he doesn't like the area – too many bad folk where we live.'

'I know someone who will come,' Angela said. 'If I have your permission I shall bring him myself, Kelly.'

'I'll ask Dad and tell you tomorrow,' Kelly said and put a cup and saucer in front of her. 'It's still hot, miss. We'd only just made it.'

'I'd better get going,' Tilly announced and stood up. 'We're rushed off our feet today.'

28

'Yes, and I must too.' Angela took a sip of her tea. 'I should like Dr Kent to see your mother, Kelly; if her health is affected by the damp conditions it will help your family move up the housing list. I can't promise anything. The charity I help out has to be fair and I'm only one small cog, but sometimes they listen to me. If your mother was better, you wouldn't have to be late so often.'

Kelly's cheeks turned even pinker and she hung her head. 'Thank you, Mrs Morton – and I'll try not to stop away too much. You see, Mammy has a little one still at home and another three at school, and if she's ill . . .'

'Yes, I do understand, Kelly,' Angela said, 'and I shan't be reporting you to Sister for staying away from work – but you must try to come in on time; you know we need you too.'

'I could always come in and make up me time when me sister gets home from school – I wouldn't mind working in the evening to make up for being late. Me da's home then . . .'

'Well, let's see what we can do for your mother first,' Angela said. 'Perhaps there is some treatment that will help her.'

She was thoughtful as she made her way to her office. If Kelly's mother was suffering from the damp conditions in her slum house then the sooner she was on their list the better. Since the end of the war more and more building was taking place, but it took time to get all the kilns and factories producing at full capacity and progress was slow. So many people had been left home- less that pulling down the old slums that had remained

29

standing was not a priority. In time it was hoped to replace all the substandard housing, but it could take years. It was the aim of the charity Angela assisted to help those who needed it most, but there were so many in bad housing and they couldn't help them all. In some quarters there was resistance on the part of the slum dwellers themselves, who didn't want to move out to the suburbs; for this reason, the charity had decided to renovate old properties rather than build new.

Families like Kelly's were often overlooked, and the terrible poverty they endured often bred cruelty, which in turn led to battered children being brought to their door at St Saviour's. If Kelly's mother died, the girl would have to leave her job to look after her siblings or they might end up at St Saviour's or some other children's home.

Determined to prevent such a tragedy, Angela resolved to speak to Dr Kent about visiting Kelly's mother. He was new to the area and keen to get to grips with the poverty and sickness he witnessed on his rounds; Angela hoped that would make him more likely to be interested in the Masons' case.

Angela had no sooner started typing up her report than the door opened and Sister Beatrice entered. She looked thoughtful and rather anxious, as if something were playing on her mind.

'Is there anything wrong?'

'Wrong with me? Why should there be? I'm perfectly well,' Sister snapped, and Angela wondered what she'd said to upset her this time. She was secretly counting the days to her forthcoming move upstairs to one of the new offices in the attic. Perhaps once their offices were no longer side-by-side and they met only to discuss business they would get on better.

'No reason at all,' she said. 'I thought you looked anxious . . . perhaps over one of the children?'

'Well yes,' Sister admitted. 'I am concerned about the new arrivals, Angela. Samantha and Sarah . . . As you know, they were discovered sleeping rough in a bombed-out house due for demolition. The police had cleared it of homeless vagrants once already, but they went back for a final check before the bulldozers moved in and found the girls close to exhaustion from lack of food and water . . .'

'Have they told you why they were there? Or given their last names?'

'Not yet. Though I've been informed they're sisters and their surname is May. Samantha seems wary. Sarah is a gentle girl, very pretty and doesn't say much, just sits there and looks at you.'

'Can she speak?'

'She speaks when she wants to – usually yes or no or thank you. They both seem to have nice manners and they haven't caused a bit of bother . . . but something isn't right. Sarah has old scarring and faded bruises, but Samantha was merely dehydrated and hungry; although when I examined the marks on her sister's body she seemed to wince, almost as if she was feeling Sarah's pain herself.'

'Could they be twins? I've heard that sometimes twins feel each other's pain and emotions.'

'Samantha says they are twins, but they aren't identical and Sarah seems younger and quieter . . . perhaps

31

she's in her sister's shadow. I think I might ask Mark to have a word with them, next time he visits.'

'Yes . . .' Angela frowned. 'We don't want the kind of bother we had with poor Terry.'

'No, certainly not.' Sister shuddered as they both remembered the frightened, troubled child who had attacked her. 'I feel so responsible for what happened. I know his sister blames herself too, but I doubt anyone could have prevented it.'

'Nancy is coping very well for the moment. Muriel was telling me she's very good at making pastry – in fact she made the treacle tart some of the children had at lunch.'

'Yes, well, I'm glad she's coming along nicely – but I don't want anything like that to happen here again, Angela. Nancy refused to be parted from her brother and Samantha is behaving in much the same way. She says her sister might be frightened if she woke in the night and she was not there.'

'Does it really matter if they stay together?' Angela asked reasonably. 'As we discussed, we're moving Mary Ellen and Marion into the new wing next week; they will have one of the smaller rooms with four beds. Perhaps we should put the twins in with them. They're much the same age, but Sarah seems younger and Samantha needs to get comfortable with us. It is very strange for children who've been accustomed to doing chores and taking care of their siblings when they suddenly find themselves having to follow our rules.'

'Do you imagine I am not aware of that?' Sister Beatrice was clearly not in the best of moods, reverting to the hostility that she'd shown when Angela first came to the home the previous year. 'I've no intention of repeating the mistakes that were made with Nancy and Terry . . .'

'None of us could have foreseen such an outcome,' Angela said. 'You mustn't blame yourself, Sister. Terry had been badly damaged by his father's brutality, not to mention the trauma of the fire that killed his parents. We shall never know exactly what took place, but Terry's mind was so badly warped by his father's torture—'

'Well, that's as maybe,' sniffed Sister Beatrice. 'Anyway, I've been informed by Constable Sallis that the police have managed to trace the girls' aunt. She may be willing to take them, in which case their stay with us will be a short one.'

'That's a good thing, I expect.'

Sister's gaze flickered and Angela thought she saw distress in her eyes, but then the older woman was turning away, leaving her to carry on with her work. The report was almost finished, which left two letters to compose and type up before she would be ready to meet Mark. But as her fingers rattled the keys of the typewriter her mind kept drifting back to Sister Beatrice's hostility, and wondering what could have provoked it.

Beatrice entered her own office, closing the door behind her and leaning against it for a moment. She had no idea why she'd been so annoyed to find Angela busily typing away at this hour; her assistant was very efficient and saved her endless hours of paperwork, something she'd found irksome in the past. Mark had assured Sister Beatrice that the Administrator's role was not intended to usurp hers and that the children of St Saviour's would continue to depend on her experience and her understanding.

She touched the heavy silver crucifix she wore hanging from a long chain about her neck, and then closed her eyes. She must conquer this feeling of anxiety and anger that came over her sometimes in the younger woman's presence.

'Forgive me, Lord,' Beatrice said. 'Pride and ambition are unworthy sins and I must submit to Thy will for me . . .'

Yet even as she mouthed the words she knew she would fight with all that was in her to retain her position at St Saviour's . . . but why was she feeling threatened? She'd thought she'd managed to put this behind her, to accept that Angela's position as Administrator was of benefit to all.

She'd felt so inadequate when Terry's illness had made him a danger to himself and others. Ever since that terrible incident she'd felt tired and strained – and there was something about the two most recent arrivals that made her uneasy.

Feeling a sudden pain in her side, Beatrice gasped and clutched at herself. Perhaps it wasn't the silence of little Sarah that had brought on this attack of self-doubt and soul-searching. These terrible stabbing pains had been troubling her for a while, and though she rose above it stoically, it was getting steadily worse – and that was what frightened her. What was the source of her pain? Had it been higher in her chest she would have thought it indigestion and ignored it, but this was low on her left side and could be severe, though it didn't last long.

She drew a sighing breath of relief as the pain receded. It was foolish of her to imagine that she had some dreadful illness. Beatrice knew she ought to visit a doctor and let him examine her, but she was reluctant. If it turned out she had something unpleasant, she might be forced to take a lot of time off work – she might lose her position here.

A quiet existence in the convent did not appeal to her after a busy life at St Saviour's, and the prospect of being forced to retire due to ill health was one that sent her into the darkest of moods. She loved the hustle and bustle of Halfpenny Street and the surrounding lanes and alleys – so many people going about their work and the rattle of trams in the distance; bicycles, horses and dray carts, and lorries as they passed, and the cry of costermongers as they pushed their hand-carts and offered fruit and veg for sale – and she was not ready for the quiet of the secluded convent. She did not have time to be ill – not when there was so much to do, and so much to lose. St Saviour's would manage without her, Angela would see to that, Beatrice had no doubt – but she needed her place here.

Her thoughts were interrupted as someone knocked at the door and then Nan poked her head round. She smiled at the woman who was her closest friend; the only person who knew anything about her life before St Saviour's.

'You're still here then,' Nan said and entered. 'I'm on duty until midnight, Beatrice. You should get home and rest. You work too hard – and you look a bit peaky.'

'I'm all right, perhaps a bit tired. I had no more than a few hours' sleep last night – but we shall be all right now. Staff Nurse Wendy is settling in well. It looks as if we've been lucky this time, Nan.'

'Yes, it looks like it.'

Beatrice nodded, her stern features relaxing as she asked, 'Have you heard from Alice recently?'

'She was well when I popped in last night, though a bit lonely with Bob away in the Army. I think she's landed on her feet there, providing she doesn't let herself brood on the past too much. We all have to accept that we can't change the past, even if we wish we could. You and I both know that, Beatrice.'

'Yes, we do,' Beatrice agreed. 'You're feeling better about your daughter now I think?'

'Yes, a bit. I shall always miss my Maisie and wish she'd chosen to stay with me, but Eddie says I must accept her decision. She's Sister Mary now and not the girl I knew at all. You found solace in becoming a nun and it seems my girl has too.'

'I found a refuge when I needed one – but then I was given the chance to nurse, first at the Infirmary, and then to become Warden here; I've never regretted it. I should hate to have to leave.'

'But why should you?' Nan looked puzzled. 'St Saviour's couldn't manage without its Sister Beatrice.'

'No, perhaps it couldn't,' Beatrice said. 'It does me good to talk to you, Nan. Where is your charming old soldier this evening?'

'Oh, Eddie is away at the moment, visiting his nephew and his wife. They run a grocer's shop in the country somewhere. They want him to live with them and help look after the shop. I shall miss him if he goes.'

'Yes, I know.' Beatrice felt better. The pain had gone

and she'd been worrying for nothing. 'I'm sure he will keep in touch though.'

'Yes . . . but letters aren't like meeting for tea or having him round for lunch, are they? Still, at my age, I couldn't expect a romance, could I?'

'Did you want one?' Beatrice looked closely at her friend, but although Nan seemed to hesitate, she shook her head.

'No, not a romance . . . but he was cheerful company. The first man I've felt comfortable with for a long time.'

'I understand. Well, I'd best go home and get some rest. It will be another long day tomorrow.'

'We never know what will turn up, do we?'

They walked down to the lift together and then parted. Beatrice made her way through the gardens to the Nurses' Home, and Nan set off on her rounds, making sure everything was quiet and as it should be in the dorms. Nan was probably right, Beatrice thought; for a while she'd been doing the work of two people and that was the reason she'd been feeling a bit under the weather. Now that the new nurse had settled in, things were bound to improve . . .

FOUR

Michelle came out of a deep sleep slowly as she heard her mother calling her. There was a note of desperation in her voice and Michelle was suddenly wide-awake as the light was snapped on and she saw her mother standing there in the doorway with tears running down her cheeks.

'What's wrong, Mum?' she asked and jumped out of bed. 'What's happened?'

'It's your father,' she said. 'He was coughing and then he sort of choked and brought up this blood and then he fell back against the pillows and I think – I think he might be dead, Michelle . . .' Her mother's eyes were wide with fear.

'No, he can't be!' Michelle cried, running barefoot through to the bedroom next door. She saw at once that her father's pillows were spotted with blood and there was more on his nightshirt. Heart racing, she rushed to him and bent over to find a pulse. Thankfully, it was there but faint. 'He's not dead, Mum. I think he's passed out – probably felt weak after bringing up that blood . . .' She turned and saw that her two young brothers had come to the door and were staring at her in distress. 'Freddie, go back to bed,' she said. 'I'll get dressed and phone for the doctor.'

'Can't you do anything for him?' Michelle's mother asked as her father stirred and moaned weakly. 'He won't thank you for fetching the doctor.'

'You look after him, Chelle,' the elder of her brothers said. 'I'll go and ring from the box on the corner.'

Michelle glanced at the alarm clock by the bed; the time was a quarter to five and the doctor wouldn't be pleased to be called out at this hour.

'No, wait,' she said. 'Dad's coming round now. Freddie, go back to bed – you too, Ben; go on now. I'll clean him up and see how he is and then we'll get the doctor later if we need to.'

'Michelle's right,' her mother said. 'No arguments. Your father hates a fuss; you know that – so go quietly now and leave this to us. I'll fetch you some warm water, Michelle . . .'

Michelle touched her father's face. He opened his eyes and she saw the fear in them as he became aware of her and then the blood everywhere. She took his hand and he gripped it tightly. His mouth moved but his voice was only a whisper.

'What . . . happened?'

'You had a coughing fit, brought up some blood and then passed out. You'll be all right in a while; it's merely the shock.'

'You didn't send for the doctor?' He clutched at her urgently.

'Not yet, but you must see him, Dad.'

'Meant to,' he said. 'Don't think I've got long, girl.

39

You'll have to look after your mother and brothers. Ben will be out to work in another few years, but Freddie's still a boy . . .'

'Don't talk,' Michelle hushed him as he closed his eyes, clearly exhausted. 'Try not to think about the blood; there's not as much as you think.'

'Yes,' he said weakly. 'Ben is sensible but Freddie needs a firm hand. Remember that when I've gone.'

'Shush . . . the doctor will help when he comes and you'll soon be better.'

'You know that's not true.' His eyes reproached her. 'My own fault, but I didn't want to let you all down – should've done something ages ago.'

'It isn't too late,' Michelle said, praying she was right and not giving him false hope. 'You'll need to go away if it's consumption – don't look like that; you know I'm right. We don't know for sure what it is – I'll look after Mum and the boys, I promise.'

'Not fair on you – should be courting . . .'

'Lie back and rest. I'm going to clean you up and make you comfortable, and then we'll have the doctor as soon as it's light.'

'I can get up and go myself . . .'

'You will stay where you are and do as you're told.' Michelle fixed him with her best Staff Nurse look. 'You owe it to Mum and the boys to get better – and the only way that will happen is bed rest in a sanatorium. I shan't listen to you, Dad, so you may as well listen to me. This attack was sent as a warning. Do as you're told, and you'll live to see the boys leave school – both of them.'

The faintest flicker of a smile passed across his mouth,

but he was too weak to do more than press her hand. Michelle's mother came back with the bowl of water and together they changed his shirt and Michelle washed away the blood, tucking him under a clean sheet.

'Shall I bring him a cup of tea?' her mother asked. Michelle hesitated, and then shook her head.

'Only a few sips of water until the doctor has been. I think he'll sleep now.'

'Yes, he looks more peaceful,' her mother said. 'I was so frightened, Michelle – I don't know what we'll do if—'

'Hush . . .' Michelle led her from the room. 'It's too soon to think that way, Mum. This has been coming on for a while now. It probably looks worse than it is . . . let's wait until the doctor tells us what he thinks; it might not be as bad as we fear.'

'Well, Miss Morris,' the doctor said as he finished examining his patient later that morning. 'You were quite right to call me. I know you think your father has TB, but I'm not too certain of that. We shall do some tests and they will give us a better idea. In the meantime, keep him warm in bed; give him milky drinks and soft foods – nothing spicy for a while at least. It may be ulcers – they cause pain, but a severe attack like this is rare; we're not sure what causes ulcers in the first place, but bad eating habits can aggravate them in certain patients.'

He was an attractive man with a pleasant smile and a way of looking at you that was appealing. Michelle had been surprised at how young and enthusiastic he was. The doctor they usually saw was much older and

41

set in his ways; this man was bound to have new ideas and theories of his own. Perhaps they'd all been wrong to jump to conclusions, but TB was prevalent in the poorer districts and she knew both her father and mother feared it. Dr Kent was new to the area; he hadn't been here long enough to understand how many people suffered from bad conditions and poor diets. Yet she would give him the benefit of the doubt and pray that he was right.

'Bert likes spicy foods,' Mrs Morris said as they stood at the top of the stairs after leaving the patient to rest. He'd been given something to help him sleep, as he was restless and kept trying to get out of bed. 'He had some food last night at the pub. It smelled awful to me, and tasted very hot, but Bert has always liked those kinds of foods.'

'Yes, and that makes me think it may be ulcers, Mrs Morris, rather than TB. I know he's had a bad cough for a long time, because your daughter told me so and she's a good nurse – but the blood he coughed up may have been caused by ulcers rather than tuberculosis.'

Mrs Morris looked at him uncertainly. 'Is that better or worse news, Doctor?'

'Better – providing you can keep him off greasy foods. Vinegary things are often as bad – so from here on it'll be rice pudding, jelly, blancmange and soft mashed potato with mince and gravy or boiled fish rather than the things he likes, Mrs Morris. However, he may have to go into hospital for tests. They will sort him out and, if I'm right, he'll have a good chance of getting over it.'

While Michelle nipped back into the bedroom to make sure that her father was resting, Mrs Morris went downstairs to see the doctor off. When she returned, her eyes were wet with tears.

'Thank you for stopping until the doctor came,' she said. 'You should get off now, Michelle. You don't want to be late for work.'

'It's all right, Mum, I'm on the early evening shift today. I rang and swopped with Paula; she didn't mind; it means she can go out with her boyfriend this evening.'

'Oh, then let's have a cuppa,' her mother said and looked at her anxiously. 'Do you think Dr Kent is right – that your father's cough is bronchitis and the blood was due to ulcers?'

'I don't know, Mum. Dad's been losing a bit of weight recently and together with the cough I thought it might be TB. Did you know he was having stomach pains?'

Her mother shook her head. 'Well, if it is ulcers he won't like rice pudding and mashed potatoes for his tea. Your dad loves a fry-up or roast beef, and those'll be on the forbidden list.'

'If it is ulcers, he'll have to be sensible and learn to stay away from the foods that upset him.'

'Well, I'm glad it happened now; it may bring him to his senses. I've been telling him to have that cough seen to but he wouldn't go to the doctor.' She wrinkled her brow. 'I don't know this doctor, Michelle. Is he new to the practice?'

'Yes, I think so. We use old Dr Simpson's practice for the children at St Saviour's sometimes, but I haven't seen Dr Kent before.' She'd thought him attractive, in a cool, remote sort of way; his hair was dark ash blond and his skin fair and his eyes a sort of greenish brown, or what some people called hazel.

'Well, he seems nice and efficient, though he doesn't smile much,' Mrs Morris said. 'I must admit I was terrified when your father brought up that blood. If you hadn't been here, I'm not sure what I would've done.'

'Well, I *was* here.' Michelle squeezed her mother's arm. 'You've got to stop worrying and look after yourself, Mum. I've noticed how tired you've been lately and I think you do too much.'

'I've been worrying about your father. I dread the winter for him and keep thinking it's time he found himself a job inside somewhere – but he says there aren't enough jobs going – and we do need more money. At times we've hardly enough for the rent, let alone the coal and our food. I wish your dad could get a steady job, something reliable.'

Michelle looked at her thoughtfully. 'If there was a different sort of job going – slow steady work – do you think Dad would take it?'

'Give him a chance! What are you thinking of?'

'I can't say too much yet; I need to talk to someone first – but leave it with me . . .'

'Can I talk to you, Angela?' Michelle hovered hesitantly in the doorway of Angela's office. 'I wanted to ask something – it's personal.'

'Of course, come in,' Angela said and smiled, indicating that she should sit in the chair opposite.

'It's a bit awkward,' Michelle said, feeling almost afraid to ask, now she was here. 'My father was ill this morning. I had the doctor in and he thinks he may have ulcers in his stomach – and his cough gets worse every winter . . . and Mum and me, we thought it was time

44

he did an indoor job. Well, indoors more than out – and I heard that the caretaker here was leaving so he could live near his daughter in the country, and wondered if, when he goes . . .'

'You would like your father to be caretaker here?' Angela looked thoughtful. 'Our present caretaker is planning to stay on until a few weeks before Christmas. Do you think your father will be sufficiently recovered by then?'

'Yes, if has treatment for his problem he should be feeling better by then,' Michelle said, her cheeks warm. It was much harder to ask for a favour than she'd imagined. 'I was hoping he might be considered.'

'I can promise you he will be considered if he applies,' Angela said. 'I'm only one of several people concerned in appointing a new caretaker, Michelle. It would have to go to the Board. I couldn't tell you now that he would get the position, but I'm sure that his application would be given every attention.'

'Thank you, that's all I wanted – just that he could be given a chance. So many men don't even get an answer to their applications for work these days.'

'Yes, I do understand . . .' Angela hesitated, and then seemed to make up her mind. She looked in her drawer and took out her notepad. 'What is your father's current job, and what work has he done in the past?'

'He was a crane driver for years, a skilled man,' Michelle said. 'He used to load and unload cargoes but then the war started and he was in the army for a while, until they invalided him out in '43. When he came back he had a weak chest; the doctor said it was bronchitis, but it has been worse recently – and he's been working as a casual worker on the docks for a long time, doing anything he can really.'

'Do you think he could put up shelves and mend broken windows – things like that?' Angela asked. 'It would involve some outside work I suppose, but our caretaker has to look after the garden and the boiler in the cellar . . .'

'I think it would be better than what he does now – and it would be regular.'

'Well, I'll see what I can do – but I can't promise anything. You know I can only give my opinion if asked – so perhaps your father would call in one day and have a chat when he's feeling well again.'

'Thank you,' Michelle said, her eyes pricking with sudden tears. 'You didn't mind my asking about the post of caretaker here?'

'Not at all; I've been given the task of finding someone suitable and if your father was willing to try, I dare say he might suit us. You are one of our best nurses, so he comes with a good recommendation . . . but it would have to go to the Board before it could be confirmed.'

'I don't know how to thank you . . .'

'Let's see what happens first. We haven't actually had any other applicants yet, though I'm sure we shall. And your father might not wish to take up the position; it isn't a great deal of money for a skilled man.'

'Mum is more interested in Dad's health than money,' Michelle said. 'I'm sure she would manage, even if she did a part time job to help out herself.'

'Then ask Mr Morris to come and see me here when he feels up to it,' Angela said. 'And now I'd better not keep you; I'm sure you'll be needed elsewhere.'

'Yes, I shall,' Michelle said, glancing at the watch pinned to her uniform. 'I mustn't be late. Thank you so much!'

'I haven't done anything yet.'

Michelle nodded, but she was feeling excited as she left the office. If her father truly had ulcers and bronchitis, then a caretaker's job could be exactly what he needed . . .

FIVE

'Hello, I'm Mary Ellen, and you're Samantha, aren't you?' The girl in the sick ward bed stared at Mary Ellen warily as she approached. 'Miss Angela asked me to come and see you. She says we're going to be sharing a dorm in the new wing soon, and she wanted us to make friends.' She sat on the edge of the girl's bed. 'It's lovely over there, all fresh and new, and the dorms aren't too big. There will be four of us. Marion, you, your sister Sarah, and me . . .' Mary Ellen glanced across at Sarah in the next bed, who sat staring at them, her eyes wide and her thumb in her mouth. 'Hello, Sarah. I think you will like it here; it's much nicer in the dorms. Me and Marion go to school with Billy Baggins, he's a bit older and good at football and running. Once you're up and about, you'll have fun here; we do all sorts of things . . .'

'Mary Ellen . . . have fun,' Sarah repeated, smiling and nodding.

'Sarah isn't well yet,' Samantha said protectively. 'She doesn't talk much but she knows everything we say – so don't think she's daft!'

'I wouldn't,' Mary Ellen said, puzzled by Samantha's hostility. 'Sarah is very pretty. I wish I had hair her colour.'

'We're twins,' Samantha said, the stiffness easing out of her. 'I thought I could look out for us both after Pa . . . but I couldn't find enough food to eat. I tried to sell what we had left but the man cheated me and would only give me five shillings for all of it . . .'

'What man?' Mary Ellen asked.

'Alf, from the scrapyard. I know it was worth more, perhaps two or three pounds, but all he paid me was five bob and he threatened to tell the police I'd stolen it if I didn't leave it with him.'

'Even two pounds wouldn't have lasted long,' Mary Ellen said. 'Don't you have anyone you could live with?'

Samantha shook her head, but Sarah took her thumb from her mouth and said, 'Aunt Jane won't have Sarah. She says Sarah idiot girl – Pa gone away . . .'

'Sarah – don't, love,' Samantha said, looking at her sadly before turning back to Mary Ellen. 'I didn't want to live with Aunt Jane. She's not kind – and she hates Sarah.'

'She sounds horrid,' Mary Ellen said. 'But you'll be all right here. It seems strange at first, but Nan is nice and so are the nurses, and Miss Angela. Sister Beatrice is a bit fierce, but she's not bad really. And we have good things to eat . . .'

'Why are you here?'

'My father died and then my mother got ill. She was unwell for ages, then my sister Rose went off to train as a nurse and we didn't have any money. Ma wouldn't tell Rose she was worse and we were so hungry sometimes

49

– and then she got really ill and they put her in hospital, but she died last Christmas. My sister couldn't look after me – so that's why I live here; I haven't got anywhere else until Rose finds us a place to live. She's always busy and sometimes I think she never will find us a new house.'

'Pa not come back,' Sarah said. She reached under her pillow and took out two pieces of what looked like rubbish to Mary Ellen, and then she saw it was a broken clay pipe with a long handle. Sarah held it to her cheek, crooning to herself, tears slipping down her cheeks. 'Pa not love Sarah . . . Child of Satan . . .'

'What did she say?' Mary Ellen was shocked.

'Our father called her that for breaking his favourite pipe. Sarah didn't mean to upset him, she loves Pa, but he doesn't care about us. He thinks she's too slow and clumsy, and he beat her until I made him stop.'

'How did you do that?'

'I threw the pee in my chamber pot over him,' Samantha said simply.

Mary Ellen stared at her in awe for a moment and then erupted into peals of laughter. 'Oh, that's so funny,' she said. 'You're brave, like Marion. When a burglar tried to steal our Christmas food she hit him with her crutch and then Angela came and fought him, and he tripped over and hit his head – and then Sister Beatrice came and stood over him with the rolling pin until Alice came and took over from her. She looked so fierce I laughed and so did Billy, even though the burglar was his brother Arthur!'

Samantha sat forward, suddenly showing signs of interest as Mary Ellen recounted the story of how Billy's brother had planned to eat their special food and then set fire to the home.

'What happened to him?' Samantha asked, a gleam in her eyes.

'Billy heard he'd been sentenced to ten years in prison. He was a thief and he tried to make Billy help him, but Billy didn't want to so he came back here and hid. That's why Arthur was intent on burning us all in our beds, 'cept he can't now, 'cos he's locked up in choky.'

'So you were heroes and saved the day,' Samantha said. She paused for a moment, then asked, 'What happens here – is it like prison?'

Mary Ellen shook her head. 'I asked Billy that when I heard my sister Rose saying I would have to come here when Mum was ill. No, it's OK, even though it's not like being in your own home. Sister Beatrice is stern and gets cross if you're naughty and break the rules, but she's all right underneath. She has to be strict, see. She's in charge of us and gets into trouble if we do bad things.'

Samantha looked solemn. 'It was easy at school when we were younger. I sat next to Sarah and explained the lessons and writing to her, but we got told off for talking – and then they separated us. Sarah was taken to a class for younger children and they didn't bother to teach her anything, but she can learn – if you tell her enough times she will remember.'

Sarah's eyes wore a glazed look, as if she were lost in her crooning. She'd stopped listening to them, and was fondling her father's broken pipe, her cheeks streaked with tears.

'You should tell Nancy about her. She's younger but

works with the carers. She'll help Sarah with reading and puzzles once you're settled in. She reads to the little ones, but Sarah could join them in the mornings rather than go to school with us.'

'Perhaps . . . but they might send her to a special school. It's what Pa was saying last year, but it didn't happen; there wasn't a spare place for her. My aunt wanted to put her in a mental institution for daft people and that's why we ran away. If they try to do that to my Sarah, we'll run away again.'

'You ought to tell Miss Angela what you've told me,' Mary Ellen said. 'I'm sure she wouldn't let them send her away if you asked her not to.'

'No, I shan't tell them,' Samantha said fiercely. 'Promise me you won't tell either, Mary Ellen. Cross your heart and hope to die if you betray us.'

'I shan't tell anyone,' Mary Ellen said. 'I think Sister would let you stay if she could, but it might not be up to her . . .' She broke off as the door opened and someone came in. It was Nurse Wendy and Mary Ellen wished she could share the secret with her, but she'd promised she wouldn't on pain of death and that was a solemn oath.

'Ah, here you are, Mary Ellen,' Wendy said. 'I'm glad you've been making friends with Samantha and Sarah, as you are all moving into the new dorm tomorrow. This afternoon, one of us will be helping you and Marion to pack your things. Samantha and Sarah, you're both perfectly healthy and will go to your dorm straight from here. You'll find your clothes and things waiting in the dorm, but I'll bring you your school clothes. You'll wear a skirt and blouse like Mary Ellen's . . .'

'What happened to our clothes?' Samantha asked, reverting to her hostile manner.

'They've been washed and you will find them in your locker with the new undies and nightdresses you've been given. Everyone has to wear school clothes unless you go out with a relative for a special treat.'

'We haven't got any relatives,' Samantha said.

Mary Ellen frowned over the fib but didn't contradict her. Her new friends had both an aunt and a father, even though one of them didn't want Sarah and the other had deserted them – but it was up to Samantha to share her story when she was ready. Mary Ellen wouldn't tell. Nothing would make her . . .

'They were talking easily when I went in,' Wendy told Angela later that day when they sat together in the staff room, 'but Samantha clammed up as soon as she saw me. I'm sure Mary Ellen knows a lot more about them than we do, but you know how loyal she is. Wild horses wouldn't get it out of her unless she thought it would save their lives.'

'We can't force her to tell us and I shan't try,' Angela said. 'We'll have to wait until the twins feel they can trust us . . . Is Sarah still clinging to that dirty old pipe?'

'Yes. She hid it as soon as she saw me, but I knew what it was. I've seen her holding it to her cheek and singing. Tears slip down her cheeks but she doesn't say anything – merely parrots whatever Samantha says if she has to answer.'

'She may simply be slow. Sarah is a sweet, loving child and Samantha is protective of her. There's nothing wrong with that.'

'As they're both girls, there's no bother about them staying together. Perhaps Sarah will have more to say when she feels comfortable with us.'

'Well, they may not be here long; you see, they have an aunt who may be willing to take them.'

'Oh, well perhaps that's best,' Wendy agreed. 'I'd better get back to the ward. I left Jean to give the children their drinks, but she's due a break soon.'

She met Tilly as she was on her way to the kitchen and greeted her with a friendly smile, but though the girl smiled back, she walked on without speaking. Wendy hadn't got to know her yet. Sometimes Tilly would join in a conversation, but more often she was quiet and wary of saying much. Wendy thought there was something sad about her . . .

Wendy had known enough sadness of her own. The only man she'd ever loved had died in the war, as had so many others – and then Wendy's mother had died of cancer. She'd spent months nursing her and afterwards she'd wanted a change from general nursing, so this job had been a godsend. Wendy loved her job here and, although it couldn't fill the empty space inside her that the deaths of her loved ones had left, several of the children had already found their way into her heart . . .

SIX

Angela filed away her reports and stretched her shoulders. She really wished that she was going somewhere nice that evening instead of a charity meeting. Her evening out with Mark had ended so abruptly; they'd hardly had time to have a drink before he was rushing off to see his patient.

'I wouldn't go, but Alan Royston is a friend,' Mark had told her. 'I told them to call me if there were complications during the operation – it's always risky, trying to remove a tumour on the brain. No matter how skilled the surgeon, it could go either way.'

'I understand, Mark,' Angela had said, swallowing her disappointment. 'You must go to your friend. If anything should happen you would never forgive yourself.'

'I was the one who talked him into having the op. The tumour had grown to the point it was going to kill him or leave him severely impaired. If he dies now I shall be left wondering if he might have had a few more months if he'd refused . . .'

Angela's heart went out to him. She suspected he

wouldn't take the death of a friend easily and she wished she could have gone with him to support him. However, Mark would never have allowed it.

She was reaching for her jacket, ready to leave for the evening, when the phone rang. Angela hesitated and then reached for the receiver. 'Angela Morton here.'

'Angela, my love,' her father's voice came down the line. 'How are you? I'm planning to pop up to town this weekend, and I thought perhaps dinner and the theatre later? I can stay overnight and we'll have lunch the next day before I go back.'

'Oh, Daddy, it is lovely to hear from you, and I'd love to go out to dinner with you on Saturday. I'll try to get tickets for a show. Shall I book them and a room for you?'

'No, I'll see to the room,' he said. 'It'll be good to see you, and we need to have a talk. It's about your mother – but we'll discuss all that when I see you.'

'Is something the matter? Mother isn't worse, is she?' Angela's mother had been drinking heavily for months before her breakdown the previous Christmas, when it had all come out. It had taken months to persuade her to go to a special clinic in Switzerland for treatment, and in the end it was Mark who had persuaded her to do so.

'No. In fact from the sound of it she's feeling better. I'll tell you all the news at the weekend. I won't keep you.'

'Yes, all right. Lovely to hear from you. I'll look forward to the weekend.'

She frowned as she replaced the receiver. Her mother's behaviour had been erratic for some time, but the breakdown last Christmas had come as a shock. Despite his attempt at reassurance, Angela couldn't help feeling anxious about whatever it was her father wanted to tell her.

Mark had known of Mrs Hendry's illness for months but he hadn't told Angela – and she'd been angry with him for that. Perhaps that was one of the causes of this rift between them. Angela had been in the wrong; Mark could not betray a confidence, and it was her father who should have told her but he'd kept it to himself. In the aftermath of the breakdown Angela had offered to give up her work at St Saviour's, but her father wouldn't hear of it.

As she set off homeward along Halfpenny Street, Angela's thoughts were preoccupied with things she could do nothing about. She turned the corner and passed the newly restored and recently reopened pub with its hanging baskets bringing a touch of welcome colour. The scent of the blooms was no longer over-powered by the tang of city drains, thanks to the efforts of the road sweeper who'd been hired to keep the pavements and gutters clean. He was an ex-soldier – his limp a relic of the war, if she was not mistaken – and he never failed to tip his cap in greeting whenever they passed on the street.

She could hear the tooting of a car horn somewhere and out on the river there was a hooter blaring from one of the barges. The vacant spaces left by Hitler's bombs made the area seem more rundown than it actually was, but some headway had been made in clearing the rubble and one or two new buildings were going up, bringing a sense that things were moving on at last.

There were still shortages, and rationing had yet to be lifted on essential items such as sugar, butter, canned and dried fruit, chocolate biscuits, clothing and petrol. Yet there was a growing feeling, encouraged by upbeat newspaper reports, that they were finally leaving those dark years of war and devastation behind.

More and more of late, Angela was aware of a vague sense of wistfulness, of needing something more in her life. She longed to be going somewhere nice for a change instead of another charity meeting. It would probably be very dull, since the housing charity was made up of a few well-intentioned people who wanted to contribute but seemed incapable of actually doing anything. Until Angela had taken over as secretary, their meetings had been spent going round and round in circles, talking endlessly and never reaching a decision. By sheer force of energy, she'd managed to galvanise them into approving funding for new housing to be built on the site they'd acquired. Now if she could only get them to come to a decision on which builder would carry out the work . . .

The Methodist hall, with its walls clad in dark oak wainscoting and drab grey paint, and a permanent odour of musty old books in the air, was not the most welcoming of venues. As usual, the old-fashioned radiators were proving unequal to the task of heating the draughty interior, and Angela was debating whether to hang her coat on the hallstand or keep it on for the duration of the meeting when she was hailed by Stan Bridges, Chairman of the Housing Society.

'Angela, just the person! I'd like you to meet Henry

Arnold,' he beamed, ushering her towards an extremely attractive young man. 'Henry, this is Mrs Morton, one of the unpaid angels who keep our little charity run—' He broke off as the door opened to admit another new arrival, then hurried over to greet them, Angela and her new companion immediately forgotten.

'Mr Arnold, I had no idea you would be coming tonight,' Angela said, extending her hand to him. 'I knew we had whittled the list of prospective builders down to three, but I thought it was to be decided this evening . . .'

'Please, call me Henry,' he said, giving her a smile that lit his blue eyes with a dazzling brilliance. 'I think I precipitated things rather. Stan Bridges is the director of a firm for whom I have recently built a block of offices and he mentioned over a drink that this project was open for tender.'

'So you thought you would jump the gun and present yourself uninvited?'

The note of annoyance in her voice was too pronounced to be mistaken, and Henry Arnold's expression betrayed a flash of pique that gave way to amusement. 'You've got me wrong, Angela,' he said, a faint northern accent discernible. 'Stan asked me to come this evening to meet you and some of the others. You see, he thinks my proposition is too good to be missed.'

'And what is your proposition, exactly?' Angela replied coolly. She didn't care for his presumption in using her first name without invitation.

'I've been invited to pitch my plans to you this evening,' he said. 'Basically, I've told Stan that I will not only match any offer from my rivals, I'll take twenty per cent off it – and give as good quality or better.'

'And what will you get out of it?'

'The pleasure of knowing six families will have decent homes to live in at rents they can afford,' he replied. 'I'm a wealthy man, Angela. My father made a fortune up north from his mills – and I've taken up where he left off. Since I came out of the Army I've gone into building on my own account and there's more work than I ever dreamed of. Once the brick ovens really get going again, we'll see houses shooting up all over the country. We're building a better Britain, and everyone must benefit from that – I hope you'll agree?'

'Yes, I do agree that we want decent homes at affordable rents,' Angela said, wondering why she'd immediately felt hostility towards this man. She knew the charity board would be likely to agree to his proposals – how could they refuse such an offer? Yet she wondered what the catch was – what he hoped to gain. He struck her as altogether too smooth, too good to be true. 'But why should you offer us such a bargain?'

'I make my money from the rich men who can afford large office buildings in the centre of London and other big cities. My firm is delighted to take every penny we can from them, but when it comes to deserving causes, I'm a different animal. I like to help those who need it – and I'm told you're the same.'

'I support good causes, but I don't have the kind of fortune I imagine you have at your disposal.'

The corner of Henry Arnold's mouth lifted in what she took to be a superior smirk. 'Not many do, Angela. My father gave me a damned good start and I've built on his work. I dare say I could live in comfort for the rest of my life without lifting a finger – but why should I? Particularly when I can use some of my money to help those that need it.'

'I can't think of a single reason,' Angela conceded, realising she was beaten. He seemed insufferably arrogant, but she supposed he had every right to be given his wealth and his good works. 'I suppose I must thank you for coming to our aid. Twenty per cent is a lot of money – but I intend to get those other estimates, Mr Arnold. I will specify exactly what we want, and I shall expect to get it.'

'Naturally. I wouldn't expect anything less of you. I've been informed you're very efficient – a dragon lady, I'm told, when it comes to protecting your children at St Saviour's.'

'A dragon lady? I'll take that as a compliment. I'm only too happy to go into battle for the home and do whatever I can to help Sister Beatrice. Now *she* is a dragon lady if ever there was one.'

'So I hear. I know the builder you employed at St Saviour's – he swears he'd never work for you again even if the alternative was going broke. Sister Beatrice questioned every last thing he did – and he caught the sharp edge of your tongue a few times, I believe.'

'Indeed?' Angela glared at him. 'I merely pointed out various areas where the work was not up to standard and refused to pay until it was finished to my satisfaction.'

'And will you do the same where I'm concerned?'

'Certainly I shall.'

'Good. If any of my men let you down, they won't work for me again I can promise you. You'll find my standards are as high as your own, Angela.'

She was about to disabuse him of the notion that they were on first-name terms, when the chairman called everyone to take their seats so the meeting could begin.

'I'll call in and see you,' Henry Arnold whispered to her as they moved towards the committee room. 'I want to see where you work. I know you're always looking for funds for your orphans and I might be able to help . . .'

Angela did not answer. Something told her that he'd come to this meeting in order to meet her and yet she couldn't for the life of her think why. Perhaps she was imagining it, but she felt he'd deliberately provoked her, trying to gain her interest. If so, his plan had backfired. She was in no mood for arrogant men who thought they were more important than everyone else.

Suddenly a meeting that had promised to be dull and tedious had Angela alert and eager to hear every word. This man would bear watching; his promises sounded generous but all too often when something seemed to be too good to be true, it was. Well, if he thought he could pull the wool over her eyes, he was mistaken. She didn't care if he were as rich as Croesus, when it came to St Saviour's she would brook no interference.

SEVEN

'It's so lovely to see you, Michelle,' Alice said as she welcomed her into the ground floor flat that her husband had rented for them. 'Bob's away at the moment – the Army sent him to protect someone at a political conference in France – and it feels strange being here on my own with the baby.'

'I expect you miss him.' Michelle gave her the small posy of flowers she'd bought in the market on her way over. 'How are you in yourself?'

'I'm really well. I get tired when she cries all night, but I know all babies do that and it's to be expected.' Alice sighed, feeling scruffy and lacklustre, especially when she looked at Michelle, who was as slim and attractive as ever. Her blue-black hair gleamed with health, whilst Alice felt hers looked dull and lifeless. 'My sister came by yesterday. She tells me I should be happy that I've got a nice home and a good husband, but Mave doesn't understand how lonely it gets when he's away.'

'I can see how you would feel a bit miserable sometimes,' Michelle smiled. 'But you've got an adorable baby girl and a devoted husband, when he's home.' She laughed as Alice pulled a face. 'Cheer up, love. Angela told me to invite you to the Church Hall on Saturday. She's having another one of her clothing sales, and she's putting food on. I said you might help out by making tea – that is, if you felt able?'

'I'd love to,' Alice said and hugged her. 'Mave might lend a hand too, if I ask her. You could both come back here afterwards for a fish and chip supper.'

'I'll be on duty in the evening,' Michelle said, 'but I'll have supper with you another time, when I'm back on days.' Then, after a pause, 'You are managing all right? I mean, you're not short of anything?'

The sudden question made Alice laugh. 'Bob makes sure I have enough money. I'm better off now than I ever was at home, Chelle. Mave asked me the same, offered me a few bob, but I'm all right. I can cook and I'm good at managing my money – but I should like to learn to sew better. Mum couldn't never be bothered to show us how to do it properly. I thought I might go to lessons at night – it's two and sixpence a week, but that's not too bad.'

'Why don't you let *my* mother teach you? She's a trained seamstress. You could come round ours, chip in for supper – and then, if I'm home I'll walk back with you.'

'Would your mum teach me? I could pay her the two and sixpence . . .'

'Do that and she'll chase you off with a chopper,' Michelle teased. 'She might be little but she's pretty fierce if you get on the wrong side of her. No, seriously, bring some fruit or cakes. You're a good cook, Mave said so at the wedding; you can make cakes. Our Freddie never has enough of them.'

'I'll do that, then,' Alice said. 'You're my best friend, Michelle. Thanks for standing by me through all this. Everyone from St Saviour's has been so good to me. Nan has invited me for tea this Sunday.'

'I love Nan. Everyone does, she's like a second mother to us all – but Sister Beatrice . . . well, I respect her, especially the way she keeps going whatever . . .' Michelle hesitated, then went on, 'I know you won't say anything – but I think she might be unwell.'

'Sister Beatrice, ill? I don't believe it – unless you mean a cold or something?'

'No, it's worse than that . . .' Again, Michelle paused as if unsure whether to continue. 'I've seen her flinch like she's in terrible pain – and sometimes her face goes very white.'

'Has she said anything? She ought to see a doctor if she's in pain.'

'I don't know whether she has seen one or not,' Michelle said. 'I daren't ask. You know what Sister Beatrice is like. And she's so irritable lately, I'll probably get my head snapped off.'

'Well, she would be touchy if she's in pain. Someone ought to say,' Alice said. 'Why don't you mention it to Angela? She won't mess about – if she thinks you're right, she'll go straight in and say.'

'Yes, she would,' Michelle agreed. 'Where angels fear to tread, Angela charges in regardless. I'm hoping she can help my father get the job of caretaker. She hasn't said she can for definite, but if his tests are all right, and he's not got TB, he's in with a chance.'

'It's time your family had a bit of luck, Michelle. Are you hungry? How about I put the kettle on and we'll have a slice of my coconut cake?'

'Good idea,' Michelle said as Alice filled the shiny new kettle one of the girls from St Saviour's had bought her as a wedding present; it had a whistle that let everyone know when it was boiling. Alice set it on her modern gas cooker, which Michelle envied on her mother's behalf. 'I like coconut cake – especially if it's moist and chewy.'

'It's moist,' Alice said, then added doubtfully, 'but I'm not sure it's chewy – it isn't one of those pyramid things you make with condensed milk. It's a proper cake with a lot of coconut. I bought a bag of the desiccated stuff at the Home and Colonial. Isn't it lovely that things are beginning to come back into the shops again?'

'Best not eat too many cakes, even if you can buy them,' Michelle teased. 'If you want your figure back . . .'

'Never was as slim as you,' Alice said and laughed. 'I'm so glad you came round, Michelle. You're a real tonic.'

'That's what friends are for. I'll always be your friend, Alice. We have to stick together, be there for each other.'

'I know.' Alice embraced her. 'Don't worry about your dad too much, love. I'm sure he'll be fine.'

'I hope you're right. He's ever so miserable since the doctor put him on that diet.' Michelle sighed. 'Oh well, he's got an appointment at the hospital tomorrow for some tests, so we should know what's wrong in a couple of weeks . . .'

*

Leaving Alice's house two hours later, Michelle was lost in thoughts of her father as she walked through the narrow streets towards her tram stop. She was vaguely aware that several of the streetlights weren't working, but when the moon disappeared behind a cloud it suddenly became difficult to see. A shiver ran through her, and Michelle registered that it wasn't so much the cold night air that had caused it as the sense that she was being followed. She glanced over her shoulder and saw a man some distance behind her. When he noticed her looking at him, he stopped walking and bent to tie his shoelace.

Michelle walked on. Determined not to let on that she was afraid, she deliberately slowed her pace. Her shadow did the same. He was following her; she wasn't imagining it. She turned into the next street, which was busy with people and traffic, then suddenly stopped within sight of her tram stop. Once again he stopped too, loitering outside a newsagent's and pretending to be interested in the window display. When he turned to look at her, Michelle saw that he was uncertain what to do.

'Why are you following me? What do you want?'

'What makes you think I'm followin' yer?'

'We both know you are . . .' At that moment Michelle saw a police constable approaching on his bike. He was within hailing distance. 'Tell me what you want and go or I'll scream and tell that policeman you threatened me.'

'Bitch!' The man grabbed her arm, his fingers pinching her flesh. 'I've been told to give yer a warnin'. We ain't forgot yer, Alice Cobb, even if yer are married to that bloody Army boy. One of these days Mr Lee will be payin' yer a visit and you'd best tell him what yer know or you'll be sorry.'

'Tell Mr Lee he should look after his own affairs instead of employing idiots who don't even know the person they're supposed to be following. I'm not Alice and I'm not frightened of you or your Mr Lee.' She glared at him. 'Now take your hand off my arm and crawl back into whatever rotten hole you came out of. If you ever come near me or my friend Alice, I'll be talking to the police about you and your Mr Lee.'

The policeman had seen them now and he shouted something. Michelle wrenched away from the man, who glared at her but then glanced nervously in the direction of the constable and set off at a brisk pace, disappearing into a nearby alley. The constable wobbled to a stop beside her, putting his feet to the floor. His trouser legs were clamped with bicycle clips, exposing shiny, thick-soled black boots; beneath the helmet that was firmly strapped under his chin, an anxious pair of eyes peered out at Michelle. He looked so young and inexperienced, she doubted that he would have been much use against the brute who'd harassed her.

'Was that man annoying you, miss?'

'Oh, it was a case of mistaken identity. He thought I was someone else.'

'You don't want anything to do with the likes of him. He's a nasty piece of work, that Big Harry. Did he upset you?'

'He gave me a bit of a shock,' Michelle admitted, 'but he didn't hurt me. I think his intention was to give me a warning, but I told him he had the wrong person.'

68

'His kind don't care who they threaten,' the constable said. 'You be careful, walking alone at night, miss.'

'It's all right, I'm catching my tram now; it's coming round the corner.'

'Off you go then. And don't worry – we'll keep an eye on him. If he bothers you again, tell us and we'll soon sort him out.'

Michelle smiled inwardly as she thought of the constable trying to sort out Big Harry, but she thanked him for coming to her assistance. Then, seeing her tram arriving, she excused herself and ran for her stop. It wasn't until she sat down that she realised how shaken the experience had left her.

She wondered why Butcher Lee and his gang still thought Alice would know something about Jack Shaw – the East End bad boy that Alice had been soft on but who had left her high and dry. After all, she was married to someone else now, and Jack hadn't been seen since the night he broke into the boot factory with Arthur Baggins, intending to rob the safe. Someone had set fire to the building while they were inside; Arthur had escaped, but Jack was presumed to have died. If by some chance he had escaped, he surely wouldn't risk returning to London knowing the Lee gang were out to kill him.

Michelle was pretty sure Alice knew no more about Jack's fate than she did, otherwise she would certainly have mentioned it. Still, if Lee thought otherwise she'd have to warn Alice to be on her guard.

The morning after Michelle's visit, Alice returned from the market to find a letter waiting for her. The sight of it sent a tingle of apprehension down her spine: it was addressed to Miss Alice Cobb rather than Mrs Manning, and she was almost certain she knew the handwriting.

For a moment she considered putting it straight in the bin without opening it, but something wouldn't let her. Though she knew she ought not to read it, she couldn't resist slitting it open and taking out the contents.

I got a mate to deliver this, Alice love. He said he knew where you were living and I daren't bring it myself. I can't come to your home, but I want to see you. I should never have left you. I think of you and my kid all the time, and now I've got things sorted we can go to America. My ship leaves in three weeks and I want us to be on it together. Please meet me, Alice. It's too dangerous for me to come to you, but if you take the train to Southend, I'll meet you by the pier. Come next Saturday and I'll be there every hour from twelve until nine at night. I've put in £2 for your fare, and the key to a locker at Euston Station. I need you to fetch a parcel for me, Alice love. No one will notice you and it's important . . . do that for me, Alice, and you'll never regret it, I promise.

I still love you, Alice. I've never stopped thinking about you, but I had to keep moving around. People were looking for me, and I couldn't let you know where I was until now.

So he was alive! Alice sat down on the nearest chair, feeling sick and shaken. Her hands trembled as she was caught by a surge of disbelief mixed with elation. He was alive, despite what everyone had told her. She felt overwhelming excitement followed almost as swiftly by despair, for it was too late. Tears stung her eyes and trickled silently down her cheeks, as she realised that she still cared for him.

She'd never quite given up on Jack Shaw, even when everyone said he was dead, but now she felt as if the breath had been knocked out of her. Alice looked at the two one-pound notes Jack had sent, staring at them as if they would burn her. She held the small key with a numbered tab in her hand and frowned. What was it that Jack wanted her to fetch? It must be important to him or he wouldn't have asked. As glad as she was to learn that he hadn't died in the fire, she knew she couldn't trust him. He'd probably put some of the stuff he'd stolen in that locker and Alice wanted nothing to do with his ill-gotten gains.

Had this letter arrived only a few months ago she'd have gone to Jack without a second thought, even though she knew he couldn't be trusted. Part of her longed to go to him even now, in spite of the way he'd abandoned her and their daughter to fend for themselves, but she couldn't. She was married to Bob now, and she wouldn't hurt him, not after all he'd done for her. He was a good, decent man and she was fond of him.

But fond wasn't the kind of all-consuming love she'd felt for Jack. A bitter sense of loss filled her and she knew that, despite everything, she still loved Jack; he was still there inside her head and her heart, even though he'd let her down. She'd tried to forget him but all it took was this letter to start up that aching need inside – but she couldn't go to him, she couldn't leave Bob.

She shoved the money and key in her apron pocket, feeling the tears sting her eyes and the angry hurt well up inside her as the shock started to wear off. If he came knocking on her door she would give him back his money and that key. It was the only thing to do – the decent thing.

Alice wouldn't be on that train on Saturday. She was going to keep her promise to help out with the teas at Angela's charity sale. She wouldn't meet Jack in Southend, she wouldn't see him ever again – but a part of her wanted to. A part of her wanted to take her child and run to the man she loved. Regret surged, and she wished that she'd never agreed to marry. If only she'd turned down Bob's proposal and stayed with Nan, then she would be free – but for what? What sort of a life was Jack offering her?

Hearing her baby cry, Alice went into the kitchen and picked her up, looking down at her with love. Her heart felt as if it were being torn in two as she held Susie to her breast and rocked her. She was Jack's child, but did he have the right to know her after the way he'd deserted them?

Besides, it was too dangerous. The Lee gang were still watching her; every so often someone would follow her when she went out with the baby, and only this morning she'd noticed a man staring at her in the market. Thus far, no one had approached her and she'd hoped that after a while they would realise it was a waste of time and give up.

No, it was stupid even to think of Jack. If he'd truly

wanted her, loved her, he would have kept his promise to send for her a long time ago. In fact, the more she thought about it, the more she suspected that the only reason he'd got in touch was because he needed her to fetch whatever was in that locker.

Bitterness swept through her as she remembered the way Jack had broken his promises in the past. He was no good, just as her father had warned at the start.

EIGHT

'That seemed to go well,' Wendy said, surveying the empty stalls after the sale of second-hand clothes and bits and pieces had finished. 'I don't know how you manage to find so many nice things to sell, Angela. I bought a good leather bag for myself.'

'I have to thank my father for a lot of it.' Angela turned to him with a smile. He was waiting patiently to take her home so that she could change for the evening. 'Dad asked our neighbours if they had anything for me to sell on behalf of St Saviour's and they overwhelmed him with stuff. He sent it up in three large boxes on the train.'

'Nan told me you've raised almost a hundred pounds from the Bring and Buy evenings you've been holding at your home, and hers.'

'It seems women like exchanging the clothes they don't want for something different, so we've done well, but once rationing is over and there's new stuff in the shops people won't want second-hand so much.'

'A lot of women won't ever be able to afford anything else.' Wendy laughed softly. 'Some of these clothes are better than anything I could afford to buy new. Besides, whatever happens in future, you'll think of something. Everyone says you've done wonders since you've been here. The children have all sorts of treats these days, and it's all down to you.'

'It's a team effort—' Angela stopped abruptly as she noticed the man standing near the hall doorway. 'I didn't know he was here.'

Wendy followed her gaze. 'Who is he?'

'His name's Arnold.' Angela's father frowned. 'He arrived at the same time as I did. You were too busy to notice, Angela.'

'I met him at a charity meeting the other night. I can't think what he's doing here though.' Angela tried not to let the others see her annoyance. 'Come on, Dad, let's go. I want to get changed before we go out this evening. Wendy will finish up here for me, won't you?'

'You know I will, Angela,' the staff nurse said, smiling. 'Have a lovely time with your father.'

'Angela . . .' Henry Arnold touched her arm as she was about to pass him. 'I was hoping we might have a word?'

'Please telephone me, Mr Arnold,' she said. 'This is my father – Mr Hendry. We have an appointment and must leave now.'

'I really do need to talk to you, Angela.'

'Another time,' Angela said. 'Please excuse us, we have to go.'

She took her father's arm and propelled him away. He looked at her, puzzled by her abrupt manner, which had bordered on rudeness. 'That isn't like you, Angela. The man was only being polite.'

'I know, but I don't like him. I may have to deal with him on behalf of the charity I represent, but I don't have to spend time with him otherwise.'

'Not like you at all,' her father said, puzzled. 'Ah, here's Adderbury. You're not going to brush him off too, I hope?'

'No, certainly not,' Angela said, but smiled hesitantly as Mark came up to them. 'You almost missed us. We had a successful afternoon.'

'I had hoped to be here sooner, but I was delayed. I'm glad it all went well for you.'

'Yes, it did.' Angela smiled at him. 'Please call me when you can, Mark. We should talk sometime, but you're always so busy.'

'I'll find the time,' he promised. 'Have a good evening. Nice to see you, Edward. We must catch up soon.'

'Drop by for a drink one weekend, when you're in the country.' The two men shook hands and they parted.

Angela opened the door of her car. She didn't often bother to drive in town but she'd had several bits and pieces to bring over earlier.

'Well,' she said as she eased the car into the steady stream of traffic. 'I think you've got something to tell me, Dad?'

'It's about your mother,' he said. 'Good news and . . . well, rather odd news too, but I'll explain when we get to your apartment. You need to concentrate on the traffic, Angela . . .'

Angela installed her father in one of the most comfortable chairs, gave him a drink and then sat down opposite, looking at him expectantly. He sipped the wine, nodded his approval, placed it on the small table at his side and assumed a serious expression.

'Your mother wrote to me. She says she feels much better and doesn't think she needs to stay at the clinic any longer, but . . . she doesn't want to come home.'

'What do you mean, she doesn't want to come home?' Angela was puzzled. 'If she feels better, why wouldn't she come home?'

'Apparently she wants to stay with a friend she met in Switzerland. She's been invited to say in a villa in the South of France and that's what she wants to do.'

'Not come home to you? Is she cured, after only a few months?' Angela couldn't believe she was hearing this properly. 'Have you been invited to this villa too?'

'No, there was no mention of it – and I'm not sure I'd want to go if there had been.' He hesitated, then, 'I'm not sure she is cured yet – but the clinic is voluntary. I can't force her to stay if she wants to leave, Angela.'

Her father was looking tired, his skin grey and his whole manner defeated, as if he was finding it all too much to bear. She hadn't noticed at the Church Hall, but now she could see that his youthful air had left him. He'd always seemed so much younger than her mother, still a handsome man and full of vitality, but now he looked drained.

'Are you ill, Daddy?' she asked quietly. 'Is it your heart?'

'Well, you know I'm not the man I was.' He forced a smile. 'I'm feeling a bit upset, that's all. I thought when your mother left the clinic she would come home to me – but her letter was that of a stranger, someone writing out of duty . . .'

'Does she know you're not well?'

'No, and I don't want her to,' he said, giving Angela a direct look. 'It's nothing serious, my love – and if she's happier staying with her new friends . . . Well, we must let her have her life. It seems that your mother was disappointed in me. I couldn't give her what she wanted. So now . . . she's decided to go her own way.'

'It sounds as if you think she isn't coming back.'

'I'll be surprised if she does. You see, the friend she's going to stay with is a man. Quite a wealthy man, I gather.'

'Oh, Daddy!' Angela was shocked at the implication in her father's news. 'After all you've done for her – for us . . .' Angela felt anger rise up inside her. How could her mother have done this to him, especially when he was unwell.

'Perhaps it is for the best, my love. You mustn't worry about me. Someone comes in twice a week to clean and she does a bit of shopping and cooking for me, so I'm well looked after and I still have you – don't I?'

'You know you do,' she said, but her eyes stung with tears and her throat was tight. Her head was running the whole gamut of emotions: love and hurt for his sake, and anger with her mother for behaving so callously. 'I'm sorry, Dad. I think she is being very unfair.'

'She thinks we're the ones who've been unfair to her. Your mother believes I love you more than her – and she might be right. In truth, our marriage has been over for some years, but I tried to hold it together for everyone's sake and the result was disaster. Mark explained it all to me; it seems that the drinking, the shoplifting and spending sprees were all symptoms of an illness that was created by deep depression.'

'But you gave us both so much, Dad.'

'I tried, but it wasn't enough for her . . . Perhaps what I gave was only money, at least as far as she was concerned. Had I loved her enough, I might have seen her despair years ago, but I was too busy – and I must admit, selfish too. Don't imagine I shall go into a decline even if it comes to a divorce. I'm sorry for your sake though, Angela; we've let you down, and people will talk.'

Angela got up and went to kneel at his side, looking up at him earnestly. 'You've never let me down, Daddy. If you need me, I'll come home,' she promised. 'Remember that, dearest. You are the most important person in the world to me.'

'I'm managing, my darling girl,' he said, tenderly stroking her hair. 'I thought you should know and it isn't the kind of thing I wanted to say on the phone or in a letter.'

'No, better to hear it from you,' she agreed, but inside she was fuming. Her mother had sent him a letter rather than tell him to his face and that made her furious, but there was no point in saying more. He had accepted it and to make a fuss would only cause him more strain. 'Now you must excuse me while I go and get ready for dinner. Tonight we're going to have a lovely evening together, Dad, no matter what.'

NINE

'I took Sarah's pinafore skirt to be washed,' Wendy told Angela as they sat drinking coffee in the staff room a few days later. 'That dirty old pipe was in the pocket and I was tempted to throw it out, but instead I gave it a bit of a wash and put it in the locker by the side of her bed.'

'That was good of you,' Angela said. 'To us it's only a dirty old thing, but it means something to that child and she doesn't have much.'

'She's a bit backward . . .' Wendy twiddled a strand of her light brown hair round her finger. She was growing it longer so that she would be able to put it back in a knot under her nurses' cap, but felt it was dull and unremarkable, and envied Angela her pale blonde locks. Angela had such lovely eyes too, the colour of an azure sky. 'Have you noticed that she agrees with everything Samantha says, echoing her like a parrot?'

'Yes, I think we all have, though she can speak independently if she wishes. Do you think they are settling into the dorm all right?'

Wendy hesitated before she answered, then inclined

her head. 'Yes, they've settled quite well. I think Samantha is happy enough here. She and Mary Ellen get on well and I think they're working on a scheme to earn some more stars for a trip to the zoo.'

'Yes, all the children like to earn points towards that trip.' Angela laughed. 'Have you settled in now, Wendy?'

'Yes, I think so,' Wendy looked sad, her soft brown eyes moist. 'It took me a while to get used to living in the Nurses' Home after Mother died – but I'm getting over that now.'

'It must have been so sad for you, nursing her yourself at home.'

'It was what I wanted to do, but it was heartbreaking.'

'I'm sure it must have been,' Angela agreed. 'Losing someone you love is terrible – but seeing them fade . . . I'm sorry, I can see it still hurts you.'

'No, not now,' Wendy said. 'I loved Mum and I'm glad to talk about her, Angela. Everyone avoids the subject – but you know what it's like to lose someone . . .'

'Yes.' Angela got up to pour more coffee but Wendy shook her head.

'I ought to be getting back to the wards, thanks all the same.'

Wendy left Angela and went out into the hall, but instead of returning to the wards immediately, she went into the new wing. It still smelled of fresh paint and everything looked modern and bright, much nicer than the old wing.

Hearing the sound of crying and screaming as she approached Mary Ellen's dorm, she hastened her step. A child was in acute distress and by the sound of it that child was one of the twins – Sarah.

81

'Stop it, Sarah,' her sister was pleading. The blanket and sheets had been stripped from Sarah's bed and were lying on the floor in a heap. Tilly had changed the sheets only that morning; now they were crumpled and it looked as if one of them had been torn. 'Don't upset yourself like this . . .'

'Want go home,' Sarah wailed. 'Don't like it here. Pipe gone, Pa gone – Sarah want go home . . .'

'We can't go back,' Samantha said, trying to catch her sister in her arms, but she pulled away and started to scream again. 'Stop it, Sarah, or they might send us away and we've nowhere else to go – please.'

'What is the matter?' Wendy asked. Samantha turned to look at her, and for a moment there was resentment in her eyes – and was that a faint trace of fear?

'Sarah's pinafore dress has gone and Pa's pipe was in the pocket. She loves that pipe because it was his. Now she won't stop crying. She's never like this . . .'

'Oh, I am sorry,' Wendy said. 'Look in your locker, Sarah love. I took your pinafore so I could wash it for you – I'll bring it back as soon as it's ironed. The pipe is in your locker . . .'

Sarah looked at her blankly, but Samantha rushed to the small cupboard at the side of her sister's bed and opened it. She saw the pipe lying on top of a pile of clean knickers and socks and picked it up, offering it to Sarah, who snatched it out of her hand and held it to her cheek, which was still damp from her tears.

'Pa's pipe come back, Pa come back,' she said, and looked hopefully at her sister as if trying to make her understand. She sat on the edge of the bed, the broken

82

pipe clutched to her cheek as she crooned the song no one but she could understand.

'Oh, Sarah,' Samantha said, wiping the tears from her cheeks with her hanky. 'Don't cry. Pa won't come back; he doesn't care about us, he never did – I'm so sorry . . .'

'I'm sorry I touched your pipe,' Wendy said, sitting down on the bed and looking at the sisters. 'I didn't mean to hurt you, Sarah. I know that it means a lot to you and I wouldn't throw it away. You must keep it safe with you all the time.'

'Pa loves his pipe,' Sarah said. 'Pa come back for pipe?'

'No, dearest,' Samantha told her, putting an arm around her thin shoulders. 'The pipe is broken. Pa doesn't want it any more – and he doesn't want us. Aunt Jane won't have us both and no one else will. We have to stop here where we're safe.'

Sarah looked at her. Her song had stopped and she seemed to be weighing up what her sister had told her. 'Pa not come back for pipe? Not come back for Samantha and Sarah?'

'No, never,' Samantha said. 'He went to sea and left us to fend for ourselves. We couldn't get any money and we nearly starved, Sarah. Remember how cold and hungry we were before we came here? We have to stay here where it's warm and they feed us.'

Sarah stared at her in silence for a moment, and then a heart-rending wail rose from deep inside her and she hurled the clay pipe against the wall. It shattered into pieces and fell on the floor.

'Oh, Sarah – your pipe!' Wendy rushed to gather up the bowl and one piece of the stem that hadn't shattered, bringing them back to the sobbing child but she refused to take them, shaking her head furiously. 'Don't you want it? I'll put it in your locker, shall I?' She bent down to place the two pieces in the locker but Sarah swooped on them and hurled them at the wall, and this time the bowl shattered into small pieces.

'Hate pipe, hate Pa,' Sarah cried and then turned her back on Wendy.

Samantha tried to put her arms around her, but she shrugged her off and jumped up, then ran towards the door. Samantha stood indecisively until Wendy asked if she ought to go after her sister.

'Sarah has to learn that we can't go back,' Samantha said, and there were tears on her cheeks now. 'Pa doesn't want us, miss; he never did. When we were born it killed our mother – Sarah was the last and our mother wasn't strong enough. My aunt says Pa will never forgive us . . .'

Suddenly she was in Wendy's arms, sobbing out her story, telling her how they'd hidden from their father after he tried to kill Sarah in his fury over the broken pipe.

'Surely he wouldn't have meant to harm her?' Wendy said, shocked.

Samantha drew back, looking at her with the eyes of a child that knew too much.

'Yes, he would, Nurse. He always hated her. It wasn't too bad when we were little; we had a lady called Melanie who came in and looked after us. She wasn't kind to us, but we were clean and we had food – and

84

Pa didn't hit us. Then one day she got cross with Sarah and hit her, so I shouted at her and told her she was wicked. When Melanie slapped my face, Sarah kicked her ankles for hurting me. So Melanie left. She told Pa she wouldn't stay in a place with evil children.'

'Oh, Samantha, I'm so sorry.' As the weeping girl buried her face in Wendy's uniform, arms wrapped tightly round her waist, the nurse stroked the girl's soft hair, encouraging her to let all the misery come pouring out of Samantha. It was as if the floodgates had opened and she couldn't hold it inside any longer. Her eyes looked enormous in her pale face, dark with anguish and remembered pain.

'I didn't mind that she'd gone, but Pa was angry and gave Sarah a good hiding for upsetting her. After that, he didn't ask anyone to come in, so I cooked what food he brought home and I did my best to look after Sarah . . . but she breaks things. She doesn't mean to – they just seem to slip through her fingers. Pa said she was a Child of Satan and threatened to put her away in a place for lunatics. Aunt Jane said that was where she'd put her too, but she'd take me in. Then I woke up and Pa was kicking Sarah, and when we ran away and hid, he went off and left us.' Samantha paused to draw breath before continuing: 'He took all the food and money and Mum's valuables, and there was only rubbish left and the man from the scrapyard wouldn't even buy the pans I took him – but he gave me five shillin's for lettin' him touch my chest.' Samantha looked up defiantly. 'I took his money and then kicked his shins and ran off. I took Sarah and we hid in a bombed-out house down by the docks . . .'

'Good for you,' Wendy said, and gave her a hug. 'In your shoes, I'd have done the same. But now you're safe here and your aunt will visit you—'

'Don't want to see her!' Samantha drew back in alarm. 'She'll put Sarah in one of those awful places!'

'No, she won't. I promise you, Sister Beatrice wouldn't let her do that and neither would Angela or any of us. You belong to us now, Samantha. You're safe here with us and we'll take care of you both. Sarah may have to attend a special school – that will be for Sister to decide – but I'm sure that she will keep you both here.'

'Sarah can do simple sums and things, if I show her,' Samantha said. 'She can help with cooking or laying tables, if I tell her what to do – and she can draw people's faces really well. She isn't daft.'

'No, she certainly isn't. I'm going to tell Miss Angela what you've told me; she will talk to Sister and decide what to do. They won't let anyone take you from us, Samantha. When I tell Angela the whole story, she will be on your side. Now, I think you'd better see if you can find Sarah, love. It's raining outside and, although it isn't cold, we don't want her getting a chill.'

TEN

Alice got the surprise of her life when she unlocked the door of her flat and went in that evening. She smelled the cigarette smoke first and her nerves prickled. Had one of the Lee gang broken into her home?

'Is that you, Alice?' Bob's voice came from the bedroom and then he strolled into the hall wearing his army trousers with braces and no shirt. His hair looked wet and she thought he'd been having a shower. He'd had one put in the bath, as he preferred a shower. 'Good, I'm glad you're home. I hope you haven't been working? I thought we'd agreed you were going to take care of yourself for a bit longer?'

'Bob!' Alice felt a surge of emotion as she saw the anxious look on his face. It was obvious how much he cared for her, and yet she'd spent the afternoon wishing she was on the train to Southend! 'I went to help out with the teas at a charity event for the home. It was only for a couple of hours – I didn't do too much, I promise. It was nice seeing all my friends.' Her cheeks turned pink as she spoke, for the letter from Jack had stirred up old feelings and she still felt torn.

'That's all right then. How have you been?'

'I've been fine.' She rushed over to give him a hug to cover her guilt. He gave her a quick hug back and then released her. 'I didn't expect you back today, Bob. How long have you got?'

'Three days. I shouldn't have been due for leave yet, but my mate wants next weekend off and so I swapped with him at the last minute. I didn't send a telegram because I thought it might put the wind up you.'

'It would have,' she admitted. 'I've only got a bit of yellow fish for tea – or we could get pie and chips from the shop, if you'd rather, then have the fish in the morning with some bread.'

'I don't go much on that sort of stuff,' Bob told her. 'You have it tomorrow, Alice. I'll take you out this evening – we'll have steak and kidney pie at that pub we went to last time I was home. They always do a good meal there.'

'Yes, all right,' Alice agreed. In truth she was exhausted after helping with the teas, even though it had been fun and all the St Saviour's girls had made a fuss of Susie, picking her up when she cried and spoiling her, but Alice wasn't about to tell Bob that she would rather stay at home. 'I'll make us a cup of tea and then get changed.'

'No, you go and put your feet up for a minute,' Bob said. 'I'll make us a cuppa and then you can take your time getting ready. Mave said she'll be over in an hour to take care of Susie for us.'

As he disappeared into the kitchen, Alice lifted Susie out of her pram and hugged the sleeping baby to her. It was a good thing that Bob had come back unexpectedly, she thought. All the way home Alice had been wondering if it was too late to catch the train to Southend – and now she was glad that she wouldn't have to think about it any more. She'd had a timely reminder that she was married to a decent man and would be a fool to throw it all away for a rogue like Jack Shaw.

Alice was aware of being watched as she and Bob ate their meal in the pub. The atmosphere was a bit smoky but that didn't stop her enjoying the tasty food and the glass of lemonade shandy she'd had with it. Bob had offered her the usual port and lemon, but Alice thought she might be better off sticking to a weak shandy, with more lemonade than beer.

'Only until the baby's weaned,' she told him with a smile. 'I don't want her to be a drunkard, do I?'

She was enjoying the unexpected treat and didn't particularly notice the man staring at them until Bob had finished his plum tart and custard. She touched him with her foot under the table and he looked startled.

'We're being watched,' she said. 'He's sitting to your right – in the corner – and he's been staring at us for a while.'

'Perhaps he's envying me my lovely wife,' Bob quipped before glancing over his shoulder. The smile was gone from his face as he turned back to her. 'I know him – he's one of Butcher Lee's henchmen. Let him look, Alice, we're not doing any harm and nor is he – but if he follows us home I'll tackle him.'

'He or someone like him has been following me for weeks, ever since you were home last time.'

Bob frowned. 'You didn't tell me. Why didn't you write and tell me, Alice?'

'I try to ignore them. I know why they follow me – in case I meet Jack Shaw.'

'How're you supposed to do that – he's dead . . .' His eyes narrowed intently. 'Alice, what's going on? Don't tell me he's alive?' She inclined her head slightly and he frowned. 'Bloody hell! How do you know – have you seen him?'

'No. I wouldn't,' Alice said, but her cheeks were warm because she knew how close she'd come to taking that train. 'It's over, Bob. He let me down and I'm with you now.'

'I can't stop you if you want to go to him, Alice, but—'

'I wouldn't go, Bob. Even if I knew where to find him.'

Bob leaned towards her, taking her hand where it rested on the table. 'You've heard from him, haven't you?'

Alice hesitated, and then nodded. 'He sent me two pounds and asked me to meet him today – but I went to the jumble sale instead.'

'What about the money?'

'It's in the drawer at home. I didn't know what to do with it. I'd send it back, only I don't have an address for him. I certainly don't want it.'

'Are you sure?'

'Yes . . .' Alice met his eyes, seeing the hurt and the fear – fear that she would leave him, and suddenly she felt wretched for even entertaining the thought. 'I did love him once, Bob, but I never trusted him. You've been good to me and I wouldn't hurt you for the world. I do care for you, you must know I do – and I trust you to look after me and the child.'

'Good,' he said and smiled. 'You leave the Lee gang to me, Alice. I'll have a word with someone I know and he'll warn them off. I don't want them bothering you again.'

'Be careful, Bob.' Alice felt a flicker of fear. 'I don't want you to be hurt.'

He grinned at her. 'I'll be careful – as careful as I need to be. I've told you before; I can take care of myself.'

Alice couldn't bring herself to remind him of the speeding car that had knocked him down earlier that year. She'd since been told that the attempt on his life had been intended as a warning to her not to step out of line, but she couldn't let Bob know or he might do something reckless.

Alice glanced at the table where the watcher had been sitting and saw he'd gone. She told Bob and he laughed, taking out his wallet to settle the bill.

'He must have known what I was saying,' Bob said. 'I'll make sure they stay away from you, love – you must keep ignoring them and I'll do the rest.'

Alice didn't answer. Being shadowed hadn't scared her, but the thought of what the Lee gang would do to them both if Bob tried to stand up to them made her blood run cold. Bob thought he could take care of himself – and perhaps he could in a fair fight – but the Lee gang didn't believe in fighting fair. They'd set the boot factory on fire to get even with Arthur and Jack for taking something that belonged to them – it didn't bear thinking about what they would do to Jack if they ever caught up with him.

*

Alice lingered as she browsed the stalls in Spitalfields. The covered market, situated off the busy Commercial Street, was open seven days a week and in all weathers. Almost everything you could want was available here, from fruit and vegetables to cheese and fish, long rolls of cloth and remnants, boots, books, second-hand goods of every description, cheap Indian rugs, umbrellas, handbags, and fresh flowers. The scent of lilies wafting from the flower stalls was so overpowering, Alice began to feel a headache coming on. As if that wasn't enough, Susie had woken up in her pram and was beginning to whimper. Alice put a dummy in the baby's mouth and rocked the pram. She would be glad to get home, because right now she was cold and tired and desperate for a cup of tea.

Alice had bought some terry towelling, which she planned to make into more nappies for Susie, and now she was ready to buy the fruit she would take with her to Michelle's house when she went for her sewing lesson. She was disappointed to see there were no bananas this week; it had been so nice to see them back after seven years without, but they were still thin on the ground. Fortunately there were some lovely big black grapes on offer, so Alice decided to buy a bag of those instead. She paid her money and was turning to leave when a young lad came up to her. He grabbed her arm, giving her an odd look.

'I reckon you dropped this,' he said, and pressed something into her hand. Alice was about to say that it wasn't hers when she realised it was a note of some kind. The lad winked at her and went off, disappearing into the crowds.

Alice glanced at it and realised it was a note from Jack. She hesitated, knowing that she should throw it away, but instead she put it into her pocket, too cold and fed up to look at it now. She was tired and her head was throbbing as she made her way quickly to the tram stop. Moments later a tram arrived and she got on, grateful to the conductor who lifted the pram on for her, folding it and tucking it in the luggage rack under the steps to the upper deck. Alice cradled Susie in the crook of her arm as she fumbled for her purse to pay her fare. Susie would be ready for her feed when she got home and then Alice would be able to put her feet up and relax with a nice hot cup of tea. Except it was hard to relax when she thought about the letter in her pocket. Jack obviously wasn't about to give up on her, but Alice had made up her mind – she wasn't going to fetch that stuff for him however many letters he sent her . . .

ELEVEN

'Angela, I want to talk to you about the new children . . .' Sister Beatrice said, entering her office as she was typing up the monthly report. 'I know they're with Mary Ellen and Marion in their new dorm now and I'd like you to bring me up to date with the situation. I'm not sure about—' Sister gasped and clutched at her side suddenly. 'Oh – I must sit down for a moment . . .'

'What's wrong, Sister? Are you in pain?' Angela asked, immediately concerned by the sight of the older woman's pale face and obvious distress. 'What can I do for you? Please let me help you . . .'

'I'll be all right in a moment. Please do not fuss,' Sister said through gritted teeth, gesturing for Angela to sit back down. 'It comes and goes – ahhh . . .' she went quiet and sank into a chair, clearly shaken by the ferocity of the pain. 'I've never known it to be this bad . . .' she gasped and clutched at herself again.

For a moment Angela was so shocked that she couldn't think. Sister Beatrice wasn't the sort to get ill; she was strong and stubborn and never allowed a child to bother her, but perhaps the strain of all that trouble with Terry had pulled her down . . . yet that was months ago and this was more than strain. She could see by the colour of Sister's face and the way she was holding her breath that the pain was bad.

'I'm going to call the doctor,' Angela said, reaching for her telephone.

'You're over-reacting,' Sister Beatrice's tone was angry. 'I'll be all right soon I tell you.' She stood up and took two steps forward, then tottered and fell to the ground, where she lay writhing and moaning in agony.

Angela knew it must be something serious to make Sister collapse in this way. The onset of pain had seemed sudden and unexpected, but then she remembered the Warden's irritability of late and her habit of hiding her emotions and anything else she considered signs of weakness. It was quite possible that she had been suffering for weeks without telling anyone.

Angela rang immediately for Dr Kent and told him what had happened. 'I'll be there as soon as I can,' he said. 'In the meantime call one of the nurses to look at her – but don't try to move her on your own unless she is able to get up herself.'

'I'm going to get a nurse,' Angela said, bending over Sister Beatrice briefly. 'Please don't try to do anything. We'll help you to get up when I come back.'

Running swiftly down the hall to the sick room, she discovered that both Wendy and Michelle were there, discussing the patients' notes. Michelle came towards her instantly, alerted by Angela's urgent manner.

'It's Sister; she's ill,' Angela said. 'I've rung for the doctor but it's going to take him a while to get here.'

'I'll come,' Michelle said. 'I've been worried about

her for a while. I thought she might simply be tired but, knowing Sister, she's probably been hiding something.'

'Yes; she would think it weak to give in,' Angela agreed.

Michelle rushed on ahead of her. As Angela entered her office she discovered that Sister had managed to get to her feet in her absence and Michelle was helping her into the armchair provided for visitors. Sister's face was grey and she looked very ill. She had her eyes closed and was holding her side, obviously in agony.

'What's wrong with her?' Angela hovered as Michelle took Sister's pulse and touched her forehead, which was sticky with sweat.

'I'm not sure, but I think from the position of the pain it may be appendicitis,' she said, looking anxiously at Sister. 'How long have you been having these pains, Sister?'

'A few weeks,' Sister said weakly. 'It wasn't so bad at first and it always went after a while but now . . . it's getting much worse.'

'We've sent for the doctor,' Michelle said, 'but if it is acute appendicitis you will need an operation.'

'I shall be all right, I tell you. All this fuss . . .' Sister gasped and could not continue for a moment. 'I can't leave St Saviour's. Who will look after things here?'

'Angela and the nurses and the carers,' Michelle answered before Angela could speak. 'We shall take care of things while you're away, Sister – but you have no choice. If I'm right and it bursts – you could die.'

Sister Beatrice looked at her. The truth was in her eyes, for she knew it as well as her staff nurse. If the inflamed appendix ruptured she could be in very serious trouble. She turned her head suddenly to be violently sick on the floor. Angela rushed to give her a handkerchief and offered a glass of water, which she accepted, looking sheepish.

'I'm so sorry.'

'Please don't worry. I will soon clear it up. Michelle, do you think she would be more comfortable in the sick bay?'

'No, I don't want anyone else to see me this way – the children mustn't be upset,' Sister said, a note of authority in her voice. 'I must get home and rest. I shall be all right in a while . . .' Yet even as she spoke, she clutched at her right side again.

'The doctor will be here shortly and you're not going anywhere but hospital,' Michelle insisted. 'Angela, could you go down and ask one of the girls to come up and clear this up? I should like a couple of minutes alone with Sister.'

'Very well; I'll get a cloth and bucket. No need to let anyone else know about this,' Angela said and went out.

She had reached the bottom of the stairs when Dr Kent rushed in, looking anxious. Stopping to explain what had happened, Angela directed him back to her office and then went off again in search of warm water and a mop. By the time she returned to her office, Dr Kent was very much in charge of the situation. He had opened his bag and was giving Sister an injection.

'This is a mild sedative to ease the pain,' he told her. 'I've rung for an ambulance and it will be here shortly. I shall telephone the hospital and let them know to prepare for an emergency operation. Acute appendicitis is very serious, Sister. You must know what could happen if there should be a rupture – I'm surprised you didn't seek medical advice before this.'

'I could not neglect my duty. Besides, it suddenly became much worse.'

'Yes, that is what happens if you neglect the warnings. It can come on very suddenly in its severest form.'

'You must see I cannot desert the children . . .'

'Nonsense! No one is irreplaceable,' he said firmly and Angela saw Sister's face twist as if he had added fuel to the flames. 'Your staff will manage perfectly well until you can take up your place here again – something you won't do if you're dead. No more arguments. I believe we may be in time to prevent the worst happening, thanks to the prompt actions of your assistant.'

Sister nodded but didn't answer. She was looking at Angela, an unspoken appeal in her eyes.

'We shall manage until you return,' Angela promised. 'I will visit as soon as you're well enough – and you can give me your instructions then.'

They both knew she did not need Sister's instructions, but it was all she could think of to comfort her. Although they did not always see eye to eye where the running of the home was concerned, Angela respected Sister Beatrice's devotion to the children.

'The children will be all right,' Michelle said as she helped Dr Kent assist Sister to her feet. 'We'll take you down in the lift and they won't see you – and the ambulance will be here soon.'

'Yes . . .' Sister had ceased to resist. She was clearly close to collapse and went with them, but at the door, she paused and looked back. 'The twins – take the greatest care of them, Angela. I'm not sure about this

aunt of theirs and someone told me—' she broke off
with another gasp of pain, unable to finish what she'd
been about to say.

'Yes, Sister Beatrice. I'll take care of them,' Angela
promised. 'Please, don't worry. We'll do our best for all
the children while you're away. You must rest and get
better soon and come back to us.'

Sister Beatrice was led away and after Angela had
cleaned up the vomit from the floor, she headed to the
kitchen knowing that she needed to let everyone know
what had happened.

'Was that an ambulance I heard outside?' Muriel
asked anxiously when she took the bucket back to the
scullery area. 'Who's ill?'

'I'm afraid it's Sister Beatrice,' Angela told her, and saw
the shock in her face. She turned pale and sat down, staring
as if she'd seen a ghost. 'I know I can trust you to keep
this to yourself, Muriel. The doctor thinks she has acute
appendicitis and will need an emergency operation.'

'God have mercy! My niece's youngest daughter had
that – it burst and she died. They couldn't do nothin'
for her – pray God, Sister don't go the same. Whatever
shall we do without her?'

'We shall have to manage as best we can until she
comes back,' Angela said calmly. 'We have good nurses
in Michelle and Wendy, and Paula too. I'm sure we shall
manage.'

'But Sister is always here,' Muriel said. 'We all turn
to her when we need her. Does Nan know? She'll be
dreadfully upset. She's very fond of Sister – as am I.'

'Yes, I'm sure everyone is,' Angela said. 'But if we all
continue to do our jobs as normal we shall manage.

99

Hopefully it won't be for too long.' Angela believed this, though she knew there would be no time for any extras, like the party to celebrate the opening of the new wing; that would have to be cancelled now.

'It might be for the best,' Cook said dolefully, dabbing at her eyes with her white apron that was smeared with some kind of sauce. 'I don't like the sound of it, though – emergency operation isn't good, Angela. It isn't good at all . . .'

'No, it's very upsetting,' Angela said. 'But I assure you, I can manage the office work as usual and the nurses will all do their duty.'

'But Sister tells me what to cook for the children – some of them have special diets and she's always the one that works out what's right for them. I'll do my best, but I'm not sure I can manage without her guidance . . .'

'I will consult with Michelle or Wendy and tell you what's needed.' Angela sighed inwardly. Sister Beatrice had no doubt been a tower of strength, but there was no reason things should collapse because she'd been taken ill. 'I dare say Sister has a record of things like that in her office.'

'Yes, perhaps,' Cook said. 'But it won't be the same. We discuss all the menus over a cup of tea and a slice of my best fatless sponge and . . . oh well, I suppose we'll manage somehow.' She sighed heavily. 'But if anything should happen . . .'

Angela suppressed a feeling of irritation. She'd thought Muriel was her friend, but it seemed that old loyalties were the strongest. She would simply have to show them all that she was perfectly capable of managing at St Saviour's without Sister's help.

'We must pray Sister returns to us soon,' she said. 'I'd better go and find Nan – she'll be terribly upset if she learns of Sister's illness from somewhere else . . .'

'I knew something was wrong with her,' Nan said after Angela had persuaded her to sit down and have a cup of tea with her in the staff room. 'I sensed it and she looked so tired – but I thought that she might not have been sleeping because of what happened with Terry. She still blames herself, even now . . .'

'Sister has been tired and anxious of late,' agreed Angela. 'I suspect she's been suffering nagging pains for a while but carried on working regardless when she ought to have gone to the doctor.'

'Beatrice is like that,' Nan said. 'She holds things inside, won't give in to whatever is upsetting her. She went through a terrible time as a young woman, before she joined the nuns, and I imagine she got used to hiding pain. I didn't know her back then, but she's told me a few things over the years . . . I do know she was married for a time, and I believe there was a child, but I can't say more than that.'

Angela didn't press her for details, even though the news that Sister had been married came as a considerable surprise. Occasionally she had wondered what Sister's life had been like before she became a nun, but it had never occurred to her that Beatrice might have been married. Though she told herself it was none of her business what terrible sorrow had driven Beatrice to give up all worldly things and enter a convent, she couldn't help wishing she knew more – perhaps if she understood more of why Sister was so passionate about her work

101

at St Saviour's and why she felt that Angela was trying to undermine her role when all she wanted was to help, then she would know how to reassure her that was not the case.

'Let's hope that holding back won't have cost her her life,' Angela said.

'I don't know what we would do without her,' Nan said in a mournful tone. 'I know you do a lot of the office work now, Angela, but . . . everyone respects Sister Beatrice: the nurses and carers, children – and the locals too. So many people stop her when she goes out, asking for her help. And every month she goes into the slums to visit families and check their health and give advice, making sure mothers know how to sterilise the babies' bottles – lots of small but significant things like that.'

'Thankfully, those visits won't be necessary now that Mr Bevan has won the doctors round and free health care is available to everyone on the National Health Service. Those poor families can call the doctor out now without having to worry how they'll find the money to pay him.'

'A lot of people don't know about the changes, and even some of those that do still refuse to go to a doctor or hospital – they don't trust them, or they're too embarrassed.'

'That's ridiculous!' said Angela, incredulous.

'You don't understand, Angela. The conditions some of these people live in are so awful that they're ashamed to have the doctor out. Some of the mothers can't even wash their children's clothes because they don't have others to put on them while they dry. Beatrice takes the poorest families a few clothes, boots and shoes, and anything else that comes her way. They rely on her for so much. She gives them food sometimes, buys it out of her stipend – and that's not much, I can tell you, but she says she doesn't need anything for herself. She'd give the food off her own plate if necessary. They don't think of it as charity from her; they trust her; she represents the Church and that's different to all the officials the government send round. People hate being told they've got to fill in a form if they want an extra five bob a week; what the Church gives is offered without question or criticism . . . only it isn't the Church, it's Sister Beatrice and Father Joe.'

'Oh, I see,' Angela said, chastened. 'I hadn't realised that things were quite that bad these days. I thought all that belonged to Victorian times when the children went barefoot.'

'Yes, perhaps you did,' Nan said, though she didn't sound critical of Angela. 'I know you do as much as you can for the charities you help, but how many slum houses have you actually visited?'

'Only a few that were going to be pulled down – and they were mostly empty.'

'Well, you should visit a family and see what they have to put up with,' Nan advised.

'I was going to ask Dr Kent to visit Kelly's mother,' Angela said. 'I told her I'd go with him, but I haven't had time. I'll telephone him later and arrange it.'

'You'll have more idea of the good Sister Beatrice has done then.' Nan smiled at her. 'You've done really well here, Angela. I know Beatrice finds it easier than before – and I know you have a good heart – but you should see some of those families. You wouldn't believe the poverty that still exists in places. I know things are slowly getting better, but it will take years to rehouse all those who need it. The shortage of housing means that more people crowd into the houses that are available. Beatrice told me about a house where five Indian families were living, sharing one toilet in the yard and one tap in the kitchen. Can you imagine what would happen if one of the children went down with an infectious illness?'

Angela nodded. 'It would spread to them all. That is truly awful, Nan. I've heard stories, but I didn't realise that Sister visited such families,' Angela said. 'No wonder Father Joe calls her an Angel. *The Angel of Halfpenny Street*.' She smiled and Nan laughed at the memory. Father Joe had waxed lyrical with a hefty tot of brandy inside him, after he'd been wounded while preventing Terry from stabbing Sister for a second time. 'Well, I must get on now. I shall telephone the hospital later and find out how Sister is after her operation.'

'I'll be going round there when I finish work,' Nan said. 'Beatrice has been a good friend to me and I couldn't sleep tonight if I didn't go myself to see how she is.'

Angela nodded but didn't say anything. It had been made clear to her in a short space of time how much the staff here thought of their Warden. It seemed that they were afraid that the wheels would grind to a halt without her, and they clearly didn't believe Angela could manage alone. Nan had been polite about it, but she obviously thought it impossible for Angela to step into Beatrice's shoes.

TWELVE

Nan left the hospital feeling slightly better than she had when Angela first told her the news. Sister Beatrice had come through the operation and was in the recovery ward. She hadn't been allowed to see her friend, but the nurse had been kind and told her not to worry.

'Sister Beatrice will recover in time. It was touch and go for a while. If they hadn't got her in quickly, I've no doubt she would have died. There is still a risk of infection, so she may have to stay here a few weeks.'

'Well, it's a good thing someone was with her when it happened,' Nan said. 'Please tell her I called and I shall call again tomorrow.'

The nurse promised she would let St Saviour's know when Sister Beatrice recovered from the anaesthetic and Nan went off to catch her bus. She was relieved but couldn't stop worrying; Beatrice wasn't out of the woods yet, and if anything happened to her, Nan knew how much she would miss her friend. And it wouldn't just be a personal loss for her – everyone at St Saviour's would be distraught.

It was hard to imagine how any of them would

manage at the home if their Sister Beatrice didn't come back to them. Nan didn't think anyone realised how much they all relied on their Warden. It wasn't so much what she did, as the fact that she was there – solid and reassuring. The death of her husband and son from diphtheria had almost destroyed Nan, but her friendship with Beatrice had pulled her through, restoring her will to live. And it was Beatrice as much as Nan's friend Eddie Charles who'd helped her see that she must accept her daughter Maisie's decision to enter a convent.

Nan's eyes stung with tears as she walked towards the bus stop through the gathering dusk. The dimly lit streets were shabby but even at this hour there were always people about, some of them with no home but a shop doorway or a cardboard box under the arches. Sometimes she dreaded returning to her home, even though she was so comfortable in her prefab. The nights could be long and lonely, despite the friends she'd made, but though she'd had years to get used to being on her own, she still missed her husband and son and Maisie. At least her last visit to the convent had shown her that her daughter was well and happy. Yet leaving her in that cold cheerless place had wrenched at her heart. Nan had longed to have her daughter home but she'd reconciled herself to the fact that Maisie was Sister Mary now and it was what she wanted. Nan had no family left, though she and her friend Eddie had decided to adopt Alice's child as their grandchild, in a manner of speaking. Eddie had suggested it in one of his letters and told her that he'd already started making wooden toys for the baby, which made Nan hope that he'd decided against moving to the country permanently. If

Eddie decided to stay with his family and work in their shop, Nan would have felt his loss far more than she'd believed possible.

Nan's job at St Saviour's was a huge part of her life now, but if they had a new warden, she might have her own ideas – and Nan could find herself looking for another job.

No, she wouldn't consider that possibility; it would mean Beatrice was no longer able to work and that would be a tragedy for her friend. Nan would not dwell on her own loneliness: Beatrice was the one that mattered now . . .

Reaching her home, she let herself in with a sigh of relief. It was good to be settled in a place she could call her own. She was about to heat some milk for her bedtime drink when the doorbell rang. Nan hesitated before going to answer it. Who could it be at this hour?

She answered the door tentatively, poking her head round to see who it was, and then wider as she recognised the woman who lived next door.

'Sorry to disturb you,' she said, 'but this was delivered for you a couple of hours ago. The florist's boy was going to leave it on the doorstep, but I thought it might get pinched so I took it in.'

'Oh, how kind of you,' Nan said and took the gorgeous bouquet of roses and scented stocks. 'Thank you so much. I should have hated it to get lost.'

'Yes, that's what I thought,' her neighbour said. 'You were a bit late home tonight, weren't you?'

'Yes, I went to see a friend in hospital.'

'Oh, well, it's a good thing I happened to see the delivery boy. Goodnight then, Nan.'

Nan took the flowers inside. The perfume was lovely and she knew even before she opened the envelope that it could only have come from one person.

'Happy Birthday, dear Nan,' the card read. 'I can't be with you tomorrow, but I shall see you next weekend. I'll be in touch before then, Eddie.'

Suddenly, the world seemed much brighter. Eddie hadn't forgotten it was her birthday tomorrow. Most years she celebrated with a glass of sherry and a slice of birthday cake with Beatrice, but tomorrow she would be on her own.

A smile touched her mouth. She was too old to be silly over birthdays. She would put these lovely flowers into water and then make herself that cup of cocoa and go to bed.

Angela sat on the edge of her bed, brushing her hair before retiring. She'd been shocked by Sister's collapse, but the more she thought about it the more obvious it was that something had been wrong the last few weeks. She was on the point of getting into bed when she recalled Sister's rather cryptic message about the twins. It had all been a bit hectic and she couldn't quite recall what Sister had said . . . something to do with their aunt. She shook her head; it was all jumbled up with Sister being taken off to hospital and everyone's reaction.

Sighing, Angela switched off the light. She refused to be annoyed despite everyone seeming to doubt her ability to cope. Naturally, she couldn't help on the nursing side, but Michelle, Wendy and Paula were capable of looking after their patients and they could always call in the doctor if in doubt. Everything would be perfectly all right, she thought as she closed her eyes. Most of the work was routine after all . . .

Sleep eluded her, her thoughts returning to earlier that evening when she'd visited Kelly's home with Dr Kent.

He had been only too pleased to accompany her and to examine the girl's mother, confirming that she had a weak chest with a tendency to bronchitis and that the dampness of her home was contributing to her poor state of health.

Kelly had shown them where her mother slept and the large patches of mildew on the walls and ceilings had shocked Angela to the core, especially when Kelly told her that she wiped them over at least once a week.

'It comes back, Mrs Morton,' she'd said. 'Whatever Da tries, it just comes back.'

'These old houses ought to be pulled down,' Dr Kent told Angela when they left the Masons' home later. 'It's no wonder Mrs Mason is ill. Her heart condition makes her more vulnerable and I think she may have some mucus on her lungs. Left untreated, she could end up with pneumonia. I shall book an appointment for her to have tests. And I'll draw up that report for you, Mrs Morton – though I'm not sure what good it will do. I dare say she isn't the only one in desperate need of a decent home around here.'

'I'm on the board of a housing charity,' Angela said. 'I do their secretarial work for free and I'm hoping to bring this case to their attention. Twelve houses have been renovated and are almost ready for occupation. With your report to support their case, I think Mrs Mason and her family stand a good chance of getting one.'

Dr Kent looked at her in surprise. 'Well, if you can manage that, I take my hat off to you, Mrs Morton. I've been badgering the council on behalf of another patient, but they tell me there's a wait of at least a year.'

'Perhaps the housing charity can do better,' Angela had replied. She'd seen disbelief in his eyes, but she had contributed to the charity in more ways than one and if she had any influence at all, she would make sure these worthy cases were at least considered for one of the first batch of renovated houses . . . Smiling at the thought, she snuggled down into her pillows and drifted into sleep.

THIRTEEN

The telephone rang in Sister's office as Angela reached it the next morning. She picked it up, listening to the crisp and rather cold tones of the voice on the other end.

'May I speak with Sister Beatrice please?'

'I'm afraid she isn't here. I am Mrs Morton, the Administrator – may I help you?'

'Yes, I dare say you can,' the voice went on. 'I am Miss Sampson from Children's Welfare. I'm ringing to confirm that Miss Jane May will be taking the May twins this afternoon. She will call at two o'clock. Please have them ready for her.'

The phone snapped off at the other end, leaving Angela staring at it in dismay. It was very short notice and she wasn't sure how the twins would take the news that they were being fetched by their aunt.

Angela made a brief search of the papers on Sister's desk but found nothing to help her concerning the twins – yet perhaps it was what Sister had been trying to say when she was struck down. Had she known that the aunt was applying to remove them from their care?

111

She hadn't mentioned the fact to Angela, but perhaps she hadn't got round to it when she was taken ill. As far as Angela was aware, Sister hadn't been consulted in the matter by the authorities, but she always seemed to know what was going on without anyone telling her. In this case she may have had her own sources and hadn't got around to sharing her thoughts with Angela before being overtaken by her illness.

Angela went in search of Nan and found her in the kitchen helping Cook with the baking. She explained about the twins leaving them and that their things would need to be readied. Nan explained that they usually allowed those children lucky enough to be fostered to take one set of clothes with them.

'It helps their new families until they can be bought new clothes,' she said. 'Would you like me to do the hand-over for you?'

'Oh no, I think Wendy might like to. She's quite close to them you know, though I shall be there to sign them out. I want to see what kind of a woman Miss Jane May is for myself.'

'Sister would've done the same, had she been here,' Nan agreed. 'Was there anything else?'

'Will you come to my office for a cup of tea at about four this afternoon – if you're free, that is? I should like to talk to you about something.'

'Yes, if you wish, Angela,' Nan said. 'Sister Beatrice was still sleeping when I telephoned this morning – nothing is wrong I hope?'

'Oh no, I was told she was satisfactory when I rang and I think that is all we can expect for the moment. No, it's just something I need to tell you . . .'

112

Angela smiled at her and left them to get on with their baking. She wanted the cake and sherry to be a surprise, but she wasn't sure that one of the staff wouldn't let it out during the day. She'd known Nan's birthday was coming up for a while. Sister had told her the date, and she'd checked the records to make certain it wasn't forgotten. Most of the carers would pop in to wish her a Happy Birthday, and Angela had arranged a special cake, cards and a present. Nan didn't realise how popular she was and everyone had been delighted by the idea of a nice surprise for the head carer.

Entering her office, Angela saw a man standing by her desk looking down at the open book she'd left there; it was a record of the accounts for St Saviour's and she was annoyed with herself for having left it there, even though she was sure she'd closed it. She was even more annoyed that he'd simply walked in and was taking advantage of her absence to look at private documents. Who did he think he was?

'What do you think you're doing?'

'Ah, Angela,' Henry Arnold said, raising his dark brows. Despite her annoyance, she couldn't help thinking how attractive he was – if he hadn't been so damned arrogant, she might have liked him. 'I must say, I'm surprised at your leaving a confidential document like this on your desk for anyone to see.'

'I left it because no one enters my office without my permission – and no one who works here would dream of doing so. How dare you walk in and look at something that does not concern you!'

'No need to get angry,' he said, a spark of amusement in his eyes. 'Actually, the accounts here may well be my

113

business in future. As you probably know, one of your sponsors has died – a belted earl, no less . . .' He smiled oddly. 'I may not quite be up to his standards in your eyes, Angela, but the donation I offered secured me his seat on the Board and—'

'You have a seat on the Board of St Saviour's?' Angela stared at him in disbelief. 'Why do you want it?'

'I told you I was interested when we met previously. Had you not been in such a hurry after that very successful jumble sale, for which I understand we have you to thank, I might have told you it had been offered.'

For which we have you to thank!

Angela's teeth grated at that remark. It infuriated her that he spoke as if he were a part of St Saviour's, a part of all that she'd worked so hard for. But if he'd been given a seat on the Board . . .

'Sister Beatrice had not been told of this new development and nor had I – when did this happen?'

'I received the letter offering it to me this morning, signed by Mark Adderbury,' he said. 'I'm sorry; I thought Adderbury would have told you. Surely you've been told of my generous donation?'

'I should certainly have been told about that,' Angela said. 'If a large sum has been deposited in the bank for such a purpose I can only be grateful.'

'Even if it kills you?' he murmured throatily. Something about his eyes seemed to challenge her, managing to get beneath her skin even though she fought against it. 'It's all right, Angela. I don't want to interfere with the way you and Sister Beatrice run this place. I admire what you're doing here and I hope I can be of even more help in the future.'

114

'How exactly?'

'If you will come to dinner with me this evening I shall tell you. Otherwise you'll have to wait for the next board meeting.'

'That's blackmail,' she said, wishing she could order him from her office. But if he was telling the truth he had a perfect right to be here – and to look at the accounts.

Angela tried to think calmly; the earl had only recently died, a few days before the jumble sale, as it happened, but Arnold must have been planning his approach for a while. What was he up to?

'So you refuse to tell me about your plans for St Saviour's unless I allow you to take me to dinner?'

'That's it . . .' His smile was maddening, but quite attractive. She was suddenly aware of the pull of his charm – if you liked that kind of arrogant man. 'It's a cunning plan, isn't it? I knew you wouldn't have dinner with me unless I made you curious – and it's worked, hasn't it?'

Angela couldn't help but laugh along with him. How often had she had dinner with people she didn't particularly like in the hope of a large donation? This man had already given several thousand pounds and he was suggesting he might do more in future. She would be foolish to antagonise a benefactor who could afford to help St Saviour's, even if he did rub her up the wrong way.

'In that case I really have no choice, Mr Arnold,' she conceded with what grace she could muster. Giving him a wry smile, she added, 'As Administrator here it is my duty to spend time with sponsors. What time do you wish to meet?'

'I could pick you up at your home – say, eight?'

'You may collect me here at eight,' Angela said to remind him that she was no pushover. 'I have a small party for one of the staff at four, but that will still give me time to go home and change and return here.'

'Still don't trust me?' His smile challenged. 'As you please. I wouldn't want to upset our excellent Administrator. Everyone tells me what a marvellous job you're doing.'

'Thank you,' she said crisply. 'Now, I really must ask you to leave. Sister Beatrice is in hospital and I have a lot of extra work . . .' As if to back up her claim someone knocked at the door at that moment. 'Come in – ah, Michelle, what may I do for you? Mr Arnold is just leaving . . .'

'I'm sorry to disturb you, Angela,' Michelle said, looking curiously at the stranger in the office. 'It's about one of our longer-term children, Sarah Morgan. She's only recently got over a nasty chill, as you know, and now she's running a fever again. With Sister Beatrice away, I was thinking I ought to ask a doctor to call . . .'

Henry Arnold had left without another word, though his eyes threw a provocative look at Angela as he paused at the door. She ignored him, giving her full attention to Michelle's worries; she would face the problem of dinner when it came to it.

'I think you should ring Dr Kent,' she said. 'As you say, we can't be too careful in matters of the children's health. Given the child's past history of chest infections, we'd better have the doctor take a look at her.'

'I'm sure Sister would say the same,' Michelle said.

'I was only wondering which doctor. You think it should be Dr Kent?'

'Definitely,' Angela said. 'He is an excellent man and decisive. If he thinks Sarah needs special treatment, he won't hesitate to say. We don't want to lose her though neglect.'

'I'll telephone him immediately.'

'Yes, you'll be able to describe her symptoms and explain why you're worried far better than I could. Telephone from here, if you wish.'

Angela picked up the account book that she'd left lying on her desk and put it away in the drawer. She'd never locked her office in the past but she would certainly consider it in future. The last thing she needed was to be accused of negligence by a man who seemed determined to have a considerable say in the way St Saviour's was run in future.

'Come along, Samantha – and you, Sarah,' Miss May's voice was sharp as she addressed her nieces. She'd arrived promptly and seemed anxious to leave as quickly as possible. 'I want to get home before it starts to rain.'

Angela noticed the way Sarah May was clinging to Wendy's hand, clearly reluctant to leave the gentle nurse. She saw an odd look in Samantha's eyes too, but then the girl went and took hold of her sister, pulling her away from the nurse.

'We've got to go, Sarah. Come on or Aunt Jane will be cross . . .'

'There's a good girl, Samantha.' Her aunt looked at her with approval, her thin grey face easing for a moment but not truly smiling. 'Now, say thank you to Mrs

Morton for looking after you while I was unwell.' She turned her pale gaze on Angela. 'I had a nasty chest infection for a while, you know. It's the reason I haven't been before – but the girls will be safe and comfortable with me now.'

'Yes, I'm sure they will.' Angela held out her hand to Samantha but the girl ignored it. 'You'll be fine with your aunt, Samantha.'

Samantha gave her a look filled with reproach and then turned to Wendy. 'You promised,' she said, a flash of anger in her eyes. Then she took Sarah firmly by the hand and led her from Sister's office, where Miss May had signed the release papers a few moments earlier.

Angela felt a distinct sense of unease as she heard the aunt's voice rise sharply as they walked away and down the stairs, her annoyance seemingly aimed at Sarah. She glanced at Wendy and saw tears in her eyes.

'What did Samantha mean?'

'She didn't want to go to her aunt's,' Wendy said. 'I'd told her she would be staying here . . . It was after I'd spoken to you the other morning. I did tell you that she said her aunt didn't like Sarah, and I meant to tell you that she'd begged me not to let her be taken away, but it was the end of my break and I had to go back to work. I didn't know it had been arranged for the aunt to take them. Samantha said that her aunt didn't want Sarah; she seemed convinced of it – and the way that woman looked at Sarah . . .' Wendy wiped a tear from her eye. 'I can't help thinking she won't look after them properly. I feel awful about the whole thing. Those girls are frightened, Angela – really frightened.'

'It wasn't your decision to make, or mine,' Angela said. 'From what I've seen today I'm not at all sure it was the best decision. Like you, I wonder whether she has their best interests at heart . . . But the authorities always prefer to keep children with relatives if they can, and perhaps it is for the best in the long term.'

'Yes, I suppose it is,' Wendy agreed. 'But I didn't like the look of her – her mouth is mean and cruel. If I had my way, they'd have stayed here with us.'

'Well, there was nothing we could do at such short notice,' Angela said, though she couldn't get rid of the unease she'd felt when Samantha looked at her as if she'd betrayed them. 'It was good of you to come in on your free day to see them off, Wendy.'

'I'm fond of them,' Wendy said, and forced a smile. 'Well, I've got some shopping to do – I want to get a present for Nan. I'll see you later . . .'

Angela returned to her own office, intending to get back to her typing, but she found it impossible to settle. There was definitely something about Miss May . . . something Angela wasn't keen on. However, there was nothing she could do, the Welfare people had decided Miss May was the best person to have the twins and the decision was made . . .

She picked up the telephone receiver and dialled Mark's number, wanting to talk to him, but the phone rang for a while and no one answered. Sighing, Angela replaced it. She would simply have to accept that the twins had gone . . .

'Happy Birthday, Nan,' Angela said, raising her sherry glass. 'I'm sure we all want to congratulate you on such a special day – and everyone contributed to the card and gift, which we hope you will like.'

'I've never had such a lovely blouse,' Nan said, and looked pleased. 'Where on earth did you buy it, Angela?'

'Peter Robinson had some rather nice things in last week,' Angela said. 'When I saw this I knew it was for you – and I knew your size because of the bring-and-buy sales we've been having.'

'It's absolutely ages since I had anything new,' Nan said. 'It feels so nice to the touch. Is it silk?'

'It's silk voile,' Angela said. 'You'll need a petticoat underneath, but that navy-and-white polka dot will suit you, Nan.'

'Michelle and I wondered if you would come out for a drink this evening,' Muriel said, and kissed her cheek. 'Alice will join us and we can have pie and chips. Angela can't be there, but the rest of us would like to treat you.'

'Well, I don't mind having an orange juice before we go home.' Nan seemed touched by the invitation. 'But I'm going to see Sister Beatrice at eight, so I can't stay long . . .'

'We didn't want you to be alone on your birthday.'

'I'm used to it,' Nan said, but her eyes were suspiciously wet. 'It's good to know I have such friends. My friend Eddie sent me some lovely flowers last night, and I got a card in the post this morning. He couldn't come today, but he'll be in town next week and we shall have tea somewhere then.'

'That's lovely,' Michelle said. 'I wish I had someone to send me flowers . . .'

'I should think Dr Kent might send you some if it

was your birthday,' Tilly teased. 'I saw 'im looking at you when I brought the drinks tray to the sick ward earlier . . .'

'Tilly!' Michelle made a face at her. 'We were discussing a patient. He was giving me his opinion of Sarah Morgan's condition. He says we worry over her too much, that she is stronger than we imagine.'

'He probably knows best,' Tilly told her. 'But the way he looked at you wasn't 'cos of Sarah Morgan . . .'

'He's done a lot for my father, that's all.'

'He wasn't thinking of your father when he smiled at you. I think you're lucky to have someone nice take an interest in you like that.' Tilly looked wistful.

'For all we know, he's married with a family. Besides, I've no intention of getting involved with anyone.'

'Well, I have to get back to work,' Nan said. 'I have the rota to prepare for my girls, and Sister isn't here to consult. What's more, Kelly's away again. It appears that her mother is ill and—'

'Yes, she really is,' Angela said, and they all looked at her. 'I took Dr Kent to see her last night and he says Mrs Mason's chest is in a bad way. He doesn't think it is consumption, which is what the family feared, but chronic bronchitis brought on by the damp conditions she has to live in.'

'You went to see the family last night?' Nan looked at her with respect. 'So you know what they have to cope with? What did you think to their house?'

'The walls were brown-streaked and running with moisture in places, and in others the plaster was crumbling. When you touched it, all sorts of creepy crawlies came wriggling out.' Angela shuddered at the memory.

121

'It was quite horrid – and the smell from the lavatory in the back yard was awful. Kelly told me she'd scrubbed it out with disinfectant the previous day, but the smell comes back almost immediately. It must be the drains. I've told her we'll send someone to see if they can do something, but that whole district looks as if it wants pulling down.'

'Now you know what I was talking about,' Nan said.

'Yes, I certainly do. I'd seen derelict houses that were about to be pulled down, but I think Kelly's home was worse. It isn't fit for anyone, particularly a sick woman, so I shall do what I can to find somewhere better for them. I've asked Dr Kent to write a full report for me so that I can appeal to the housing charity on their behalf. There are others waiting, and I can only recommend that the Masons be given priority. Kelly's father seems a decent sort – but his wage barely covers the rent and food they need. Kelly's wage is important so it would be a shame to get rid of her, and she's promised to put in extra hours at night when her sister is home to look after the younger ones. She could clean the offices and rest room when we've all gone home.'

'Yes, well, I'll make allowances for her, but she needs to pull her socks up,' Nan said, though she clearly agreed.

'It's difficult for the girl with her mother so ill.'

'It's a pity Kelly's family has to wait,' Nan said. 'It's obvious that her mother needs to move as soon as possible.'

'Unfortunately, charities like the one I help out cannot hope to meet the need we see around us,' Angela said. 'We do what we can, but it's time the Government did more to rehouse people in council houses. If they did their job properly perhaps people wouldn't need to live in squalid conditions. It's no good blaming the war for the slums – they weren't much better before the war, from what I've been told. Anyway, I've done what I can for Kelly's family, but I can't guarantee it will mean they get a new home.'

'You'll have to go into Parliament, Angela,' Nan teased.

Angela shook her head. 'No thank you! I couldn't stand all the dithering and the hypocrisy. At least working with various charities I can help get things done. All the Government seems to do is set up committees – they talk endlessly, but nothing ever changes.'

'I still think we need people like you to stand up and say what's needed.'

'Well, I must get on,' Angela said. 'There's a lot to do and I'm going out this evening!'

FOURTEEN

Mark rang the bell of Angela's apartment, feeling annoyed and frustrated when there was no reply. He should have phoned and saved himself the bother of coming out here for nothing. It was the second time he'd called on the chance that she might be at home, but so far he hadn't found her. So much for her saying she hardly ever went out with friends! Mind you, he knew she did a lot of extra charity work these days. Her time was divided between the post at St Saviour's and the various good causes she'd taken up. Naturally, she was at liberty to do whatever she pleased when she wasn't working, but he hoped she wasn't overdoing it.

As he turned away, Mark was frowning. He hadn't been out much himself lately; it had taken him a while to get over the affair with Carole. It wasn't that he'd been madly in love with her; in fact he'd only started going out with her when he'd thought his hopes of a relationship with Angela were dead in the water. He'd mistakenly believed that she might be in love with Nick Hadden, but she'd told him that had been merely friendship. Mark had been a fool to let himself be drawn into that flirtation with Carole, because that was all it had been to him. She'd claimed to be in love with him, but he suspected that was as false as her claim that she was having his baby. He'd only proposed to her for the sake of the child; he'd seen too many men shirk their duties, abandoning the infants they'd fathered – he'd seen the suffering it caused. No matter the cost to his personal happiness, he'd been prepared to go through with marriage to Carole so that his son or daughter would know what it was to have a father. Though it had come as a relief when Carole's lie was exposed and the engagement was broken, there was disappointment too that fatherhood had once again been snatched away from him.

Mark's first marriage might have survived had their little boy been born healthy, but he died within days of being born. Edine, unable to have another child, succumbed to depression and recklessly neglected her health, dying in a diabetic coma. Ever since, Mark had felt empty, living only for his work – until he'd started seeing more of Angela after her husband was killed. He'd lost a good friend in John and out of respect and love he'd given Angela all the support he could without demanding anything in return – but perhaps he'd been wrong to wait so long before speaking. He wanted to speak now, to tell her that he loved her . . . but would she want anything to do with him after his affair with Carole? She would have every right to be angry, to dismiss his claims of having loved her for years. Looking back, he could not imagine why he'd fallen into Carole's arms like an immature fool, when it was Angela he wanted – but perhaps it was because Angela had wounded his pride and Carole's flattery had made him feel good. Mark wasn't proud of the way he'd behaved, but honest enough to face the truth.

He was too good an analyst to pity himself and had no illusions about what a fool he'd been. Mark was thoughtful as he got back in his car and drove home. He'd been a fool to delay. It was time he talked to Angela, made her aware of his feelings for her – but for that he needed to be alone with her, to spend time in her company. Recently, he'd been far too wrapped up in his work – and the fate of one of his closest friends. Alan had come to him complaining of severe headaches and worrying loss of memory. Suspecting a brain tumour, he'd sent his friend to see a consultant. Roberts had given him the bad news – the tumour was large and would eventually kill Alan unless he had a potentially fatal operation.

Thwarted in his attempts to see Angela, Mark decided he would visit Alan in the private nursing home, as he had been doing every spare moment since the operation. Mark's patients always played a large part in his life, but lately he'd been working flat out and the visits to his friend left him no time for a personal life.

If Angela was annoyed with him for neglecting her, he would have to explain how busy he'd been. Once she knew, he was sure she would understand. Mark would send her some flowers in the morning and then he'd telephone and ask her out to dinner at the weekend . . .

Angela frowned as the huge bouquet was delivered to her office. If this had come from Henry Arnold she had a good mind to send it straight back. However, when she opened the card attached she saw it was from Mark. He'd promised to ring her and spoke of dinner at the weekend. She smiled as she put the flowers in some water in a vase and stood it on her desk. Until this moment she'd been annoyed with Mark. He hadn't told her about the seat on the Board being offered to a man she was unsure was right for the position.

Her thoughts returned to the previous evening. Only when they reached the coffee stage had Henry Arnold unfolded the plan he had in mind. Angela's first reaction was to dismiss his idea as ridiculous – move St Saviour's to a brand-new home in the country and a large building designed specifically for the purpose? Nonsense!

'Don't you see, you will never be able to give your children the fresh air and space they need unless you move out into the countryside. These children are taken on visits to the zoo or a park sometimes, but in a new home in the country they would have so many advantages. Running in the clean air, for starters . . . but you could give them riding lessons at a local stable and take them swimming and lots of hikes around the beauty spots. You could teach them to play cricket and arrange football matches . . .' Henry Arnold leaned towards her, the smile on his lips so charming and inviting that briefly she was swayed to his opinion despite her belief that now was completely the wrong time for such a move.

'Billy Baggins would like that,' Angela said, dazzled by the shining prospect he dangled before her eyes. When he chose, Henry Arnold could be a charming and attractive companion, she realised, and the children could do with better facilities for sport. But moving the home was too drastic a course for Angela to accept out of the blue. 'Yet I'm not sure it's what is needed – at least not for some years yet. We've only recently opened our new wing at St Saviour's. Besides, we are at the heart of the problem where we are. The police bring us any children they find in trouble and . . .'

'Sometimes that leads to more problems,' Henry Arnold said, his direct gaze making the back of her neck tingle. 'Some children aren't right for St Saviour's; they're too damaged and violent, like the boy who attacked Sister Beatrice.'

'I know, mistakes have been made in the past.' Angela gazed into her delicate wineglass and thought of poor damaged Terry. It seemed bizarre to be discussing the poverty of the East End while dining at Simpson's, one of the finest restaurants in London.

'Had he been properly examined, you would have known that he was not a suitable child for St Saviour's. While the local police continue to think of you as their own private depository for every destitute child they pick up, you will always be at risk of something similar. The children should be assessed first by a committee and then sent on as is considered appropriate to the right home.'

'That's rather cold and clinical, isn't it?' Angela looked at him in disgust. 'St Saviour's was set up on compassionate values and to meet the needs of the most vulnerable children. Mark was making arrangements for Terry to be moved to a suitable place as soon as possible . . .'

'He should have sectioned him instantly he realised there was a danger.'

'Mark would not agree with you. He believed it could

send the child over the edge and wanted to avoid damaging his chances of a decent life . . . to give Terry every possible chance.'

'I take it you also disagree?' He nodded, looking thoughtful. 'I would say that Sister Beatrice is a trifle old fashioned and might be replaced – but we need people like you to bring new ideas for the future. Perhaps she was at fault in her attitudes to the children—'

'I think I've heard enough of this,' Angela said. 'It might interest you to learn that many people feel St Saviour's could not operate without Sister Beatrice. She is considered to be the rock we all cling to.'

'Surely that is not your opinion, Angela?' His eyes mocked her. 'I have heard that you find her authority irksome. Suppose I told you that in *my* home you would be my first choice as Warden for St Saviour's?'

'I do hope that you don't expect me to jump at the offer,' Angela said calmly. She might be itching to fly at his throat, but she wouldn't give him the satisfaction of knowing it. 'For one thing, as far as I recall, St Saviour's is an independent charity home; with some grants from the Government and generous donations – we hope to keep it that way. You may be rich, Mr Arnold, but that doesn't give you the right to walk in and take over.'

'Angela, there's no need for us to quarrel over this . . .' He reached to touch her hand. She pulled back as if she'd been stung, knowing that she was physically attracted to him even though her instincts told her not to trust this man. 'You know it is a generous offer. Now that I have a seat on the Board I shall make my views known and I think most of my fellow committee members will agree with me.'

'Yes, perhaps they may in principle,' she agreed, wondering why his touch sent a tingle down her spine. Surely she disliked him? 'There may come a time when a home in the country might be the right move, but personally I feel that many of our children would resent being taken from the environment they've been brought up in. When they grow up, their lives will be in London – most of them have a good idea of what they want to be when they leave us. London has so many excellent opportunities for them.'

'There you and I part company,' Henry Arnold said. 'I believe that away from the dirt and noise of the city they will learn to appreciate the better things in life. I am not saying the home should be built in a wasteland – I was thinking perhaps on the edge of a country town in Essex. They would then have the advantage of being able to choose whether they preferred rural or town life. Those who wished could return to London if they so desired, but many of them might become farmers or builders or even doctors rather than dock workers or labourers.'

'Have you any idea of the kind of children we take in?' Angela asked, smiling now. 'I've tried to interest the older ones in trips to museums and the ballet, but few are interested; they prefer the zoo, Madame Tussauds or the picture house, followed by tea at Lyons. It is only now that they are beginning to take an interest in competitive team games and their own concert—'

'So I understand and much of that is due to you. Until you arrived only their bodily needs were seen as important; their minds were left to stagnate. I grew up amongst the smoke and the factories of the North of

England, Angela. My father started out as foreman of another man's business and worked his way up. He sent me away to the right school to learn that there was another way of life – and I did. That is what I want for our children.'

'Yes, I do too – to a certain extent,' Angela agreed. 'It's possible that some of them may go on to something better, rise up from their humble beginnings and make a good life for themselves, but it isn't possible for all of them. These children have a taste for fish paste, not caviar.'

'Not as things stand, no,' he said, a faint smile playing on his lips at her joke. 'I have a view of a better future for all our children, Angela – and I mean more than the orphans at St Saviour's. I want to see a revolution in education and living standards, to bring the lower classes up to a new level and give them a chance to be more . . . to open ignorant minds to the possibilities that are out there. There is a new world coming and it shouldn't be open to just you and me and people like us – it should be there for all our children.'

'I know there is so much to be done, and people like you and Mark – and me, in my own small way – we're trying to help all we can, but it's a huge job.'

'And one mainly for the Government,' he said. 'I shall keep lobbying for improvements for the working man and his family through my connections with the unions – but we have to start with the children, to bring them up to recognise the failings in society that gave us slums and poverty . . .'

Angela looked at him, seeing the light in his eyes as he spoke of his hopes and dreams of a better future.

He was undoubtedly an attractive and dynamic man and he seemed to have the right ideas. Perhaps she'd misjudged him, due to his arrogance and his irritating manner of assuming that what he saw as right was automatically so. Yet she was level-headed enough to know that what he was describing was very difficult if not impossible to achieve – certainly in one man's lifetime.

'I agree with your principles,' she offered at last, 'if not with all your ideas.'

'Well, at least I've made some headway,' he said and looked pleased. 'So I can count on your support when I raise the matter with the Board?'

'I didn't say that,' Angela backed off as he threw the challenge at her. 'I might agree to the home being moved one day in the distant future, but that isn't now – and I could never agree to replacing Sister Beatrice as Warden. Everyone loves and depends on her too much. I'm sure you have no idea how much she does to help those in need.'

'Well, Rome wasn't built in a day.' Henry Arnold's stern features relaxed into a smile. 'I think we've broken the ice at least. What do you fancy for pudding? I rather like the idea of spotted dick and custard; it always used to be a favourite of mine as a child . . .'

'Coffee for me please. I couldn't eat another thing.'

After their meal, he'd driven her home but Angela hadn't asked him in. She'd thanked him formally and seen the disappointment in his eyes. Henry Arnold had made no secret that he found her attractive, and she acknowledged that he was a sensual, good-looking man – but she had no wish to begin a relationship with him, despite the knowledge that she needed more than friendship in her life. She wanted love, a close physical relationship, but not with Mr Arnold: despite his undoubted charm, Angela simply didn't trust him.

She frowned as she put a new sheet of paper in her typewriter after mentally reviewing the previous evening. She'd thought about what he'd said and something was nagging at her, though she couldn't put a name to it. In all his enthusiastic ranting about a wonderful new life in the future, Henry Arnold had neglected to mention what he hoped to get out of all this . . . and somehow something about him didn't ring true.

FIFTEEN

Michelle was thoughtful as she walked through the deserted market. Rotten fruit lay abandoned in the gutters, slowly turning to a foul-smelling mess, and she thought how dilapidated the area looked; Bethnal Green was still showing signs of the war damage it had suffered. At least Alice's home was in a fairly new block of flats, which is where Michelle would like to live if she ever had her own home, not that it was likely she would, given that there was no special man in her life. Alice's cousin Eric had told her he was interested in marrying her, but she'd been holding him off for ages – even though she wasn't sure why. Eric was decent and nice – but Michelle wasn't sure how much she could trust him. She wasn't sure she could trust any man again.

Alan had let her down so badly and the pain of his lies and deceit had lived with her for too long. She ought to have been over it by now; it had been years since he came into her life, right at the start of the war, as she was finishing her training as a nurse. Michelle had been running for her bus one wet and windy day and she'd dropped her exercise books. Alan had saved them from being blown into the filthy water filling the gutters and handed them over with a flourish.

'Thanks – those books contain three years' work,' she'd said, her breath catching as she looked up into his deep blue eyes. He was so handsome, she'd thought she would die, and his smile had caught her fast. It had pretty much been love at first sight, but only on Michelle's side. Alan had been married, but he hadn't told her that until she discovered it for herself – just as she'd been on the verge of going away with him for a long weekend.

If someone hadn't seen her with him and told her that he was married with a small son, Michelle might have found herself in the same boat as Alice: pregnant and shamed. Thank God for the nosy neighbour who'd made it her business to put Michelle right!

Alan had denied it at first when she'd accused him of deceiving her, but she'd known he was lying. She'd seen it in his face, even though he kept telling her that she was the one he loved.

'I'm getting a divorce. I promise you, I'll leave her,' Alan had said when she'd told him the weekend was off and she wouldn't be seeing him again. 'I love you, my darling; please don't be like this. What does it matter? She doesn't care about anything but the boy—'

'And that makes it all right?' Michelle asked, feeling cold all over. 'What happens when you get tired of me – will you tell the next girl that I'm only interested in my children?'

Alan had pleaded with her, tears running down his cheeks, but they'd been false. When he'd realised that he wasn't going to get his own way, he'd sneered at her for being a fool. They'd parted badly and Michelle's wounds had taken a long time to heal. It didn't hurt as much now, but it had left her with a deep distrust of men in general.

She crossed the road towards the block of flats where Alice lived and glanced over her shoulder, but no one seemed to be hanging around that night. Perhaps Butcher Lee's thugs had got tired of their games.

Alice let her in. She smiled and welcomed Michelle into her lovely flat; it was as clean as a new pin, everywhere smelling of polish and fresh washing, very different from the old house that Alice had been brought up in, which had always smelled of foul drains. For a moment Michelle envied her friend her lovely home, wishing her mother could have a place like this, but then she registered that her friend seemed tense, not her normal cheery self.

'What's wrong? Mum said you seemed a bit down when you came for your sewing lesson.'

'Nothing . . . a bit fed up, that's all.'

'Bob was home recently, wasn't he?'

'Yes, but . . .' Alice caught back a sob. 'I had a letter from Jack . . . he wants me to go to America with him.'

'Jack Shaw? But I thought he died in the fire.'

'He's alive, Michelle. I told you I didn't believe he was dead; I had a feeling and now I know. I've no idea how he managed to get out, but his letter came recently, asking me to go away with him.'

'You won't go?'

'I couldn't do that to Bob, even if I wanted to . . .'

'Oh, Alice, you know Jack was a bad lot.'

'I wouldn't hurt Bob . . . I couldn't . . .'

'No, of course not,' Michelle agreed. 'The last thing you want to do is let him down.'

'And I wouldn't; he stepped in when Jack left me in the lurch,' Alice said.

'You're not even a bit tempted, then?' Michelle thought she could see some uncertainty in her friend's eyes. 'I know you were soft on him.'

Alice smiled ruefully, 'Yeah, well, fat lot of good that did me. No, I'm with Bob now, and that's that. I made him a promise when we wed and I'm not going to break it. But, don't let's talk about me,' she said. 'What about you, Michelle? When are you going to get married?'

'And who would I marry?' Michelle asked, arching her brows playfully while inwardly noticing that Alice had turned away from the subject of Jack Shaw a bit too quickly.

'I know Eric keeps hoping he'll wear you down, Michelle. He really loves you and wants to marry you – but if you don't love him, then don't marry him.' Alice paused then added, 'What about that doctor you told me about – the one who came round to your dad? Dr Kent, isn't it? You've seen him several times since, haven't you?'

'He visits St Saviour's sometimes, but I don't know him – for all I know he could be married . . .'

'No, he isn't. He lives with his mother and she's a widow . . .'

'How do you know?'

'The nurses were talking about him at the clinic when I took Susie for her check-up yesterday. He works there sometimes and I've seen him. He's very good-looking – I think half of them are in love with him, but he never seems to notice, keeps his distance and doesn't flirt, unlike most of the doctors – at least, that's

137

what they say. They were hinting he might be . . . you know, the other way. But I'm sure he isn't. Bob showed me some of them once at a pub we went to and Dr Kent isn't a bit like that . . .'

'Of course he isn't,' Michelle said, annoyed. 'Those nurses are only jealous because he doesn't notice them and probably has a lovely girlfriend they don't know about.'

'Perhaps,' Alice said, then changed the subject. 'Bob says he's getting leave again soon and he might take me for a holiday. I get so lonely here when he's away. No one talks in the street like they used to when I lived at home in Spitalfields. I've been here a few months and yet I hardly know anyone . . .'

'Why don't you bring Susie in to see the staff at St Saviour's? I'm sure they would love to see you.'

Alice looked wistful. 'I will bring Susie for a visit, but I don't know if I'll ever get back to work there now. It takes a lot of time to look after a baby and it isn't easy to find a child minder – not one I'd trust, anyway.'

'Mum might, for a couple of days a week – if that would be enough,' Michelle offered.

'Do you think she would?' Alice's eyes lit up at the idea. 'I do like your mum, Michelle. You're so lucky . . . even if Ma had been willing to look after Susie, I'm not sure I'd trust her. She was too handy with her fists, even when we were small.'

Alice's mother had thrown her out when she learned she was pregnant, and she hadn't even attended her wedding, though the rest of Alice's family had been there to support her.

'I'll ask her – I'm pretty sure she'll say yes.'

'Well, thanks for suggesting it,' Alice said and sighed. 'I'm glad I've got my Susie, and I wouldn't part with her for the world, but I used to enjoy the company at St Saviour's. It's not much fun being at home with Bob away . . .'

'Why don't you come to St Saviour's tomorrow afternoon? We could go for coffee or something after I finish my shift.'

'Oh yes, I'd like that,' Alice agreed. 'Thank goodness for you, Michelle. Sometimes I think I shall go mad here all alone.'

'You've got Susie, and Bob comes home when he can.'

'Yes, he comes when he can . . .' Alice turned away but not before Michelle had seen the sheen of tears.

Alice was hankering for that rotten Jack Shaw. Michelle wanted to take her and bang her head against the wall to make her see sense. Why couldn't she see that the man she had was worth ten of that charming rogue who had made her pregnant and then deserted her?

'Well, Eric is coming home on leave soon,' Michelle said. 'I'll ask him to babysit and we'll have a girl's night out somewhere – what do you reckon?'

'I reckon Eric won't think much of that,' Alice said, laughing. 'Maybe Nan would babysit one night so we can go out together. I'll ask her.'

'You do that.' Michelle grinned. 'Put the kettle on, Alice. I'm dying for a cuppa.'

*

'Can you come please, Nurse Michelle?' Mary Ellen tugged at her uniform skirt the next morning at work. 'Only it's Matty. He isn't very well. I don't know what's wrong with him, but he's gone all funny, making strange noises, and he can't breathe.'

'Yes, I'll come at once,' Michelle said, looking at the child's anxious face. 'Where is he?'

'He's on the floor in the playroom. He and Billy were having a game of football . . .' Mary Ellen stopped guiltily. 'I know they're not supposed to play in the house, and Sister would be cross, but Matty loves football, same as Billy, and he was showing him how to score a goal, but then Matty fell down and started twitching. He was kicking and frothing and I didn't know what to do. Billy put a hanky in his mouth 'cos he thought he might bite his tongue . . .'

'That was quick thinking,' Michelle said, letting Mary Ellen lead the way. She and Billy had been a couple of rebels when they first came here, but these days they seemed very responsible. 'Matty might be having some sort of a fit. I'll see what I can do – but perhaps we shall call the doctor.'

Michelle saw the child lying on the ground. By the time they arrived he'd stopped fitting but lay staring up at them with glazed eyes, as if he didn't know what he was doing. She knelt by his side, stroking his forehead and talking to him softly. If she was not mistaken, from Mary Ellen's description, the child had had some kind of nervous fit that had affected the use of his limbs, which might possibly be an epileptic fit. If that was the case, he would need to be on tablets for the rest of his life – and the effects could be unpleasant, especially for a child that liked to run and play football. She could only pray there was some other explanation for his fit.

He was coming round now, staring at her uneasily, clearly frightened by what had happened to him. Michelle decided not to make snap decisions; it might have been a harmless spasm or nervous fit of the kind children suffered sometimes when they got over-excited or too hot.

'What happened?' Matty asked, wide-eyed. 'Did I get sick?'

'You had a bit of a turn,' Billy told him. 'You're all right now, mate – nurse is here.'

'Yes, you've been sick and dizzy,' Michelle said, making up her mind to discuss the child with Dr Kent before she made any judgements. 'I'll take you up to the sick ward and clean you up. Do you think you can walk for me – or shall I get someone to help me carry you?'

'I can walk if you help me,' Matty said, making a brave attempt to get to his feet and falling back. He seemed very unsteady as he tried to walk, as if he had no control over his limbs.

'Run and fetch Tilly, please, Mary Ellen,' Michelle said. 'We'll have to carry you, Matty. I expect it was all that running about. You'll be right as rain after you've had a nice drink of water and a rest.'

She wiped the sick from his mouth with her apron, talking to him gently until his mind cleared. By the time Tilly arrived to help, he was able to walk with a helping hand on each side of him, albeit a bit jerkily.

Twenty minutes later, Matty was in bed and resting. Tilly followed Michelle as she went through to the rest room, which was between the sick and isolation wards, to wash her hands and put on a clean apron.

'He had a fit, didn't he? Me da's uncle's an epileptic – Uncle Derry. He comes from Dublin and he married me da's auntie, so he's not a blood relation. She's had a time with him, I can tell you. Once the fittin' starts it can 'appen anywhere, but she got killed in the war and he's in some sort of home for disabled folk now . . .'

'Well, we don't know it was an epileptic fit,' Michelle said. 'Children can have fits for all sorts of reasons. Please don't talk about it, Tilly. I'm going to contact the doctor and ask him to look at Matty – but until then, keep this to yourself please.'

'Of course, but the children will know he had a fit,' Tilly said. 'You can't keep nuthin' quiet when there's kids about.'

'I know – but we don't have to gossip, do we?'

'All right, I was only sayin' . . .'

Tilly looked annoyed as she went off to check on the drinks trolley for the children, which was late coming up. Cook was probably short-handed in the kitchen again.

Michelle sighed. Perhaps she had been a bit sharp with Tilly. She was still very new here and Michelle wasn't sure she could trust her, as she'd been able to trust Alice and Sally. She would get used to her eventually, but it took time to train a girl to do things the way they should be done, and Tilly seemed prone to some odd moods . . .

Tilly felt really fed up as she went into the kitchen to fetch the drinks for the kids in the sick bay. Everyone

142

seemed to get on to her and there were days when she couldn't do a thing right. It had started that morning at breakfast. Her mother had still been in bed after a late night out with her husband, Arthur Mallens. Roddy had been in a rush to leave, because he had football practice at school, and Mags was sulking. She'd glared at Tilly when she'd asked her to take a cup of tea up to Ma, then sullenly refused.

'Take it yourself or let her come and fetch it.'

'Mags, you wretch! You know I've got to get to work. I was lucky to get this job and I don't want to lose it.'

'I ain't goin' up while he's still around.'

'He went out ages ago,' Tilly said. 'If you're referring to Arthur?'

'Oh, all right then,' Mags said. 'Give it 'ere. I'll probably be late for school, but it don't matter. I'm never goin' ter do anythin' but work in a bleedin' factory.'

'What makes you say that? I thought you wanted to take your exams and be a nurse?'

'He told her I ought ter be out earnin' me livin' – said he wasn't goin' ter keep all of us – not unless it were made worth his while.'

Tilly looked at her suspiciously. 'What do you mean?'

Mags shrugged. 'Dunno. I'll take the tea. You'd better go if you're late. I don't care long as he ain't here . . .'

Tilly couldn't stop thinking about the look in her sister's eyes. If she hadn't been in such a hurry to get to work she would've made Mags tell her what she was getting at. Probably it was simply Arthur flexing his muscles, making sure they all knew he was the big man who kept a roof over their heads.

If she'd had a choice, Tilly would rather have lived

143

anywhere else but under the same roof as Arthur. But there was no way she could walk out on her mother, brother and sister; especially if . . . No, surely Arthur wouldn't try his dirty tricks on her younger sister? It was Tilly he was after . . . wasn't it?

Yeah, of course it was. He never left her alone, followed her into the scullery or the back yard when she went out to the toilet, and upstairs. If she didn't make a habit of locking her door, he'd have followed her into her bedroom – and Tilly knew that one day he'd be too quick for her . . .

SIXTEEN

'We were hoping you might take him in,' the police constable looked at Angela, twisting his helmet in his hands as he went through the tangled explanation. 'The boy's father is in the Navy and will be away at sea for the next few months, and his mother isn't considered fit to care for him, especially as he's a difficult case.'

'What do you mean, difficult?' Angela asked. 'Is he naughty or mentally unstable?'

'No, Timmy is a bright boy,' Constable Sallis said. 'Truth is, we've tried a couple of places already and they wouldn't take him. He's a victim of polio – caught it swimming at the pool with his father, they reckon. It was a severe case and he's had to spend months in an iron lung, but now he's no longer infectious and the hospital want to release him. Trouble is, it's left one of his legs weaker than the other, so he has to wear a leg iron and he'll need to be taken to hospital for treatment every so often. We thought with you having a regular staff of nurses here, you might be able to look after him . . .'

'Poor child,' Angela said. 'We certainly have room to

take him in, Constable. As you know, Sister is away for the moment but I'm sure she wouldn't refuse.'

'We should be grateful, Mrs Morton. As I said, the mother has had a breakdown – the doctors think it was too much for her, seeing her son suffering the way he did – so she isn't able to care for him. I'm not here in an official capacity, but I happen to know the family and I thought, seeing as you've got that new wing . . .'

'What about the council? Have they not made an order for his care?' In July of that year the Children's Act had been passed, which meant that there was now a Children's Officer and a committee to look into this sort of thing. It had made a considerable change in the way children's welfare was managed; these days requests to take children in were more likely to come from the council than the police.

'No, the case hasn't come to their attention as yet, and we're hoping it needn't. My sister is friendly with Mrs Bent – the lad's mum – and she offered to look after him, but the hospital won't allow it. They say it must be a children's home or a relative, and the only relative is Timmy's grandmother and she isn't up to it. Poor old girl is willing, but she ought to be in a home herself.'

Angela hesitated; a child with Timmy Bent's affliction would need a great deal of extra care and the nurses already had enough to do, but how could she refuse? She wished she could discuss his case with Sister Beatrice, but with the Warden in hospital it was down to her to make the decision.

'You are certain that the infectious stage is over? I understand that poliomyelitis is a very contagious disease.'

'May I suggest that you go along to the hospital and discuss it with the doctors there?' Constable Sallis said. 'I know you have to think of all the other children here, Mrs Morton, but the doctors know what they're talking about. They wouldn't send the boy out unless he was ready, would they?'

'No, I'm sure they wouldn't,' Angela said. 'I shall visit him and talk to his doctors, discuss what extra treatment he is going to need, and then I must consult the nurses. However, if at all possible, we shall be pleased to take Timmy in at St Saviour's.'

'You don't know what a relief it is to hear you say that, Mrs Morton. Mrs Bent would hate it if her boy was sent off to some sanatorium in the country somewhere she couldn't visit – and I think Bert would go mad when he got back from sea. Timmy will be all right here – and it's only temporary. The family will want him back once they're on their feet again.' He smiled at her. 'When will you speak to the doctors at the hospital?'

'I'll visit this afternoon and I'll pop into the station and leave a message for you when I've made my decision.'

'Thank you. I can rest easy now I've done my bit. He's a good lad, Mrs Morton. It's a rotten shame what's happened to him.'

'Yes, it is a terrible disease,' Angela agreed. 'I only wish someone would come up with a vaccine for it.'

'According to what I've heard, there's no cure,' Constable Sallis said. 'It takes its course and the victims either get over it or die. Too much of it about around here, I can tell you.'

'Well, there's nothing we can do about that, but if we can help Timmy we shall,' Angela promised.

'I don't know what we'd do without St Saviour's, and that's the truth. You know what they call you around here?' Angela shook her head. 'The 'Alfpenny Angels,' he said, and grinned.

Angela smiled but made no reply. Constable Sallis had confirmed her view that St Saviour's was needed here, right in the heart of the East End where dirt and poverty were still the twin enemies. It was all very well for Henry Arnold to talk of fresh air and the benefits of the countryside, but here in Halfpenny Street they were accessible to children like Timmy Bent – and here was where they must stay.

Abandoning the letters she'd been about to write, Angela went in search of Staff Nurse Michelle. She would have a chat with her before she went to the Infirmary to determine Timmy Bent's future . . .

'I'm really glad you asked me out this evening,' Angela said as Mark held the door of his car for her. 'I needed to get away and relax for a few hours.' Her visit to the hospital and the ward where children suffering with terrible diseases were lodged had distressed her, though she'd made up her mind to take Timmy Bent into St Saviour's. Her brief visit to his bedside with the comics and sweets she'd bought for him had instantly convinced her that she needed to help. It wasn't so much that Timmy needed to be at St Saviour's, it was the fact that Angela couldn't leave him where he was to save her own life. One look at his pale wan face and her heart was won. She would have moved heaven and earth to help him.

'Work getting you down, Angela?' he asked as he tucked the skirt of her smart dress in so that the door did not damage it as it closed. He went round and slid across into the driving seat. 'I know the feeling. Sometimes it simply overwhelms you and everything seems too much.'

'I've been working all hours to catch up on my reports. I don't think I realised quite how much of a load Sister Beatrice was carrying,' Angela said with a wry smile. 'There isn't an hour in the day when someone doesn't have a question or some decision that needs to be made. The staff come to the Warden on all sorts of matters, whether it's a child who keeps leaving the bathroom in a mess or one that's been caught playing truant from school. And then there's the staff themselves: Michelle came in late one morning; she had to look after her brothers while her mother went to the hospital with her father, so I had to ask Paula to work longer. Next week will be even worse because Sister was due to make her monthly visits then, and I haven't the faintest idea what I ought to do . . .'

'Monthly visits?' Mark eased the car out into the traffic, frowning as he listened to Angela's account of the nun's mercy visits to various poor families in the district. 'I don't think that comes within your remit, Angela. Strictly speaking, it isn't part of the Warden's duties. Sister Beatrice has obviously taken it on herself to help out in her own time.'

'So you don't think I should visit these families in her stead?'

'Not unless you feel confident,' he said. 'Have you

been to see Sister Beatrice – consulted her as to her wishes in the matter?'

'Nan says she's still quite unwell and not up to visitors. I don't want to bother her – but that isn't what I wanted to ask you about.'

'No? Fire away then,' he said. 'I'm listening.'

'Why didn't you tell me that Henry Arnold was being offered a seat on the Board of St Saviour's?'

'I didn't know myself until I was asked what I thought. It happened very quickly. Arnold is a major contributor to the charity, so we thought he ought to be asked, considering the large donation he offered.'

'I'm ready to make the contribution I mentioned to you a few months ago,' Angela said. 'Shall I be offered a seat?'

'Are you requesting it?' Mark sounded surprised. 'I didn't think you wanted the bother?'

'I don't trust Mr Arnold.'

'Is this feminine intuition, or do you have a good reason for your suspicions? And if so, may I know what they are?'

'I can't put it into words. I suppose you could say it was intuition,' she admitted ruefully. 'He coerced me into having dinner with him the other evening – and it turns out he wants to build a new and I imagine expensive home in the country and move St Saviour's.'

'Yes, he has put a proposition in writing to the Board,' Mark said, glancing at her as he indicated and then turned off on to the road leading to one of his favourite restaurants. 'It isn't set in stone by any means, Angela.'

'But you think it's a good idea to move away from Halfpenny Street . . . from London?'

150

'Don't you – eventually?'

'I can see why it would be considered a step forward – in time,' she agreed. 'But I know that many of our children would resent being taken out of London – as would the staff. I'm not sure that either Nan or Sister Beatrice would care for the idea . . .'

'No, I'm certain they wouldn't. But as the population grows and traffic intensifies London is only going to get busier, dirtier and the air more polluted . . . surely the country will be a better environment for children who've only ever known poverty and the squalid conditions of the slums?'

'Even if I agreed that might be the way to go in the future . . .' Angela paused as he drew up outside the ancient inn by the river and stopped the engine '. . . seriously, Mark, I don't think it would be sensible to trust everything Mr Arnold says.'

'Your instincts are usually good,' Mark said, looking thoughtful. 'It might be worth doing a bit more investigating – but Arnold is entitled to that seat after the amount he donated. I'm sure the Board would agree that you are too, once you make the donation.'

'I'll send the cheque in the morning, together with my request. As Administrator I think I should have a say in policy-making – and I think Sister Beatrice should be invited to join the Board too.'

'I doubt she'd be interested,' Mark said. 'She finds the monthly meetings a chore and prefers to leave them to you.' He quirked an amused eyebrow at her. 'Hoping for an ally to help you block a future move, Angela?'

'Would you vote for it regardless of my views?'

'I haven't said I'm definitely for it, though I have

151

some ideas of my own.' Mark leaned in closer, his breath warm on her face as he touched her hand. 'I certainly wouldn't want this to come between us,' he said. 'You know I value your opinion, Angela. Your friendship means a great deal to me and I would always listen to your arguments – just as I hope you would consider mine.'

His touch made her heart miss a beat and her breath caught as she felt something spark between them. She knew instinctively that Mark was ready to move forward in their relationship, and she believed she might be too. At last she could contemplate loving a man again, and the sexual tension was there between them in that moment. She felt it and welcomed it, her mouth slightly dry and the slow rhythm of her heart like a drum beat, as if she were being drawn from the darkness into the light.

Angela hesitated, and then smiled and squeezed his arm. 'You mean a great deal to me too, Mark. I would hate to lose you – but I have a bad feeling about this business with Mr Arnold. I know he speaks highly of St Saviour's and appears to be genuine in his concern for the children, yet I cannot shake off the suspicion he has an ulterior motive, even though it's hard to see what's in it for him. He referred to St Saviour's as *his* home, and more or less offered me the post of Warden. I felt as if he were trying to bribe me – as if he were riding roughshod over the rest of you.'

'In a few years, if you still wanted it, I'd probably recommend you for the post of Warden,' Mark said. When Angela shook her head, he raised his eyebrows. 'You wouldn't want that?'

'I am suited to the role of Administrator – I get

things done, and I'm good at raising funds – but you need someone like Sister Beatrice at the helm. Aside from the fact her nursing experience is invaluable, she has an understanding of the children and people of London that comes from intimate knowledge of what they've suffered. I love the children, and I spend as much time with them as I can, but I doubt they could ever trust me the way they trust her. Besides, it's too much work for one person, especially now we have the new wing.'

'It sounds as though you admire Sister Beatrice.'

'Yes, of course – don't you?' Angela blushed as his eyes quizzed her. 'That doesn't mean that we shan't end up arguing once she's fighting fit again – I've no doubt we shall – but I do know that she does a good job.'

'I think the two of you make an excellent team. Although marvellous in her way, Beatrice was struggling to cope until you arrived – St Saviour's was stagnating, behind the times. We had to bring it up to date, move foward. And once the country gets through this austerity period, the pace of change is only going to pick up. You've done a lot since you arrived, gone a part of the way there, but there's so much more to do. The NHS will revolutionise health care in this country. It is my belief and hope that the life of the working man will also improve. Yet some evils will never go away; men will go on getting drunk and beating their wives or abusing their children. We need to create a safe environment for those youngsters – and we could take on more in the space and freedom the countryside offers.'

'Yes, but in Halfpenny Street, St Saviour's is right at the heart of the need . . .'

Mark had come round to the side of the car; he offered his hand and she took it, gliding elegantly from the car. For a moment as he looked down at her she thought he might kiss her and found that she was hoping he would, but he merely smiled, closed the car door and offered her his arm.

'Shall we forget work for once and enjoy ourselves, Angela? I know you're passionate about St Saviour's and I'm glad it has turned out so well for you – but I'd rather like to talk about us for once.'

'Oh?' Angela looked up at him as they walked towards the lights and warmth of the restaurant. 'We are still friends, I hope?'

'Yes, of course, and always will be – but I was hoping there might be something more. I know you loved John, and I was frightened of speaking out for a long time – too long, but I should like to clear the air. I care for you a great deal and I'd like us to be more than friends one day . . .'

'And Carole?' Angela gave him a questioning look. 'You have no regrets? I thought perhaps you felt something for her?'

'It was an affair, nothing more. To my shame, I used her – she was young and pretty and seemed to like me. I was flattered . . . and you didn't seem interested. I thought your heart might be set on Nick Hadden?'

'Only as a friend,' Angela replied. 'I'm not sure you used Carole, Mark. I think it was the other way round: she knew you were comfortably off and she wanted the prestige of being your wife. It was a rotten trick she played, lying about being pregnant with your child.'

'Yes, perhaps,' he agreed ruefully. 'Fortunately, you were not taken in by her.'

'I might have been if she hadn't tried to sabotage Sister Beatrice.' Angela smiled. 'I'm pleased you weren't hurt by her, Mark.'

'As I said, it was merely a flirtation – and you and I seemed to have drifted apart. I suppose I felt shut out, which is why I got involved with Carole.'

'Did I shut you out?' Angela gazed deeply into his eyes.

'You were angry with me because I didn't tell you that your mother was ill, weren't you?'

'Yes,' she admitted. 'That was unfair of me, Mark. I know you can't talk about your patients.'

'Your mother particularly asked me not to speak of it to you. I did ask if you were going home last Christmas – if you'd said no, I would have told you that you ought to. That was as much as I could do. The truth had to come from your mother, or your father.'

'Father wouldn't have told me if he hadn't needed help with the fees for the clinic in Switzerland,' Angela said, feeling a shadow pass over her. 'She has left there, did you know?'

'Yes, I was informed as a matter of courtesy by the clinic.'

'Dad says she's going to stay with a friend in his villa in France . . . It isn't fair on him. Did you know he has a heart problem?'

'Yes. He has asked my advice . . .' Mark's hand reached for hers. 'Again, I was asked in confidence. I'm sorry, Angela, I know it's all been pretty rotten for you

155

since John died. The split between your parents is awful, especially at a time when your father needs someone.'

'I'm so angry with her. I'd like to go over there and tell her what she's done to him – but of course I can't.'

'Perhaps she had her reasons,' Mark said. 'A marriage fails over several years and for many reasons. Mine failed after my son died, but perhaps it was falling apart long before that . . . I've always wondered if Edine felt that I'd let her down, failed her in some way.'

'I'm sure you did everything you could to help her.'

'Perhaps . . .' His strong features reflected vulnerability, as if the past hurt too much to be reopened. 'Thank you for believing in me, Angela – but every one of us has something in our past that we regret, do we not?'

'Yes, I'm sure you're right,' she agreed. 'Tell me, how is that friend you were anxious about? Is he recovering from his operations?'

'Yes, though I fear that he may find life harder to cope with now . . . it looks as if he may be physically impaired. For a man like Alan, that is worse than you can imagine. His music means everything to him, and he may never again play as he once could – oh, he can make music, but for an artist like him that isn't enough. I feel guilty, and yet the advice I gave him was the best I could offer in the circumstances.'

'I'm so sorry, but I know you will help him all you can.'

'I will indeed. Yet I wonder if that is enough . . .'

The lights were soft and discreet as they entered the restaurant. As she took her seat opposite Mark, Angela was unaware of the man rising to his feet a few tables

156

away, having just paid his bill. Although she didn't see him as he escorted his very pretty blonde companion from the dining room, Henry Arnold observed Angela laughing at something Mark had said to her.

'I'm glad you've decided that you like and admire Sister Beatrice,' Mark said after he'd ordered their meal. 'I've always thought she was an excellent nurse . . .'

'I certainly admire her and appreciate what she does,' Angela said with a little grimace. 'But as to *liking* her . . . well, I think the jury is out on that, and I'm sure she feels the same way. Before she was admitted to hospital I couldn't do anything right and I dare say it won't improve her mood having to stay there for a few weeks.'

'No, perhaps not, but have you ever wondered why she's so tetchy?'

'It may have had something to do with her feeling ill,' Angela said.

'Undoubtedly that was a factor, but I think she was also nervous of the future. After all, she isn't young any more and in you she has a formidable rival.'

'I'm not a rival,' Angela said. 'I've already told you that I wouldn't want her job as warden.'

'Yes,' Mark said and smiled, his brows lifting. 'But does she know that?'

SEVENTEEN

Beatrice's body ached all over. Her head was throbbing and she felt as weak as a kitten, but at least the pain in her side had gone and she no longer felt that dragging sensation that she'd been vaguely aware of after the operation. It had been as if her limbs were made of lead and it was too much trouble to move, drink or eat. She'd been aware that Nan had visited a couple of times, and her bedside table was bedecked with flowers and cards from the children and staff at St Saviour's, but everything seemed so distant, as if it was happening in another time, another life. She could only recall having felt like this once previously in her life . . . but that was so long ago, when she'd reached rock bottom after losing the only thing that mattered: Tommy, her beloved son. She'd never loved her husband, but after Tommy's death she'd hated him, blaming him for the way her son died . . .

She shook her head, refusing to dwell on the unhappiness that had so nearly destroyed her. On that previous occasion when she'd occupied a bed in the Infirmary she'd wished for death, believing that life held nothing for her but emptiness and misery. Then she'd sought

158

the forgiveness and mercy of God, and in return she'd found comfort at the convent. She trained as a nurse and through helping others she'd come to terms with the tragedy that had almost destroyed her. St Saviour's had given her back the contentment she'd lost all those years ago . . . giving her love and respect, and lending purpose to a life that had once lost all meaning.

Beatrice glanced at the clock on the wall. It was almost eight in the evening and she'd had no visitors. Nan had told her she couldn't come tonight, but Beatrice had expected a visit from Angela. She needed to see her, to hear how things were going at the home – to be reassured that they missed her and needed her back.

Nan told her these things, but she'd also told her that Angela was managing very well. 'I never expected she'd cope half as well as she has,' Nan told her cheerfully. 'There's no need for you to worry about rushing back, Beatrice. The doctor said you should take a couple of weeks at the seaside to rest and get your strength back, and I'm sure Angela will be fine.'

Nan's intention had been to reassure her, Beatrice knew that, but it wasn't what she wanted to hear. She needed them to miss her, to be desperate to have her back. Her greatest fear was that the Board would decide she was too old and invite Angela to replace her. What would she do then – return to the convent and work in the Infirmary? But what if they decided she was too old for that, too?

Hearing a cry from two beds down, Beatrice turned to look at the woman who lay there. Old and homeless, she'd been found lying on the pavement, her body wasted and spent. The nurses whispered that she'd had a stroke and her mind was affected.

'Please help me,' she cried weakly. 'My eyes . . . I can't see . . . it's my eyes . . .'

Beatrice looked for a nurse but there were none in sight. Every bed was occupied and the nurses had been rushed off their feet all day. At this hour, they were most likely getting ready for the changeover, the day nurses briefing the night nurses on new admissions to the ward and each patient's particular needs.

'Please help me . . . it's my eyes . . .' the pitiful wail stirred Beatrice into action. She swung her legs over the side of her bed, feeling slightly dizzy for a moment but immediately steadying herself. Discovering that she could walk slowly, she found her way to the woman's bed and bent over her, touching her hand.

'What is wrong, dear?' she asked.

'Oh, Nurse, will you bathe my eyes?' the woman pleaded. 'I can't see – and it's so much better when you bathe them.'

Hesitating for a moment, Beatrice picked up a tissue from the box beside the bed and damped it with water from a jug. It was tepid, because it had been left there all day and in Beatrice's opinion was not fit to drink. Her patients would not be given liquid that had been standing in the ward all day! She wiped the woman's eyes a couple of times, soothing with gentle kindness as best she could, and her hand was seized and kissed.

'You're so kind,' the old woman said, 'so kind, Nurse . . .'

Beatrice patted her hand and withdrew it. She was feeling decidedly odd as she left the old lady, who had quietened now, and began to walk back to her own bed. Realising vaguely that she was weaving from side to side, Beatrice sighed and sank to the floor in a faint before she could quite reach her bed. The next thing she knew, a nurse was standing over her, scolding her for getting out of bed.

'What did you think you were doing, Sister Beatrice!' the nurse admonished. 'You could have opened your stitches and harmed yourself – and after all the trouble Doctor's gone to, making you better.'

Beatrice allowed herself to be helped back into bed. She felt foolish for making a show of herself, and made no attempt to excuse what she'd done or give a reason for it. Closing her eyes, she lay back against the pillow. She felt the sting of tears behind her lids but she would not let them fall. She would not allow herself to cry, even if she did feel weak and old and alone.

Her action had been one of compassion; it was what she did, and she wanted to be able to do it again, to be back at St Saviour's where she was needed and appreciated. To be loved was too much to expect, but at times she had felt loved when she nursed a sick child back to health. That old lady had been grateful for her kindness and Beatrice knew that her impulse to help had been right, but she wasn't strong enough yet. She could only pray that she would recover her old stamina and be able to return to the job she loved . . . assuming they still wanted her. If Angela was coping well, they might think it was time Beatrice retired . . .

Angela had paused for the first time that morning, grateful for the tray of tea Nan had carried up to her room. She invited Nan to share, but the head carer shook her head, hovering in the doorway.

'Not this time, Angela. I know how busy you are and I've got a lot on myself today. It's just I wanted to say that I visited Beatrice again last night and the nurses told me she'd had a fall the previous day. They were concerned as she got out of bed for no reason – though she told me she went to help one of the other patients.'

'Yes, that is exactly the sort of thing she would do if someone was calling out and the nurses weren't about. Did she harm herself?'

'No, but they said she was very tired. The thing is, I think she wants to see you – she's been fretting about it.'

'I've been putting it off because I didn't think the hospital were keen on her having too many visitors and I didn't want to upset or tire her,' Angela said. 'If I'd known she would fret, I'd have called in much sooner.'

'I'm sure it would set her mind at rest if you were able to drop by. I keep telling her everything is fine here, but you know how she worries.'

'Well, I'll pop in and see how she is this evening – take her some fruit and a few flowers. Are you going tonight?'

'I won't if you are,' Nan said. 'They don't like too many people round the beds, and she will want to talk to you, I'm sure.'

'Well, it sounds as if she's on the mend at least,' Angela said. 'If she made the effort to get out to attend to that patient, she must be feeling more like her old self. She shouldn't have done it, but it wouldn't have been Sister Beatrice if she hadn't, would it?'

'No, I don't suppose it would,' Nan said, still hesitating. 'I told you once that St Saviour's is my life these

162

days, but I do have some outside interests . . . The thing is, I don't think Beatrice does. There's the convent, naturally, but she needs more than that.'

'Yes, I dare say you're right. You know her better than anyone.' Angela looked thoughtful. 'Mark said something the other evening when we had a meal and I think perhaps he's got a point. There's something I ought to make clear to her . . .'

'She needs to feel wanted here.'

Angela nodded her agreement. 'She *is* needed here, Nan – and she has to get well again so that she can return to us.'

Sister Beatrice was relaxing back against her pillows, her eyes shut, as Angela approached the bed. She opened them when Angela reached her and a flicker of uncertainty showed in her face.

'Angela, it's good of you to visit,' she said, a little stiffly.

'I thought you might like some grapes – and this magazine. It's about gardening. There are lovely photographs . . .'

Sister Beatrice waved an impatient hand, dismissing the magazine and grapes. 'What is happening at St Saviour's – is everything as it ought to be?'

'We are managing. We've had some new arrivals, but they were quite healthy, though a bit malnourished,' Angela told her. 'I think everything is ticking over nicely, but there are certain things that will need your attention when you're well enough to return.'

'Indeed? Is something wrong?' Beatrice sat forward, an eagerness about her that hadn't been there moments earlier.

'Oh no, nothing wrong, but I'm worried about the May twins. Samantha told Wendy that her aunt didn't want Sarah, that she might try to put her in an institution for the mentally retarded.'

Beatrice frowned. 'But Nan said she had taken both children? The Welfare people made an order in her favour, didn't they? I was given to understand the aunt wanted them the morning I was taken ill, but I'd hoped you might have managed to change their minds. As it happens one of the mothers I visit from time to time had previously mentioned Miss May in passing and not in complimentary terms. I had hoped to discuss the situation with you more fully . . .'

'Ah, I see, that explains your anxiety concerning them when you became so suddenly ill. I was given only a couple of hours' notice and there was nothing I could do once the order was in place – I had no idea at that time that Samantha was fearful of her aunt. She'd told Wendy but Wendy didn't think to tell me all of it – until it was too late . . .'

'I'm not sure what you could have done even if you had known,' Beatrice said. 'Maybe the child's experience has made her wary. Besides, surely the woman wouldn't take the child from us and then abandon her?'

'We've seen worse, haven't we? Perhaps agreeing to take both was the only way she could have Samantha. She was very sharp with Sarah when she took them away – with both of them, really – but she obviously had no patience with Sarah. I presume that the Children's Welfare will have followed things up, but I wondered if I should go round to the house and make sure they are all right.'

164

'It may be the only way – we cannot allow that child to be incarcerated in one of those dreadful places.' Beatrice shook her head. 'It would be a crime – you must not allow it, Angela.'

'I shall certainly do what I can to help the twins. Whom do you suggest I should contact in the event an attempt is made to put Sarah away?'

'Do not wait for the aunt to act – you must pre-empt her,' Sister Beatrice told her authoritatively. 'We must make a case for having the twins in our care permanently. Write a report and get Mr Adderbury to give his opinion on the child. You'll have to deal with the council or possibly the magistrates, and they will doubtless have their own views on the matter.'

Angela nodded. 'I'll compose the report and type it up tomorrow. Would you be willing to put your signature to it?'

'Absolutely.' Sister Beatrice sighed and leaned back against the pillows once more. 'I wish I could be of more help, Angela – but this affair has pulled me down more than I realised.'

'You mustn't worry. Mark will help me,' Angela assured her. 'But you're sorely missed, Sister. Everyone keeps telling me you would do this or that, and they're all eager to have you back.'

'Are they really?' Beatrice gave her a straight look. 'I know what you're doing, Angela. It is extremely thoughtful and kind – but I dare say you have everything under control.'

'Even so, I would appreciate your advice. It is reassuring to have the benefit of your experience. We've been asked if we'll take in a young boy – a victim of polio. His father is away at sea and his mother is too ill to care for him, but it would only be until the father returns and can make alternative arrangements. He needs special treatment, so it would make more work for our nurses—'

'Naturally, we must take him. He is precisely the kind of child that needs us – but you knew that . . .'

'Yes, but please remember I can't do everything, any more than you could before I was appointed. It's a two-woman job, Sister. Besides, I shall need you to fight my corner quite soon . . .'

'What do you mean?'

'I think someone wants to move St Saviour's away from London – and I don't trust his motives. He speaks of building huge new premises in the country, and it all sounds wonderful, but I sense something is wrong. I want you there with me if it comes to a fight to save our home, to keep it where it should be in Halfpenny Street.'

A spark of her old energy showed in Sister Beatrice's eyes. 'I would never allow them to close St Saviour's, not while I have a say in it,' she said. 'Don't they understand that we need to be where we are, in the streets where those children live? Take them away from the place they belong and you will destroy a part of them.'

'Yes, that is what I feel, Sister,' Angela said. She smiled at her colleague. 'We may have our differences, but we stand united on this, don't we? St Saviour's will always be needed in London, no matter what happens elsewhere. Even if in the future they do build that new place, we should continue in Halfpenny Street, perhaps as a halfway house if nothing more.'

'On this we are united,' Sister Beatrice said, taking

the hand Angela offered and gripping it strongly. 'I shall return as soon as my body has healed. The spirit is as strong as ever, Angela, even if I have been given a salutary lesson that I am a mere mortal.'

'I wouldn't say mere,' Angela replied, smiling. 'At St Saviour's we all believe you are superhuman!'

EIGHTEEN

'Good morning,' Nan said when they met in the hallway two days after Angela's visit to Sister Beatrice at the hospital. 'I'm glad I've caught you – there's someone waiting for you in the staff rest room. I put her in there, as I didn't think you would want her to wait in your office. I did tell her she should have made an appointment, and I told her you might be a while, but she insisted on waiting – so I gave them a cup of tea and some biscuits.'

'Them?' Angela's fine brows rose. 'More than one visitor is waiting?'

'It's that Miss May, and she's brought Sarah with her. Sarah looks as if she's been crying, and I think she's frightened . . .'

'I'd better go to them right away. Thank you, Nan,' Angela said, quickening her stride. At the mention of the May twins' aunt she had a cold sensation at the nape of her neck that told her there was something wrong. On reaching the rest room she paused in the doorway to survey the scene before entering. Sarah was standing with her thumb in her mouth, staring vacantly into space, while Miss May perched on the edge of her seat looking impatient. She stood up hastily as Angela entered.

'I'm sorry to keep you waiting. It would've been better to make an appointment—'

'I haven't time for messing about,' Miss May snapped, her features cold and disdainful. 'I can't cope with this child. Her father called her a Child of Satan and that's exactly what she—'

'Miss May! That is not appropriate language to use about Sarah – I would ask you to have more care for her feelings.'

'She doesn't know what I say.'

'We found Sarah intelligent enough, though somewhat reticent—'

'Well, here she is then.' The woman glared at Angela defiantly, pushing the child towards her. 'I've brought her back to you while her sister is at school; Samantha is strong-willed and she would kick up such a fuss if she knew – but I've had enough of this one and that's the truth.'

'Sarah was never any trouble here,' Angela objected. She saw the woman's mouth twist sourly and felt a surge of anger. 'What has she done that's so terrible?'

'She's stubborn and wicked, that's what she is,' Miss May said furiously. 'She deliberately broke my Copeland vase – threw it down in a tantrum. And that's not all. She's wet the bed, knocked orange juice all over my best tablecloth, and left the lavatory without pulling the chain – and she won't wash herself unless Samantha stands over her. I need Samantha to help me in the mornings, not spend her time running after this sinful girl.'

'This is highly irregular. The Children's Welfare officer will have to be informed and I'm sure they will want to discuss it with you.' Angela wanted the woman to understand that sending a child back to the home was a serious matter.

'I'll tell them precisely what I've told you: this one's a wrong 'un and no mistake.' Miss May's mouth was set in a thin line; clearly she would brook no argument.

'Well, we shall certainly take Sarah back,' Angela said and reached for the girl's hand. Sarah glanced up as she took it and she smiled and nodded to her, before turning to look at her aunt once more. 'You'll have to sign that you're willing to let Sarah return to St Saviour's, and that you relinquish your rights to her.' Angela knew she would have to square it with the Welfare people, but if she could get this awful woman to sign that she didn't want Sarah, perhaps they would accept that she was better off with them at St Saviour's.

'Give me the paper and I'll sign. I've no more time to waste on the ungrateful child. My brother always said she wasn't right in the head – singing those strange songs.'

'It's a French lullaby, I think,' Angela said. 'Was her mother French by any chance?'

'What has that got to do with anything? She died straight after this horrible girl was born.' Miss May scribbled her signature on the form Angela produced and glared at the child, who was crying silently. 'There's no need to bawl, Sarah. You're back where you wanted to be, so stop your grizzling.'

'Sarah want Samantha,' Sarah said, before putting her thumb back in her mouth.

'Well, you'll have to want in vain. I'll leave her to

you now – and I hope you have better luck with her, Mrs Morton. The child is an imbecile, if you ask my opinion.'

'I didn't,' Angela said and restrained herself from saying something she might regret. 'Sarah will be safe and looked after here. We should be glad to have her sister, too, if you wish to return her. It's cruel to separate them.'

If looks could kill, Angela would have been instantly slain, but Miss May turned tail and flounced out angrily without another word.

Sarah's tears continued to slide down her cheeks as Angela wiped them with her handkerchief and wondered what she should do next. If only Sister Beatrice had been here; she would have dealt with the situation so much better. Still, at least one sister was safe now. Angela had seen enough of Miss May to know that poor Samantha could not possibly be happy in her care.

'It's all right now, love. You're here with us. Let's go and find Staff Nurse Wendy,' she said, offering her hand to the child. Sarah considered and then nodded, sliding her hand into Angela's. 'You like Wendy, don't you?'

Sarah nodded, but didn't answer. Angela's heart wrenched at the sight of her distress; she wished she could have told that awful woman what she really thought of her, but she'd been afraid she would exercise her right as the child's legal guardian and snatch Sarah back. Thank goodness she hadn't taken her off to a mental institution. She probably would have, if not for the paperwork and effort involved: two doctors were required to give their agreement before the papers could be signed, and Jane May wasn't the kind of woman who would waste her energy or money on such an enterprise. Instead she'd chosen to dump Sarah back at St Saviour's, and Angela could only rejoice that she had taken the easy way out.

'But what about Samantha?' Wendy asked when Angela brought Sarah to her. 'Isn't she coming back too? Sarah won't settle without her.'

'Miss May seems determined to keep her,' Angela said. 'I'm not happy about the situation, Wendy, but for the moment there is nothing I can do except let the Welfare people know. I promise you I do not intend to leave it there though. I'll seek advice from the authorities and see what more can be done.'

'Why send one back without the other? I don't understand . . .'

'I think Miss May has a use for Samantha. She mentioned needing her help in the mornings.'

'You think she wants the child to wait on her?' Wendy was horrified. 'Samantha isn't old enough to look after anyone, except perhaps her sister – she ought to be with people who will love her and care for her.'

'I agree with you,' Angela said, 'but Miss May has the law on her side, so I can't force her to surrender the child to me.'

'No, I suppose not,' Wendy said. 'But it doesn't seem right – you only have to look at Sarah sitting there, rocking herself. She's distraught.'

'Perhaps now she's with people she knows and trusts, and once she's had something to eat . . .' But deep down, Angela shared Wendy's anxiety. Sarah relied so heavily on Samantha; how would she manage without her twin.

And how would Samantha manage, living with an unfeeling aunt and no sister to love?

'Sarah like Nurse Wendy,' the child said, and slipped her hand into Wendy's as she finished dressing her in a clean skirt and blouse, and turned her to brush and plait her hair. Sarah's hair had grown very long and Samantha had told Wendy before that her sister had always wanted it done in a long plait at the back. 'Wendy not go away?'

Wendy's throat caught as she saw the yearning appeal in the young girl's eyes. Sarah was such a beautiful child, with her pale hair, wide, innocent blue eyes and clear complexion, and the idea that anyone would want to hurt her was beyond Wendy's comprehension.

'No, I'm not going anywhere,' Wendy said, and squeezed Sarah's hand. 'I'm going to take you down to Nancy. You like Nancy, don't you? She came and told you stories – do you remember?'

Sarah nodded and sucked her thumb. Her aunt was a cruel woman to abandon her here, separating her from her sister and implying that she was an imbecile. Wendy knew she wasn't stupid; she'd listened avidly to Nancy's stories, particularly the ones about the Big Hairy Spider who vanquished giants and looked after lost children.

Looking at Sarah now, so lost without the person she loved, reminded Wendy of her own loss. Jim Bracknell had been her feller for such a brief time. They'd hardly got to know each other before he was shipped off to France, only to fall at Dunkirk.

Her throat tightened, but Wendy knew she was only one of thousands of women who'd lost the man they loved to that awful war. She didn't know why, but there had never been anyone else since. Perhaps it was because she was too busy being a nurse and then looking after her mother, but she'd never looked at another man – and she didn't think anyone had looked at her twice. She wasn't exactly a Brighton beauty queen: there was nothing remarkable about her at all, at least in her own eyes. Yet Jim had loved her and she would always be grateful for the memory.

'Wendy sad?' Sarah pulled at her sleeve and Wendy looked down. Sarah had picked up on her mood. She was such a sensitive child. 'Wendy not cry . . .'

'No, darling, I shan't cry,' Wendy said, and bent to hug her, flinging away years of being told she mustn't be too soft over the children. 'I've got you to love now, haven't I?'

Sarah hugged her back. 'Wendy not be sad. Samantha and Sarah love Wendy.'

'Wendy loves you too, darling.'

'Sarah want Samantha.'

'Yes, I know, but she's at school,' Wendy said. 'Perhaps she'll come when she can.'

Blinking back her tears, Wendy thought about everything Sarah had had to put up with in her young life, yet she remained gentle, sweet and loving. She resolved to do whatever she could to help Angela in her fight to make sure the child stayed with them.

Somehow she didn't feel anywhere near as lonely as she had when she first came to St Saviour's. It was as if this place had something enchanted about it, reaching out to embrace them – children, nurses, carers and all – like a special kind of family.

174

She turned as the door of the sick room opened and Nan came in, carrying a tray. 'I thought you could do with a nice cup of tea – and there are a few buns I baked myself. I thought you might like them for the children . . .' She bent down to offer one to Sarah. 'Hello, lovey; I'm glad you're back with us. Eat your bun and I'll take you down to Nancy, shall I?'

'You're so kind and thoughtful,' Wendy said. 'I'm really glad I came here to work.'

'Good, that's what we like to hear,' Nan said, smiling back at her. 'I'm pleased you're settling in, Wendy. We need nice kind nurses like you.'

'Thank you.' Wendy watched as the head carer gathered up some dirty glasses and cups. In most places a woman in Nan's position wouldn't dream of doing the jobs she did, but Nan was more like a mother to her girls than a boss.

As she left the room, talking to Sarah and encouraging her, Wendy thought it was Nan and people like her that made this place what it was. She hoped that, with time, perhaps she and Nan could become friends. She needed a few of those, having given up her own life to look after her mother. Maybe now she could start to live for herself again . . .

Angela put the letter she'd finished writing into the file she'd started on the twins. She must contact Children's Welfare and get some legal advice today to see what they could do about Samantha. Miss Jane May must surely have been aware of her brother's neglect of his daughters and his brutality toward them when he was drunk, so why hadn't she taken the girls away then?

She'd sensed Sarah's fear of her aunt and her instincts told her that Miss May was not a good person. If she'd kept Samantha, it was because the child was of use to her, and not because she cared about her happiness. Yet Angela had no proof that the woman was unkind, even though her sharp tongue had upset Sarah.

If she was to convince the authorities to intervene, Angela needed to prove that the spinster aunt was not fit to care for Samantha – and to make certain that the twins could be reunited at St Saviour's. As things stood, the law was on Miss May's side, despite the cruel manner in which she'd relinquished responsibility for Sarah. Even if Angela were to argue that the woman's motive for keeping Samantha was a selfish one, the Welfare people would insist the child was better off with a relative. Miss May would no doubt tell them that Sarah was backward and needed special care, while Samantha could benefit from a loving home – as if that woman were capable of offering a loving home! And how could Samantha be happy without her sister? Judging by the way she'd cared for Sarah, she would be distraught when she got home from school and realised what her aunt had done.

'I've got to get her away from that woman!' Angela muttered as she left the office. She would have liked to consult Sister Beatrice but the nun still wasn't well enough to be troubled. In the meantime, Angela had a mountain of work to get through and no idea how to start the long campaign she suspected would be needed to wrest Samantha from that woman's grasp.

Angela began her rounds with the sick ward, where two children were laid up with a tummy bug. At the moment the isolation ward was empty. Timmy Bent, the boy who was recovering from polio, would be occupying that ward soon. Angela had consulted Sister, who thought it best to keep him isolated until they were certain he was well enough to mix with the others. At least now that the new wing was open they had the luxury of empty beds, and for the past week there had been no new arrivals to fill them. Angela suspected it was the lull before the storm, but she could only be glad of it. They could do without emergency admissions right now.

Wendy was still on duty in the sick ward when Angela entered. She had been preparing a trolley with various bowls, towels and soap, and was apparently about to give one of the children a wash. As she turned to greet Angela, the small boy in the third bed made a retching sound and was sick all over his sheets.

'Oh dear, that's the third time Dickon has been sick since Nan asked me to take him in this morning.'

'So that's why we have three patients now,' Angela said. 'What is this tummy trouble, Wendy? Is it something they've eaten or a bug that's going round?'

'I think it's a vomiting bug that is going round the schools. I was talking to Tilly earlier and she says that several of her neighbours have children down with it, so I suppose we were bound to get a few cases. Try not to worry, Angela. It's normally not serious and only lasts a day or so, but it may spread through our children. We could have several more cases go down before the week's out.'

'It's just as well that I've secured the services of another qualified nurse then,' Angela said. 'She'll start in a couple of weeks – on a purely temporary basis, until Sister Beatrice returns. I'm assured she has experience in treating polio victims, and Timmy is going to need help with his leg. Let's hope this bug doesn't turn into an epidemic in the meantime.'

'Indeed,' Wendy said. 'Be sure to wash your hands before you leave the ward, Angela – and don't go near Dickon – he's still at the infectious stage.'

Angela nodded. 'We shall have to set up a strict no-entry policy for members of staff that do not need to come into the ward – and that includes me, unless I gown up.' She smiled at Wendy. 'Where is Sarah?'

'With Nancy,' Wendy said. 'Tilly has put her back in Mary Ellen and Marion's room.'

'Good idea; she knows them and she may settle,' Angela said, dutifully washing her hands before leaving Wendy to clear up after her young patient. The nurse had only been in the job a few months, but she was proving herself now, thrown in at the deep end with no Sister Beatrice for guidance. Angela only hoped they didn't get a flood of new admissions while the vomiting bug was taking its course.

When she made her way into the new wing there were only a handful of children in the playroom, today being a school day. Nancy was with them, overseeing their games and keeping them in order. Like Wendy, she was doing very well in her new role, probably because she'd spent years caring for her brother Terry before they were brought here. No doubt she would make an excellent carer when she finally left school. At the moment, Nancy was training for her future by taking some classes in school and doing practical work, like cooking and sewing, at the home. The arrangement had been Sister Beatrice's idea, and it seemed to be working well.

'Good morning, Nancy,' Angela said as the girl turned to greet her. 'How is everyone? None of your charges are sick, I hope?'

'No, they all seem well,' Nancy said. 'We've been reading books and working on puzzles. Some of the children want to make their own, so I've been helping with that.'

'What a lovely idea,' Angela said.

Nancy smiled, pleased at the compliment. 'Tilly's been really nice to me, helping me to come up with ideas and suggesting things the children can do to earn points. I like her.'

'Well, I'm sure a puzzle would be worth a couple of stars,' Angela said, looking round and spying Sarah sitting alone near the toy box. 'How is Sarah?'

'She seems to have taken to that broken doll, the one with the cracked face. We've been making some clothes for it.'

'At least she's stopped crying.'

'Yes, but she simply sits holding the doll and singing to herself.'

'She misses her sister. If you notice anything unusual about her behaviour – tell me or one of the nurses, Nancy.'

'How do you mean, "unusual"?'

'I'm not sure.' Angela frowned. 'I'd be grateful if you'd keep an eye on her, that's all. I'm worried about her.'

'Yes, she does look pale, doesn't she.'

Angela couldn't be certain, but she sensed that Sarah had been badly treated by her aunt. If only the twins had never been handed over to that woman – Angela hadn't liked her from the start and she wouldn't put anything past her – which made it all the more urgent that she find a way of getting Samantha back to St Saviour's.

As she walked back to her office she made up her mind to ask Mark over. If anyone could help her find a way to ensure Samantha was safe, it was him. She would have dearly loved to invite him round this evening, but unfortunately she had to attend another charity meeting. It wasn't something she was looking forward to. More than likely, Henry Arnold would be there. And, for all his charm, she still couldn't bring herself to trust him.

NINETEEN

'I hear you've requested one of the newly restored houses for a family you've taken an interest in?' Henry Arnold raised his brows. His dark good looks were enhanced that evening by the navy pinstripe suit and crisp white shirt he wore, his tie blue and held by a gold pin. Something about his smooth air of assurance made Angela glad that she'd had her own hair cut recently into a stylish bob; it suited her and the heather-blue skirt and pale blue twinset she had on reflected the azure of her eyes. Worn with Cuban heels and her pearls, it made her look what she was: an intelligent, efficient woman from a middle class background, and if there were faint lines at the corners of her eyes they didn't detract from the image she wanted to convey.

When she spoke it was with crisp purpose and confidence. 'Yes, the Mason family. Kelly Mason works for us and her mother is always ill, thanks to the damp conditions they live in, so I'm hoping to move her to the top of the list.'

'Well, you can count on my support,' he said and

smiled, his gaze seeming to draw her into his orbit. 'We've no need to be enemies, Angela.'

'No, of course not . . .' Angela hesitated. She needed advice and she'd rung Mark twice that day without success. 'Tell me, Mr Arnold – do you know of a good lawyer who does not ask the earth for his advice?'

'Are you in need of some?'

'It's on behalf of one of the children at St Saviour's,' she said. Now that he'd been accepted as a member of the Board she could hardly keep secrets from him. 'We had twins with us. Their father was abusive and they had been neglected. Their aunt subsequently took them both in, but now it seems she only wants one of them; she claims the other girl, Sarah, is retarded and ought to be put away. Mark Adderbury disagrees; the girl is sweet-natured and responds well, given kindness and patience. Thankfully, she is back with us once more – but I fear she is pining for her sister. And I'm certain Samantha is equally unhappy at her aunt's. We feel it would be better if the twins were together at St Saviour's.'

'You don't think the other girl is better off with her aunt?'

'No, I'm convinced the aunt only wants to use her. I'm not saying she abuses the child, but she stood by when their father did and made no attempt to intervene. And she was so sharp with both girls when she came to St Saviour's to collect them, I don't believe she is a fit person to have charge of the child.'

'I might be able to help you with that,' he said and looked thoughtful. 'I don't believe you need the services of a solicitor, Angela. It will be quicker and simpler if I speak to someone I know.'

'This is a matter for Children's Welfare, but if they refuse to listen I may have to go to the magistrates – and for that I need legal advice.'

'No, you need someone who knows someone and can have a quiet word. What is the aunt like? Have you done any research into her background?'

'I haven't had time as yet,' Angela admitted. 'I won't rest until I do, though. I saw the look in Samantha's eyes when her aunt came for her – she felt we'd let her down. Unfortunately our hands were tied: Miss May had an order from the Welfare people.'

'I'm sure the welfare officers would not have given the girl to her aunt if they thought she might harm her. I happen to know one of the senior officers in the Children's Welfare department: Miss Ruth Sampson. Let me speak to her – but I'll need you to draw up a report on the case, as well as one from Mark Adderbury.'

'I've already typed up my report and can give you a duplicate, but I would need to retype the report Mark did for us when the girls were first admitted to St Saviour's.'

'One of my office staff will do that. I'll collect the papers tomorrow.'

'Well, I suppose . . .'

Henry Arnold frowned at her. 'Surely you can trust me not to do anything that would harm the interests of the children, Angela? I know you and Sister Beatrice consider yourself their guardians, but I'm not Lucifer, you know.'

His eyes seemed to mock her and Angela felt herself colouring. She was making her distrust so obvious despite the fact he was offering to save St Saviour's the cost of a solicitor's time.

'Well, yes, I suppose it would be all right – but I was hoping to see the Welfare officer myself. I want to explain my reasons for believing the twins are better off with us . . .'

'I could probably arrange that, but I'd like to see those reports first. I suppose it hasn't occurred to you to get another doctor's opinion on the girl?'

'Why? Mark gives his services free of charge and he is a well-respected psychiatrist—'

'Despite failing to identify the threat posed by a dangerous child who went on to violently assault Sister Beatrice?'

Angela felt her hackles rise. How dare he criticise Mark?

'That was hardly Mark's fault. He erred on the side of mercy and caution. We none of us wished to condemn Terry to life in an asylum. And none of us foresaw that he would attack Sister Beatrice.'

'Yet perhaps Adderbury should have been prepared for a violent reaction, based on the child's troubled history?'

'You are speculating. There was no way of foretelling what the boy would do – I think you should speak more carefully.'

'Are you aware that Adderbury will have to face an inquiry over the incident? I am merely suggesting that his judgement is liable to be called into question. Perhaps if another opinion was sought it might be helpful, in the circumstances.'

Angela held back the furious retort that trembled on her tongue. She hadn't realised that Mark was facing a hearing. He had not neglected his duty and she was certain that his name would be cleared – but if the council wished to be difficult over this business of Samantha and Sarah they might bring it up; it might be suggested that the same thing could happen again, though Sarah was the gentlest of souls.

'What do you suggest?' Angela asked, swallowing her indignation that anyone could doubt Mark Adderbury's judgement. If he'd waited too long to remove a troubled boy from St Saviour's, his motives had been kindness and concern, not neglect.

'I could send someone I know to talk to the girl,' Henry Arnold said. 'He's a consultant psychiatrist at a London hospital. I will arrange everything – and settle his fee.' Seeing that she was still hesitating, he reached across and took her hand. 'I only want to help, Angela – to make certain that you get your wish and that no terrible consequences result from it. Mr Yarwood will visit you in your office and then observe the child at play, perhaps talk to her for a while. If I let him have Adderbury's report he will know what he's looking for and it should take only one brief visit to confirm Adderbury's assessment – surely you can see the merit of having two opinions rather than one?'

Angela withdrew her hand from his grasp. She was very aware of the sensual pull of his personality; the very arrogance that she disliked was what made him attractive as a man – or a lover. She crushed that thought immediately.

The twins' welfare was paramount; if another psychiatrist confirmed Mark's diagnosis, it would certainly help rather than hinder – hard as it was for her to accept the insult to Mark's integrity.

'Very well, please send your friend to see us. And I will see that the reports are ready for you tomorrow. As a member of the Board you are entitled to see any documents you wish.'

'Good, I'm glad you see the sense of it, Angela – and I'm sure I can get Ruth to view your request in a favourable light. If we can make a case for the girls being together it would seem clear-cut. This aunt returned the vulnerable child to you and in doing so may have forfeited her rights over the other – provided we can prove that both may suffer as a result. I believe she would be forced by the Welfare department to give Samantha up. I'll set it all in motion at once.'

'Thank you.' Angela felt the words would choke her, but she got them out and again saw laughter in his eyes. He was obviously well aware of her feelings and amused by her reaction.

He was the kind of man she might have liked in other circumstances, but she wasn't convinced by those lingering, meaningful looks. He was trying to make her feel she could trust him – and on another level he seemed to be implying that he found her attractive – but Angela's instincts were usually reliable and they were telling her to be wary of this man. His flirting and his intimate smiles were intended to draw her in, but there was a voice inside her warning that underneath all the charm he was quite, quite ruthless.

'Three more children have gone down with the vomiting bug,' Wendy said when Angela visited the sick ward the next morning. 'I was afraid it might spread. If too many

186

children go down with it, we shall need to close one of the dorms and use it as a sick ward.'

'Let's hope it doesn't get that bad,' Angela said. 'The new nurse will be starting next month, so that should help. I'm sure some of the carers will put in extra hours if we need them, but let's hope it doesn't come to that . . .' She turned as the door opened and someone entered. Tilly had not put on an apron to cover her uniform of pink gingham, which made Angela frown. 'Haven't you been told not to come in here unless you put on a gown that you can remove when you leave, to stop the spread of infection?'

'Sorry, I needed to speak to you and forgot. I'm not going to touch anything,' Tilly said. 'I thought you should know the police brought in two children a few minutes ago. By the look of them they need a good bath – and a nurse will have to check them over. Nan has them in the bathroom now. She sent me to inform you and I was told you were here, Mrs Morton.'

'All right, Tilly. I just wanted you to understand that we must try to keep this horrid infection from spreading,' Angela said. 'Please wash your hands in the rest room and then tell Nan I'll be there in a few minutes.'

'Do you want me to look at the new children?' Wendy asked.

'No, I think Michelle is due in shortly. I'll have a look at them myself . . .'

'But you're not a nurse – are you?'

'I did have some first aid training, during the war, and I helped look after wounded men on the wards, in emergencies. We were so short-staffed during one air raid that the nurses couldn't cope . . .' Angela sighed. 'This is where we miss Sister Beatrice so much. She would have been first on the scene, making all the necessary decisions. Now I've got to work out where they can go – usually we keep new arrivals in isolation for a couple of days until we're sure they're not carrying some kind of infection.'

'I'm afraid the isolation ward is filled with my tummy bug cases,' Wendy said. 'Don't you have a room free in the new wing?'

'Yes. I was keeping it in case we had some urgent admissions – but I suppose that is where we shall have to put them. If Michelle comes in, please tell her about the new arrivals.'

Feeling harassed, Angela went off to greet the new children and help Nan check them over. When she arrived, she discovered that Nan was busily scrubbing the hair of one small boy. The smell of strong disinfectant told Angela that the children had probably been carrying lice.

'And who have we here?' Angela asked as a small thin face appeared through the neck of one of St Saviour's shirts. Apart from some nasty scabs on his mouth, the boy looked angelic; his cheeks were pink and shiny and his blond hair bright after Nan's thorough scrubbing.

'This is Jimmy Ross,' Nan said, smiling gently down at him. 'And this is his brother Robert. Jimmy is nine and Robert is seven – and their mother has been taken into hospital after an accident. They're hungry – they've been on their own for five days and had hardly anything to eat.'

'Me dad went off to find work six months ago,' Jimmy sniffed, wiping his nose on the back of his hand. 'He said he'd come back wiv a pocketful of money, but he ain't nivver come. Dot next door, she give us a crust nah and then, but she can't feed us 'cos she's got five bleedin' nippers of 'er own.'

'Jimmy, that's not nice language now, is it?' Nan reproved but her eyes were bright with laughter.

'Nah, sorry, missus,' Jimmy said. 'Me ma would clip me ear if she heard me – but it's what Dot said.'

Jimmy obviously had plenty to say for himself, and something in his manner reminded Angela of Billy Baggins when he'd been rebelling against the routine at St Saviour's the previous year.

'We're going to put Jimmy and his brother in the new wing,' Angela said to Nan as the head carer gave him a nudge and told him to finish dressing himself. 'Did you notice any signs of fever? Or any obvious bruises . . . anything untoward?'

'Both of them look healthy enough, though a bit underweight,' Nan said. 'I know Wendy is busy, but I think Michelle will be in soon. They can't go into the isolation ward, but they should be all right in a room of their own over on the new wing. Michelle will take a look at them later.'

'I sometimes think we need two nurses on all the time,' Angela said. 'The budget doesn't quite run to it, but we are stretched when we have children down with chills and bugs.'

'Yes. If Beatrice were here it would be all right; she was always ready to step in, day or night. She hardly ever took time off – and that makes all the difference.'

'She is certainly missed,' Angela said. 'I could probably take their temperatures, if that would help.'

'Oh, I've already done that,' Nan said cheerfully. 'I'm pretty certain this pair are healthy. I think their mother looks after them when she can – but they've been neglected for a few days, or a week or two at most.'

'Ma ain't well,' Jimmy said. 'She's bin 'avin' 'eadaches and they reckon she had a turn and fell in front of the bus. I don't know if she's hurt bad – the police didn't tell us nuffin' until Dot told 'em we wus on our own . . . then they said Ma was sick and we couldn't see her 'cos we're only kids.'

'I'm afraid a lot of hospitals are like that, Jimmy,' Angela said. 'They don't let children on the wards. It's unfair, I know, but they think it might upset your mother.'

'More like she'll fret over us if she don't see us,' he said, turning his head as his brother emerged from the bathroom wrapped in a thick towel. His hair was wet and once again there was a strong smell of disinfectant shampoo. 'All right, Nipper?' Jimmy asked.

'That rotten old stuff stings somefin awful.' His brother scowled. 'Bleedin' cow, she rubbed me skin until it felt as if it would burn!'

'Shut yer mouth, Bobby,' his brother said. 'They don't want none of that language 'ere. We've got ter behave 'till Ma comes to get us.'

Bobby sniffed hard and rubbed at his eyes. 'I want me ma. I want ter go 'ome.'

'If you know which hospital your mum is in, I will visit her,' Angela said. 'Then I'll come and tell you how she looks and what she says.'

'Would yer really, miss? She's in the London.' Jimmy looked at her hopefully. 'I'll keep the nipper right if yer go and see me ma.'

'You have my promise,' Angela said, and exchanged glances with Nan. 'You know where to put them? I need to get back to my office.'

She was leaving the room when Michelle arrived, looking sheepish and apologising for being late. 'I missed the first tram and had to wait for the next. I'm sorry to let you down.'

'It's only that we have a bit of a crisis. Is something wrong at home, Michelle?'

'My youngest brother was sick this morning so I had to take him to the doctor – I think he's got the bug that's going round. I'll work a bit later this evening if that helps?'

'No, it's all right. But don't make a habit of being late, please.' Angela smiled at her and went out. Michelle was one of their best nurses and she couldn't scold her too much, but it was difficult running St Saviour's with the minimum of staff. Sister Beatrice did so much in the background and everyone, including Angela, took it for granted. It was hardly surprising that Sister hadn't wanted to give in to her illness. She was in the habit of thinking herself indispensable and, if the truth were told, she was.

Returning to her office, Angela discovered that she had a visitor, her door wide open. A man was standing by the window. He turned and smiled at her as she entered, offering her his hand.

'I'm sorry to have intruded but one of your carers said I should wait inside for you. She didn't think you would be long – and you haven't been . . .'

Angela kept her annoyance to herself. Nan and Tilly were the only carers on that morning so it had to have been Tilly who had told him to wait inside. She'd been warned never to enter Angela's office unless invited, but obviously didn't think it important that a stranger should follow the same rule; Angela would have to have a few words with her. Tilly needed to start being more thoughtful if she wanted to go on working here.

'I was overseeing some new arrivals. We're rather busy at the moment, Mr . . . ?'

'Forgive me.' He extended his hand. 'I'm Yarwood – I believe Henry Arnold told you I would call.'

'Oh yes; I had thought you would telephone first . . .'

'I'm sorry. I was in the general area and thought I'd call in to see if it was convenient, but if—'

'No, no, it's good of you to call,' Angela said quickly. 'I'll take you to see Sarah. She plays with the under-fives, even though she is actually eleven. She likes dolls, you see.'

'Why don't we go and observe them? Henry allowed me to read the report my colleague did for you. I must tell you, I respect Adderbury – he's a good man – but I understand this is a delicate matter in the circumstances.'

'Yes, thank you. I'll take you to the playroom. If you're with me the children will accept it as normal; they're quite used to my popping in and out, and I occasionally take visitors to see them – it helps with the fundraising. We always need money, you see, and if people see the children they are more inclined to give. I'll point out Sarah to you; she's the most beautiful child, but quiet and sad.'

'In that case I doubt she'll need pointing out,' he said.

They made their way to the playroom where Nancy was sitting with a group of children, reading them a story. Several others were playing with toys; Sarah was sitting apart from the others, nursing the doll with the cracked face. She seemed to be far away, crooning to herself.

'Yes, I see,' Mr Yarwood said. He did not immediately go towards Sarah, but stood for a while listening to Nancy read her story and smiling over it. He then proceeded to a small boy playing with a wooden train, pausing to ask a question, and then moved on to Sarah, crouching down to speak to her.

Angela tried not to watch. She nodded to Nancy to continue reading and went to look at some of the work the children had been doing. After several minutes, Mr Yarwood stood up, touched Sarah briefly on the head and walked back to Angela, stopping once or twice to speak to other children who had chosen to play rather than listen to the story. He then nodded to Angela and they left the room together, walking in silence towards her office.

Closing the door, Angela turned to him. 'From what you were able to observe, do you feel in a position to give an opinion?'

'From my observations, I am perfectly certain the child is neither violent nor an imbecile,' he said, looking thoughtful. 'Tell me, was their mother French?'

'Because of the lullaby?' Angela nodded. 'It's odd, isn't it? Some of the words are not quite correct, but the tune is perfect – and I think it is an old French lullaby.'

193

'Yes, that is my own opinion. The French has been slightly corrupted, as though whoever taught Sarah did not quite know it herself.'

'I believe their mother may have been French, but she died in childbirth so she could not have taught them anything. From what I can gather, the woman who looked after them did not care for Sarah.'

'I wonder . . .' He shook his head. 'This is merely a theory that I've come across in my work, Mrs Morton – but it's possible the lullaby may have been something that the twins' mother sang to herself when she was carrying the children. You say she is dead – is there anyone who might know more?'

'Their father has gone away to sea and their aunt, Miss Jane May, is a most unpleasant woman.'

'I should like to speak to her nonetheless,' Mr Yarwood said. 'I'll need to speak to Samantha, too. I'll ask Miss Sampson to arrange it with the aunt. As regards Sarah, I agree with everything Adderbury says. She should remain at St Saviour's and attend a special school for a few hours once or twice a week; there is certainly no need for her to be shut up in a mental institution. I shall endorse Adderbury's report and send you a copy of my own.'

'Please let me know if you discover anything more about the girls. I was curious about the song too. It seems to comfort her.'

'Yes, and that is good. I think she's had more to bear than most – but we must see if there is a way to unlock her mind . . .'

'Do you think it possible?'

'If we could find the key, it might well be possible,' he said. 'Adderbury was puzzled because she seems to

194

understand what is said to her yet cannot form words or opinions without help. It's a mystery, Mrs Morton – and I like solving puzzles.'

'Thank you, Mr Yarwood.' Angela offered her hand, completely won over by his open manner. 'It was good of you to give up your time.'

'I shall make no charge, even though Henry Arnold offered a generous fee,' he said with a smile. 'If there is ever any other matter in which I can be of service, please do not hesitate to ask.'

Angela thanked him again and saw him to the door. She was feeling much better as she went back to her office. With Mr Yarwood on her side she was confident that the Children's Welfare officers could be persuaded to allow both twins to live at St Saviour's.

She supposed that she ought to be grateful to Henry Arnold for introducing her to his friend, but that still didn't excuse his arrogant manner or the way he imagined he was always right – let alone the way he'd blamed Mark for what had happened with Terry . . .

If she didn't know better, she could almost have accused him of being jealous of Mark Adderbury's influence at St Saviour's. Yet why should he care enough to try to discredit a man Angela liked?

TWENTY

'Staff Nurse Michelle,' Dr Kent said, approaching the desk where she was writing up her notes. 'I'm glad you called me in to look at young Matty. He seems physically well, but it sounds as if he has some kind of nervous disorder. It may be epilepsy, as you suggested, but there are other disorders that affect the nervous system.'

'Do you mean a muscular disease?' Michelle looked at him anxiously and handed a box of used dressings to Tilly, who had been cleaning the ward. 'Take these and dispose of them in the proper way; they have to be burned in the cellar.' She looked again at the doctor. 'As far as I know, he's only fitted once.'

'Sometimes the symptoms are slight, hardly noticeable at first,' Dr Kent said. 'It may be very serious, Michelle.' She flinched with shock and distress as she understood what he meant. 'I can't be certain without further tests.'

'But you think it's to do with the nervous system?'

'I suspect it may be, yes.' He touched her hand in sympathy. 'I know, it's always so much worse when it's a child, but if we've caught it in time, we may be able to at least control the progress of his illness. There are some good people at Great Ormond Street – as you know, they've always relied on charity to keep going, as you do here.'

'It's a wonderful place, but all the same I can't bear to think of Matty having to go there.' Michelle couldn't stop the tear that trickled down her cheek. He hesitated then reached out and offered his hanky. She took it and smiled, resisting the urge to weep. Sometimes being a nurse was too damned painful! 'The children they treat are so ill . . .'

'It's the best place if he has something nasty, Michelle – and the sooner they get to work, the better his chances.'

'I'll prepare him for the ambulance,' she said, and would have moved away, but he laid a hand on her arm, holding her steady.

'I was hoping perhaps you might be able to go with him, Michelle?' His eyes held her, making butterflies flutter in her stomach. Yet in another moment, he'd released her and his gaze was no longer locked with hers. Perhaps she'd imagined that temporary connection.

'Wendy is due back from her break in half an hour. I could go with him then.'

'I shall arrange it,' he told her with a smile.

Michelle looked at him uncertainly; something in the way he'd looked at her when he offered his hanky had made her catch her breath. It had been a long time since she'd felt this attracted to a man and she was trying to resist it.

'Thank you – we're rather short-staffed with Sister Beatrice away, you see. And with so many children sick with that bug, I couldn't leave without someone to cover.'

'I do understand . . .' He hesitated, then, 'I should like us to meet away from work – could we do that? Perhaps this evening . . . if you'd like to go for a drink?'

'Yes, why not?' Michelle said, and her heart raced with excitement. In that moment she noticed a few silver hairs amongst the gold at his temple, but they only served to make him more attractive in her eyes. In his mid-thirties, he had an air of having known suffering and conquered it, a worldly manner that some of the younger men she'd met didn't have. 'I'll speak to Wendy when she comes back from her break in five minutes and I'll have Matty ready to leave when the ambulance arrives.'

'Thank you,' he murmured, and his smile warmed her. 'Shall we meet near here – at that rather nice pub at the end of Halfpenny Street?'

'The Lion and Lamb?' Michelle nodded. The pub had received a direct hit during the first year of the war and had only recently reopened. 'I shall come straight from work. At about seven? Will you have finished surgery by then?'

'It's my night off. I'm not even on call,' he said. 'We'll talk later, Michelle.'

'Oh good, that will be lovely.'

'I shall look forward to it – and now I must speak to Mrs Morton. In Sister Beatrice's absence, she stands as guardian to Matty and she will need to sign the consent form should he need treatment.'

Michelle stared after him as he left the ward. She'd considered visiting Alice that evening to deliver some things she'd made for baby Susie, but that could wait. Dismissing Alice's problems from her mind, she went to sit on the edge of Matty's bed. Somehow she had to break the news to the boy that he was going into hospital to have tests; she didn't want him to be frightened at being put in an ambulance and taken to a strange place with nurses he didn't know. She took his hand, choosing her words carefully and keeping her manner calm and reassuring; it was going to be a traumatic experience for a young lad – especially if Dr Kent's suspicions were right.

Michelle was glad that she'd worn a pretty yellow gingham shirtdress to work that morning. The white piqué collar and short sleeves suited her, and she'd cinched the waist in with a wide white belt. She'd had time to comb her raven black hair, which was much easier now that she'd had it cut into a shorter style that framed her face. She'd put on some fresh lipstick and a touch of face powder and knew she looked as good as she could after a day working at the home.

Inside the pub the smell of fresh paint mingled with the stronger odour of beer and spirits. The square oak tables with Windsor chairs set at various angles about the large saloon bar were attractive and decorated with small vases of artificial flowers and lamps with red shades that gave subdued lighting to what would otherwise have been a dark room. The oak beams running across the ceiling were not original, but they'd been stained to look old and looked good against the white of the ceiling and walls. The pub had been taken over by a husband and wife; the new landlord had been a captain in the Army and limped, but his wife was beautiful, with dark hair and eyes, and looked a bit Italian. She was offering bar food, salads and bowls of pasta, unusual cheeses and slices of what looked like sausage, and fresh crusty bread, very different from the tasteless meat pies that had been sold here before the war. If this was an example of what things would be like now the war was over, Michelle decided she liked it; the East End needed something to haul it out of the neglect and poverty of the last few years.

Dr Kent had found a table near the window, which was slightly open. He saw her as she entered and lifted a hand to greet her. Michelle's heart jumped as she returned his smile; he smiled so seldom that it was all the more welcome when it occurred. She wondered what had happened to him to give him that habitually sombre air.

'I'm not late, am I?'

'No, you're not late,' he said. 'I was early – I thought I might as well reserve a table. This place gets busy in the evenings.'

'Yes, I suppose it does. We came in for a drink on Nan's birthday, but I haven't been for a meal here. I imagine they do decent food.'

'Would you like something to eat? Are you hungry?'

'No, not at all. We're well fed at St Saviour's – and my mother will cook supper when I get home. I was only wondering what it was like here. Some of us go out as a group occasionally – though Alice is married now, and Sally left us . . . but I expect I'll get to know the new girls soon enough.'

'Yes, I dare say,' he agreed. 'Do you get a lot of girls leaving?'

'The carers come and go. Sally had been with us longer than anyone except Nan. I don't know if you heard what happened to Mr Markham?'

'Yes, I did – terrible accident. Such a shame. I understand he was a brilliant surgeon.'

'He wrote children's books too. We still read them to the children,' Michelle said. She sipped the cool lemonade shandy she'd ordered and wondered why he'd asked her out. Was it just to talk about work? She'd thought he might be interested in her personally, but now she wasn't sure. When he smiled he seemed a different person, and sometimes, when their eyes met, she thought he liked her, but there was some inner reserve that was like a barrier between him and the rest of the world.

'I think perhaps it's time for me to go,' she said after they'd talked some more about St Saviour's and her colleagues. 'Thank you for the drink. It was very nice.'

'Please, call me Richard,' he said. 'Perhaps not in the wards, but outside. I've enjoyed our time together, Michelle. We must do it again one day.'

He stood up and offered his hand as Michelle rose to leave. His clasp was firm and strong and she was thoughtful as she left him standing there, gazing after her. She wasn't sure what Dr Kent wanted from her. A quiet drink with a colleague – or something more? Shaking her head as she tried to work out why she'd been asked for that drink, she ran to catch her bus home. Dr Kent was still as much of a mystery to her as he had been before that evening . . . and she would be an idiot if she let herself think about him too much. She didn't want to get caught up in another affair that was going nowhere.

TWENTY-ONE

Alice had been down and depressed. It was lonely in the flat with no friends or family to talk to. She'd been brooding over the business with Jack Shaw and missing Bob's company. Her mood lifted when she opened the front door of her flat to find Nan there. 'I'm so pleased you've come,' she said. 'I was sitting here wondering what to do for a couple of hours. I've put Susie down for the night and there's nothing on the radio I want to listen to – I don't feel like knitting or reading.'

'I've been sorting out some things,' Nan explained. 'I found this doll down the market and thought your Susie might like it – I think it's a rag doll, old fashioned, but it looks as good as new.'

'It's lovely. I'll give it to her when she's old enough to appreciate it – thank you for thinking of me. Everyone has been so kind since my baby was born. I've had loads of presents. Mave is always bringing me things. She dotes on Susie.'

'Well, she is beautiful,' Nan said. 'I've got the night off so I thought I'd pop round and see how you were – are you managing all right, Alice?'

'Yes, thanks, Nan,' Alice said, trying to be cheerful. 'You'll never believe what I did today – I popped in to see Sister Beatrice. She was sitting up and feeling much better, so she said – and she's looking forward to returning to work.'

'She'd come back if she could, but the doctors won't let her.'

'Yes, she said they've told her she has to take a holiday by the sea first.' Alice sighed. 'I'm hoping to get back to work too, once Susie is a bit older and off the breast. Only for a few hours a day – Michelle's mum is going to look after her two days a week. It's not the money – Bob gives me all I need. It's more that I enjoy the company.'

'Yes, you should come back if you can. In the meantime, bring Susie in sometimes to show her off. Everyone would love to see you both,' Nan said. 'We've had a new girl on the carers' staff. I like Tilly, but she's not as thorough as you were. Angela had to reprimand her today, but I dare say she'll settle when she knows us.'

Alice was putting the kettle on. She lit the gas and then smiled at her. 'Do you want to see my Susie?'

'Yes please,' Nan said and followed her into the small bedroom, where the cot was standing. Alice had painted the room white and decorated the walls with pictures of ducks and kittens she'd cut out of a magazine and pasted on blank paper; her curtains were a pretty pink cotton and the bedcovers white.

'I've been making things nice for her since she arrived. Michelle's mum is teaching me to sew. I go twice a week – I look forward to having someone to talk to as much as the lessons. The neighbours here keep themselves to themselves and I don't see much of them. Still, Michelle comes to visit after work quite often.'

'She was planning to come this evening, but someone asked her out so I said I wanted to visit you.'

'Has Eric come home on leave?'

'I think she was meeting Dr Kent.' Nan smiled down at Alice's baby, who was looking up at her with sleepy big blue eyes. 'She was upset over one of the children – Matty went into hospital this morning and they think it may be serious.'

'Oh, that's awful,' Alice said, immediately concerned. 'Michelle always pretends she doesn't get upset if the children get really sick – but she frets inside.'

'I think we all do,' Nan said. 'I lost my son and husband to diphtheria; it happened years ago, but when a little one's sick it brings back the memories.'

'That must be terrible for you,' Alice said, bending over the cot to hide her emotions. 'Isn't she beautiful?'

'Oh yes,' Nan leaned towards Alice's baby to touch the child's tiny fist. 'She is adorable, Alice. Eddie loves her. He hopes you'll let us be her nanny and grandpa – he's back in London now and has made up his mind to stay.'

'I like your Eddie, Nan.' She tipped her head to one side. 'Are you going to marry him?'

'Goodness me, no!' Nan said. 'We're just good friends – but neither of us has much family now and we'd like to see more of you and the baby – and Bob too, when he's home.'

'Yes, of course, I'd like to come round,' Alice said. 'I miss being at home with my sister – and you know Mum still won't speak to me.'

'Your mother is a foolish woman,' Nan said. 'It's true

you shouldn't have gone with that Jack Shaw, Alice, but you're not the first lass to get in trouble. Your mother is missing so much: all these early months of Susie's life, her first smile, and then when she starts to walk and talk . . .'

'Dad comes now and then. He's miserable at home, but he tried leaving her once and it didn't work. Mave is fed up too; she wants to get married but her boyfriend says they can't afford it yet.'

'What about you?' Nan asked as Alice poured them both a cup of tea and brought out some almond short-bread biscuits she'd made. 'Are you happy, Alice?'

'Yes, most of the time,' Alice said, her eyes not meeting Nan's. 'When Bob is home it's fine, but when he's away I sometimes think . . . But that's all in the past. Jack must be in America now. I hope he is. He'll forget about me and make a new life out there – and I'll forget in time.'

'Try not to think of him,' Nan said. 'You chose to marry Bob, Alice – and he's given you so much.'

'I know,' Alice said, stifling a sigh. 'I'm lucky – but I loved Jack, I really did. It's hard to get over something like that.'

'It took me ages to get over losing my husband and my son, so I understand how you feel.'

'Oh, Nan; I shouldn't moan. I'm sorry if I said some-thing to bring all those memories back – I wouldn't do that for the world.'

'It's all right,' Nan smiled. 'I don't often think of it these days – but sometimes it comes back and then I feel their loss as if it were yesterday . . . and my daughter is in that convent and I accept she's happy there and will never come home . . .'

205

'I'm so sorry, Nan.'

'Don't be sorry, my love.' Nan smiled at her. 'I've got you and your little one now, Alice, and that makes up for a lot.'

'Oh, Nan, I'm glad I've got you,' Alice said and poured her another cup of tea. 'And yes, I'd love you and Eddie to be Susie's nanny and grandpa – and you'll be one of her godmothers too when we have her christened, won't you?'

Alice closed the door behind her visitor and shot the bolt across. She wouldn't have any more visitors at this time of night. Returning to the kitchen, she washed the cups and rinsed out the teapot, before hanging the cloth up to dry. About to switch out the light and go up to bed, she heard heavy banging at her back door and froze. No one came that way, because it meant climbing a high wall into her yard, but she'd always been afraid someone might. Had one of Butcher Lee's men come calling at this hour?

For a moment she couldn't move, but then she walked towards the door, saying in a loud voice, 'I'm not going to let you in. Go away, whoever you are or I'll call the police.'

'Alice, it's me. I had to come this way. I couldn't be seen at the front.'

Her breath caught and for a second she thought she might faint. She pressed closer to the door, listening hard. 'Is that you, Jack?'

'Yes, of course it's me. Let me in, love.'

Alice drew a sharp breath and turned the key, opening the door slightly so that she could see him in the light of the street lamp behind the wall. Yet she knew that voice; it couldn't have been anyone else but Jack.

He pushed the door back quickly, entered, shut it and locked it behind him. Alice's breath caught: with his black hair and blue eyes he was every bit as handsome as he'd always been.

'I don't think anyone saw me, but we'll make sure they can't surprise us. Is the front door locked?'

'I locked it after Nan left – she's from St Saviour's . . .' For a moment she stared at him, her heart beating wildly, then, 'Oh, Jack, is it truly you?'

'Pleased to see me, Alice?' he laughed, then grabbed her, looking down into her face before he kissed her on the mouth. Alice felt her whole body tingle. For a moment she clung to him as the need and longing surged through her and she remembered how much she'd loved him. She wanted so desperately to hold him to her and never let him leave her again, but after a moment she drew away, looking at him suspiciously as he asked, 'Why didn't you come to meet me?'

Alice avoided his question by asking a few of her own. 'Everyone thought you'd died in that fire. Arthur told the police it was you that blew the safe – how could you have got out? The fire was so fierce . . .'

'The bloody safe was empty,' Jack said, and glared at her as if it was her fault. 'All that effort and they'd put the money somewhere else. I got out down the fire escape at the back. I always make sure there's more than one way out before I do a place. No one saw me. They were all round the front looking at the fire and running round like scared rabbits!' He laughed as if amused by the memory.

Alice stared at him, feeling cold all over. 'What about the man who died at the factory? They found a body at the bottom of the stairs – who was it, Jack?'

'Some down-and-out sleeping rough; the watchman let him come in to keep warm and he was going to give the alarm. We had to keep him quiet.'

'Arthur Baggins told the police it was you that killed him before the fire, Jack.'

'He would, wouldn't he?' Jack said. 'Who would you rather believe, Alice – a petty thief or me? You know I wouldn't lie to you, love.'

She wanted to believe him, of course she did, and yet she couldn't ignore the chill at her nape. 'I believe you.' Alice's fingers touched lips that still tingled from his kiss. 'Jack, you shouldn't have kissed me – I shouldn't have let you,' she croaked. 'I'm married to Bob now, didn't you know?'

'Someone may have told me,' he said carelessly, but his gaze narrowed and she saw anger in his face. 'Why didn't you wait for me, Alice? I told you I'd come for you and the kid. You've had a girl, ain't you?'

'Yes,' she whispered, her throat tight. Her heart was beating so hard that she could hardly breathe let alone think. 'It was so hard, Jack. Ma threw me out and I was going to have to leave my work. You left me all alone without a word to let me know you were still alive, what was I supposed to think? I didn't know what to do and Bob got me this place. He offered me marriage . . .' She let a small sob escape. 'I couldn't come to meet you after that – could I?'

'Why not?' he demanded. 'You could at least have told me yourself, instead of letting me find out from

208

someone else. I wasn't going to sell you off to the white slave traders, was I?'

Alice gave a weak smile. 'I was afraid of what I'd do if I came . . .' she stopped, the tears welling. 'It wouldn't be right, Jack – not after all this.'

'He took what belongs to me,' Jack said fiercely. 'You're mine, not his. I've come to get you, Alice. I want you to pack your stuff and I'll take it with me. You can leave in the morning and meet me in Southend. You must shake off those shadows Butcher Lee sent to follow you or you'll lead them to me, but if you've only got the baby they won't take so much notice. I'll get your stuff away and join you at this address . . .' He handed her a scrap of paper. 'You've still got the key I sent you, haven't you?'

'Yes and the money – I'll give them back to you . . .'

'No, Alice. I want you to fetch the stuff from that locker like I asked you. It's important to me – to both of us.'

'It's that pinched stuff, isn't it?' Alice stared at him reproachfully. 'I daren't, Jack. The Lee gang are watching me. I wondered why they still kept watching me if you were dead and now I know. It's because they know you aren't dead and they think you will use me to fetch the stuff . . . and it's that they want, isn't it?'

'That stuff is the only reason they haven't killed me already. They know I've got it hidden somewhere and they want it.'

'Why don't you just send them the key and leave England? Go to America – get away while you still can . . .'

'Not without what I came for. I want what's in that

locker, Alice – and I want you and my daughter. You belong to me – both of you.' He took hold of her upper arms, looking at her intently. 'Where is she? What did you call her? I want to see her.'

'Susie, I called her Susie, but she's sleeping and it took me ages to get her off. I don't want to wake her.'

'All right, but remember she's my kid and you're mine too, even if you have got that Army bloke's ring on your finger.'

'Oh, Jack . . .' Alice felt the tears welling inside her. He was persuading her, as he had so often in the past, sapping her will with his eyes and that smile, but could she believe him? She wanted to go with him, but she mustn't – she mustn't! She couldn't trust him to take care of her and Susie. 'No, I can't – I can't do that, Jack. It would be cruel and hurtful to Bob.'

'What about me? Doesn't it matter what I feel?' Jack demanded. His fingers tightened about her wrist. 'I thought you loved me.'

'I did, I do love you,' she said brokenly, 'but I'm not coming to Southend.' She looked at him urgently. 'You've got to get away; don't you understand that, Jack? The gang think you've come back and they will kill you if they find you; they'll make you give them what they want.'

'And whose fault is it that they're after me, Alice? I wouldn't have tried to get out so quickly if it wasn't for you. You were the one that wanted to get away from them. You made me break away from Lee.' He grabbed her by the shoulders and shook her. Alice sobbed as his fingers dug into her, but then he pulled her close and kissed her roughly. 'You do care about

210

me. I know you do,' he said. 'I'm telling you, Alice, I shan't give you up—'

He was interrupted by banging at the front door. Alice looked at him in fear, her heart thumping as she heard the voice calling to her through the letterbox.

'They know you're here, Jack,' she said urgently. 'You've got to go quickly or it will be too late.'

Jack swore furiously. 'Don't bother with your things, Alice. I'll buy everything you need. Bring the baby to the zoo – make it Sunday and I'll meet you at the cafe. They will follow you for a day or two, so you can't pick up the stuff from the locker yourself. Ask that friend of yours to do it for you. I'm relying on you, Alice. Now give me a couple of minutes to get away and then speak to them through the door – but don't open it whatever you do.'

'You'd better go, Jack. If I'm not there on Sunday you'll know I couldn't get away from them.'

'You will come?' His eyes lit with excitement, clearly thinking he'd won. He believed she would come and bring the jewels. 'I love you, Alice. I'll always love you until the day I die.'

'Go now,' she urged. 'I loved you, Jack. I don't want you to die . . .'

In a moment Jack was gone. She stood at the window with the light off and saw his shadow scale the wall at the back of her yard. Then she walked into the hall and shouted through the door.

'Go away, you'll wake my baby. There's no one here but me – and if you don't stop making a noise, my neighbour will phone the police!'

'We know Jack Shaw is in London,' the voice said

through the letterbox. 'If we find out you've been helping him, you'll be sorry, Alice Cobb.'

'I'm not Alice Cobb,' she said, and tears streamed down her cheeks. 'Go away and leave me alone. I haven't seen Jack Shaw and I'm not going to.'

At least that last bit was true, Alice thought as she went through to the kitchen to make sure the back door was secure. She'd let Jack think she would meet him knowing he wouldn't leave otherwise, but she wouldn't go to him – and she wouldn't fetch that stuff or ask Michelle to fetch it for her. She wouldn't meet him; she knew Jack had lied to her about the man who had died at the factory. Arthur Baggins hadn't killed him; Jack had. And that made him a cold-blooded murderer.

For a moment when he'd kissed her, when he'd told her he loved her and wanted to see Susie, she'd almost believed him; she'd wanted to believe that he'd come back for her – and a part of her still did. But the sensible part told her that the only thing Jack wanted was the jewels. He was merely using her.

Perhaps it wasn't too late. She could meet him at the zoo with Susie and they could go away together, start a new life in America – but once Jack had what he wanted he wouldn't want to be bothered with a child. No, he was a liar, a thief and a murderer, and even if a part of her longed for him, she knew she had to resist.

She had loved Jack so very much and she'd kept his memory enshrined in her heart all this time, but now it would fade – it must, because he wasn't and never had been the man she'd believed. She had to forget him . . . didn't she?

212

TWENTY-TWO

Kelly finished washing the dishes and turned to look round the kitchen with a pleased smile. She'd been tired when she got home from work, but her mother was in bed again and the children had left their things all over the place, dirty cups and plates and bits of crust left from their thick slices of bread and dripping. Kelly couldn't let her father come home to that after he'd worked all day. She had a fish pie in the oven for him with some mashed potatoes and a bit of cabbage, which she would chop up with margarine, salt and pepper when he got in. Hearing the sound of his boots on the cobbles outside in the yard, Kelly drained the cabbage and started to chop.

'Your mammy not well?' he asked with a slight frown as he glanced about the kitchen. 'You've got this place decent again, girl. I don't know what we'd do without you.'

Kelly shook her head as her brothers came bursting into the room, fighting over a ball and throwing their coats on the floor as they quarrelled over whose ball it was.

'Anythin' to eat, our Kelly?' Michael said and helped himself to a cup of water from the tap. 'That smells good . . .' He looked enviously at the pie, mashed potatoes and cabbage she placed before her father. 'Ain't yer got a bun or anythin'?'

'You had your tea earlier, Michael. You can have some bread and dripping if you want?'

'You can have a bit of my pie,' his father said. 'Bring your plate here, lad.' He cut a wedge of the pie and slid it on to the boy's plate. 'What about you, Robbie?'

'I had bread and jam for tea – and they gave us minced-beef pie at school today.'

His father nodded, but Michael was growing fast and he wolfed down his share of his father's meal, wiping his hand across his mouth afterwards in satisfaction.

'Off with you now, I want to talk to your sister,' he said, and the boys left the kitchen without protest.

'Is something the matter, Dad?' Kelly asked, sitting on the chair next to him as she poured tea for them both.

'I might be on short time after next week,' he told her. 'You mustn't say a word to your mammy, love, but if it happens we'll be a bit short in the rent. I don't suppose there's any way you can do extra hours at your job?'

'I've offered to go in in the evenings to make up for being late sometimes when I have to get the children off to school,' she said and bit her lip. 'I'd like to be one of the carers; they're always taking on new girls – but I don't think they would trust me.'

'Why not, may I ask? You've had plenty of experience with your brothers and your sister,' her father said. 'Cate is nearly ten and it's high time she helped her mother more. I'll speak to her and tell her she has to help in the mornings. You ask Sister Beatrice if she'll give you some extra hours – as a carer or in the kitchens.'

'Sister Beatrice is ill – I might ask Mrs Morton,' Kelly said slowly. 'She's been kind, bringing the doctor here and putting our name on that list for a better house . . .'

'No news on that, I suppose? If we had a decent place to live your mammy might not be sick all the time.'

'I'll ask Mrs Morton tomorrow,' Kelly said, smiling at the father she loved. 'And I'll see if there's any chance of being taken on as a carer – but I don't think I've much chance.'

'Well, maybe I shan't get put on short hours,' her father said. 'I'll find a bit of labouring or something if all else fails . . .'

'I know it's a lot to ask,' Kelly said when she spoke to Angela the next day. 'I was taken on as a kitchen girl but I'm good at looking after kids. I have been late a few times, and taken days off, but only because Mammy was ill. I promise I'll work hard – and I'm happy to do nights or evening shifts. Some of the girls grumble about being on nights, but I wouldn't mind what I did so long as I can earn a bit more while my dad's on short time.'

'Yes, I do understand why you've been late, and hopefully your mother will improve if we can get you that new house, though I still can't promise anything,' Angela said. 'But I don't know about making you a carer, Kelly. I should have to talk to Sister Beatrice first . . .' she hesitated, then, 'I'm going to take some of the children to the zoo one Sunday soon – would you like to volunteer to come with us? It will mean being here earlier in the morning to get your work done first, and it will be a long day . . .'

'Me, come on the trip to the zoo?' Kelly stared, hardly believing her ears. 'I'd love the chance, miss.'

'Well, it would give us an opportunity to see how you are with the children,' Angela said. 'There are no guarantees, but I shall put your name on the list for the trip. Now you'd better get back to work or Cook will be cross with me for keeping you talking.'

'Yes, Mrs Morton. Thank you so much,' Kelly said, feeling slightly dazed as she hurried back to the kitchen. It wasn't a promise, but there was a half-chance she would get to go on the visit to the zoo and then, if she could prove herself and be made a carer, her wage would go up by at least a pound a week. Yet she hardly dared to hope, because things like that didn't happen to girls like her – did they?

Angela sighed as the door closed behind Kelly. She'd asked about being made a career and the rise in wages would undoubtedly help at home, but would it be wise to go out on a limb for the girl? She'd been late so often, and yet Angela knew that Kelly had tried much harder lately and she'd put in extra hours at night to make up for any lateness in the morning. After all, everyone deserved a chance in life and they did need good carers, especially one happy to work at night . . .

The telephone shrilled beside her and she answered it to hear her father's voice.

'Angela, are you too busy to talk?'

'No, I always have time for you. How are you, Dad?'

'Not too bad, my love; much better for the sound of your voice. I'm coming up to town on Friday. Would you be free to have dinner with me?'

'Absolutely. Will you be staying in London for the weekend? I'm taking a party of about twenty-five children to the zoo – a few of the carers will be coming too, of course . . . I don't suppose you fancy joining us?'

Her father hesitated for a moment, then, 'Do you know, I should enjoy that, Angela. What a splendid idea. I think the weather is set fair for a few days.'

'And how do you know that?' she teased. 'Have you been consulting your seaweed?'

'I don't need seaweed; my arthritis is a far better barometer,' her father said. 'You sound happy, Angela.'

'Yes, I am. I'm feeling better in myself than I have for a long time – although it's difficult here with Sister Beatrice in hospital.'

'Yes, it means more work for you . . .' A sigh escaped him. 'I was going to break the news on Friday, but I may as well tell you now: I've had another letter from your mother. She wants a divorce.'

'A divorce! Daddy, she can't,' Angela cried, distressed. 'It isn't fair to you. What have you ever done to deserve being treated like that?'

'According to your mother, my sins are many and varied. I shall have to engage a solicitor to sort this mess out – which is why I'm coming up to London. I don't feel my firm should handle it. No, I shall speak to an old friend of mine and let him deal with your mother's solicitors – though I'm not going to argue with her unless she demands too much. I want you to have your share when I've gone, Angela.'

217

'Please, don't. I've no interest in money. I want you to live for ages – and I don't think this is fair of Mum. If she knew you weren't well, she wouldn't do this to you, Dad.'

'Wouldn't she?' Angela's father sighed deeply. 'I'm not sure what I did to make her hate me, but it seems she does. Apparently, everything she did when she was suffering from strain was my fault. It's my fault she ran up bills and my fault she stole things . . .'

'I think I should talk to her,' Angela said, feeling angry and protective. 'How could it be your fault? You've always been good to us – both of us.'

'Not in your mother's opinion,' he said. 'Please, my love, don't try to interfere. I don't want to make your mother unhappy – or rather, more unhappy than she already is. I would prefer to settle this through a third party. Whatever the law says she is entitled to, she must have – but I don't want to give up the house. I would prefer to sell the practice and pay her out of the proceeds.'

'But being a family solicitor is your life, Dad.'

'I don't think I can go on for much longer in any case, love. I was thinking of selling up – and that's what I'll do if need be. I've had a couple of offers but I wasn't quite ready. However, I think it may be for the best – rather than leave it all for you to sort out when I go.'

'Daddy, darling . . .' Angela's heart felt as if it would break as she heard the tiredness and the sorrow in his voice. It wasn't fair on him. Of course she didn't know all the details of her parents' lives. Perhaps something had happened years ago that had caused the slow parting of the ways, but all her sympathy belonged with her father. 'Do what you have to – but don't consider me.

You know John provided all I need for myself and more.'

'Yes, I know, but you're a generous woman and you give much of your income away to others,' her father said. 'I would never interfere – but promise me that you won't give away your home. I want you to have security, somewhere to go if you ever need it.'

Again, Angela's eyes were wet with tears. Her knuckles were white as she gripped the phone, but she kept her voice steady as she promised.

'I like the idea of a country retreat,' she said, trying to sound upbeat, 'but I prefer that you're there when I come down, dearest. And I'm definitely coming for Christmas. I'll give you a list of what we need and I'll be down late on Christmas Eve, as I was last year.'

'Goodness, I hadn't started to think about that yet.'

'It's creeping up on us,' Angela said and laughed. 'I'll see you on Friday – and don't work too hard. I don't want to lose you, Dad.'

'Oh, I've no intention of going anywhere yet,' he said. 'This is all just so that you know what's going on, my love.'

'Yes, I see,' Angela said. 'I still think you should tell Mum that you're not too well.'

'Please promise me you won't.'

'You have my word.'

'Good. I shan't keep you any longer. I'll see you on Friday.'

'I shall look forward to it – and our day at the zoo.'

'That will be like old times, when you were young, Angela.'

'Yes, it will . . .' Angela replaced the phone, her eyes

stinging as she fought to hold back her tears. Sometimes, it hurt to think of her father living all alone, but at least she would be joining him for Christmas, and the thought of cooking him dinner banished the tears. Her father had always been special to her and she couldn't forgive her mother for hurting him the way she had.

She picked her telephone receiver up almost immediately and asked for Mark's office number. He might be at the hospital or one of the clinics, but she needed to hear his voice. A surge of relief went through her as she heard his voice at the other end.

'Mark, can you come over to mine this evening? I'll buy some steak or chops or something and we'll have a salad . . .'

'Yes, lovely,' he replied. 'Is anything wrong, Angela love?'

'I'll talk to you this evening. I'd rather not discuss it on the phone.'

'Then I'll be there,' Mark said. 'Tonight you can tell me everything.'

Replacing the receiver, Angela sat very still as Mark's reassuring words sank in. She'd told him she needed him, because her father's phone call had left her wanting to weep on someone's shoulder and she'd known that Mark was the only one she could turn to . . .

TWENTY-THREE

Wendy looked at the child sitting forlornly on the side of her bed; it was a bright morning and she ought to be outside, running about with the other children, getting some fresh air, but she looked so pale and distressed that Wendy couldn't chide her. Instead, she sat down beside her.

'Something is wrong, isn't it, Sarah?' Wendy asked and reached for the delicate hand, cradling it in her own. 'Can't you tell me?'

'Sarah want Samantha,' she said and two tears welled and spilled out of her wide eyes.

Wendy wiped them away with her fingers, longing to cuddle the child, but knowing she wouldn't be helping. Unless they could get Samantha back, Sarah was going to have to learn to cope without her twin.

'Samantha can't come love; your aunt won't let her, but I'm sure she will one day . . .'

Sarah shook her head and then clutched at her tummy. 'Hurt bad,' she said, 'Samantha not well.'

'Do you mean you're not well?' Wendy asked,

221

looking at her in concern. 'Do you have a tummy ache?'

Again Sarah shook her head. 'Not Sarah, Samantha hurt bad . . . hurt all over like when Pa beat Sarah. Samantha crying.'

'Samantha is crying because she's hurt?' Wendy looked into the wide innocent eyes and felt a jolt when she saw the utter despair there. 'How do you know? Have you seen her?' Sarah's head shake was angry, impatient. 'Then what makes you so sure, love? Perhaps you don't feel well and you think it's your sister?'

'No!' Sarah jumped to her feet in sudden temper and gave Wendy a look of what could only be disgust. 'Wendy not understand. Sarah feel Samantha's pain always!'

Then, before Wendy could answer, she ran out of the room.

Too stunned to think, Wendy was slow to follow and when she did there was no sign of the child. Frustrated and distressed, she'd run off somewhere. Wendy's heart went out to her; Sarah had seemed genuinely in pain, but how could it be possible that the hurt she was feeling was actually her twin's? That wasn't possible, was it? She'd heard stories about a kind of telepathy between twins, but this seemed so far-fetched. She wondered whether she might have misunderstood; Sarah was a bit backward, which made it difficult to be sure that she knew what she was saying.

Yet supposing she was right? Supposing Samantha was unwell or in pain? Was it an illness or . . . Wendy went cold all over. What if the child was being ill-treated by her aunt?

It was Wendy's day off. Perhaps if she asked Angela for the aunt's address she might go round there and ask to speak to Samantha . . .

'Wendy, may I speak with you for a moment?' Wendy turned as Nan came up to her.

'Yes, Nan. What can I do for you?'

'Nurse Paula telephoned a moment ago; she has terrible toothache so she won't be coming in. Could you do the evening shift? I'd ask Michelle, but she's been on all day so Angela suggested I speak to you.'

'Of course I will,' Wendy said. 'I was thinking of going somewhere this afternoon, but it can wait. I'll head off home and get some sleep.'

'Yes, you do that.' Nan smiled at her. 'I'm sorry to spoil your plans, but I'm sure Angela will arrange for you to have a day off in lieu.'

'I'm not bothered, really,' Wendy said. She pushed the faint worry about Sarah to the back of her mind. It was unlikely that the child really had picked up her sister's pain, after all. In all probability it was all in her mind . . .

'I came to tell you that Matty has had his tests and he's feeling more comfortable.' Richard Kent had approached Michelle in the sick ward at St Saviour's as she was about to leave for her lunch break. 'I know how worried you were about him, so I wanted to give you the news as soon as I heard.'

'We could go for a cup of coffee,' she suggested. 'I'm on my break now for half an hour.'

'Yes, if you like,' he agreed, falling in beside her as they made their way down the stairs to the small staff room.

As Michelle had expected, the room was empty; at this time of day, most of the carers were in the dining room overseeing the children's lunch. She filled the kettle with water and switched it on, turning to him with a plain white mug in her hand.

'Tea or coffee?'

'Tea – unless it's real coffee?'

'Not a hope,' Michelle said, and picked up the teapot. 'Angela sometimes treats us if she can get hold of some real coffee, but mostly it's that awful chicory stuff in a bottle.'

'No thanks,' he said, 'I'll stick with a strong cup of tea. Now, my news – Matty has had all the tests. We do not have all the results yet, but from preliminary findings it seems that he has a problem with his spine – most likely it was the pressure on his vertebrae that caused him to have a fit. The most likely explanation is a tumour—'

'Oh no,' Michelle said, turning to look at him. 'The poor child – that's absolutely awful, Richard. Could the tumour be malignant?'

'I'm not a specialist, Michelle. Like you, my mind's racing and I know nothing for certain, but I do know the prognosis isn't good if it is indeed a tumour. He could begin to lose mobility over time and end up confined to a wheelchair, he could suffer more fits . . . Until the tests are complete, the hospital can't say for sure what the outcome will be. The boy is going to need love and kindness to help him through this. Does he have any relatives?'

'No, I don't think so. Poor Matty; he doesn't deserve to have to suffer so much.' Michelle tried to focus on pouring milk into the cups while the tea brewed in the pot, but she was picturing Matty, trying so hard to be brave as she'd helped him up after his fit. 'It makes me so angry when I see children suffering with an illness like that – it isn't fair, Richard. He's had no chance to live and be happy.'

'No, it isn't fair,' he agreed and smiled at her as she offered sugar. 'One lump, thank you. I must admit that it upsets me too when I visit the children's ward and witness how sick some of them are, but we have to realise that they are in the best place.'

'I think the nurses and doctors at Great Ormond Street are fantastic.' Michelle smiled sadly. 'I don't think I'm made of strong enough stuff. It breaks my heart when a child dies, and they must see it happen all too often. At least here, most of our children have less severe ailments, most of the time.'

'Yes,' Richard looked thoughtful. 'I understand that Angela has arranged for a polio victim to come here?'

'She consulted me first, naturally. She was worried about the added workload with Sister Beatrice still off sick, but I told her I thought we'd manage.'

'As I understand it, the boy has made a good recovery from the disease but it has left him with a wasted leg.'

'So Angela said. We'll be able to help him with gentle exercises to build up his wasted leg.'

Dr Kent nodded. 'As far as his respiratory condition is concerned, he seems fine. You'll need to keep an eye on him if he picks up colds or coughs, because he may have a weakness in his chest – but you'll know more once you've seen the boy. I'll come in and check him over, if you wish?'

'I expect Angela will ask you to keep an eye on him,'

Michelle said, taking a sip of her tea. There wouldn't be time for lunch now, so she opened the biscuit tin hoping to take the edge off her appetite, but there were only a couple of plain biscuits and they looked soft so she left them. 'I'll have to get back soon.'

'I've taken up your lunch break, haven't I?' said Richard.

'It doesn't matter; someone will bring me a sandwich if I ask.'

'How about I take you out for a meal this evening to make up for it?'

Michelle hesitated, then, 'You don't have to do that . . .'

'I should like to,' he said, giving her a surprisingly uncertain look. 'I thought perhaps we might be friends? I don't often have time to go out – I work late most nights, and I don't like to leave my mother alone for too long as she's quite fragile – but this evening she has a friend coming, so I could pick you up at eight . . . if that isn't too late for you?'

'No. I'll be changing to evening duty tomorrow, so this is my last free evening until next week, when I have Saturday and Sunday off.'

'So, will you come?'

'Yes, thank you,' she said and smiled. 'I like going out with friends, Richard – as long as it is just friends. I'm not interested in a romance.'

He looked serious for a moment. 'Any particular reason – or does that apply only to me?'

'No, it applies to everyone,' Michelle replied, looking him in the eyes. 'I was hurt badly once, and since then . . .'

'You think men are a lot of cheating bastards?' he asked, one eyebrow raised questioningly.

'No, of course not!' she laughed. 'I know it doesn't make sense.'

'Now on that we're in perfect accord,' he said, amusement dancing briefly in his eyes. 'I'm content with friends for now, Michelle. I'm not sure I could cope with more myself, given my situation at home; since my father died, my mother has come to depend on me. I'll pick you up at your home at eight this evening. Don't be late – and wear that pretty blue frock of yours . . .'

Michelle stared after him as he went off whistling cheerfully. So now he was telling her what to wear – he had a cheek! She had a good mind to refuse to go with him – and yet she was already looking forward to it. If she wasn't careful, she might find herself liking him too much . . . Wasn't that precisely what she'd been afraid of? If she relaxed her guard and let herself like Dr Richard Kent, she might end up with a broken heart again.

There'd been no danger of that when she was going out with Alice's cousin Eric. Although Eric wanted more than friendship, he hadn't pushed it. He was a decent man – and she tried not to think of the hurt and disappointment in his eyes the last time she'd turned down his offer of marriage – but she wasn't in love with him, so she couldn't be hurt. However she had a feeling that she could easily fall for the mysterious but charming Dr Kent . . .

'Why did Rose have to go and say she wanted to come to the zoo this Sunday?' Mary Ellen said, scowling as

227

she and Billy sat on the back stairs and shared a sherbet dip. Billy had broken the liquorice stick in two and they tipped a little of the sharp sherbet onto their palms and rolled the end of the stick in it before sucking it clean. It was sticky and Billy had a line of white powder above his mouth. His red hair had been slicked down with water that morning, but it was sticking up at the crown and his socks were down around his ankles, his shoes scuffed and needing a polish. 'If you come on the trip looking like that, Billy, she'll stick her nose in the air and call you *that Baggins boy*.'

'She can't stop me coming,' Billy said cheerfully. 'We'll find a way of being together, Mary Ellen. I ain't gonna let your Rose ruin things for us, don't you worry.'

'No, she can't stop you coming,' Mary Ellen agreed. 'And if she gives me any money, I'll share it with you, Billy – but I still think it would've been more fun if Nan had come instead of Rose.'

'Yeah,' Billy agreed. 'I used to like Sally, but she's gone off to be a nurse like your Rose. I think that Tilly is all right, but she can be a bit moody.'

'She looks sad sometimes,' Mary Ellen agreed. 'Miss Angela said her father is coming to the zoo with us as well. I've seen him with her once and he seems nice – so maybe it will be all right, even if our Rose does come.'

'Did you see that new boy come in this morning?' Billy asked. 'They brought him in an ambulance as I was leavin' for school. He's in a wheelchair, and it looks like he's got an iron cast on his left leg.'

'Oh, poor him,' Mary Ellen said. 'Do you think he's in the sick room? Should we go up and see him – tell him it's all right here? You know how it feels when you first come . . .'

'His name is Timmy,' Billy said, then frowned. 'I'm not sure, but I think I heard Staff Nurse Michelle say he'd had polio. Do you remember that kid down our lane who died of polio? I reckon Timmy must be pretty miserable if he's got something awful like that.'

Mary Ellen didn't remember the boy who died – it must have happened before Ma had taken them to live near the Docks – but she agreed that Timmy must be feeling miserable.

'I wonder if he's coming on the trip to the zoo . . .'

'I bet they won't let him; they're sure to say it would be too much for him,' Billy said. 'I'm goin' to see if I can sneak in and have a word with him before lights out, but you don't want to come. If I get caught, I might be in trouble.'

'If Sister was here she might say you couldn't come to the zoo. Remember how she stopped me going to the pantomime last Christmas? Do you think there'll be a trip to a panto this year?'

'Dunno, but as I remember you did all right last year – Miss Angela took you to the pictures to see *Bambi*.'

'Yes, but I was stopped the pantomime treat – and it might happen to you if you get caught sneaking into the sick ward.'

'Not unless I did somethin' bad. I'm only goin' to see him, Mary Ellen – cheer him up a bit.' He finished his sherbet dip and sighed. 'I've got a penny's worth of Tom Thumb drops. I'd share them with you, but I think I'll give them to Timmy.'

'All right,' Mary Ellen said and stood up, brushing

some white powder from her skirt. 'I'm going to find Nancy and ask her if she'll mend my coat. One of the girls at school tore it and I don't want Sister to find out.'

'Why did she do that, Mary Ellen?'

'She called me a charity 'alfpenny kid and pulled my hair, so I kicked her ankle and she went for me and tore the front of my coat.'

'You should have told me,' Billy said. 'I'd have given her a black eye.'

'Then Miss Angela *would* have stopped you going on the treat,' Mary Ellen said. 'You mustn't hit girls, Billy. Boys who hit girls are bullies; I'm a girl so it's all right for me to hit her – and I did, right on the nose. She went crying to teacher, but she said it was six of one and half a dozen of the other, and made us both stand in the corridor for the whole of reading – and it was a lovely story about a ballerina too.'

'You didn't miss much there then.'

Mary Ellen pulled a face at him. 'I love books about the ballet. We're doing a scrapbook project at school and I want to make one about ballerinas . . . I should like to be a dancer when I'm older.'

'I thought you wanted to be a teacher?'

'I do – but I'd like to dance, too. It's all right; I know it's only a dream.' Mary Ellen grinned at him. 'Go on, if you're going to see Timmy you'd best be on your way – I'm off to help Nancy with the under-fives . . .'

Billy glanced in the sick room. Nurse Paula was on that evening and she was busy giving out drinks and medicines. He waved at a boy he knew and went out, closing

230

the door after him. No sign of their new admission there so he must be in the isolation ward; it was empty again after the sickness bug cleared up, but he might find the new boy there. Billy knew he wasn't allowed in, because it was for children with serious illnesses – but he wasn't going to let that stop him. Timmy couldn't be infectious or the nurses would have been wearing protective clothing when he was brought in, and they hadn't been.

He opened the door cautiously and peeped round the corner. Only one bed was occupied, by the window at the far end, overlooking the garden. Billy couldn't see anyone else and knew that the nurse was next door. She was busy and he reckoned he had time to sneak in and have a few words.

Timmy looked at him in surprise as he walked up to him and grinned, before sitting on the edge of the bed.

'I don't think you're supposed to be here,' Timmy said.

'I'm Billy Baggins, and I've brought you these,' Billy said, and handed over the Tom Thumb drops. 'I reckon you're feelin' a bit lonely, ain't yer? It seems awful when you don't know anyone – but you'll be out of here soon and then you can join my team. We do all sorts of things to earn stars and then we go on trips to the zoo and things.'

'It's nicer here than it was where I've been,' Timmy said. He looked in the bag and smiled. 'Thanks, I like these. Do you want some?'

'Nah, they're for you,' Billy said nobly. 'We're goin' to the zoo this weekend – have you ever been?'

'Only once. Will you come and tell me about it when you get back?'

'Yeah, 'course. I'll bring you something. It won't be much, 'cos we only get threepence a week pocket money. Miss Angela is taking us to the zoo.'

'I think I've seen her,' Timmy said, remembering. 'She brought me some strawberry jelly and ice cream for tea. I can eat more now, but I still find it difficult to eat solid food. It isn't easy to swallow hard things – the polio affected my throat and I had to be fed by drip for a long time . . .'

'Yeah, that's rotten for yer, mate. Mind you, I like jelly and ice cream – but I like ham sandwiches and plum tart and custard too.'

'I used to like me ma's bread-and-butter pudding before I got ill—' Timothy said, breaking off as the door opened and Angela entered. She was wearing a white apron over her dress and carrying a tray with a glass of orange juice.

'Hello, Billy,' she said. 'Have you come to welcome Timmy to St Saviour's?'

'Yes, Miss Angela,' Billy said warily. 'I was telling him about bein' on my team when he leaves the ward – and the trips out. I promised to bring him something back from the zoo.'

'Yes, we shall certainly do that,' Angela said and gave him a look of approval. 'I think you should go now – please wash your hands before you leave the ward. We think Timmy is over the infection, but you can't be too careful.'

'Yes, Miss Angela,' Billy said and went over to the sink. He winked at Timmy as he gave his hands a perfunctory wash and then went out, shutting the door after him.

Miss Angela was all right. He reckoned she was a brick for not getting on to him just because he'd bent the rules a bit. Smiling to himself, he went down to the dining room to have his cup of cocoa before going to his dorm.

TWENTY-FOUR

'I'm sure Billy thought he would be in trouble for breaking the rules,' Angela said later that evening when she welcomed Mark to her home, 'but he meant well and his visit certainly cheered Timmy up a lot – besides, there can't be any risk of infection. I would put Timmy straight into one of the dorms, but I thought he needed to get used to us a little at a time. After all, he has been very ill and I think he's more at risk of catching something from the others than they are from him.'

'He was lucky to come out of it with just a weak leg,' Mark said and smiled at her as he relaxed in one of her comfortable chairs, his long legs stretched out in front of him. 'Some victims don't survive, as you know, and some have to be in an iron lung for a long time merely to breathe. Apart from the partial paralysis in his leg, Timmy seems to have come through it well.'

'Dr Kent said the same thing when he visited this afternoon,' Angela said, filling his wineglass. 'He was sure the boy wasn't infectious – but he agreed that Timmy will need to find his way slowly. He can walk a few steps with the help of the leg iron and a couple of sticks, but he can't swallow solid food yet and he's a long way off keeping up with the other boys. I'm not sure where I ought to put him.'

'Why don't you put him with Billy Baggins?' Mark suggested and sipped his wine. 'He was obviously ready to make friends – and he won't let the others bully him.'

'No, he would give anyone who tried a black eye,' Angela said and laughed as Mark raised his eyebrows. 'I've heard him threaten it a few times since I made him a monitor. I'm not sure Sister would approve, but it seems to keep the younger boys in line. He would make a good sergeant major.'

'Yes, he certainly would,' Mark agreed. 'This is lovely wine, Angela, but I'm certain you asked me over for a purpose . . .'

'My father telephoned today. He's coming up this weekend – but his news is rather disturbing, Mark. My mother wants a divorce – can you believe that?'

Mark was silent for a moment and then inclined his head. 'Well, yes, I'm not that surprised, Angela. I think this has been coming on for a long time.'

'What do you mean?' Her voice betrayed her annoyance; for her the news had come as a tremendous shock.

'You know your mother talked to me in confidence, Angela. I can't tell you what she said – but it was my opinion that she'd been unhappy for a long time. I believe your father will confirm that the rift happened years ago. I dare say they stayed together for your sake.'

'That's ridiculous!' Angela got up and went to pour more drinks to cover her distress. Mark seemed to be implying that she should take the divorce in her stride.

Why couldn't he see how upset that idea made her? 'And to do it now, when my father isn't well . . .'

'I doubt if she knows,' Mark said. 'I'm not sure how serious his illness is, Angela, but if two people feel they no longer love each other, there isn't much point in prolonging the agony, surely? Besides, it may be best for both of them in the long run. Your father may be relieved when it's over.'

'Why do you always take her side?' Angela demanded, and then regretted it as she saw his frown. 'No, I'm sorry – you weren't taking sides, merely trying to reassure me.'

'I like both your parents, Angela – but it's you I care about. I realise the divorce will hurt you; it's not as if you're not a child, though.'

'No, of course not.' Angela sat down with her wineglass and took a sip. 'I'd rather not quarrel with you, Mark.'

'We shan't quarrel,' he said and his smile caught at her heart. 'At least, I shan't. I do want us to be friends again, Angela. It hasn't been the same since Carole – has it?'

'No. I think we've both felt awkward . . .'

'Well, I know I was embarrassed,' Mark said. 'I made such a fool of myself—'

'No, she deceived you,' Angela said. 'I never thought she was good enough for you, Mark – and if that annoys you, I'm sorry.'

'I feel rather flattered, actually,' Mark said. 'I'd like to have dinner one night – we shall have to consult our diaries. I know you're busy most of the time.'

'Come to the zoo with us this weekend,' Angela said suddenly. 'My father is coming and some of the carers; we can take them out for tea afterwards.'

Mark moved towards her, taking her hands in his and pulling her to her feet. For a moment he looked into her eyes and then he sighed. 'You know I want to make love to you, but deep down, you're still angry with me and I want it to be right for us when it happens, and it will happen, Angela. You must admit there's something between us, my dear. However, I've waited this long and I can wait a bit longer.'

'Mark . . .' she felt regret as she saw the withdrawal in his eyes. 'I do care for you, you know that—'

'Yes, and perhaps one day you will trust me,' he said. 'I'll come to the zoo with you on Sunday, Angela. Think about what I've said and try to understand that you mean too much to me to let these disagreements over your mother sour our relationship. I don't want an affair with you, Angela. I want far, far more . . .'

He bent his head, kissed her softly on the lips, turned and went out, leaving Angela to stare after him.

'Angela, may I have a word with you, please?'

'Yes, of course, Wendy. Please come in,' Angela said, looking up from the report she was typing. 'What seems to be the trouble?'

'It's Sarah May,' Wendy said anxiously. 'She seems to be fading away, Angela. She told me Samantha is hurting and she can feel her pain. I know that sounds unlikely, but she's in such distress and she got cross with me when I didn't believe her immediately. This morning she isn't talking to me at all, and she's so thin and pale that I'm worried she's pining for her sister. Is there any news about Samantha?'

'Nothing more as yet,' Angela frowned. 'Mr Yarwood

was going to see what he could do for us, but I haven't heard from him.'

'Well, I thought you should know that Sarah isn't right. I can't say she's ill – but I'm worried about her. She keeps on saying "Samantha hurts", and I'm not sure whether she means that she hurts or whether she really feels that Samantha is ill.'

'I'll telephone Mr Yarwood and ask him what is happening,' Angela promised. 'But there's nothing much I can do beyond that. As things stand, Miss Jane May has the Welfare people's blessing. Much as I might disagree with their decision—' She broke off and sighed. 'I will do what I can, Wendy, but I'm afraid this is going to be a long drawn out process. The Welfare department won't act unless it can be proven that Miss May is actually causing the twins distress by keeping them apart and it is affecting their health.'

'It's so unfair!' Wendy blurted, unable to contain her anger. 'The poor child needs her sister, and that heartless woman won't let them be together . . .'

'Yes, I realise it's very hard on Sarah. But for all we know, Samantha might be getting on well at her aunt's, she might be relieved at not having to look after her twin.'

'I bet she hates it there,' Wendy said passionately. 'I've a good mind to go round there and tell that woman that Sarah needs her sister. I'll go this afternoon, if you'll give me the aunt's address.'

Angela shook her head. 'No, Wendy, I'm sorry. I can't do that. For one thing, I doubt it would help. You must wait until the law takes its course.'

'It might be too late by then,' Wendy said, and closed the door with a bang as she left Angela's office.

Angela was taken aback; Wendy was usually so gentle and even-tempered. Clearly, Sarah's distress had upset her a great deal. Angela too was upset to think of Sarah pining for her sister and believing that the pain she was feeling was Samantha's. Though she'd heard about the special understanding that existed between twins, she'd never encountered a case like this. And given that Sarah was somewhat easily confused, they had to be wary of setting too much store by what she said. All the same, it was worrying.

She decided to telephone Mr Yarwood to see if he had any news for her. As she reached across her desk to pick up the receiver, it rang. She snatched it up and listened as Henry Arnold's voice came over the line.

'Angela, how are you? I have some news concerning the May twins – I wondered if you would meet me for lunch today?'

'Oh, what time?' Angela asked and glanced at her watch. 'It's twelve now – perhaps if we met near here?'

'What about that pub on the corner?'

'Fine. Shall we say one o'clock?'

'One it is. I'll look forward to seeing you then.'

'What—' Angela started, but he'd hung up.

What sort of news did Henry Arnold have and why did he need to see her to deliver it? Couldn't he have told her over the phone? She was annoyed with herself for giving in so easily; it was obvious Mr Arnold wanted her to be beholden to him, though she had no idea why. Her instinct was still telling her that he wasn't to be trusted; something about his proposals for St Saviour's was ringing alarm bells in her brain, though she couldn't for the life of her think why that should be.

At least she knew one thing that he didn't, and Angela had the distinct feeling Mr Arnold wouldn't be too pleased to discover that she was expecting to be promoted to the Board herself.

'I've spoken to Miss Sampson about Samantha,' Henry said as they sat down at the table in the corner. He looked around him. 'It's not bad in here – is the food any good?'

'It's all right for a simple meal,' Angela replied. 'I always have a salad if I come here at lunchtime. What news do you have concerning the twins?'

'Well, after reading the various reports, Miss Sampson has agreed that St Saviour's can keep Sarah on a permanent basis. However I'm afraid at the moment she is holding out for the other girl remaining with her aunt. She believes that children should be with family whenever possible.'

'I'm glad they're not going to try to take Sarah away from us – I would fight tooth and nail to keep her. But the fact is, she needs her sister. One of my nurses was telling me only this morning that she is pining for Samantha. Can't these fools in the Welfare department see that twins need to be together? All children fare better if they have their siblings with them at that age, and Sarah is even more dependent on her twin than most.'

'Yes, I do understand that, but in the end it might be better for both of them, don't you think? I know you see it from Sarah's side, and I can't blame you for that, because I've been told she is a lovely child . . .' Henry gave her a winning smile and reached across to touch her hand. 'Don't treat me as the enemy, Angela. You must know how much I like you? I appreciate you as a colleague and I know you have the children's happiness at heart – and I'm going to keep trying. I've asked Ruth to let you put your case to her and she's agreed – but she does need proof that Samantha would be better off with her sister. You see, it is the accepted norm that relatives should care for the children if they can . . .'

'Miss Sampson has agreed to see me?'

'Yes. She's a busy woman, Angela, as you are – but she's promised to telephone and make an appointment soon. So you see, I have done as I promised.'

'Yes, you have, and I do appreciate it.' Angela relaxed. 'I know you're not the enemy, Henry.'

'Thank you.' He couldn't keep the triumph from his eyes. 'I'm rather hoping we can be friends – good friends. Perhaps even more . . .'

Angela was about to inform him that she would never be interested in more than a casual friendship, but something held her back. Her instincts told her that Henry would be a bad enemy. She preferred him to be friendly, even if she wasn't interested in taking friendship as far as he was clearly hoping.

Angela was deep in thought as she sat down at her desk after lunch. She was pleased that Sarah was being allowed to stay at the home, but the problem of Samantha still remained. If Sarah was pining for her, they needed to get Samantha back here as soon as possible. Miss Sampson might be prepared to give her a fair hearing, but even if she agreed to take action it could take months to wade through all the red tape. Perhaps if she rang Mr Yarwood he might be able to suggest something that could get their case pushed to the front of the queue.

She reached into her top drawer for the small book of addresses and telephone numbers she kept there, but the compartment it usually occupied was empty. Frowning, Angela closed the drawer and opened the next one down; the book was lying on top of a bundle of papers. The back of her neck prickled; she would never have put it in there – this was where she kept all the receipts that had yet to be entered into the accounts.

Had someone taken the book out to find a number or an address? If so, Angela suspected she knew the culprit. Yet surely Staff Nurse Wendy would not be so foolish? She'd asked for Miss Jane May's address and Angela had refused it – she couldn't reveal confidential material like that . . . besides, it would only make things worse if Wendy went round to the aunt's house and made a scene.

Angela was on the point of going in search of Wendy when the door opened and Nan came in looking worried.

'Are you busy, Angela?' she asked. 'Only I wanted to talk to you about Tilly . . .'

'Has she been careless again?' Angela asked. 'She seems such a pleasant girl, Nan – but she is inclined to go her own way at times.'

'Muriel was complaining about her. Apparently, she helped herself to a sandwich and tea without asking when she got in this morning – and you know how Muriel feels about her kitchen.'

'I do indeed,' Angela said. 'Would you like me to speak to Tilly again? I would rather not let her go – we've lost too many of our girls recently.'

'Alice will soon be coming back for a few hours twice a week,' Nan said. 'But I don't want you to sack Tilly. I was hoping you could get her to tell you what's wrong. I've tried talking to her, but she says she's fine and apologises if she's done something she shouldn't.'

'Well, if she won't tell you . . . but of course I'll try. Will you ask her to come and see me?'

'She's in the staff room,' Nan said. 'If I'm not mistaken, she's been crying.'

'All right. I'll go now,' Angela said, smothering a sigh. It looked as though she would have to wait until this evening to talk to Wendy about going round to Miss Jane May's house.

Tilly looked up as Angela entered the staff room. She had obviously been crying; her eyes were red and she had a handkerchief in her fist and was rubbing at her face.

'You'll make it worse, Tilly,' Angela said gently. 'You need to wash your face with cold water – but before you do, I'd like you to tell me what is making you so unhappy.'

'I know you're going to sack me,' Tilly said defiantly. 'I didn't know I wasn't allowed to make myself a sandwich—'

'I think you must have known,' Angela said, her voice slightly sterner. 'Please don't lie, Tilly. You must be aware that Muriel has a very tight budget and needs to keep a check on things, especially with butter and cheese still rationed.'

'I was hungry. I didn't get any breakfast and I didn't think one sandwich would matter.'

'It's the principle,' Angela said. 'Why didn't you have breakfast before you came – trouble at home?' Tilly nodded but avoided her gaze. 'Can't you tell me, Tilly? I really don't want to sack you. At St Saviour's we prefer to keep our staff – but you do need to learn the rules and to be more careful. We can't have carers forgetting to put protective aprons on in the sick ward or we'll have everyone ill, and Cook doesn't like girls helping themselves to food without asking her.'

'I wasn't thinking, Mrs Morton,' Tilly sobbed. 'I've quarrelled with my mother and *him*, and now I've got to leave my home.'

'Why – and who is this "him" you've quarrelled with?'

'Me stepdad – and he's a filthy brute, no matter what Ma says,' Tilly said with a flash of defiance. 'For months now he's been tryin' it on . . . pawing at me and leering. Well, this morning he grabbed me and shoved me up against the wall and stuck his hand up me skirt. I went for him and Ma heard – and we had a terrible row. I walked out and I shan't go back.' She shuddered, a look of such disgust and anger in her eyes that Angela immediately felt for her.

'Nor should you,' Angela said. 'Did you bring your clothes with you?'

'Some . . .' Tilly stared at her. 'Why?'

'We have a spare room at the Nurses' Home and I'm going to let you have it – at least for a while, until you decide what you want to do.'

'You'd do that for me?' Tilly seemed stunned. 'No one's never done nothin' for me before.'

'Then it's time someone did.' Angela smiled. 'I'm going to give you another chance to prove yourself to us, Tilly – is that a deal?'

'Yeah, I reckon so,' Tilly said and grinned. 'You're all right, Mrs Morton. I give yer my word I'll work hard and I won't be careless. I've 'ad so much on me mind . . .'

'Yes, I expect you have,' Angela said. 'I think you've made the right decision. Now let's go and see that room, shall we?'

TWENTY-FIVE

'Well, will this do?' Angela asked as she unlocked the door of the vacant room. 'I think the bed needs making up, but if you tell Nan about the new arrangements she'll give you clean linen and towels. It means you'll join the children for breakfast in the mornings and you'll have all your meals with us.'

'Do I pay for them, Mrs Morton?'

'No. Our live-in girls get all their meals free, but they are expected to be in earlier in the mornings and stay later if need be – so will this solve your problem, Tilly?'

'Yes, miss. I can't thank you enough!'

'In that case, I'll leave you to hang your clothes up,' Angela said. 'If you need to fetch more things, you should ask one of us to go with you.'

'I'll make sure I go when he's out,' Tilly said. 'I'm not afraid of me ma. She only took his side 'cos she can't manage without him.'

'Well, you know best,' Angela said. 'But we look after our girls and I'm perfectly prepared to come with you if you need moral support.'

Leaving Tilly to settle into her new room, Angela

246

hurried down the stairs, intent on getting back to her office and telephoning Mr Yarwood. As she opened the back door, she saw something across the small garden that separated the Nurses' Home from the children's home that made her break into a run. Wendy had reached the foot of the main stairs when Angela caught her – and she was holding the hand of Samantha May.

'What do you think you're doing, Wendy?' Angela asked in as calm a tone as she could manage. 'Samantha, does your aunt know you're here?'

'She wasn't there,' Wendy said, taking a firmer hold of Samantha's hand and ushering her forward so Angela could see her. 'Look at her, just look at the state of her! Tell Mrs Morton what happened, Samantha. Don't be afraid . . .'

Angela frowned as she saw that the child's skirt was stained and her hair looked as if it hadn't been washed since her aunt had fetched her weeks before.

'Aunt Jane went shopping two days ago and I haven't seen her since,' Samantha said. 'She told me to stay where I was and not move until she got back – but there's no food in the house and it was cold.'

'Didn't you go to school?'

'No, miss. Not yesterday or today. Aunt Jane would've been cross if I'd gone out – and when she's cross she canes me.' Her head dropped and she clung to Wendy's hand.

Angela was momentarily lost for words. Having seen the hopeless look in the child's eyes, she didn't doubt Samantha was telling the truth.

'She has marks all over her back,' Wendy said. Her eyes were brimming with tears, but she met Angela's gaze defiantly. 'I'm not sending her back there, Angela. She's staying here at St Saviour's with Sarah – and . . . and, I'll go to prison before I let them take her back.'

Angela suppressed the urge to hug Wendy. 'You shouldn't have gone there without permission, Wendy – but it's just as well you did. I suggest you take Samantha to her sister and then get her some food and drink. She'll need a bath too.'

'What will happen when her aunt goes back and finds Samantha isn't there?' Despite her brave words, Wendy looked nervous. 'I couldn't leave her there – and Sarah needs her.'

'Indeed she does. Take her upstairs and leave the rest to me.'

Angela watched the two disappear up the stairs. Wendy had acted impulsively; she couldn't bear to see Sarah declining for lack of her sister – but it was a good thing she had; if Miss Jane May had stayed away much longer, the child might have starved. Angela was going to have to start phoning a few people. Mr Yarwood might be helpful, and Mark . . . Yes, she would ask Mark for his advice. She certainly didn't want to involve Henry Arnold any more than she had to.

'Where Samantha?' Sarah burst into the bathroom as Wendy was helping Samantha out of her stained clothing. She'd sent Tilly to tell Sarah that her sister was here, thinking it best if Sarah didn't see her until Samantha was feeling better. But as Samantha broke from her and ran to catch her twin in her arms, she knew she'd been wrong. These two had been kept apart too long as it was; the feeling between them was

248

much stronger than any outsider could possibly understand.

'It's all right, Sarah,' Samantha said, kissing her. 'I'm here with you now, love. I'll never go away from you again, I promise.'

'Promise,' Sarah said, looking at her intently, tears rolling down her cheeks. She reached out and touched her sister's face. 'Samantha hurt so bad. Sarah feel her pain . . . Sarah hurt for her . . .'

'Yes, I know,' Samantha said and put her arms about her again. 'Get in the bath with me – she can, can't she, Nurse?'

'Yes, if it's what you want,' Wendy said, watching as Sarah hastily undressed and then the two climbed into the warm water and Sarah began to tenderly wash her sister's back. Wendy went out and left them alone; it was so touching, seeing the two of them together, that she couldn't hold back her own tears a moment longer. As she dabbed at her eyes with a hankie, a murderous rage welled up inside her. She would like to make Miss May suffer for what she'd done to those children. Well, she wasn't getting her hands on Samantha again! Not if Wendy had anything to do with it . . .

'Constable Sallis says the aunt is very ill,' Angela told Mark an hour or so later. 'As Mr Yarwood was out of the country when I phoned him recently, I asked the constable to make inquiries about Miss May. He spoke to her neighbours and discovered that she has fits which cause her to black out and she is frightened of living alone in case no one finds her until it's too late – and that of course is why she wanted Samantha around.'

'She has no business relying on a young child,' Mark said. 'She should be in a home where she can be taken care of. This alters the case considerably, Angela.'

'There's more,' Angela said. 'Samantha told us that her aunt canes her if she gets cross – and she has the marks of a beating on her back. They aren't deep and her skin hasn't been cut, but I've told Wendy I want photographs and her testimony to the state the child was in when she found her. There wasn't a fire or any food in the house when Samantha let her in, and she hadn't even dared go to school for two days for fear her aunt would punish her.'

'I think your case is proven,' Mark said. 'The Welfare people can't go against evidence like that – Samantha will not be going back there, but that doesn't mean they will let us keep her.'

'Well, I'm not going to let her go again unless Sarah goes with her – and it has to be to someone who will love and care for her.'

'I'm with you all the way,' Mark said. 'Do you want me to speak to anyone for you?'

'I'm going to make an appointment with Miss Sampson,' Angela replied. 'I've been told she is willing to hear my case and I think it's a much stronger case now. I'll fight them through the courts if I have to, Mark – and if it comes to that I'll need all the help I can get.'

'Well, you know you can count on me,' Mark told her. 'That nurse used a bit of initiative, didn't she?'

'Wendy shouldn't have done it,' Angela said, 'but she cares for the children – especially Sarah – and I'm glad she did. Samantha was so frightened of making her aunt cross that she might have stopped there until she became ill – and she's lost weight too. I think Wendy acted in the nick of time.'

'It's a difficult case, because the aunt has the excuse of illness. She may not have intended to leave Samantha for so long.'

'Whatever her intention, the child was left alone in that house for two days – and I hope Miss Sampson will see that she can't go back there under any circumstances . . .'

'Yes, I quite see your point, Mrs Morton,' Ruth Sampson agreed when Angela visited her office the next day. 'Inquiries have been made and Miss May is in hospital. She has been in a coma for two days, but she came round earlier this morning and told someone that the child was alone. It was not a case of wilful neglect.'

'Perhaps not, but she isn't fit to have care of a child – and these photographs show that Samantha has been beaten . . .'

'The law states that guardians must discipline children as they see fit—' Miss Sampson winced at the photographs Angela was spreading out across the desk in front of her. 'Not that I agree with such punishment, Mrs Morton. No, it would appear that a mistake was made by our department, but Miss May seemed to be the only living relative.'

'We are happy to care for both of them,' Angela told her. 'Naturally, if a loving relative came forward, we should not stand in the way of adoption. But I hope you agree that Miss Jane May is not a suitable guardian?'

'I do not think she will be well enough to leave hospital for a long time – if ever. So, until such time as other arrangements can be made . . . yes, you must keep them at Halfpenny Street. As I said before, I can only apologise if a mistake was made . . .'

If a mistake was made! Angela would have liked to tell her what she thought in no uncertain terms, but this woman still had the power to send the twins elsewhere and Angela had no choice but to smile politely and express her gratitude before taking her leave.

A tragedy had been averted thanks to a gentle girl who had stood up for what she believed was right, even though she had broken several rules and regulations in the process. Angela hadn't had the heart to reprimand Wendy for going to that address; she could only feel relieved that the twins were back together. And if she had anything to do with it, they would stay that way . . .

'So she gave in?' Mark asked as they sat talking by the glowing fire at their favourite inn. 'I'm glad, but I knew she would once you presented her with the facts.'

'She's only granted temporary custody,' Angela sighed. 'But at least that means they're safe for the time being.'

'That's all that matters for now,' Mark said and reached for his wineglass. 'It's time to discuss Christmas in detail, Angela. I think we should have the carol service and a tree – with a visit from Santa Claus, just as we did last year, don't you?'

'Yes, the children loved the tree and the presents, and everyone enjoyed the carols – but why don't we go one better?'

'What do you mean?'

'Well, we've never officially opened the new wing. So why don't we give a carol service there, followed by drinks and nibbles – on Christmas Eve? Make it a double celebration . . .'

'Yes, I think that's a wonderful idea, Angela. We did intend to have a party back in September, but then Sister Beatrice fell ill . . .'

'Hopefully she will be well enough to come back to us by Christmas,' Angela nodded. 'We have a few weeks yet to plan it all.'

'Is there any chance of a pantomime this year?'

'Last year the tickets were given to us, but I can't ask again,' Angela said. 'I do have a Christmas fund, but it won't stretch to more than about twenty of the younger children.'

'Supposing I were to chip in with a few quid?' Mark said. 'Do you think you might get a better deal at the theatre if we took them all?'

'Take all of the children that are well enough?' Angela smiled at him. 'What a lovely idea, Mark. Yes, that sounds marvellous – I might get a discount for such a large party.'

'Good. I do like to give the children a good Christmas. I suppose it comes from having no one of my own to spoil.'

'Oh, Mark . . .' Angela's throat caught as she saw the sadness in his eyes and knew he was remembering the son who'd died soon after being born.

'You'll be going home on Christmas Eve after the party I expect?'

'Yes, I couldn't leave my father to cook his own Christmas dinner . . .' A sigh broke from Angela as she remembered the previous Christmas when she'd discovered her mother's secret drinking.

'Your father isn't as helpless as you imagine,' Mark said. 'I think you'll find that he wouldn't be on his own, even if you didn't go home – although I know you will.'

'What do you mean?' Angela frowned, sensing that Mark was hinting at some deeper meaning.

'Simply that he has a great many friends, Angela. He must receive several invitations over Christmas.'

Angela wasn't entirely convinced by this explanation, but she didn't want to quarrel with him again. She felt a surge of longing, an intense need to be close to him, to be held in his arms and kissed. It was so long since John died and, despite her busy life, Angela was lonely. As she looked into Mark's eyes she felt the physical pull between them and her heart raced. Perhaps now they were both ready to begin a new phase of their relationship.

'Mark . . .' she began, but before she could continue a shadow loomed over them and a man spoke.

'How nice,' Henry Arnold said. 'I was hoping to see you, Angela – and you, Adderbury. Ruth Sampson was telling me about that business with the twins . . . shocking, quite shocking. I'm so glad you've managed to settle the matter, Angela. I really cannot imagine how it happened that they approved the aunt's application to have the children in the first place.'

'It's obvious that they didn't make enough inquiries about Miss May,' Mark said, then he glanced at his watch and frowned. 'I think we shall have to make a move soon, Angela – if we want our table . . .'

'Of course; I mustn't delay you,' Henry said smoothly. 'Angela – I'll call you soon? To talk over a few things.'

'If you wish,' she replied politely, trying to disguise her reluctance.

'Good, I'll be in touch,' he said, giving her what she could only interpret as an intimate look. What was he trying to imply? Nothing had passed between them that he should look at her in that way. What was he up to? Not for the first time, Angela felt infuriated by Henry Arnold.

'The waiter has signalled to us twice,' Mark said, a little irritably. 'We'd better go into the dining room, Angela. Excuse us, Arnold.'

'Good night, Mr Arnold,' she said firmly. But as she got to her feet and followed Mark, she sensed that his mood had changed. The invisible barrier that had been there since Carole's departure from St Saviour's had slipped back into place. If only Henry Arnold hadn't intruded . . . but he had, and Mark seemed annoyed. Surely he didn't imagine that there was anything more than business between her and that man?

For the rest of the evening Angela struggled to get back their former mood of intimacy, but it had been shattered. Mark kept steering the conversation back to business, and when he dropped her outside her apartment, he did no more than graze her cheek with his kiss.

As she went inside, Angela was aware of a feeling of disappointment, of longing for something that had been missing from her life since her husband's death. Suddenly, she realised that the years were slipping by – and she wanted more than her job and the satisfaction she got from helping the orphans of Halfpenny Street. She wanted love and marriage and perhaps children of her own . . . and for a time that evening she'd felt that Mark was telling her it was what he wanted too.

TWENTY-SIX

'This is lovely,' Michelle said, looking round the large dining room. Richard had brought her to an inn out in the country some miles from London and she was feeling a bit overwhelmed by her surroundings. 'I've never been anywhere like this before.' The oak tables were covered by spotless white cloths and the chairs were wheel-backs with U-shaped stretchers and looked as old as the inn itself; through the window she could see wintry sunshine dappled on old brick walls. 'How old did you say it was?'

'Seventeenth century, I think,' Richard replied. 'I've only been here once – it was during the war. I came here with some friends and we had a party . . .' Sadness flickered in his eyes and Michelle wondered what memory the reminiscence had stirred, but everyone had bad memories of the war, didn't they? In a moment the shadow had passed and he was smiling. 'The food was good even then, and I understand they do a very good game pie – if you like that sort of thing?'

'I haven't eaten game often,' Michelle admitted, feeling that this place was a bit out of her league. She was an

East End girl and the nearest her family ever got to game was a rabbit from the butcher's. 'I don't mind trying it though.'

'Well, let's have a look and see, shall we?' Richard perused the menu and nodded. 'Good, they have either game pie or pheasant for main course – and some kind of fancy fish cakes with vegetables . . .'

'Oh.' Michelle hesitated. She wasn't sure she fancied pheasant, or the game pie. 'I'm not sure . . . perhaps I'll have the fish cakes.'

'Really – are you sure?' Richard looked disappointed in her choice. 'I'm having the pheasant . . . what will you have for starters? They have tomato soup or pâté . . .'

'The soup please,' Michelle said, relieved that there was something ordinary on offer. 'Yes, soup and fish cakes, please.'

Richard gave their order to the waiter and discussed the wines without consulting Michelle. She wondered what he'd ordered, because she didn't much like dry wine. Alan had liked dry wine, but Michelle preferred the sweeter variety even though she knew it was supposed to be drunk with dessert.

'How is Matty getting along?' Richard asked as the waiter departed with their order. 'I haven't had time to get in to see him myself.'

'I went yesterday, after work,' Michelle said, pleased that they had common ground to meet on. 'He seems better in himself, though the nurse told me he'd had a fall when he tried to go to the bathroom by himself.'

'That doesn't sound promising,' Richard frowned. 'Do you know when they are going to do those tests?'

'I think they've done some already,' Michelle said, 'but they haven't told me anything yet.'

'Well, we must hope that it isn't too serious,' Richard said. He paused as the waiter returned with their wine, tasted it and nodded. Michelle tasted hers tentatively. It felt dry on her tongue and she took a very small sip; she couldn't drink wine like that unless she had food to help it down. 'Now, tell me about yourself, Michelle – I know you're a good nurse, but what is your ambition?'

'Ambition?' Michelle hesitated, trying to think of something that would qualify as an ambition. 'I just want to look after the children and help my parents . . . but if Dad gets that job as caretaker at St Saviour's and they move into a better house, they won't need as much help from me.'

'Do you hope to become a nursing sister – or will you marry and leave the service?'

'I'm not sure I'll ever marry.'

'Do you mind my asking why? Did someone let you down?'

'He was married,' Michelle said, deciding to be honest about it. 'We had a brief affair but when I discovered he had a wife and son, I broke it off.'

'Is that why you don't trust men?'

'It's why I'm careful,' she said and smiled at him. 'I don't want it to happen again.'

'No, but it doesn't have to, if you give yourself a chance to find love,' Richard said. At that moment their food arrived and he smiled. 'I hope this is as good as it smells . . .' He lifted his wineglass to toast her. 'To the future and happiness . . .'

Michelle lifted her glass in return and took a tiny sip. 'Thank you – and these fish cakes are delicious, much like my mum makes when she can get the proper fish . . .'

'This is a bit of all right,' Billy said, licking the ice cream that Angela had bought at the kiosk inside the zoo gates. It was a bit cold for ice cream, but the children had had their choice of what they wanted from the man selling bags of popcorn, sweets and ice cream cones. 'Look out, here comes your Rose.'

'Haven't you finished that yet?' Rose asked. She'd left them staring into the monkey enclosure while she went to the toilet. 'It smells a bit here. Why don't we move on? Angela said she was taking everyone to the café for a cup of tea. I don't know how you can eat ice cream on a day like this, Billy.'

'It ain't cold – not proper cold, anyways,' Billy said. 'We get used to the cold playin' football, Rose. Play in all weathers, we do.'

'Yes, well, I'm cold – what about you, Mary Ellen?'

'I'm all right,' Mary Ellen said without looking round. 'I've been watching that keeper take the elephant for a walk. Do you think he'd let us touch it?'

'What on earth would you want to touch a smelly thing like that for?' Rose O'Hanran looked at her sister and shuddered. 'You're a funny girl, Mary Ellen. We'll ask him where the café is and see if he'll let you get a closer look at the elephant – but be careful. They are wild animals you know . . .'

'Come on, Mary Ellen, I'll race you,' Billy said and started running to be the first to reach the keeper who was walking the elephant.

Mary Ellen ran after him, but Billy was too quick for her. He'd been one of the fortunate few that Angela had taken to the Olympics in the summer, and since then he'd been running every chance he got, having decided he was going to run for England. At least, that was his ambition when he wasn't dreaming of playing for West Ham football club.

'Can we stroke him, mister?' Billy asked the keeper. 'He's big, ain't he?'

'Yes, she's an African elephant,' said the keeper. He was used to children asking if they could stroke the gentle giant. 'Why don't you give her this?'

He held out a banana to Billy. 'Offer it to her and she'll take it in her trunk – she won't hurt you, so you needn't be afraid.'

'Billy isn't afraid of anything,' Mary Ellen said, coming up to them. 'She's lovely, mister – what's her name?'

'Got a posh name has her,' the keeper said with a smile. 'She's called Matilda.'

'That's a daft name for an elephant,' Billy said, holding the banana tentatively as she took it delicately in her trunk and then dropped it into her mouth. 'It tickled!' he laughed in delight. 'How many bananas does she eat, mister?'

'As many as she can get,' the keeper said. 'She only gets a few a day now – they're still in short supply – but we give her all sorts of things. Matilda loves her fruit, but she'll eat whatever we give her. She didn't get bananas at all during the war.'

'Come along,' Rose said. 'I'm sure this gentleman has plenty to do without talking to you two. We've got to find Angela and have that cup of tea . . .'

260

'It's part of my job, talking to the young ones,' the keeper said, and touched his cap to Rose. He was a young man and his eyes were warm as they lit on her, making Rose blush. 'Nice to meet two such pleasant children.'

'Thank you,' Rose said and pushed them ahead of her.

Billy had taken off again, running ahead. He was some distance in front of Rose and Mary Ellen when he appeared to trip and fall over.

'The stupid boy!' Rose exclaimed and quickened her pace when she saw he was sitting on the ground rubbing at his knee. 'Now you've cut yourself . . . look, no wonder you fell. Somebody left a bit of metal lying there and you've cut yourself on it.'

'It's nothing,' Billy said bravely, but when he moved his hand they could all see the blood.

'It's a good thing I always bring a few bits and pieces in my bag,' Rose said, and opened her large black bag to take out a roll of bandage and some safety pins. She wiped the blood away and nodded. 'Yes, it's a nasty cut. I've cleaned it as best I can – but you must ask nurse to put a fresh dressing on when you get back home, Billy.'

'Billy never makes a fuss,' Mary Ellen said as Rose used some antiseptic cream that stung and then wrapped his knee in a white bandage. 'But it's a good thing you've got that bandage, Rose. We don't want to miss the rest of the treat.'

'No – and I want to find Angela and the others,' Rose said. 'Look, there's the café. Come on, we'll see what the others are having.'

261

'What would you like?' Mr Hendry asked Billy and Mary Ellen as they joined the others at his table. Samantha and Sarah May were sitting with him and the waitress was waiting for their order. 'You can have whatever you choose, Billy. I think you and Mary Ellen deserve a treat for what you did last Christmas. Angela told me how brave you all were.'

'It weren't nuthin',' Billy said. 'I'd like a sticky bun and a glass of orange, please, sir.'

'Yes, all right – and you, Mary Ellen, what would you like?'

'Tomatoes on toast and a glass of orange squash, please, Mr Hendry.'

'Good, sensible girl – and what about you, Samantha – what will you have?'

'I'd like toast and tomatoes too,' Samantha said. 'What do you want, Sarah?'

'Same as Billy,' Sarah said and blushed, looking shy.

'I'm having one of the pink ones,' Billy said and looked at the glass case where the cakes were sitting. A small queue had formed; there were always a lot of people wanting a hot drink, especially when it was cool like today. As Billy scanned the people waiting for a table, he saw a face he recognised and a shiver went down his spine.

What was Jack Shaw doing here? Billy looked about him quickly. He ought to tell someone; Jack Shaw was a bad one and had been involved with Billy's brother Arthur in several big robberies the previous year – but who should he tell? Even as he hesitated, he realised that Jack had seen him and recognised him. Immediately, he left the queue and went out without ordering anything.

'Is something the matter, Billy?' Mr Hendry asked.

Billy shook his head. Mr Hendry didn't know Jack the way he did and he might think Billy was mistaken – after all, the papers had said he was dead – but Billy was afraid of Jack and he knew it was him. Perhaps it was best if he kept it to himself. Jack had gone now and there was no point chasing after him, he could have gone anywhere . . .

'You were lucky, Billy,' Michelle said the next morning as she gently smeared ointment onto his knees and put a nice soft bandage round it. Her work was neat and efficient and the bandage felt a lot better than the one she'd taken off earlier. 'Rose cleaned the wound well and I don't think you'll take any harm. I didn't need to stitch it, but don't run around too much for a few days. If it hurts worse, come straight in to the sick ward to see whoever is on duty.'

'Yes, Nurse,' Billy said. His knee had stiffened up overnight and it still felt a bit sore as he hobbled from the sick room and stood uncertainly in the hall.

Billy wished that Sister Beatrice was in her office, but she'd gone away to recuperate after her illness. He'd fretted all night and had come to the conclusion he had to tell someone what he'd seen at the zoo; if he didn't, Jack might come here and threaten them. He knew Billy had recognised him and he'd threatened him a couple of times when Arthur had made Billy keep watch for them when they were breaking into that factory. In Billy's opinion he was as big a bully as Arthur.

Taking a deep breath, Billy marched up to Angela's door and knocked. He was invited to enter. She was sitting at her desk typing and looked surprised to see him.

'Anything the matter, Billy?' she asked.

'Yes, miss – at least . . . I'm not sure. I think I ought to tell you . . .'

'Please, come in. If you think it is important I have time to listen.'

Billy approached the desk, his hands clenched behind his back. 'I'm not a snitch, miss – but I saw him. The police were never sure if he died in the fire or got away, but I know it was him . . . yesterday, in that café when we was having tea. It was Jack Shaw, miss. I reckon the police might want to know, don't you?'

'Yes, I do, Billy.' Angela frowned. 'You're quite sure it was him?'

'Yes, miss. I know it was – he saw me and cleared off sharpish soon as he knew I'd seen him.' A shudder went through him. 'I shall never forget what they done, miss – that Jack Shaw and my brother. They killed a man the night of the factory fire . . . and they threatened me more than once. Arthur wanted to burn us all in our beds and I don't trust that Jack. If he came here—'

'I'm sure he won't, Billy,' Angela reassured him quickly. 'I'm going to let the police know at once. Constable Sallis might want to talk to you – but you won't mind that?'

'No, miss. Not if it helps . . .' He hesitated, then, 'I took Timmy some fudge we bought at the zoo, and he sucked a piece and said he wished he'd been with us – can he come on other outings, miss? Our team will soon have enough stars for another trip to the zoo, and Timmy's only been once with his father. He misses his mum and dad, Miss Angela – and I should like to have him on my team.'

'Yes, Billy, I'm sure he does miss his family. I asked Timmy if he felt well enough to sleep in your dorm and he said yes, so I'm going to move him in next week . . . but you do realise that he isn't properly over his illness yet, don't you?'

'Yes, miss. We'll look after him. He said he will be having that horrible thing off his leg soon. He's been having exercise and massage to help strengthen his leg, hasn't he?'

'Yes, Billy, but it is a long, slow recovery from an illness like polio. Timmy is lucky that his leg is the worst of his problems. He will need to wear the leg iron for some weeks, perhaps months yet, despite the massaging and the exercises. He may need to be in a wheelchair if we take him on outside trips.'

'I'd push his chair and look after him, Miss Angela.'

'Well, we'll see. I hope it won't be too long before Timmy is able to get about more easily, but we have to be patient and let him do it in his own time.'

'He's in a hurry to get up and join in everythin'.' Billy grinned. 'He wants to come and cheer me on at the football when I start playin' again.'

'Ah yes, that reminds me,' Angela said. 'Father Joe has found a club where you can train with other boys. They do athletics – running and jumping, throwing javelins and things. We wondered if you might like to join? Father Joe will take you there and enrol you. He has a converted van for transporting you all. So, would you like to join the club?'

'Me, miss?' Billy's face lit up. 'Yeah, I'd like that!'

'Are there any other boys at St Saviour's you think would like to join?'

'Mebbe one or two,' Billy said. 'Shall I ask round, miss?'

'Yes. I think it would be nice to have a St Saviour's team. Father Joe told me there are competitions you can enter with children from other parts of London – and teams from the country, too, I think. If enough of you want to join he will take you and the others and enrol you all.'

'Can girls join too, miss?'

'I suppose they could.' Angela smiled. 'Yes, if anyone thinks they could run fast or jump a long way – or throw things – yes, why not girls as well?'

'I bet I get you a long list,' Billy said, beaming with pride as he turned away, but at the door he stopped and looked back. 'You won't forget to tell the police what I saw?'

'No, Billy. I'm going to leave a message for Constable Sallis immediately.'

'Jack Shaw wants locking up, miss.' Billy closed the door behind him.

He soon forgot his brother's accomplice in crime as he started running, ignoring the soreness in his knee. It would be great to join an athletics club. He could train with other boys whenever he wasn't playing football . . .

TWENTY-SEVEN

'You were sitting next to Billy Baggins at tea yesterday, weren't you, Dad?' Angela said when her father came to have coffee with her before catching his train home. 'He thought he saw one of the criminals involved in that factory burglary that went wrong last year. He didn't say anything about it to you?'

'No – but it was a bit odd. One minute he was chatting away, talking to Sarah and helping her choose what she wanted for tea, and then he suddenly went very quiet, though it didn't seem to affect his appetite.'

'It takes a lot for Billy not to be hungry,' Angela said with a smile. 'He came to tell me he'd seen Jack Shaw waiting in the queue for drinks. Apparently, he went off as soon as he saw Billy. I rang the police this morning and they confirmed what Billy said. They are certain he wasn't killed in the fire and they've had reports that he has been seen in London, but they haven't been able to find him.'

'Let's hope they do – and soon. You don't want more trouble with that sort here, Angela.'

'No, we don't,' she said. 'How are you feeling now, Dad?'

'Much better for having that wonderful day out with you and Mark – and the children. I like your Billy Baggins, and Mary Ellen . . . and that child Sarah is delightful if you take the time to communicate with her. She certainly isn't an imbecile. Yes, I had a lovely time and it did me the world of good.'

'I wondered if you would like to come when we take the children to the pantomime this Christmas. Why don't you come up for a few days and we can travel home together on Christmas Eve?'

'I suppose we could . . .' He appeared to consider it for a moment. 'I could ask someone to come in and get things ready for us at home – and we can order the food and have a hamper delivered.'

'There's no chance Mother will be back, I suppose?'

'None whatsoever. I think we both have to accept that she has decided to make a new life for herself, Angela. And now, I really must leave if I'm going to catch my train.'

'Yes, of course. I'll telephone you this evening.'

'My taxi will be here any moment . . .'

'I'll see you very soon then.' She kissed his cheek and went to the door with him, watching as he entered the lift and disappeared from sight.

Sighing, Angela collected the cups and took them into the kitchen. She didn't see enough of her father these days, and she worried about him being alone in that house. As she was washing the cups, her doorbell rang. She went to answer it, wiping her hands.

'Did you forget something?' she said, thinking it must be her father.

Angela frowned as she saw the man standing outside her door.

'Hello, Angela. I hope I haven't called at an inconvenient time?'

'I thought you were my father . . .' She stared at him, reluctant to ask him in and yet knowing that it would be rude not to. 'We've just had coffee. It may still be warm – or I could make some fresh . . .' She hoped her reluctance wasn't too obvious.

Henry Arnold followed her in, looking about him with interest. 'I heard you'd bought one of these apartments. Not a bad job – not bad at all, but I still prefer new build to old patched up.'

'It depends what it is,' Angela said, annoyed once more; she really loved her apartment. 'Please sit down, if you wish. What did you want to ask me, Mr Arnold?'

'Henry, please.' He didn't sit down, his smile rather forced. 'I hope I'm not keeping you from something important?'

'I'm going into work shortly.'

'I shan't keep you long,' he replied. 'I wanted to tell you the good news – I've found the perfect place for the new St Saviour's. It's a couple of miles outside Newmarket – I've been able to get us an excellent price on the land and I can't wait to give my news to the Board at the meeting this week.'

Angela frowned. 'I wasn't aware that we were that far advanced with plans to build a home in the country. I'm not at all sure it's the right time to be thinking of

269

moving the home. We've not long opened the new wing—'

'I dare say you could get a decent price for the building. In fact, I could probably help with that; I have lots of contacts in the trade. Nothing has been agreed yet, though my proposals have been approved in principle – but with this offer, I'm sure that the Board will want to at least secure the land. They would be mad not to.'

'We're a long way from having funds to purchase the land and build the kind of place you suggest,' Angela said. 'In time, a move to the country might be a good thing, but I think it would be better to wait for a few years and then, when we have all the funding in place, we can think about where it should be situated. Perhaps somewhere in Essex.'

'I'm not sure I agree with you there. Besides, if you leave it until then you will miss the opportunity of a lifetime. The land is available at a good price, but in a few years it will have become more expensive.'

'Even so,' Angela said, 'I couldn't recommend going ahead with a large purchase at this stage, I'm afraid. Personally, I'm not convinced that it would be a good move for our children.'

'Still against me, Angela?' he asked, a tiny nerve flicking at his temple. 'Tell me, why don't you like me?' He stared at her in frustration for a moment, then grabbed hold of her by the arms and brought her in close. Before she had time to protest, he was kissing her, kissing hungrily, passionately, and for a moment she felt her reserve melting and her lips softened beneath his, but then, suddenly, she felt a surge of revulsion and pushed him away.

'What the hell do you think you're doing?'

'Don't pretend you haven't felt it. It's been there from the first – I want you and I know you feel the same way about me. Why fight me, Angela? We could be a damned good team if you'd only try to see things my way.'

'I've given you no reason to treat me this way,' she said coldly. Perhaps she had found him attractive, but that kiss had told her all she needed to know. Henry Arnold wasn't the man for her. She didn't like him and she didn't want him to touch her. There was only one man Angela wanted. 'I'm sorry, Mr Arnold, but I think you should apologise – and then leave. I have no interest in a relationship with you, and I'd be grateful if we could keep matters on a strictly professional basis.' She tried to keep the tremor out of her voice. 'I shall give your proposal for St Saviour's the consideration it deserves.'

'In other words, you intend to turn it down flat,' he said, and there was an angry glint in his eyes now. 'By George, you're a damned cold fish!'

'What I am is none of your affair,' Angela said. 'Please leave now and don't call here again.'

'I'll get my way, see if I don't,' he said, and walked to the door, stopping to turn and deliver his parting shot: 'I could have helped you with your orphans, Angela. You'll be sorry you turned me down. If you want to have any hope of keeping your job when we move St Saviour's to Newmarket, you'd better not try to make trouble for me.'

'I haven't started yet,' Angela said coolly. 'But I intend to discover exactly what your little scheme is, Mr Arnold. And when I do, I shall inform the Board.'

'Oh, I do hope you won't,' he said in a soft voice that sent shivers down her spine. 'I should hate it if I were asked whether or not I felt you were right for the post of Administrator and I had to say I wasn't sure.'

'I think I've proved myself and my loyalty.'

'We could have been lovers, Angela,' he said in that soft voice of his and reached for her hand. She snatched it away from him and his eyes narrowed. His handsome face was marred by a look she could only describe as threatening. 'I should have liked to be more than a friend – but you've obviously made up your mind to oppose me. Believe me, I don't take kindly to enemies.'

Angela was silent. He stared at her for a moment, turned and left her standing in the hall. The door closed behind him with a sharp snap. Her mouth felt dry and her heart beat loudly in her chest. Why had he been threatening her? Why should it be so important that the Board approved the purchase of a piece of land for the future? What did Henry Arnold expect to get out of it? He would earn a small profit on the building of a new children's home, but that was surely not important to a man who made no secret of the fact that he was very wealthy?

There must be more to it. Angela felt the icy tingle at the nape of her neck. She'd been uneasy about Arnold from the start, but now she was utterly convinced that something underhand was going on.

She went back into the kitchen and finished drying the coffee cups, then paced up and down the room trying to get her thoughts in order. Desperate to talk to someone she could trust, she ran through the possible candidates: her father was on his way home, Sister

272

Beatrice was convalescing . . . which meant there was only one person she could turn to: Mark. She only hoped he would be at his apartment.

Picking up the receiver, she dialled his number and waited. It rang for several minutes and then, as she was about to replace it, Mark answered.

'Mark, I was afraid you were out . . .'

'Is something wrong, Angela? I was having a shower after my morning run.'

'I didn't mean to get you out of it, but I really need to talk – if you've got time to come round?'

'I have the rest of the day. I'll be there in half an hour. You can tell me what's on your mind and then we'll have lunch – if you'd like?'

'Yes,' Angela said and gave a shaky laugh. 'I'd love that, Mark. I'll get changed and be ready when you arrive.'

TWENTY-EIGHT

Alice hesitated outside the police station. A week had passed since she'd arranged to meet Jack at the zoo. She could never really have gone, of course, and in her heart she'd known what she had to do. Despite that, it had taken her a while to make herself come this far, and then she'd hovered outside, unsure whether she was doing the right thing – and yet what else could she do? She'd approached the door three times and then changed her mind, torn between doing what she believed was right and fear of what she might start if she went through with her decision to hand in that key.

'Can I help you?' a police constable asked, and with relief Alice realised that she knew him, because he'd been to St Saviour's to talk to Sister Beatrice.

'Constable Sallis?' He was a stalwart young man, solidly built but with a pleasant face. 'I used to work at St Saviour's . . .'

'You're Alice Cobb – or you were. Didn't I hear that you'd got married?'

'I'm Mrs Bob Manning now. My husband is in the military police.'

274

'Ah yes, I know of him. We sometimes have to work with the military police when there are important people in town. Is something bothering you?'

Alice made up her mind and thrust the envelope at him. 'I think there's something hidden here that you might be interested in,' she said. 'I don't want anything to do with . . . pinched stuff. I think you might be pleased if you open this locker, Constable Sallis.'

He took the envelope and saw the number of the box at the railway station written on the outside. Holding it in his hand without attempting to look inside, he asked, 'Where did you get this, Mrs Manning?'

'Someone I used to know sent it to me and asked me to fetch the stuff in that security box – but I don't want to; it ought to go back to the people it belongs to.'

'Did Jack Shaw give you this key?' he asked, and caught Alice's arm as she turned away. 'We know he's still alive, Mrs Manning. He's been seen in Southend – and recently in London.'

'It might have— Yes, it was,' Alice said, deciding she might as well go all the way. 'I think that stuff once belonged to some dangerous people, but where it came from before that I don't know. They've been following me around, and I think it's because of whatever's in that locker. Jack and Arthur Baggins stole it from them and they want it back. If they knew I had that key . . .' Alice shivered. 'Please, will you take it and do whatever needs doing?'

'Yes, I'll take it,' he said, looking serious. 'I believe you, Mrs Manning – but the inspector might want to talk to you about this.'

'Please, I don't want any trouble,' Alice begged. 'I'm

married now. I don't want anything to do with Jack or his gang.'

'I understand,' Constable Sallis said, his expression serious. 'You've done the right thing, Mrs Manning – but if the gang know you've handed in this key you could be in trouble. I suggest you take care to keep your doors and windows locked, and if you go out at night, make sure you don't walk home alone.'

'I'm no use to them if I haven't got the key,' Alice said, but his warning frightened her.

'If you think you're being followed, let us know. We'll keep an eye on you.'

'Yes, all right . . .' Alice turned and wheeled her pram away. She was glad she'd handed in that key but she hoped it wouldn't cause her trouble either with the police or the Lee gang.

Jack wouldn't keep on waiting for her to join him. She'd been tempted for a while, and she'd even got Susie ready, but it was as she was packing a bag with her daughter's stuff that she'd seen the little teddy bear Bob had bought for Susie. She'd broken down and wept, knowing that she couldn't leave her husband. Bob didn't deserve to be treated like that, and even though it had cost Alice, she'd stayed home and baked cakes instead of meeting Jack. By this time he would surely have given up on her and bought himself a passage on a ship to America. She certainly hoped so, because if he came looking for that stuff he would be very angry when Alice told him she'd given the key to the police.

Glancing over her shoulder, Alice started to walk home. The constable's warning had her worried. If only

Bob was around more – when he was there, she felt safe. Feeling nervous and lonely, Alice decided she'd go round to Nan's house later. She needed to talk to someone she could trust . . .

Alice heard the knock at her door and stared at it uncertainly. For a moment she was almost afraid to answer, fearing it might be one of the Lee gang.

'Who is it?' she called.

'It's me, Nan. Alice, are you all right?'

Nan's voice was reassuring and Alice opened the door, smiling with relief at the sight of her friend. 'Come in, Nan. I'm so glad you're here,' Alice said, standing aside to let her through. 'I just put the kettle on . . .'

'I could do with a cup of tea,' Nan said, then stared at her, eyes narrowing. 'You're shivering, Alice love. What's wrong?'

'Nothing, it's just . . . I felt a bit lonely,' Alice said, leading the way into the kitchen. 'Nothing important.'

'Now you're being untruthful,' Nan said. 'Whatever it is, Alice, you can tell me. I'm your friend. If you're in trouble, I'd like to help you.'

Somehow, Alice found herself pouring out her troubles. How Jack had sent her that key then come to see her, wanting her to fetch the stuff for him, asking her to run off with him.

'Surely you wouldn't think of leaving your husband, Alice? I like Bob. He's a good man and he loves you.'

Alice nodded. 'Bob is a better man than I deserve, Nan. It took me a while to realise what I've got, but I know it now. I'm very fond of him and I've no intention of leaving him for a rogue – that's why I handed the

277

key in. Constable Sallis told me to be extra careful for a while, not to go out on my own after dark. Now I'm frightened.'

'But these men don't know you had the key, Alice. If they've been trying to find Jack Shaw, they must think he has what belongs to them. You've no idea what's in that locker, you say?'

'No.' Alice took a deep breath. 'Thanks, Nan. You've made me feel a bit better. All the way home I kept wondering whether I'd done the right thing, giving the police that key.'

'Of course it was the right thing to do, Alice. Jack isn't worth a tenth of Bob. He's a thief and a liar and goodness knows what else. I know it's hard, but you have to try and forget about him.'

'Yes, I'm going to,' Alice said. 'What made you come round?'

'I wanted to make sure you're ready to start doing a few hours for us again. Jean has had a nasty cold and we've been a bit short-handed. I could do with you for a couple of hours every day, to tell you the truth.'

'I should like to, but it's finding someone to look after my Susie.'

'Nancy is very good with the younger ones,' Nan said. 'She will be leaving school this Christmas and I expect her to stay on at St Saviour's, helping out where she's needed until she's ready to move on. Sister Beatrice hasn't decided on her job yet, but she seems good with nursery-age children and I dare say she'll do a bit of this and a bit of that for a while. I think she might be willing to take charge of your baby for a few hours a couple of times a week, and if Michelle's mother has her there a couple of days, that would do nicely. Once your Susie is a bit older, she can play with the others in the mornings. With a home to run and a baby, I think a few hours in the morning would be all you'd really want.'

'If I could bring Susie with me, it would be perfect,' Alice said. 'Have you heard from Sister recently?'

'She sent me a postcard from Bournemouth. The boarding house is Church-run, I think she is quite enjoying her retreat, though she said there was a cold wind off the sea – "bracing" was the word she used. I'm sure it must be pleasant for her to have a bit of a break at the seaside; we Londoners seldom go further than Southend.'

'Bob's taking me to the seaside soon,' Alice said. 'He has leave coming up and he wants us to go visit his auntie – she helped bring him up when he was a boy and his mother was ill. She lives on the coast so we'll stay nearby and visit her, but have a few days for ourselves.'

'Good. It will be nice for you to get away.'

'Yes. It's our chance for a proper honeymoon. We didn't get one the first time, because I was expecting Susie . . .'

'You should make the most of it,' Nan said. 'When I got married there was a war on and we had only a few nights together . . .' She smiled at the memory. 'It was wonderful all the same. I kept hoping my Archie would come back to me and he did – until I lost him and my son to diphtheria . . .'

'That was sad for you, Nan,' Alice said, pouring her a second cup of tea. 'But you've still got your

279

memories, haven't you? No one can take those away from you.'

'No, they can't,' Nan agreed, smiling. 'That is perfectly true, Alice. We keep our memories – at least until we get old and senile . . .'

TWENTY-NINE

'Michelle, I wanted a word, if you have time?'

Michelle had paused on the steps of St Saviour's to pull up her coat collar. Although the weather was mild for November, the evening air was cold on her skin. She'd decided to walk home across the bridge, taking the road that followed the river; the money she'd save on her bus fare would help buy Freddie the new football boots he needed for school.

'Dr Kent . . . Richard,' she said and smiled. 'Yes, I have time. Was it something to do with the children?'

'It concerns Matty,' he said. 'Do you have a bus to catch? I could take you home if you wish?'

'I was going for a walk by the river – it's good to get a breath of air after work.'

'Yes, I'm sure it is,' he said. 'Your hair looks lovely. Have you had it cut again?'

'Yes, a bit shorter this time; it was getting long and this is easier for work. I'm not sure I like it brushed back off my face, but it doesn't take as long to wash and set in the mornings.'

'You have lovely hair,' he said, falling into step beside

her. 'I'll walk with you, Michelle, but we could go somewhere, take the bus. Perhaps we could have a drink in that pub by the river, it's a nice evening for it?'

'Why not? Yes, I'd like that, it'll make a change for me,' she said as they caught a bus and found seats near the back. Richard paid their fares and they smiled at each other, chatting easily as the bus negotiated the busy streets. It was a short walk to the pub once they left the bus. In summer there were tables outside and lights strung in the trees, but inside it was low-ceilinged and smelled strongly of spilled beer – and yet Michelle felt at home, far more than she had at that posh hotel they'd gone to in the country.

'You were going to tell me how Matty is?' she reminded Richard.

'Feeling pretty low, I'm told,' Richard said. 'They've given him several tests and he's been feeling very ill. He also misses his friends from St Saviour's. I couldn't advise taking any of the children to see him, but I wondered if you could visit . . . not as a member of staff, but as a friend. Perhaps you could take some comics or a few grapes?'

'Well yes, of course I will,' Michelle said. 'Have they told you what is wrong yet?'

'They've found a small growth on his spine, and they think that's what has been causing the fitting and the falls.'

'Does that mean it's cancer?' Michelle asked, upset at the idea.

'Not necessarily,' he said. 'They operated this morning to remove the growth, so we shall soon know. If it is malignant, he will need further treatment, but anything related to the spine is risky. It may just be benign tissue, in which case, now that they have cut it away, he should start to recover.'

'I do hope so,' she said, looking intently at him. 'But there's more, isn't there? What haven't you told me?'

'The surgery to remove the tumour may have damaged his spinal cord. It could have a lasting effect on mobility – his ability to walk . . .'

'You mean he could end up in a wheelchair?' She sipped her drink as she contemplated the awful outcome if the child suffered such damage.

'It is a possibility,' Richard said. 'A terrible prospect – but the surgeon didn't have much choice. If they hadn't removed the growth, Matty would have continued to suffer fits and severe discomfort – and if it was cancerous, he would've died anyway.'

'He's such an energetic child . . . it would be awful for him to be paralysed.'

'Let's hope that's not the case,' Richard said. He finished his drink. 'Well, I shan't keep you any longer. Perhaps we could go out again one day – somewhere a bit better than this?'

'Yes, when we both have time,' Michelle said vaguely. She wasn't sure she wanted to repeat the experience of that trip to the country, although she couldn't have said why. Richard Kent was a gentleman and generous with his money – but perhaps that was the problem. Michelle wasn't sure she wanted to go on with a relationship that seemed wrong for her. He was attractive and seemed interested in her, but he was hard to get to know, there seemed to be something amiss, something she couldn't quite put her finger on. 'Do you think I should put off visiting Matty for a little while, if he isn't feeling well?'

'It doesn't matter if he is unwell when you visit; he needs someone to make a fuss of him, care for him. He doesn't have anyone else to visit him and I'm a doctor. He needs someone he knows well – someone who can be more than simply a visitor to him . . .'

'I'll visit then,' Michelle said. 'I'd better get off. My mother will be expecting me home soon.'

'Yes . . .' he hesitated, then, 'I've been asked to help take a party of St Saviour's children to the British Museum this weekend. Mrs Morton said you might be going?'

'Well, yes, I have said I will,' Michelle agreed. 'So you're coming too?'

'It looks that way,' Richard said. 'I thought we might get a moment to ourselves afterwards, but I dare say the children will take up most of your time.'

'And yours,' Michelle replied. 'Don't imagine Angela will let you get away with simply being there. I expect you'll be on drinks duty or taking the boys to the toilets.'

'I dare say you're right.' Richard made a wry face. 'We shall have to find time for a day out ourselves again, Michelle.'

'That sounds lovely,' Michelle said politely, because she didn't like saying no. 'Not this weekend though. I promised Mum I would help her on Sunday. She wants new curtains in the front room and it takes two of us to hang them, though she has made them all by herself.'

'Perhaps the following week, or the week after,' he said vaguely. 'I promised my mother I'd take her visiting a week on Sunday – and I have surgery on the Saturday.'

'Oh well, some other time then,' Michelle said. She finished her shandy and set the glass down. 'That was very nice but I ought to get home now. My mother will worry if I'm late.'

'I'll see you on Saturday for the museum trip,' he said. 'Take care of yourself, Michelle – and don't forget about Matty, will you?'

Michelle promised and they parted company. It was as she turned to look back at Dr Kent that she saw Eric with some Army friends. They had taken the table Michelle had vacated and Eric was watching her, a disappointed expression in his eyes. She lifted her hand in greeting, hesitated and then walked on.

She knew he must have seen her with Richard Kent, which explained the way he'd looked at her, as if he felt she'd let him down, but she hadn't promised him anything. Michelle walked on, feeling vaguely guilty. She liked Eric. He was attractive in his quiet way with his sandy hair and greenish eyes, and she knew he was keen on her – at least, he'd claimed to be enough times, but she'd never led him to expect anything more than friendship, though she knew he was hoping for a lot more.

She liked Eric and she liked Richard – but she wasn't sure that she wanted to go steady with anyone . . . In her experience, getting to like someone too much could only lead to heartbreak.

'I'm going to visit Matty this evening and take him some comics and a few grapes, not that he will be able to eat them,' Michelle told Wendy the following day. 'If he's feeling sick all the time I think he will probably leave them – but I wanted him to feel that someone cares.'

'I've got the morning off tomorrow, so I'll go,' Wendy said. 'I'll take him a sherbet dip – he used to love those – and I'll buy him a puzzle book too.'

'That will please him . . .' Michelle hesitated, then, 'How do you feel about going out to the flicks when we both have a free evening? Paula will start the evening shifts next week.'

'I'd love to go on a Thursday, if that suits?'

'Great. I'll look forward to it.'

'I'll be sure to take my turn visiting Matty. It's awful having to go through that kind of treatment with no one to visit you. Timmy Bent was telling me about the time he was in the hospital and his mum could only come once or twice a week, because she wasn't well. He's so much happier now that he's at St Saviour's – and Billy has taken him under his wing. I saw Billy pushing his chair down to the park this afternoon. When I asked what he was doing, he said it was a special event for his school – a special sports day or something.'

'Oh well, as long as he doesn't tip him out of the chair – as he did Marion when her leg was still sore.'

'Yes, I heard about that, but Billy is a lot more sensible these days,' Wendy said. 'I'd best get on with the drinks and medicines now.'

'I'd better be off too. I'll have to change buses a couple of times to get to Great Ormond Street and I want to be there for the start of visiting hours.'

Michelle said goodbye to her colleague, collected her coat and went down the stairs. As she left St Saviour's, she saw Eric waiting for her. He was leaning against a wall, smoking, but he put the cigarette out as he saw her and came to greet her. His open and honest face looked uncertain, but it was hard to resist and Michelle found herself smiling.

'Hullo, Michelle, I thought I might catch you. I don't suppose you feel like coming out with me somewhere?'

'I'm visiting a small boy in hospital,' Michelle said. 'He has no family and doesn't get many visitors. He's recently had an operation so I think he will be feeling pretty rotten. If you want to come with me, I'll go for a drink afterwards, if you like?'

Eric's face lit up. ''Course I'll come. What's wrong with him?'

'He had a growth removed from his spine. They aren't sure whether it was malignant – and even if it was benign, he could have damage to his nervous system and might end up in a wheelchair.'

'Poor little blighter,' Eric said instantly. 'I've got a bar of chocolate in my pocket. I was going to give it to me sister's kids, but they can wait for next time. Is he allowed sweets?'

'I imagine so, if he can keep them down. We'll ask when we get there,' Michelle said. 'I think he might be pleased to see you. His dad was a soldier, killed in the war like so many others – and his mum died in an air raid; he doesn't have anyone of his own.'

'Rotten buggers, those Germans,' Eric said. 'If Hitler wasn't already dead I'd strangle the blighter with me bare hands.'

'Eric!' Michelle shook her head at him, but she couldn't help smiling. 'I think we did some pretty dreadful things at the end of the war ourselves . . . but then, war is horrible altogether. I don't know why you want to be a soldier now the war's over.'

'I thought it was a safe bet for a job,' Eric said, 'but I'm a trained mechanic. I've been thinking of giving up next year. I signed on until the end of '49 and then it's up to me whether I carry on.'

'Would you like to work in London?' Michelle asked, looking at him curiously.

'I'd work anywhere if it meant you would marry me, Michelle. Surely you know you only have to give me the nod and I'll do whatever you want.'

'Eric, I've never said— you know it's friends, nothing more.'

'I know you've been let down bad,' he said, catching her arm and swinging her round to face him. Her heart quickened as she saw the passion in his face. 'I swear I'd never let you down, Chelle. I love you. I'd be good to you, if you'd give me the chance.'

'Oh, Eric, you know I like you – and thanks for asking me, more than once!' Michelle said and smiled at him. 'Look, this is our bus coming. I know I can trust you – but don't push me and don't expect too much. I'm not sure what I want yet.'

'I'm patient, I'll wait,' Eric said, 'but I'd rather you tell me if I've got no chance. If there's another bloke . . . well, I'd rather you told me straight.'

She jumped on the bus and found two seats at the front. Eric came to sit beside her, and when the conductor churned out two tickets he paid the fare. Michelle sat in silence for a moment, then, 'You're a lovely bloke, Eric, and perhaps if we do get married it might work – but I'm not sure yet. There is someone else I like –

he's a doctor – but I can't be sure of my feelings about him either. I know it isn't fair, but I didn't think I'd ever get over what happened before – my heart was broken and I don't want that to go through that again; and I don't want to break your heart, Eric. I'm not that sort of girl. I'll have to be sure . . . you said you wanted me to tell you straight.'

'Look, I've got a year before I can leave the Army,' Eric said. 'Take your time, love. I saw you with him so I've told you how I feel; maybe if he's a doctor you'd be better off with a man like that – but I want you to know that I love you. I'll always be around, whenever you need me.'

'Thank you, Eric,' Michelle said, finding that she meant it. She smiled at him again. 'I appreciate you coming with me to visit Matty. I think he liked Sally best of all the carers and nurses – she was the one who looked after him before he was sick. The carers are closer to the children sometimes, because they stand in for a mother with those who need it, but I can't bear to think of him going through so much and no one there to comfort him – Sally is doing her nursing training, so she won't have much time for visiting anyone.'

'I've got a few days' leave,' Eric said. 'I'll ask if it's all right for me to visit – and I'll go in as often as they let me while I'm home. But we'll have to see if he likes me first . . .'

Michelle could tell that Eric would make a great father. She felt warmed as she remembered the previous evening and their visit to Matty. He'd been in a small ward with two other children, both of whom had mothers and fathers visiting. Matty's face had lit up when he saw them come in and realised that he had visitors too. He was delighted with his gifts, especially the chocolate, and he'd sucked a tiny piece. Apparently, he'd been sick earlier but was feeling better at the moment, though he'd been told he had to lay straight and not move too much, and he was finding that irksome.

Eric had got on with him instantly. Matty had wanted to know what regiment he was in and whether he'd been in the war. Eric told him that he'd joined up towards the end and had been one of the invading forces that drove through Germany when the enemy was retreating.

'Did yer give them what for?' Matty asked eagerly. 'Me dad were killed at Dunkirk. One of the boats took him off, but he was wounded bad and me ma said he died in the 'ospital in Portsmouth.' Tears gathered in Matty's eyes. 'Me ma weren't never the same after Dad died – and then she went too, in a bombing raid.'

'I'm sorry about your dad and your mum, Matty,' Eric said. 'A lot of our brave soldiers were killed that day at Dunkirk.'

'I'm goin' ter be a soldier one day,' Matty said, and then his face clouded. 'If they ever let me out of this bloomin' place.'

'You'll come back to us when you're better, Matty,' Michelle told him. 'It won't be for ever, I promise you.'

'Will you come and visit me again?' Matty was looking at Eric as he spoke. 'The other kids have families, but I've got no one.'

'No uncles or aunts?' Eric asked, and the boy shook his head. 'Well, then, why don't I be your uncle? I can visit you here, bring you things – and when you're well again, I'll still visit you at St Saviour's. When I'm home on leave, we can go to the zoo – or to watch the guard changing at Buckingham Palace.'

'Would you take me there when I'm better?' Matty's face lit up. 'My dad said only the best soldiers get to be the guards at the palace.'

'Well, they're good at drilling and marching,' Eric said. 'Your dad was a real soldier. He went to war to defend his country, Matty. You can't get braver or better than that.'

'Dad was going to get a medal, but it never arrived – at least, the house was bombed and me ma . . .' Tears trickled down his cheeks.

'I tell you what, I bet they don't know where to send that medal,' Eric said. 'I'll ask someone about it. If your dad won a medal, it should be yours, Matty. I'm going to make sure you get it.'

Once again, Matty's face lit up like a candle. He talked to Eric most of the time and when the ward sister arrived and told them it was time to go, Matty caught hold of Eric's sleeve.

'You will come again?'

'Cross me heart and hope to die if I tell a lie,' Eric said and grinned. 'You won't get rid of me now, mate – and when I'm away I'll write to you and you can write back. Promise now! I want proper letters telling me what you're up to, Matty.'

Matty had let him go then. His eyes followed them down the ward and he waved when Eric turned and gave him the thumbs up. Outside the ward, one of the nurses spoke to them.

'You've cheered him up a great deal. The sick children in our wards do need parental visits to help them through what is a dreadful experience for anyone.'

'I'm not a relation,' Eric said. 'But I've taken to Matty and I should like to visit while I'm on leave, and to bring him things. What can he have?'

'We make no restrictions on what our children can have, but he may not be able to eat certain foods if he's having treatment. If you can bring some lemonade for him, please do. Lemonade does help them when they are feeling sick. Most of the parents bring that – and perhaps an ice lolly. It depends on what sort of treatment he is going to need. He was a bit better tonight; it may not always be that way.'

'Was the growth malignant then?' Michelle asked. 'Will he have to have treatment for cancer?'

'We expect the results tomorrow,' the nurse told them. 'I was told that it looked as if he may have been lucky – but there is still the other question . . .'

'Of whether or not he will be able to walk again.' Michelle bit her lip. 'He's going to be devastated if he can't; he's been such an active child.'

'Well, I'm sure the doctors have done their best.'

'I'm sure they have,' Eric said. 'Don't worry, Nurse. We'll be visiting – if you're happy for me to visit. I'd like to be his friend.'

'Well, if you and your girlfriend visit, I'm sure that will be fine – and yes, I am certain it will do him good to know he has a friend he can rely on.'

'Thank you, Nurse. I'll be in again tomorrow . . .'

'That was very nice of you, Eric,' Michelle said as

they walked to the bus stop. It had turned much cooler now and she shivered. 'Matty really took to you.'

'He's a brave lad,' Eric said. 'I liked him – and I'm going to make sure he gets his dad's medal.'

'You're taking on a commitment for life,' Michelle said. 'Once you become his adopted uncle, as you suggested, he will expect you to keep it up.'

'Well, why not?' Eric grinned confidently. 'I like kids. I want plenty of my own – and I dare say there would always be room for another nephew round my house.'

Michelle smiled and nodded. She'd liked the way Eric talked to the boy – not as a soldier who was doing a favour to a sick child, but as a favourite uncle or a big brother might. Matty had clung to his every word and she'd seen the way his eyes lit up when Eric made him promise to write to him when he was away.

It was what all their kids needed at St Saviour's: someone to cling to when things were bad, and someone to have fun with when they were good. Without love, life could be pretty bleak, Michelle realised. She glanced at her companion sideways, and then hugged his arm as they walked briskly to keep warm.

She liked it that Eric had given hope to a child who had so little to anticipate. If Matty had his father's medal, it might give him something to look up to – and that could only help him to endure whatever happened to him . . .

THIRTY

Hearing a loud cry from the kitchen next morning, Michelle hurried downstairs. Her mother was holding an opened letter in her hand and looking stunned.

'What is it – is it bad news about Dad's tests?'

'No, he had the all clear from Dr Kent yesterday – didn't the doctor tell you? I was sure you'd see him at work, and you were so late in last night I didn't get a chance to tell you . . .'

'No; the doctor would tell you and Dad first – so what's wrong?'

'It's from Mrs Morton – she's written to tell us that your father has been given the job as caretaker. It seems that there were three who applied for the job, but at the interviews, they considered your father by far the best candidate. Well, that's a feather in his cap and no mistake!'

'Oh, Mum,' Michelle cried and hugged her. 'We hadn't heard anything and I thought someone else must have got it – but this is wonderful.'

'Yes, it is,' her mother said, but still looked slightly stunned. 'To tell you the truth, I never expected it when you told me he'd got that interview, and he never said a word when he came home. I thought it was no good. It looks as if our luck has turned.'

'Yes, particularly if the council picks us for a new flat,' Michelle said. 'I don't mind moving out into the suburbs if it means we get a new house.'

'I've given up on that.' Mrs Morris sat down at the table and looked about her. 'I'm not sure I'd want to move; this has been our home since we married.'

'But a new council flat would be better, and there's a couple empty in that block they built in Bethnal Green.' Michelle leant over to kiss her on the cheek. 'I may be late home again this evening, Mum.'

'Going to visit that sick child again – or are you going out with Eric? He's a decent lad, Michelle. Why don't you bring him home for tea one day, love?'

'I'm not sure how long a leave he has,' Michelle prevaricated. 'Besides, he's only a friend, Mum.'

'That's what you always say.' Her mother shook her head. 'It's time you thought of settling down, Michelle. I want some grandchildren before I get too old to enjoy them!'

'Mum, you've got years left yet! And so have I.'

'Yes, but if you're not careful they will slip away and you won't know what's happened,' Mrs Morris said. 'Please go and thank Mrs Morton for me, Michelle. It was ever so good of her to put a word in for us.'

'Dad must have impressed the Board,' Michelle said. 'He got the job on merit, Mum, and don't you forget it – but I shall thank her.'

'You'd best get off then. You don't want to be late for work – and don't forget to ask that nice young Eric of yours for tea one day.'

Michelle was thoughtful as she left the house and then ran to catch her bus as it pulled up at the stop. Perhaps her mother was right – perhaps it was time she started to think about the future . . .

Angela was making notes on the campaign she intended to hold for St Saviour's before Christmas. The Board had told her she could spend a certain amount on advertising and she'd made a heading on her page:

CHRISTMAS ORPHANS' CAMPAIGN

Flag Day or collecting envelopes? How could we distribute the envelopes countrywide? Picture of orphans in the paper or . . .

As yet she hadn't got much further. She was contemplating something different, perhaps a traditional Christmas story the children could act out, with a few carols at the end, with tickets on sale to their supporters or even the general public. Father Joseph would help with the play, and she could ask Nan and the carers to organise teas and perhaps a raffle – or perhaps that would be better at some other function. Maybe she could hold a Tombola evening or a themed fête – or would that clash with the church's own Christmas functions?

Her pen was poised over the paper when the telephone rang. She reached for it absent-mindedly, 'Yes, Angela Morton here . . .'

'Angela, this is Mark. I have a couple of tickets for the ballet this Friday evening. It's *Swan Lake* and I wondered if you would like to come?'

'I should love to, Mark. I really enjoy that particular ballet,' she said. 'I've been making notes about Christmas. I know it's only November, but time slips away and I've decided to put on a nativity play before the carols and the party we spoke about. I've also managed to secure a good discount on tickets for the Christmas pantomime this year – it's *Mother Goose* . . .'

'For all the children, as we discussed?'

'Yes, and six adults – though we'll have to pay full price for our tickets.'

'Well, that's pretty good I think,' Mark said. 'I'll look forward to the ballet then, Angela. We'll have supper afterwards.'

'Yes, that sounds wonderful.'

'Oh, and I thought you'd like to know that your donation was well received and everyone is looking forward to having you on the Board – a fresh eye and all that . . .'

'Oh, good! I did wonder if they'd think I was presumptuous.'

'Not at all. The Bishop told me it was time we had someone of your calibre on board. I'll see you soon.'

Angela was smiling as she replaced the receiver. She looked down at her list and wrote a few words and then picked up the receiver again. It was best to get the church hall booked, and then she must have a word with Muriel about Christmas supplies for the kitchen . . .

A knock at the door made her look up. Michelle stood in the doorway, beaming with delight.

'I take it you got the letter?' Angela asked. 'I hope your father was pleased.'

297

'My parents are both over the moon,' Michelle said. 'We can't thank you enough, Angela.'

'I didn't do much, apart from give my recommendation. I thought he was by far the best candidate of all the applicants we had, and it seems the Board agreed with me.'

'Well, he wouldn't have dared to apply if you hadn't given your blessing first, so we're grateful to you,' Michelle said. 'I'm on duty in a few minutes, so I'd best be off. I don't want to keep Wendy waiting . . .'

'No, that wouldn't be fair,' Angela said. 'She told me she's going to pop in and see Matty today. You haven't heard the verdict yet, I suppose. '

'Not yet. Last night the nurse said they should have the results today, so maybe Wendy will have some news for us later and I'll be visiting myself again soon, to see how he is. We're trying to make sure he has at least one visitor every day.'

'Yes, you must,' Angela agreed. 'And let me know how he is getting on please . . . oh, are you still coming on the British Museum outing this weekend?'

'Yes, I wouldn't let you down,' Michelle said. 'We're still a bit short-staffed here, though, aren't we?'

'Yes, we are, which is why I have to drag anyone I can in on these trips,' Angela said, her eyes twinkling naughtily. 'I'm afraid Dr Kent got caught in my net this time, but he was very good about it – and I think a visit to the museum is more in his line than the zoo, don't you?'

'Yes, I suppose it is,' Michelle said. 'Well, you can count on me to be there on Saturday – and thanks again for helping my dad.'

As the door closed behind her, Angela's telephone shrilled. She reached to answer it, the smile leaving her face as she heard the voice of Miss Ruth Sampson.

'Ah, Mrs Morton, I'm glad I caught you.'

'What can I do for you?'

'Well, it's a bit awkward, actually . . . you see, we've had an inquiry about the May twins.'

'What sort of inquiry? I thought the matter was settled and you'd agreed that they should both stay here?'

'Yes – for the time being, at least. Miss Jane May is still convalescing and will not be able to have them, – but it appears there is another aunt—'

'The girls only mentioned one aunt.'

'Their father had only the one sister – but this inquiry came from France. I wasn't aware that their mother was French, were you?' Angela asked.

'No, I had no idea . . .'

'Sarah sings her own version of what I think is a French lullaby, but when I asked their aunt she refused to be drawn on the subject. I don't think the children know of any French relatives.'

'Nor did we, but Mr Yarwood made some inquiries and followed up the information on Mrs May's marriage lines. He got in touch with a lawyer in her own town and they were able to trace her family – or her sister, because the parents are dead. Apparently, he learnt to speak and write excellent French during the war. I thought he might have been in touch with you?'

'Good gracious, no he hasn't. I knew Mr Yarwood said he liked puzzles, but I didn't realise he'd gone to all that trouble.' Angela felt a bit annoyed, because the last thing she'd expected was for a French aunt to start claiming the twins. 'So is the aunt interested in the twins – and who is she?'

'Apparently, she is the mother's sister, a Madame Bernard. Her letter says that she has been searching for her sister since the war ended. The children's mother left France some years ago after an argument with her father, who is now dead; she sent a letter home to say she was married, and then another letter to say she was expecting a child, but then nothing more . . .'

Angela took a deep breath. 'What does their aunt want? Is she asking to take the children?'

'For the moment she simply wants to meet them. She will be in England at the end of the month. Perhaps one of your nurses could tell the children about their French aunt – get them used to the idea? I don't know what Madame Bernard intends, but she may have the right to take them from the home – if she proves a proper sort of person, of course, and she is actually their aunt.'

'Yes, I see.' Angela thanked her for letting them know and replaced the receiver, her heart sinking. She'd thought the matter of the May twins was settled, but now it looked as though the girls' ordeal was far from over . . .

THIRTY-ONE

'It was wonderful,' Billy told Mary Ellen when he saw her that evening after the group of children who had joined the athletics club returned to the home. 'We did running on the new cinder track, and the long jump – and there were men doing the pole vault – like they did at the Olympics!'

'What's the pole vault?' she asked, listening in fascination as he described the event where the men ran up and pushed themselves high in the air with the aid of a pole, to seemingly fly over a high bar.

'It was so exciting. An American called Guinn Smith won it at the Olympics; I told you then, but you've forgotten. I'm going to practise all the time, Mary Ellen, and one day I'll be in the Olympics.'

'You'll be a great runner – you're always running.'

'Yeah, I could run faster than any of them at the track tonight.'

'Did our runners win anything in the Olympics?'

'Nah. We came second and third in some things,' Billy said excitedly. 'I'm goin' to win a gold medal runnin' for England one day. I think I shall go for the sprints – the one hundred or two hundred yards.'

'It's a pity you couldn't have run this year, Billy,' Mary Ellen said and offered him half her sherbet dip. 'We might have got a medal then, 'cos you're better than any of them.'

'Yeah, I'm the best in all the school championships!' Billy grinned cockily. 'You wait until I get going, Mary Ellen. I'll show them all. Now Miss Angela has arranged for me to join that athletics club, I'll be able to train proper.'

'I wish I could run fast like you, Billy.'

'Father Joe is goin' to take some of us to the swimming baths,' Billy said. 'He says we ought to learn while we're young. I've got me name down and I reckon you could come too if you wanted – Tilly and Jean will be there. Jean's good at swimming.'

'I think I should like it, but I haven't got a costume to wear.'

'Father Joe says we can borrow some at the pool until we get our own. I think it would be fun.'

She smiled at him. 'I'll ask if I can come too. I'd like to learn to swim – it would be like going to the seaside. I've never been, but I should like to, shouldn't you?'

'I've never been either,' Billy said, 'but one day I'll take you, Mary Ellen. We'll go on holiday together when we get married.'

'Yes, let's!' Mary Ellen said. 'We'd better go; it's almost time for supper and Jean is on duty. She doesn't like it if we're late. Besides, Father Joe is comin' later and he's going to tell us about the Christmas play. I want to see who he chooses to be Mary.'

302

'If you're Mary, I'll be Joseph,' Billy said. 'I reckon we'd be good as them.'

'I think Samantha would be better as Mary,' Mary Ellen said. 'But I want to be there and see who gets chosen, so I don't want to be late . . .'

'No, we mustn't be late or we'll lose stars, and we're saving up for another trip to the zoo so that Timmy can come with us. I'm getting good at pushing his chair now and I bet Miss Angela will let him come next time.'

'I'm glad I'm not going to the museum tomorrow,' Mary Ellen said. 'Michelle is going, and so is Dr Kent, but I reckon all that old stuff must be boring, don't you?'

'I'd rather go to the zoo or the waxworks – but the sea would be better than anywhere. We'll definitely go there when we're older, Mary Ellen – you wait and see if I don't take you as soon as I start work!'

'I warned you that you would be on drinks duty,' Michelle said and laughed as Richard handed round the glasses of squash and mugs of cocoa. They had spent the morning looking round the museum and were now in a café. The party of children from St Saviour's had filled most of the tables and Richard had taken on the duty of fetching the drinks while they waited for the meal to be prepared. 'How does it feel to be a stand-in father for this lot?'

'Not quite up my street,' Richard grimaced as he made his way back for another load of drinks. 'Can I bring some tea for you, Michelle?'

'Yes, please,' she said. 'What are you eating, Richard? I'm having sausages and chips like most of the children.'

He pulled a face. 'I think I'll stick to a cup of tea and a biscuit. I'm not too keen on these places for food, though it looks clean enough.'

'You're too fussy,' Michelle said, and saw him wince with distaste as a waitress passed him carrying a tray loaded with plates of sausage, chips and beans.

Richard might turn his nose up at the simple fare, but so far as Michelle was concerned it was a treat to be able to order sausage and chips again. She sat down with the children, keeping order as they grabbed for the brown and tomato sauces on offer. For years sausages had been in short supply, and if you could get them they were mostly breadcrumbs, but as soon as she bit into hers Michelle knew it was a proper banger with a lot of meat, and very tasty.

'You don't know what you're missing,' she told Richard as she smeared HP sauce on her chips and ate them. 'It is ages since I had a sausage as good as this.'

'I dare say,' he said, an odd smile playing on his lips as she continued to eat her meal with as much enjoyment as the children. 'You would be an example to your children, Michelle. I think you will make a good mother.'

'Doesn't every woman who gives birth?'

'You know that isn't true,' Richard said. 'Surely you've seen enough neglect to know that too many children are ill-treated?'

'It isn't always the mother's fault,' Michelle said. 'Most women love their kids and the neglect comes from poverty and illness.'

'As I said, I think you would be a good mother from what I've seen this morning.'

'Would you be a good father, Richard?'

'I'm not sure I would. Oh, I'd provide for them properly, and I suppose that's most of it, isn't it? A mother loves and a father provides.'

Michelle wasn't sure that she agreed. 'Some men are wonderful with kids. Eric is like that – he loves them. He met me from work one night and I took him along to the hospital. Matty took to him instantly because he's a soldier, and Eric has promised to keep in touch, even when he's back at his base. We've been visiting regularly since . . .'

'This Eric is a friend of yours? You must trust him if you took him to the hospital.'

'Yes, he's a good friend, and I do trust him. He was brilliant with Matty the other evening. We've been visiting regularly and we were both there when they told Matty he would be in a wheelchair for a while. They'd waited to tell him until we visited, naturally . . .' Thankfully, tests had revealed that the growth was not malignant, but Matty's spine had suffered some trauma during surgery and the doctors were not sure whether he would walk properly again. The child's eyes had brimmed with tears until Eric took his hand and told him they could still do lots of things together, even if the worst happened.

'Doctor says your nerves may right themselves, lad – so there's no sense in cryin', is there? We'll sort you out whatever happens, don't you worry,' he'd promised, giving Matty's hand a squeeze. And remarkably Matty had grinned and said he bet he could still beat Eric in a game of table tennis in a wheelchair. Even though his bottom lip wobbled a bit, he was being brave because he wanted Eric to be proud of him.

'He stopped crying when Eric talked to him and they started teasing each other.'

'I see . . .' Richard looked thoughtful. 'You know this Eric well?'

'He's Alice's cousin – she's my best friend – and he'll make a wonderful father one day. I think Matty has already adopted him. He told Eric that his father was supposed to get a medal from the war but it never came to him. Eric is going to make sure he gets it.'

'You sound as if you approve of Eric. What did you say he was – a soldier?'

Was Richard criticising her choice of friends? Michelle looked at him as he sipped his tea and pushed it away. While it wasn't the best tea she'd ever drunk, it certainly wasn't the worst and she drained her own cup. Looking round at the other carers and Angela, she saw they were all joining in the fun, ordering ice cream or jelly and looking at the souvenirs they'd bought from the museum that morning.

Nan's friend Eddie was explaining something to one of the boys about the dinosaur remains they'd seen earlier. Michelle found herself comparing his easy manner with Richard's aloofness. Nan's friend was a lovely man, kind and generous, though he was forever dropping things and seemed very absentminded at times. He was certainly doing his share when it came to looking after the children though. It was clear he was taking a genuine interest in them, enjoying their company. Richard merely looked uncomfortable, as if he wished he were elsewhere.

If only it had been Eric who'd come on this trip rather than Richard. Dr Kent was an attractive man and a good doctor, but she had begun to see quite clearly that he wasn't for her. Michelle was an East End girl through and through; she'd done her training and she had a good education, but she belonged here, among her own class – and Richard didn't. She felt far more comfortable with Eric.

That discovery made, Michelle suddenly felt as if a weight had been lifted. She enthusiastically joined in a game of I-Spy that had started at the table, and was soon laughing with the rest of them. When she noticed that Richard had left the table and was at the counter paying for a packet of cigarettes, it didn't bother her. He took the cigarettes outside and lit one, clearly bored with the whole affair.

Michelle put him out of her mind. Richard might be a snob and above enjoying himself with the kids, but Michelle wasn't and neither was Nan's Eddie, who was fetching more drinks. Remembering that Eric had told her he would meet her at the hospital that evening, Michelle smiled. For a while she hadn't been sure which of the two men she liked best, but now she knew.

'You look lovely,' Eric said when she met him outside Great Ormond Street Hospital later that evening. 'I've only got a couple of nights of my leave left – why don't I take you for a meal somewhere after we've been in to see Matty?'

'Yes, I'd like that,' Michelle said and smiled at him. 'I don't want much to eat – we had bangers and chips with the kids after the museum visit – but I'd like to have a drink somewhere and then perhaps go for a nice walk, if you're not in hurry?'

'Suits me. I'll buy a packet of fish and chips, and you

can pick at them if you like . . . then we'll see where our fancy takes us.'

'Lovely,' Michelle said and followed him into the hospital. She couldn't help wanting to smile at him, and felt happier than she could remember for ages. Suddenly life seemed so much better. 'Has anyone ever told you that you're a nice feller, Eric?'

He grinned at her and Michelle's heart skipped a beat as she saw the warmth in his eyes. 'Might 'ave done, one or two,' he said. 'But I told yer – I'm savin' meself for me best girl.'

'Am I your best girl, Eric?' Michelle asked, lifting her eyebrows at him.

'You know you are,' he said. 'Come on, we'd better see how the lad is – he'll be waitin' for us to keep our promise. I've got him that football book I told him I'd bring.'

'You'll spoil him,' Michelle said, but she hugged his arm.

'Nah, the boy needs a bit of love,' Eric said. 'I like to see him smile. Kids and family is what it's all about – isn't it?'

'Yes,' Michelle agreed. 'I reckon it is.'

'I really liked your Eric,' Michelle's mother said to her over breakfast on Monday morning. 'He'll have gone back to his base today, I suppose?'

'Yes, last night was the end of his long leave, but he often gets a half-day. Sometimes he comes home and sometimes he stops on the base instead.'

'You want to let him know if you like him, Michelle. He won't wait around for ever – but he seems to like you and you could do a lot worse, my girl.'

Michelle stopped in the middle of washing one of her mother's best china cups. 'Don't push me, Mum. I'm almost sure, but I haven't told him yet.'

'Well, you should,' her mother. 'If you're thinking of your dad and me, don't. We'll be all right now he's got this steady job. Once the boys have left school I could take a few hours' work, if I felt like it.'

'I can't see Dad agreeing to that,' Michelle told her. 'He's old-fashioned and doesn't think wives should go out to work. Eric is different. He knows I'd want to work if we married, at least until I had children, and even then I'd like to do a few hours if I could.'

'You'd be surprised about your dad,' her mother said. 'He wouldn't stop me doing a few hours, as long as it wasn't hard manual work and I was happy, but I'd only do something like cooking for the kids at the preparatory school. I know some of the dinner ladies there and they used to be friends of mine before I met your dad.'

Michelle looked at her mother in surprise. She'd never thought of her mother as having a life other than as a wife and mother, but of course she'd been young and single once. Both Michelle's parents had gone without treats to put her through nursing college and she'd always felt grateful for the sacrifices they'd made and wanted to contribute to the family budget. Now her mother was telling her that she should get married and Michelle was aware that she wanted a family of her own. For too long she'd thought she couldn't trust men, but now she was beginning to think that perhaps there was one she could trust not to let her down . . .

THIRTY-TWO

'No, don't want to see her!' Samantha said, setting her bottom lip stubbornly. She was clinging to Sarah's hand and looking at Wendy defiantly. 'Sarah and me, we want to stay here. You promised she wouldn't make us go away again . . .'

'It isn't your Aunt Jane who is coming to see you next week,' Wendy said, her throat tight with emotion as she saw the fear and tension in the girls' faces. She'd become so fond of them and it would break her heart if the twins were sent to live with someone who would mistreat them and perhaps put Sarah in a home for retarded children. 'It's your mummy's sister from France.'

'Ma's sister?' Samantha looked at her blankly. 'Pa never mentioned her having a sister. Please don't let them send us away again, Nurse Wendy.'

'Your auntie is coming a long way to see you,' Wendy said. Although it broke her heart to see Samantha upset, she knew that if the aunt was suitable nothing she or even Angela could do would prevent the authorities from giving the children into her care. 'Let's wait and

310

see what happens, shall we? Your mummy was lovely – didn't your father tell you that?'

Samantha nodded warily. 'She died when Sarah was born. Pa hated her because of it, but it wasn't Sarah's fault.'

'How could anyone hate Sarah?' Wendy said and shook her head. The thought of the cruelty they'd endured made her want to run away with them to keep them safe, but she knew it wouldn't help them in the end. 'You don't have to worry about going away yet awhile, Samantha. Your aunt is going to visit so that you can get to know her first. You never know – you might like her.'

It was the only comfort she could give, but Wendy could see by the expression in Samantha's eyes that she wasn't convinced.

'You'd better take Sarah down to Nancy,' she said, resisting the urge to hug them and promise she would never let them go. Wendy didn't have a home of her own or a family, and she certainly couldn't afford to support two children – especially if she broke all the rules and ran off with the twins. Despite all the love inside her, she knew it would be foolish to promise something she couldn't give, but as she watched the twins walk away with their heads down, her heart felt as if it were splitting in two.

As she turned back to the wards and started to make beds and take the drinks round to her patients, Wendy made up her mind to speak to Angela, asking her to be vigilant and not let the twins go to this aunt unless she was kind. Surely even that Miss Sampson wouldn't risk

311

letting the twins suffer again as they had at the hands of their father and then his sister . . .

'It's so unfair!' Wendy had waited until the end of her shift before going to Angela's office, but her anger hadn't abated. 'You should have seen Samantha's face when I told her that her aunt was coming next week. Poor mite's terrified they'll be taken away from us and end up separated from each other again. They're happy here and they want to stay – why doesn't anyone ask the children what they want?'

'I agree that it seems unfair,' Angela said. 'And I wish I could do more, but I've spoken with Miss Sampson on three occasions now and she seems to think the late Mrs May's sister is a good person who will give the children a better life than they have here. Madame Bernard and her husband live on a farm in France. Apparently, she is unable to have children of her own, and she is very keen to give her sister's children a home.'

'Oh . . .' Wendy faltered and looked at her uncertainly. 'I suppose . . . as long as she isn't unkind to them . . .'

'She'll be here next weekend and she wants to take them to the country for two days, to try to get to know them. All her credentials have been checked – so I don't really see how we can prevent her.'

'Supposing she tries to leave the country with them?'

'I don't believe she would do that . . . but perhaps I can arrange it so that you would go with them for the weekend?' Angela looked thoughtful. 'If I explained what happened before, tell her that they are nervous of strangers . . . I don't know whether I'll be able to persuade her to agree, but assuming I can, would you be happy to go with them?'

'Oh yes, I'd love to!' Wendy said. 'I'm off next weekend, so you won't have to change the rota.'

'Well then, I shall speak to Madame Bernard when she arrives and let you know what she has to say.'

Wendy smiled, thanked her and left. Angela, too, felt a glimmer of hope; the twins' fate had been preying on her mind ever since Miss Sampson had told her about Mme Bernard's visit. If Wendy came back from the weekend visit satisfied that the girls' aunt would give them a good home, it would be one less thing to worry about.

With Sister Beatrice unlikely to return from convalescence much before Christmas, Angela was still working all hours. At least now she had all the clerical work under control, and on the whole she was happy with the way things were going. The staffing levels bothered her, though. The nurse she'd engaged to help out until Sister Beatrice returned had let them down at the last minute. Since then she'd interviewed several nurses, but she'd yet to find one who was suitable for this work. If they were hit by winter flu epidemic, she dreaded to think how they would cope . . .

'If they try to part us again, we're going to run away,' Samantha told her twin that evening as they were getting washed to go to bed. 'Our mother's sister is coming to visit from France. I reckon if we're not here, she'll go back home and they will let us stay at St Saviour's.'

Sarah looked at her solemnly and sucked her thumb. 'Sarah not want to run away,' she said. 'Sarah like it here with Nurse Wendy. Nurse Wendy kind. Sarah love Nurse Wendy.'

'Yes, I know. I like Nurse Wendy too,' Samantha said. 'But don't you see? They might make us go with her – Ma's sister.'

Sarah started to sing the lullaby she always sang when she needed comfort. Samantha sighed and blinked away her tears. She loved her twin dearly, but Sarah could be stubborn and she didn't want to leave St Saviour's. Samantha knew it would be difficult to make her understand that they might have to run away and hide so that they couldn't be forced to go with this aunt.

Samantha turned away, fighting her tears and her fear. She didn't want to leave this place where they were better fed than they had ever been and it was warm and safe. Besides, she wanted to be here at Christmas and take part in all the lovely things Miss Angela had planned. It wasn't fair that people could decide that they belonged with someone they didn't know. Why didn't anyone ever ask them what they wanted? Tears stung her eyes; it didn't matter what Nurse Wendy or Miss Angela said – nobody really cared how they felt. If they did, they wouldn't let them go.

'Busy day?' Mark asked when he arrived at Angela's that evening. 'I hope you're not too tired to go out?'

'No, really, not at all,' Angela shrugged off the suggestion even though it had been an exhausting day. 'I'm looking forward to this evening. I could do with a good laugh and Bing Crosby and Bob Hope will be just the tonic I need.'

'Having problems at work?' Mark asked, offering the

314

bottle of wine he'd brought. 'I believe this is the one you like?'

'Yes, very much so, thank you. I already have one cooling in the fridge – perhaps you'd open it for me while I fetch my bag and coat.'

'Of course,' Mark followed her to the kitchen and dealt with the wine while she went into the bedroom to fetch her bag and velvet evening coat. He handed her a glass as she reappeared. 'So how about you tell me what's troubling you?'

'It's the May twins again. I've heard from their aunt and she is definitely coming this weekend. She hopes to take them to the country for a couple of days. Wendy was going to go with them, but we've got several children sick at the moment and I don't think she will be able to leave St Saviour's.'

'Well, insist that the first meeting takes place at the home and postpone any visits out of St Saviour's for a while. I think you have the right to do that much, Angela.'

'Yes, I think I must after that fiasco with Miss Jane May.'

She took a sip of her wine. 'I shouldn't get so upset, but Wendy is distressed over it and I've been trying to reassure her, even though I know there isn't much we can do if Children's Welfare decide the aunt can take them.'

'Well, you've done all you can for the time being. Tonight you must relax and think about having fun,' he urged. 'You look beautiful, Angela.'

'Thank you.' Angela smiled. 'I suppose I worry about them too much. I just don't want them to be hurt again.'

'That's something we shall face when we get there,' Mark said. He hesitated, then, 'I've done some digging on Henry Arnold, as you suggested . . .'

'What have you discovered?'

'Nothing remotely helpful as regards discrediting him, I'm afraid.'

'Oh, so it looks as if the Board will need to decide if they like his ideas.'

'I think so far they're evenly split. It has always been the intention of some of my colleagues to fund a home in the country, Angela. If I'm honest, I'm inclined to agree with them – the fresh air and the availability of open spaces to run about in is obviously advantageous. That said, I can see why you and Sister Beatrice are in opposition.'

'She will resist with everything she has,' Angela said, 'and so shall I. Right now, we're needed where we are. It's the wrong time, Mark. Why is Henry Arnold in such a hurry to push this through? He's acting as if it has to be now, and this piece of land he's found is the only one that will do – doesn't that seem odd to you?'

'The land is certainly being offered to us at a bargain price,' Mark said. 'All the same, I cannot see why we can't wait a few years . . . In that regard, I agree with you and Sister Beatrice.'

'I read the notes, and as you know, the Board put his suggestion forward for consideration last time they met, and I've prepared a case against an immediate move, which I intend to present at the next meeting – but I'm sure Henry Arnold will have prepared one that looks irresistible.'

'I've no doubt you're right. And like you, I wonder

why he's so determined to have his way.' Mark finished his wine. 'I'll keep digging, Angela, but so far he seems whiter than white – and the Board won't turn down a gift horse. Even if they're not ready to build for a few years, I suppose there's no reason they shouldn't acquire the land.'

'Provided it really is suitable. But I cannot help thinking that, given the lengths he went to just to get me on his side, he must be up to something underhand.'

'If he is, I haven't found it yet, but there are still some avenues to try – and you can be certain I shan't give up, but that's enough of business for one evening. I told you to relax and we've done nothing but talk shop. From now on it's forbidden. I want to enjoy your company, Angela. And you really do need to relax.'

'Thank you,' Angela said. 'You're such a good friend, Mark.'

'Perhaps I'll be more, one of these days,' he said softly. 'We'd better go, my dearest girl, or I shan't want to go at all and it would be a pity to miss the film . . .'

Angela laughed softly. It was the first time for ages that she'd felt this close to him and she wasn't about to let anything spoil their evening – particularly that odious Mr Arnold . . .

THIRTY-THREE

'You'll have to stay off school for once and look after Mammy,' Kelly said to her younger sister. 'I can't take another day off work or I shall get the sack. I've been warned several times, Cate, so don't look so miserable.'

'It's choir practice for the carols,' Cate said and gave her sister a defiant stare. 'I've got the solo part and I don't want to lose out on that – it's not fair!'

'I'm sorry, but Mammy needs help and it has to be you this time.' Kelly met her sister's sulky look with determination. 'You know what Da said, Cate. You're old enough to take your turn helping Mammy, and I have to go to work so stop being selfish and do as I ask.'

'You're mean and I hate you.'

'I'm truly sorry.' Kelly looked at her sister's hunched shoulders but there was no point in giving in; they needed her wages with Da on short time at the Docks. 'Please, just this once think of someone but yourself, Cate – and promise me you won't run off the minute I've gone and leave Mammy to cope alone.'

'I shan't – but only because Da said,' Cate muttered. 'You're the selfish one in this house, Kelly – and if I lose my solo in the carol concert I'll hate you for ever.'

Kelly sighed as she pulled on her coat and left the house. It was bitterly cold out and she had to turn her collar up to keep out the biting wind. She felt mean about making her sister stay home to look after her mother and the little one – Cate's singing voice was so lovely that it would be cruel if she lost the chance to shine as a soloist in the school concert – but Kelly was on probation at work after all the time she'd had off. Besides, she didn't want to let Angela Morton down after she'd done her best to help; it wasn't Mrs Morton's fault that they were still waiting for a house, or that her mother's chest was bad again. Kelly wished she could work in the evenings and help her mother during the day. Her father wasn't one of those men who went out drinking every night, so between them they'd see that Mum had someone with her all the time.

Kelly had to put on a sprint to catch her bus. It was about to move off and she took a flying leap, barely managing to get on board, but she swayed back danger-ously and if a man hadn't reached out and caught her arm she might have slipped off the platform.

'Watch it, miss,' he said and grinned at her. 'Do you often risk life and limb for the sake of catching a bus?'

Kelly did a double take as she looked at her saviour. He was young, perhaps in his mid-twenties and attractive with dark blond hair and blue eyes. Dressed in working clothes, he looked as if he'd come straight from work; there was a smear of oil on his cheek and his hands were grimy. He saw her looking at them and nodded.

'Yes, I look a bit mucky, lass. I'm on maintenance work for the railways and we had some overhead cables come down – bit of a storm last night. We had to work all through the night to clear the line by morning.'

'Oh, you work for the railways,' Kelly said, feeling her cheeks heat as he continued to stare at her with interest. 'I work for St Saviour's – the children's home in Halfpenny Street.'

'Are you one of them 'Alfpenny Angels?' he asked, nudging her towards a vacant seat. 'You take it; I'll stand and grow good.'

'You don't look like the sort to grow good,' Kelly responded to his joke cheekily, though she wasn't sure why – she didn't flirt with lads as a rule. There wasn't much point when she never had time to go out on dates. 'No, I work in the kitchens – but I'd like to be a carer one day. I don't suppose I'll be lucky enough, though.'

'Why not? Bright, pretty girl like you,' he said and gave her another of his confident grins. 'I should've thought they would take you like a shot. I would, if I were the boss.'

'I'm on probation at the moment as I've been late so often,' Kelly said. 'Mammy isn't too well again this mornin' and I almost missed my bus.'

'Good thing I was there to catch you then,' he said, looking round as the bus started to slow up for the next stop. 'This is where I get off – see you around sometime.'

Kelly smiled but didn't answer. She knew it was only a chance encounter. Even if he were interested in her, she didn't have time to go courting – more's the pity. He was cheerful and good-looking, and she'd have liked to see him again . . . but it was never going to happen.

*

'Do you like living in the Nurses' Home?' Kelly asked when Tilly joined her for a cup of tea later that morning. 'I don't much like our house, but I'd miss my family too much to leave them and live in one room.'

'You wouldn't if you had my life,' Tilly said and sipped her tea. 'I hated it after me mother got married again, but she couldn't cope on her own . . . and she likes men, if you know what I mean. I could hear them in the bedroom and it made me sick sometimes . . . after what he was tryin' on with me.'

'Oh . . .' Kelly looked at her with sympathy. 'It must have been awful for you.'

'I don't think I could have put up with it much longer,' Tilly said. 'I don't mind lookin' after my sister Mags and me brother, but it's him I can't stand. Mrs Morton asked me what was wrong and she got me the room – and I'm grateful to her. She's all right, even if she isn't really one of us.'

'I know she speaks posh,' Kelly said, 'but she isn't stuck up with it – and she got that doctor to come and see Mammy. The trouble is, Mam'll never be any better until we get a decent house.'

'If you worked with the children, you could do nights and then you could help her during the day,' Tilly said. 'We're short-staffed again since Julia left last month – it's just Jean, Nan and me at the moment. If one of us was ill, we couldn't cope. Nurse Wendy often gives us a hand if she's off duty, but it isn't her job to change beds and clean floors.'

'We never seem to have enough staff in the kitchen either,' Kelly said. 'I don't think I've got a chance of being promoted to being a carer.'

'Why not? You should ask Mrs Morton, ask her to help you,' Tilly said. 'You never know, she might give you the chance.'

'I did ask. She said maybe—' Kelly said, breaking off when Cook came in from the scullery.

'Gossiping again, Kelly? Have you scrubbed those jacket potatoes yet? And I want you to clean those ox hearts again. I'm going to stuff them and I'm not satisfied that you've washed them thoroughly.'

Kelly grimaced at her friend as she got up to return to the back scullery, even though she still had five minutes of her break left. There was no arguing with Cook, especially when she was on the warpath. Cleaning offal was one of Kelly's least favourite jobs and she never ate the stuff herself; it turned her stomach to think of eating anything from the insides of an animal. However, she had no choice but to clean them when Cook was able to get what she considered a nutritious treat for the kids. The shortages during the war had meant that everyone had been forced to eat more offal: tripe and onions, liver, or chitterlings fried and eaten with vinegar. Heart stuffed and roasted in the oven was one of her father's favourite dishes.

Holding the hearts under a running tap, Kelly forced the gruesome task from her mind and thought instead about the man who had saved her from a nasty accident that morning. He hadn't even told her his name, and she hadn't told him hers. She knew he worked on the railway, and he knew she worked here in the kitchen – but that was all. A sigh left her as she realised that, even if he'd told her his name, even if he'd asked her out, she wouldn't have been able to go. Her family needed her at home and she couldn't see that changing anytime soon . . .

Kelly emerged into the cool night air and pulled up her coat collar. Her bus was pulling up at the stop and she started to run for it when a hand reached out and caught her arm, making her jump. Startled, she looked at the man who had hold of her arm and for a moment thought him a stranger, but then she realised it was her saviour from the morning.

'It's you,' she said, surprised because he looked so different in his suit with his hair slicked back and smelling of a nice citrus scent from the lotion he'd used. 'I didn't recognise you.'

'Look a bit different when I'm clean, don't I?' he said and grinned at her. 'I hope you don't mind me coming here like this – but you didn't tell me your name and all I knew was that you worked here.'

'I'm Kelly Mason,' she said. 'You didn't tell me your name either.'

'Steve Jarvis,' he said. 'Railway engineer, single, live at home with me mother and sisters. I'm honest, hard-working and I've got a good job . . .'

Kelly giggled. He made her want to laugh and be happy. There was something about his carefree manner that she really liked, and she didn't object when he walked beside her.

'Were you running for that bus?' Steve asked as it drew away from the stop. Kelly nodded and he looked apologetic. 'Sorry I made you miss it, but I've been standing here for hours, and I didn't want you to run off before we'd introduced ourselves. Have you got far to go?'

'Standing here, on a cold night like this? You daft thing,' Kelly said, staring at him in surprise. 'Why didn't you come in and ask for me? Oh, you didn't know my name.'

'Will you come for a cup of tea?' he asked. 'I'd ask you for a proper date, but after tonight I'll be working all hours.'

'I wish I could, but I have to get home,' Kelly said, knowing there was a pile of ironing waiting for her. She saw the disappointment in his face and relented. 'Well, maybe just a quick one, but I've got a lot of jobs to do this evening. It's Mammy – she's not well and there's three still at school and one at home, besides me and Pa.'

'I've got five sisters,' Steve said. 'Me pa died two years ago so I took over as the breadwinner – but Maggie's at work now and Sheila starts after Christmas at the jam factory. Still, I know what it's like havin' a family to look out for.'

Somehow his confession made it seem all right. Steve had commitments of his own. He wouldn't expect her to drop everything to go out with him all the time, and with his family to keep he couldn't afford to get married, so perhaps they could be friends.

'What are your sisters like?' she asked and tucked her arm through his. 'Our Cate is nearly eleven, but she's a proper lazy little madam.'

'She sounds like our Ally,' Steve said and smiled at her. 'I reckon it was my lucky day when I hauled you on that bus, Kelly Mason . . . We'll have that cup of rosy lee and then I'll walk you home.'

THIRTY-FOUR

'This is lovely, Bob,' Alice said as she looked round the holiday cottage that her husband had hired for them in Bournemouth. 'Much nicer than being in a hotel.'

'I thought it would be easier for you with Susie,' he said. 'It's cheaper too, especially this time of the year, but we're lucky we've got a nice spell of weather. It's cold but it's better to be frosty than raining.'

'It's not cold at all, but lovely fresh air.'

'We can eat out in hotels in the evenings, Alice. The couple that owns this cottage also runs a baby-sitting service to look after the holidaymakers' kids. We can leave Susie for a few hours and then pick her up when we get back. I checked them out and they have a proper nurse in charge, so she'd be quite safe.'

Alice nodded; he'd been very good about Susie, helping her to change nappies and walking about with her in his arms when she cried. The first time he'd set eyes on her, he'd decided she looked very like Alice and not one word about the girl being another man's child had passed his lips since. People assumed he was Susie's father and when he was asked a question about his daughter, he answered naturally as if he was the proud dad. Alice felt grateful and a little guilty.

She hadn't told him that Jack had come to the flat or that he'd given her a key. Alice hadn't heard a word from the police, so she supposed that whatever they'd found in the locker wasn't of much importance. She'd decided to keep it to herself and was trying to put it out of her mind so she could enjoy this holiday that Bob had chosen for them. He'd been talking about this trip for months, but he'd been unable to get home for long enough to make it worthwhile. Now he had two weeks to spend with her, and Alice was excited at the prospect.

Walking into the bedroom, where a large double bed took up most of the room, Alice felt a tingling inside. This was the first time that she and Bob would sleep together since she'd recovered from Susie's birth. Until a few weeks earlier, she'd been too sore and Bob hadn't even tried to touch her when he'd come home for a brief leave. It would be different now. They were on holiday, which meant they had nothing to do but enjoy themselves – and Alice was perfectly able to be a wife to Bob for the first time since their marriage.

Despite feeling a bit nervous, Alice wanted it to happen between them now. She was over Jack at last. It had taken a lot of thinking and a deep internal struggle when he'd asked her to go away with him, but she'd resisted and knew she'd made the right decision. Perhaps she wasn't in love with Bob, but she liked him and respected him, and he was good to both her and Susie. She was ready to be a proper wife and she was going to try to be happy with her life.

'There's another bedroom,' Bob said, coming up behind her.

Alice swung round quickly. 'You'll sleep with me, Bob. I want us to be together, now I'm over it all.'

Bob seemed pleased and slightly amused. 'I meant for Susie. I asked for a proper cot, so she'll be comfortable, and we can leave the doors open so you'll hear her if she cries.'

'She doesn't cry much,' Alice said. He was still smiling at her. Emboldened by the warmth in his eyes, she moved closer to him. 'I mean it, Bob – it is all over, all that nonsense. I don't feel anything for him now. I want us to be together properly . . . as man and wife.'

'Sure you're ready? Not still sore after Susie? You had a bit of a rotten time with her, love. I told you I'd wait until you were ready.'

'I'm ready now,' Alice said and moved closer. She put her arms about his waist. 'I'm going to be a proper wife to you, Bob. I want to have more children, perhaps a boy next time, if we're lucky . . .'

'Alice, love,' he said and put his arms about her, kissing the top of her head. 'Don't feel you have to give me a child. Susie is ours. I shall love her as much as any children you give me. Naturally, I'd like a son one day, what man wouldn't? But most of all I want my Alice to be well. You're barely over it and the doctor told me that you shouldn't have another baby for at least eighteen months to two years.'

'What do the doctors know?' Alice protested. 'You won't let it stop us being together?'

Bob laughed softly, looking down at her with love. 'No, I shan't, Alice, but I'm going to take care of you.

It's my responsibility to make certain you don't fall for a child too soon. I've seen women who give birth year after year until they're worn out and their health has gone. I love you too much to let that happen to you, love. We'll have a baby, but not for a year or two. I want my pretty Alice to myself for a while . . . you look so lovely in that dress. You should wear blue often, Alice. I don't think I've ever seen you look so pretty.'

'I'm not pretty, Bob,' Alice said, blushing. 'You can't really think—'

She got no further because he took her into his arms and kissed her, his mouth gentle and sweet as he caressed her. His tongue ran softly between her lips, teasing and arousing. Alice gave a sigh and melted into his body, wanting the kiss to go on and on. Bob ran his finger down her cheek, a smile in his eyes as he stroked her hair back from her face.

'I've always thought you the prettiest thing I've ever seen,' he said. 'I love you, Alice. I wasn't sure you would ever look at me, but I was smitten that first night at the dance Eric dragged me to. I never thought I had a chance with you then, but when you married me I knew you would be faithful – at least, I hoped it would be that way.'

'I wouldn't leave you, Bob,' Alice vowed. 'I liked you at the start, but now . . . I want it to be you and me always. You have to believe that, Bob, believe that I do care for you . . .'

'Say it, Alice. Say you love me.'

Alice hesitated, and then she knew as she looked up at his face. Bob would never be the dashing hero that Jack Shaw had appeared to be, but he was steady, dependable, and loving – and she'd come to appreciate him. A tiny lie wouldn't do any harm.

'Yes, Bob, I do love you. I didn't expect to, but I—'

Alice gave a shriek as he suddenly swept her off her feet and carried her to the bed. He dropped her down and she laughed, gazing up at him as he bent over her, beginning to strip off his shirt. She caught a glimpse of firm, tanned flesh and then, even as she started to fumble with the buttons of her gingham shirtdress, they heard a wail from the next room.

'Oh, Susie, not now,' Alice cried. 'She's ready for her feed. I'm so sorry, Bob.'

'Get your things off and settle in bed, and I'll bring her to you,' Bob said, and shook his head as she tried to apologise. 'Babies need feeding and they always have to come first. Once she's settled, I'm coming in that bed with you and I'm not getting out again until the morning!'

THIRTY-FIVE

'I'm glad you asked me over this evening,' Mark said as Angela filled his wineglass. 'I wanted to talk to you about the Board meeting tomorrow.'

'Yes, I've been meaning to ask if you've discovered anything more about Henry Arnold's reason for offering us this "marvellous deal", as he calls it.'

'On the face of it, the deal is sound enough,' Mark said, 'but I have a feeling it may turn out to be conditional on the Board agreeing to sell Halfpenny Street.'

'Oh no, they can't – they won't?' Angela looked at him in alarm. 'Even if they want to build this splendid new home in the country, we can't sell St Saviour's. Surely they know how important it is to be where we are, at the centre of need? If we weren't there, the local police wouldn't have anywhere to bring the children. I thought that we should stay where we are for some years yet, even if we're only a halfway house and most of the children eventually pass on to the country home.'

'Several of the Board think it's too good an opportunity to miss – especially as we've received a large offer for the building at Halfpenny Street.'

'What offer – why haven't I heard of this before?'

'I wanted to make some inquiries before telling you, Angela,' Mark said. 'I was certain there had to be a reason for the offer, but it's taken me a while to get answers to my questions.'

It took an effort to control her anger. How long had he known about this, and yet he'd not said a word to her. 'Does Sister Beatrice know?'

'If she doesn't, she will tomorrow. She wrote to inform me that she will be attending the Board meeting, and she will be back at work soon after.'

'I can't tell you how pleased I shall be to see her back, Mark.'

'Been feeling the pressure?'

'Yes, sometimes . . . but please, go on.'

'They've offered fifteen thousand for the property and another five as a contribution towards the move.'

Angela gasped: it was far more than she'd expected, surely more than the property was worth. 'I don't understand. They could buy any number of properties in the Spitalfields area for that price.'

'Yes, but we're in the way,' Mark told her with a frown. 'Apparently, there is a scheme under discussion to pull two whole blocks down and rebuild – new shops, mainly, but also a large hall for the council and various other projects, including a health centre. St Saviour's stands dead in the middle of the whole scheme. I doubt if it could go ahead if we refused to sell.'

'Why Halfpenny Street? Why not build somewhere else? There are plenty of areas that need renovation.'

'The consortium already own quite a few properties that need to come down in the area. I gather they've been engaged in discussions for a while with a firm that wants to build a huge shopping centre. I'm told it's the coming thing for the future – a sort of super-market.'

'Well, they can jolly well go and build their shopping market somewhere else!' Angela glared at him. 'The Board won't take the offer, will they?'

'What's to stop them?' Mark arched his brows at her. 'On one hand, they've got this generous offer, the like of which will probably never come again – and on the other Henry Arnold has promised them a large plot of land in the country. The money would build a new home for us and quite possibly keep it running for a couple of years. I know some of the Board are going to think it a splendid offer. I'm surprised you don't.'

'You know what I think,' Angela said. 'We do wonderful work where we are – in the slums, where we're needed. I'm quite certain Sister Beatrice will not agree to a move. The staff are Londoners and won't want to move—'

'What about you? A nice country house and a less stressful job as the Warden . . .'

'No!' Angela stared at him in horror. 'Oh, Mark, you can't think I'd want that – to leave Halfpenny Street? Besides, I don't want Sister Beatrice's job; we're a good team. And the children would hate being carted off to the country, away from everything they know. Yes, a country holiday would do them good, and I'm hoping to take them on trips to the sea next summer, but—'

'Good,' Mark said and smiled at her. 'Then I can count on your support when I come up with an idea of my own for the Board to consider.'

She looked at him warily. 'I'm not sure what you mean . . .'

'Oh, Angela, I do love you,' Mark said and laughed out loud. 'You adore those children, don't you? And you're willing to fight like a tigress for them – and believe me, my darling, we do have a fight on our hands. I agree that we need Halfpenny Street for another ten years at least, but I'm hoping we can find enough money to fund a cottage – in Norfolk, perhaps, somewhere near the sea and big enough for, say, twelve children at a time, if four share a room . . .'

'A holiday home?' Angela said. 'Oh, Mark, do you think we could?'

'I think we might. I have somewhere in mind – but first we have to win the Board over to our way of thinking. Henry Arnold is involved in this shopping market business, Angela. I'm not quite sure how at the moment, but I'm hoping to have the answer by tomorrow.'

'You can't tell me now?'

'No, at this stage it is only a suspicion, but I think he has more reasons for pushing this move than he has declared to the Board.'

Angela nodded. It was clear that Mark had said all he was prepared to say, and she wasn't about to quarrel with him tonight. They'd been moving closer of late and she didn't want to do or say anything that might spoil it.

'In that case, I shan't press you,' she said softly. 'You see, I do trust you, Mark.'

He smiled strangely. 'That's good. I'll see you to-morrow then. Goodnight, Angela . . .' And then he was gone, leaving her wishing that he had stayed.

*

Angela looked at the people grouped around the long shining oak table. Every member of the Board was there, including Sister Beatrice, an invited member for this extraordinary meeting. She appeared very much fitter, if a little thinner, and there was a new sprightliness in her manner. Like everyone else present, she was looking expectantly at the man who had called this meeting.

Henry Arnold had put his motion to buy the land for building a proposed new home some weeks previously and, on Mark's advice, had been outvoted by five to two on agreeing the purchase there and then. It hadn't gone down well with Arnold when the Board agreed to give Mark the time he requested, and now he asked his question in a tone that failed to mask his irritation.

'Is Mr Adderbury ready to tell us why he wanted the delay? Or are we to be asked to wait yet again? I need an answer and this delay is ridiculous!'

'I propose to tell you all exactly why I asked for the delay,' Mark said and rose to his feet. 'Mr Chairman, Bishop, honourable members . . . I would beg your indulgence while I tell you a story—'

'Can't we get to the vote?' Henry Arnold asked. 'I don't have all day to waste.'

'I shan't keep you too long,' Mark smiled at everyone else but didn't look directly at Mr Arnold. 'I've been investigating the offer made for our property at Halfpenny Street . . . and I have discovered two things—'

'I fail to see what this business has to do with the land and the new building proposed,' Henry Arnold interjected tetchily.

'Give Adderbury a chance and you will,' the Bishop said, frowning at the interruption.

334

'One day, I hope that St Saviour's will move to a splendid new home,' Mark said and smiled easily at Angela. 'Accommodation for up to two hundred children, a playing field, sports hall and perhaps even a small swimming pool. However, that will not be for some years—'

'I'm afraid I cannot undertake to hold my offer open for years, Adderbury.'

'Well, I dare say the Board won't wish you to, once they hear what I have to say.' Mark cleared his throat. 'It appears that the premises we occupy in Halfpenny Street are at the centre of a large area that is being considered for demolition so that the council can build new housing and shopping facilities. The council owns some derelict properties in the district, with the rest being owned by private individuals and businesses – of which we are one. It seems that the land we occupy is key to the major development that is under consideration. I've been told that if we refuse there are other owners who will also hold out, which could put the whole project in jeopardy.'

'Have you considered that the council might put an order on St Saviour's, forcing you to sell?' Henry Arnold said.

'You have clearly gone into this in detail,' Mark replied as the room fell silent. 'But that is only to be expected, given that you own quite a few buildings in the area which would be sold under compulsory purchase. I imagine you stand to gain a great deal of money if the proposals go through . . . and I believe you also have a promise on the contract to carry out the rebuilding, which would be worth a huge amount of money for your company, and yourself—'

'I hardly think that is your affair!' Henry Arnold glared at him furiously. 'You would be fools to turn down such an offer.'

'That decision must be put to the vote, but I am making my opposition known now both on the grounds that you have a conflict of interest and because this home and the other historic buildings in the area need to be preserved – and I would like to say that I have alternative plans to put to the Board concerning our future . . .'

'Perhaps I might have a word . . .' the Bishop rose to his feet and Mark sat down. 'Sister Beatrice only heard of the offer two days ago and she immediately brought something to my attention that I wasn't fully acquainted with . . .' He smiled at Sister Beatrice, who remained seated, her expression giving nothing away. 'As it turns out, the land on which St Saviour's was built many years ago belonged to the Church and there is a significant clause in the deeds which states the buildings on the said land may only be used for certain purposes – and that does not include anything of a commercial nature. St Saviour's was, as some of you may know, a grand private house and then it became a hospital for fever patients. We bought it cheaply, in a dilapidated condition, partly because of the clause—'

'An outdated covenant that could be overturned in the courts by any lawyer worth his salt!' Henry Arnold blustered.

'Possibly,' the Bishop agreed. 'However, in the circumstances, I could not agree to the proposals on the table. I do not believe we are in a position to purchase and build a country house without the sale of Halfpenny

Street – and therefore I think we should carry on as we are until some future date when things seem more propitious for our eventual move.'

'Don't you see what a chance this is for your charity? You could get enough out of this to cover the building of a new home for the kids and money in the bank. I don't see what difference it makes if there is an old covenant . . .'

'Perhaps you don't, sir,' the Bishop said mildly with a faint lift of his brows. 'It is an ethical matter and one of conscience, I believe.'

'That's damned insulting!' Henry Arnold's voice was sharp and cold. 'This is a business matter, and in business everyone looks out for themselves. No wonder you're forever in debt at St Saviour's, and likely to remain so unless you start to live in the real world. I brought you a fantastic deal and if you let some stupid covenant stand in your way I can only think you have no sense of reality. You could make a donation to the Church, if that eases your conscience . . .'

'For my part I consider the matter closed, but we'll take a vote on it if you wish . . .' He looked round the table. 'Is anyone in favour of accepting this deal?' Not one hand was raised other than Henry Arnold's. 'It would seem that you are outvoted, Mr Arnold. I am sorry, but we do not wish to accept your offer.'

'Fools, damned fools!' Henry Arnold spluttered, furious at the murmur of approval from the rest of the Board. 'In the circumstances I have no wish to be associated with your charity and I resign my seat. However, I do not intend to leave it there. The council may very well put a compulsory purchase on your property and any others that stand in the way of progress. Good day.'

There was silence as he left the room, and then the Bishop cleared his throat. 'Never liked the fellow. Well, Adderbury, perhaps now you can tell us what you have in mind?'

'I've been wondering if we might raise funds to buy a holiday cottage where the children can take turns to have a week or two at the sea. It would bridge the gap until we can build the substantial new home we all want and give our children the fresh air and excitement of visiting the sea.'

'I believe we ought to take a vote on that suggestion,' the Bishop said, and a show of hands duly approved the proposal. 'That seems to be agreed. No doubt you will make inquiries, Adderbury, and when we have the funds we shall progress along the lines you've drawn.'

'As a matter of fact, I have been talking to someone,' Mark said. 'He is an old friend of my father and we recently met at a function we both attended. Sir Martin Harkness is a rich man but childless, and most of what he owns will go to his nephew. He was, however, very interested when I mentioned that I hoped to get the children of St Saviour's away from London for some fresh air. Apparently he owns a cottage in Old Hunstanton, Norfolk. Nothing has been agreed as yet, but I believe he would sell it to us very cheaply if not actually make us a present of it.'

'That is extraordinarily generous, if he means it.'

'We spoke last night and he confirmed that he was willing to complete the exchange if we wished to accept. He has offered us the cottage for fifty pounds – but I believe it will need some renovation. If the Board agrees,

I will seek estimates as to the cost of getting the place into reasonable order.'

'And where is the money to come from?' Sister Beatrice asked. 'What funds we have are needed for the running of the home we have – how are we to afford this wonderful holiday cottage?'

'Yes, Sister has a point,' the Bishop said, looking at Mark.

'I shall be funding some of it myself. The repairs and furnishings will be my contribution to this project. As to the rest, I'm going to try to take our fundraising countrywide, much as Barnardo's do. I cannot see why we shouldn't, as a fully registered charity, collect on a much larger scale, rather than confining our appeals to private sources as we have in the past.'

'I have been thinking along the same lines,' Angela said. 'I have several rather daring ideas for fundraising for the Christmas treats this year – and I don't see why we shouldn't continue to innovate when it comes to supporting both St Saviour's and the holiday cottage. Halfpenny Street is our main concern, of course, but I believe the fundraising will continue to support our needs there for some years to come. I had an inquiry only yesterday from a large firm with branches all over the country, asking me what they could do to support us.'

'As long as St Saviour's does not suffer, I am content,' Sister Beatrice said.

Angela met Sister's gaze and a nod passed between them. The Chairman called the meeting to order and it was formally closed. As everyone rose to leave, Sister Beatrice touched Angela on the arm.

'I shall be back in my office tomorrow,' she said. 'I shall want a full report to bring me up to date, Angela.'

'I'll have it on your desk first thing,' Angela promised. 'I'm so glad you're ready to come back to us, Sister.'

'I've been ready for weeks, but the doctors would not agree. However, I feel much better and eager to get back to work.'

'I can only say how glad I am. In fact, there is a matter I need to discuss with you as soon as possible.'

Sister Beatrice inclined her head, and said nothing, but Angela saw the smile of satisfaction on her face as she turned away. A feeling of peace descended on Angela. It was good to have the determined Sister Beatrice back at the helm; much as she loved St Saviour's and its children, there were a few personal issues that needed Angela's immediate attention . . .

'Why didn't you tell me what was going on?' Angela asked as Mark drove her back to her flat after the meeting. 'I couldn't believe it when you told us how much Henry Arnold stood to gain if that deal had gone through.'

'Your instincts about his motives were correct from the start, Angela. Had he persuaded us to go ahead, he stood to gain thousands of pounds, one way or another.'

'Do you think the council will try to force the sale?'

'Why should they? Large parts of London need renovation. No, they'll simply take their plans elsewhere, especially if the Church are opposed to the Halfpenny Street development.'

'Henry Arnold was very angry. I think you've made an enemy, Mark.'

'Men of that ilk do not frighten me,' Mark shrugged her concern off. 'I am not interested in his world of big business, Angela. In my own sphere I have the respect of my colleagues; whatever Arnold chooses to say or do is a matter of indifference to me.'

'He told me you were facing an inquiry over Terry's attack on Sister Beatrice – he tried to suggest you were at fault. That was why I was forced to take advice from Mr Yarwood on Sarah's behalf . . .'

'Yes, there was a hearing.' Mark frowned. 'I am very aware that I may have delayed too long in the matter, and I told the hearing of my doubts and regrets. It was decided that I had acted in the child's best interests and that the outcome was unfortunate . . . it should not have happened, but no one could have foreseen it.'

'You didn't tell me any of this,' she said, looking at him doubtfully. 'Didn't you trust me?'

'You've had enough to worry over, without my adding to your concerns,' he said and touched her cheek. 'I still intend to talk to Nancy about it one day. If any compensation is due, it is due to her – and I'd like to help her get started in life if at any time she chooses to leave St Saviour's.'

'That would be a nice thing to do,' Angela said. 'Wait for a while, Mark. She's only just ready to leave school and for the moment she's happy where she is – but one day she might want to do something else, like having a place of her own, and then perhaps we could help her.'

'Yes, I think we should put all this other business out of our minds,' Mark said. 'Unfortunately, I've got a lot on and I have to leave London for a while, but when I get back we must spend some time together, Angela.'

'Yes, that's what I want too . . .'

'Dearest Angela,' Mark said and bent his head to kiss her softly on the lips. 'Please hold that thought. I have to go now, but I will telephone you and we'll go out and then, after Christmas we'll go abroad for a few days . . . perhaps skiing, if you would like that?'

'That sounds wonderful,' Angela agreed and reached up to kiss him on the mouth. For a moment he held her and her heart soared. She felt as if she had come home after a long and stormy journey. 'Oh, Mark, I hope you know how much you mean to me . . .' A shaky sob escaped her. 'I've been so lonely for you.'

'Have you, my love?' He smiled, holding her pressed tightly against him and his kiss this time was very different, strong and passionate, filled with promise of the love to come between them. 'Then you've been feeling some of my despair; there were times when I thought you would never love me the way I love you . . .'

'What a pair of idiots,' she said, a little breathlessly.

'We're both so committed to our work that our feelings get brushed under the carpet, but after Christmas we'll make time just for us, Angela.'

'Promise?' she asked and looked at him, almost shy as she saw the burning heat in his eyes.

'Promise,' he said, kissed her once more in a way that nearly tore her heart from her body and then left . . .

THIRTY-SIX

'Nan,' Wendy approached the head carer as she was leaving her room the following afternoon. 'I was hoping I'd catch you.'

'Is something wrong?' Nan asked. 'Has Tilly done something foolish? She has a good heart but she isn't used to helping on the sick ward yet.'

'Tilly's fine – Michelle and I will teach her all she needs to know. I was wondering . . .' Wendy took a deep breath, then, 'I've got two tickets for the theatre – it's a musical. I wondered if you might like to come with me.'

'Me?' Nan looked surprised. 'Are you sure you wouldn't prefer to go with one of the other nurses – a girl of your own age?'

'I've been to the flicks with Michelle once, and no doubt I'll go out with her and some of the others now and then – but I thought it might be nice to get to know you.' Wendy's cheeks were turning pink. 'That is, if you were interested?'

'Well, that's very nice of you, Wendy. I should like to come if I can. When are the tickets for?'

'This Saturday. I think that's your night off, isn't it?'

'Yes, and my friend Eddie won't be coming round this weekend, so I'd love to come, Wendy.'

'I'm so pleased,' Wendy said. 'It takes a while to make friends when you move your job. I didn't want to keep my mother's flat on after she died, and the Nurses' Home is very nice, but it does get a bit confining always in one room. You have to get out sometimes.'

'You must join some clubs,' Nan advised her, then nodded her head. 'I do know how you're feeling, Wendy. When my home was bombed I lived in one room until the house I was staying at got bombed as well. I was lucky enough not to be at either place when it happened or I shouldn't be here to tell the tale – but then I was allocated one of the new prefabs. It has two bedrooms, so my daughter could come home and stay if she wished . . .' Nan sighed. 'I don't think she ever will, because she's happy where she is – so perhaps I should take a lodger.'

'It's awful when you lose people you care for, isn't it?' Wendy smiled in sympathy. 'I lost my mother to illness and my boyfriend to the war.'

Nan hesitated, then, 'Why don't you come to tea at mine on Saturday afternoon? We can have a good chat and then go on to the theatre later.'

'Oh, that would be lovely,' Wendy said. 'I suppose I ought to get on. I promised Samantha and Sarah that I would take them to the park for half an hour if it was fine this evening and I don't want to let them down.'

'You're fond of the twins, I think?'

'Yes, particularly Sarah,' Wendy sighed. 'Their aunt is coming here tomorrow to see them and I know

344

Samantha is fretting over it. She thinks it will be like it was with her father's sister.'

'I'm sure the Welfare people have checked Madame Bernard out properly. They wouldn't make the same mistake again.' Nan frowned, then, 'I hope you asked Sister if it was all right to take the twins out to the park this evening? Sister doesn't like the children being taken anywhere unless we know.'

'Yes, I did ask and Sister said yes, provided I thought I could cope. It's only half an hour in the park . . .'

'Yes, I'm sure that will be good for them,' Nan smiled. 'Well, off you go then and enjoy yourself . . .'

'I shall look forward to Saturday,' Wendy said and walked off.

Nan's eyes followed the nurse. Wendy had just confirmed her suspicions. The girl had no family and was lonely. Nan could understand why she wanted to make friends, and why she'd become attached to the twins. While there was nothing wrong in Wendy becoming fond of the children, Nan could only hope that she wouldn't let herself care too much. She'd seen children like Sarah before; beautiful, loving and fragile. Sarah had been ill with what would probably have been merely a slight chill in a sturdier child. If anything were to happen to her, it might break the young nurse's heart – and by the sound of it, she'd had her heart broken more than once.

Nan was pleased that Wendy had asked her to the theatre. She'd been considering whether she should ask the girl to tea, because her intuition had told her that Wendy was lonely; it was a look in the eyes, something you became more aware of with age.

Well, Wendy had invited her to the theatre and she'd invited her to tea. It was a start, and if they got on well together . . . Nan had that spare room and she'd accepted that Maisie, or Sister Mary, as she was now, was never coming home. She wasn't sure whether she wanted a permanent lodger, but she had felt a bit lonely herself over the years . . .

She'd wait a while before she jumped in feet first again, but if Wendy proved to be the lovely girl she seemed to be – well, what would be wrong with getting closer to her?

Nan had always longed for more children, and Wendy had lost her mother. A smile touched Nan's mouth as she set out to begin her inspection of the wards. It would be her last night on duty for a while, because Beatrice would take her share of the night watch now that she was better – back to her old self, in fact.

Nan felt a warm contentment inside. She'd been so worried when Beatrice had that dreadful infection. For a time she'd been afraid that her old friend might never return to St Saviour's, but she was back now and that had set Nan's mind at rest. Angela was a good Administrator and she did a lot for the children, but in Nan's opinion Beatrice was the heart of their little family and they'd missed her too much . . .

She saw Staff Nurse Michelle leaving the sick room and smiled at her.

'Off home, Nurse?'

'Not yet. I'm visiting Matty at the hospital first. He was having more treatment on his spine today and he'll need a friendly face . . .'

'Yes, poor boy,' Nan said, 'but when I was young he

probably wouldn't have had a chance, Michelle. At least they've removed the growth and it wasn't malignant. We must pray that he will be able to walk again soon. Give him my love and tell him we're all thinking of him.'

'Yes, I shall,' Michelle promised. 'Goodnight, Nan.'

'May I speak with you, Miss Morris?' The sister in charge of Matty's ward came up to Michelle as she was leaving after the visit. The child had tried to respond to her, but he'd looked wan and listless, and he'd only sucked his ice lolly a couple of times before giving it to her to throw away. 'I know you're busy, but this concerns Matty and I need to know your thoughts on his future.'

'Yes, of course, Sister Norton,' Michelle said. 'I'm going home but there's no rush.'

'It will only take a few minutes of your time,' Sister said, leading the way into office. 'Please sit down. I can offer you a glass of sherry if you would care for it?'

'No thank you,' Michelle said, aware that she was being honoured but unsure why. 'Matty isn't any worse, is he? He seemed very down this evening.'

'It's the soreness in his back, because we've been giving him exercises. He'll feel better tomorrow. For the moment he seems to be making good progress.'

'For the moment – what does that mean?'

'At this time we are not sure whether he will recover the full use of his legs,' Sister Norton said, looking grave. 'While we have observed a marked improvement in Matty's general condition, we're worried by his apathy. Since his uncle has stopped coming to see him he seems very down and we were wondering what you were planning for the future.'

'I'm not sure what you're saying? He will return to us at St Saviour's, of course.' Michelle wondered what was coming next when she noticed the speculative look in Sister Norton's eyes.

'I'm not sure that is the best outcome for Matty, Miss Morris. The boy looks forward to the letters, cards and small gifts his uncle sends him. He told the doctors that he was going to live with his uncle and aunt, and his uncle has promised to show him the changing of the guard at Buckingham Palace, take him to football matches, and teach him to box . . .'

'Matty told the doctors that?' Michelle was shocked. She didn't think Eric would have promised the child he would live with him. 'Eric is in the army for another year. He couldn't have the boy to live with him in the meantime, and even then it wouldn't be suitable: Eric isn't married.'

'Is he your fiancé? We always find that sick children like Matty respond and recover best when they are part of a loving home. Are you and Sergeant Wright intending to marry? If so, it offers the chance for Matty to live with you, doesn't it?'

Michelle hesitated. One part of her wanted to tell Sister Norton it was none of her business, but she knew it was; Matty's future happiness and wellbeing was at stake, and she'd invited the nurse's outspokenness by choosing to visit regularly and bringing Eric when he was on leave.

'Eric and I are very good friends,' Michelle said. 'Nothing has been decided yet. If Matty is ready to leave hospital he would return to St Saviour's – at least for the present.'

'Yes, I thought that was the case – but is it possible that you would consider taking him into your home one day?'

'Yes,' Michelle said without thinking. She realised that Sister Norton needed a positive answer and the idea that they could offer Matty hope and be a real family seemed almost possible. 'If Eric and I were to marry, I believe we should very likely apply for custody of Matty. Adopt him as our own. I know he adores Eric.'

'Yes, he does. We hear of nothing but his uncle these days, Miss Morris. He sometimes speaks of you or another nurse who visits him – but the only one who truly matters is Sergeant Wright.'

'They get on very well,' Michelle said, realising that Sister Norton thought Eric was his real uncle rather than merely an adopted one. Eric had obviously allowed the nurses and doctors to believe he was Matty's uncle and there was no harm in it. She thought of what marriage to Eric would mean and she felt a tingle at the thought of being intimate with him. Eric never made any secret of his desire to make love to her, though to give him his credit he hadn't gone beyond a kiss or two. Eric had laughed when Michelle pushed him away after a passionate kiss and told her there was no need to worry, because he was saving himself for marriage. The wicked gleam in his eyes told her he was teasing her, but she was glad that he was prepared to be patient.

Michelle also knew that her attitude towards Eric had changed since the night she'd brought him to see

Matty. Whereas before she'd seen him just as the tough East Ender, who had made the Army his career, she now saw a generous caring man who wanted kids and a home – which, she'd begun to understand, were the things she really wanted deep down. Not that she would give up her nursing; she might have to for a while if she had kids of her own, but it was something you never lost – a job you could go back to when the children were older, if the hospital would take you on. She recalled her wandering thoughts, realising that Sister Norton was speaking.

'Thank you, Miss Morris. Matty isn't quite ready to leave us. We are going to keep him here for some time yet, and then I imagine he will come back to St Saviour's – until your happy event. However, we should like to think that eventually he will live with his uncle. It will be a long slow job, my dear, and as a nurse you understand what he will need . . .'

Michelle didn't contradict her. She knew it was best to be careful, because Matty had become very fond of Eric and if the doctors thought he was not going to keep up the care and friendship he'd offered, the child might be moved away from his influence – and that would break Matty's heart. He truly loved his adopted uncle and Michelle believed Eric was fond of him. It might be possible to adopt the boy properly if . . .

Her mind was churning with all kinds of thoughts as she walked home. It was a lovely mild night for the time of year and Michelle walked past the river, watching the boats chugging up and down the sluggish and rather smelly water, not wanting to go home at once. She knew Eric wanted to marry her. He'd promised to leave the army next year and find work in London if she became his wife.

For a while Michelle had felt confused; torn between two men that she liked, her resolution not to let another man into her heart had wavered. She'd thought that nursing children would be enough – that she did not need a home of her own or children and a husband, but now she wasn't sure.

What about Richard? She was attracted to him, but kept getting mixed signals from him. He'd seemed to take an interest in her, but he hadn't been the same since that visit to the museum. She'd met him once when she was leaving St Saviour's, but apart from a brief inquiry about Matty and her parents, he'd had nothing to say to her.

If she wanted to get married, she should talk to Eric and discover his feelings about adopting Matty. If Eric was in favour, he would find them a house then Matty could live with them. He could go to his school with the other St Saviour's kids and come back there for his tea when she was working, and afterwards Michelle would take him home. She would be able to give him the physical exercise he would need at home and, if they were lucky, in time his spine would heal and he would walk again.

Michelle's mind began to think of the practical things. She wasn't ready to give up work altogether and once Eric got his release from the Army, he'd be around more and he would be able to meet Matty after school sometimes – and in time, she'd probably have a baby of her own.

She could see all the advantages and she'd been

coming round to the idea that Eric would make a good husband and father – all she had to do now was to make up her mind whether or not she could love him as he undoubtedly loved her, because to marry him for other reasons wouldn't be fair . . .

Running the last few steps to her home, Michelle put all such thoughts out of her mind. She wanted to do the right thing for herself, for Eric and for Matty, but she couldn't be sure what that was yet. She would have to give it some more thought – perhaps have a talk to Alice. She and Bob would be back from holiday this weekend . . .

'Where are you going, Samantha?' It was pure luck that Wendy was in time to spot the twins leaving St Saviour's by the back door. She'd popped across to the Nurses' Home for a clean uniform after one of her patients had been sick over her and was on her way back when they appeared. Both had their coats on and Samantha was carrying a bundle of clothes under one arm. Her guilty look told Wendy everything. 'Oh, Samantha, Sarah, you're not trying to run away are you?'

'I don't want to see her,' Samantha said, and her mouth pulled down at the corners. 'I won't let them take Sarah away, I won't . . .'

Sarah sneezed suddenly and Wendy saw that tears were running down her cheeks. 'What's wrong, love?' she asked. 'Are you not feeling well?'

'Sarah's head hurt,' the child said and pulled her hand from Samantha's. 'Sarah not run away from Wendy . . . Sarah want to stay here . . .'

Wendy placed a hand on her brow and frowned in

concern. The child was burning up, clearly running a fever. 'You're not well,' she said, and looked at Samantha. 'Sarah needs to be in bed. I'm going to tuck her up in the sick ward – I think she has a nasty cold coming on. Please don't run away, Samantha. Let me look after you – and let your auntie talk to you. She won't be taking you anywhere yet, because Sarah isn't well enough.'

Samantha looked at her for a moment, and then inclined her head. 'All right,' she agreed. 'But if they try to separate us we shall run away and hide until she goes back to France.'

'I think perhaps you should have a day off school too,' Wendy said. 'You can get in bed near Sarah and I'll make you both a nice hot drink . . . it's too cold for you to go out and you might be catching a cold too.'

Taking Sarah firmly by the hand, Wendy led them back into St Saviour's. She was secretly pleased that their aunt wouldn't be able to take them out that weekend after all. It would take time for Samantha to trust her mother's sister and the best thing for them all was to remain at St Saviour's until they knew what kind of a woman Madame Bernard was – and if Wendy had to pretend that both sisters were sicker than they actually were, she would do it . . .

'Madame Bernard?' Angela said and offered her hand to the young woman who had just introduced herself. 'I'm very pleased to meet you at last.'

'As I too am pleased,' Françoise Bernard spoke in a soft musical voice. 'I 'ave long wanted to find my sister's babies and at last I am 'ere . . .'

'Unfortunately, the twins will not be able to leave St Saviour's this weekend as they are suffering from colds . . . and Sarah is running quite a nasty temperature.'

'For this I am so sorry,' Françoise said, looking upset and disappointed. 'I may see them, yes?'

'Yes, certainly, Madame. They are both in the sick ward and at the moment we do not have any other cases, though we have three children down with a vomiting bug, but they are in the isolation ward.'

'I do not quite understand . . . what ees this place?'

Angela explained they kept children who had infectious diseases separate from those suffering less serious illnesses, and the young woman nodded. She was in her early twenties, rather pretty and she looked a little like Sarah, with the same unusual pale hair, but her eyes were a deeper blue and her skin had a delicate tan from living in a much warmer climate.

'What is your intention in visiting the twins, Madame Bernard?'

'If they like me, I 'ope to take them 'ome to France with me very soon.'

'Do you have the paperwork necessary to take the twins with you, should you wish to?' Angela asked as they walked along the hall. 'I realise they are your sister's children, but I'm not sure how easy it is to take adopted children back to France.'

'My 'usband ees nephew to the . . . how you would call it? . . . the lawyer,' Françoise said. 'You forgive please. My English is not so good as I would wish. I 'ave the papers I need to take my sister's babies 'ome to France, yes.'

'I see.' Angela was thoughtful. Madame Bernard

seemed pleasant and was obviously eager to take her sister's children. 'You have been told that Sarah is very dependent on her sister, and we could not consent to them being parted . . .'

'But of course I wish for both Samantha and Sarah,' Françoise said. 'My sister would wish it. When she left us to marry her sailor, my 'eart, it broke. I was still a child when she died, but when I learned of her death I vowed that one day I would find them . . .' Tears glistened in her eyes. 'My 'usband 'e consents to 'ave the little ones with us. We 'ave no babies of our own and we will love them.'

'Yes, well, Samantha and Sarah have had a bad experience, so please give them some time to get used to you before you tell them you want to take them away from us.'

Angela pushed open the door and saw Wendy taking Sarah's temperature. The nurse turned; a defensive wary expression on her face as she saw the woman with Angela.

'Sarah still isn't very well,' she said. 'She needs an aspirin and a nice warm drink.'

'*Ma petite*,' Françoise said and moved eagerly towards the bed. 'My poor little one, you 'ave the nasty 'eadache, no? Eet ees like your poor *maman*, she always have the 'eadache – when she was child she 'ave many 'eadaches. And the ear, she too is bad . . .'

Sitting on the edge of Sarah's bed, she reached forward and stroked her head gently, and then she began to sing softly, a lullaby in French. Sarah looked surprised and then began to sing the words with her, their words slightly different, but the tune exactly the same.

'You know your *maman*'s favourite song!' Françoise said, and leaned down to kiss Sarah's cheek. 'She always sing to me when I was baby – and she sing to you her song, yes? Your *grandmère*, she teach us both. When she carry her little ones inside, she think of them with love and she sing to them . . . my poor Jenni she do the same, this I know . . .'

Samantha had got out of bed and was sitting on the opposite side of Sarah's bed, staring at her aunt oddly. Françoise turned to look at her and smiled. Samantha stared back but didn't smile.

'And you are my so brave Samantha,' Françoise said and reached across to touch her hand. 'I 'ear all 'ow you look after ma petite – you are 'er big sister, no?'

'We're twins,' Samantha said. 'Did you know my mummy?'

'She was my big sister and when she went to England with 'er sailor to be married I cry all night, because I think I no see her again, and I break my 'eart – but now I see my Jenni again in you and Sarah . . .' Tears had started to run freely down Françoise's cheeks and she made no attempt to check them as she held out her hand to Sarah, who took it trustingly. 'I pray always to find you well . . .' She held her other hand out to Samantha. For a moment the child held back but then she moved slowly to place her hand in her aunt's.

'I won't come to live with you unless Sarah comes too,' she said, her face set stubbornly, still not quite able to trust.

'But of a certainty Sarah must come also,' her aunt told her. 'My 'usband has a big 'ouse and a farm with many animals. For you and Sarah he has waiting a puppy and a little 'orse you can ride. 'Ee cannot wait to show you all the animals. And, for me, I show you all the things that belonged to your *maman* when she was child . . .'

'My mother's things? Did she have a doll?' Samantha asked, her interest aroused. 'And pretty clothes?'

'My Jenni had a doll and a rocking 'orse, and I 'ave kept them for you,' Françoise told her and smiled. 'When you and my precious Sarah are well, you come with me to France, yes?'

Samantha removed her hand and looked warily at Wendy, who was standing a few feet away watching. 'Can Wendy come too?' she asked.

Françoise turned to look at the nurse and nodded. 'If your friend want to come for a holiday to help you, she will be welcome – and to visit you whenever she wish.'

'Oh . . .' Wendy blushed. 'I don't know. It's very kind of you, but . . .'

'Please come, Wendy,' Samantha begged. 'Sarah wants you to come too, don't you, Sarah?'

Sarah nodded, looking very solemn. She had watched and listened, but now she looked at Françoise and said, 'Sing *Maman*'s song to us, please.'

Angela turned away as Françoise began to sing softly to the children. She touched Wendy's arm and they walked to the door together.

'I think you should go, for ten days or so. I'll help you with the passport and pay your fare there and back.'

'If you think . . .' Wendy faltered. 'I've never been to France or anywhere much.'

'Well, this is an opportunity for you,' Angela said. 'I should feel easier in my mind if you went with them,

Wendy. Madame Bernard seems truly delightful, but I want you to see what her husband is like – and to make sure the children are happy there before you come back. Will you do that for me?'

'Yes, of course,' Wendy agreed. 'But what about my job – what will Sister Beatrice say about my taking a holiday so soon?'

'I'm sure the other nurses will be willing to do extra hours while you're away. Besides, Sister Beatrice is back now and she's always ready to step in.'

'In that case I'll tell Samantha that I can go with her and Sarah,' Wendy said. 'I think their aunt truly wants and loves them, but I should feel easier if I could see them settled.'

'Then I suggest we get everything in order so you can go.'

'If we leave on Monday, I should be back for Christmas.'

'Yes, well, that would be nice, but first you must be sure in your own mind that the twins are safe and happy.'

'Absolutely,' Wendy said. 'I feel as if a cloud has lifted, Angela – and it will be quite an experience for me.'

'I'm sure it will – and we can all be easier in our minds.'

Angela left the ward and made her way back down to the kitchens. That was one worry off her mind, and now she could really start to make arrangements for a good Christmas for them all. And afterwards . . . well, perhaps she would have even more to make her happy in the New Year . . .

THIRTY-SEVEN

'That was such a lovely holiday,' Alice said as she dumped all her parcels and the bags they hadn't been able to get into the cases on the kitchen table. 'I've never had so much fun or enjoyed myself so much, Bob.'

Bob smiled at her. He'd taken the suitcases into the bedroom, and left Alice to bring the small bits. Susie was in her carrycot in the kitchen and Alice bent down to take her out as she started to grizzle.

'She's wet and tired, Alice love. I'll change her nappy and put her in her cot . . .' He placed a white envelope on the kitchen table. 'That came for you while we were away. I picked it up in the hall.'

Alice stared at the envelope and recognised Jack's hand. 'No,' she said without thinking. 'Throw it away, Bob. I don't want it. I'm not going to open it.'

Bob looked at her curiously, but took Susie through into the bedroom and gently deposited her in her cot. She'd stopped grizzling as soon as she was dry and clean, settling down in the coolness of familiar surroundings, and he returned to the kitchen. Alice had filled the kettle and placed a couple of plates on the table.

'What do you fancy?' she asked as she took knives and forks from the drawer. 'Poached egg on toast? They look lovely, those eggs we bought from that farm on the way home. Or would you rather have some chips and Spam?'

'We'll have the eggs, but not yet,' Bob said. 'Sit down and have a cup of tea first and tell me why don't you want to open that letter.'

'I know who it's from and I don't want to see what it says.'

Bob frowned, picked up the letter and tore it open, ignoring Alice's gasp of protest. He read it and then handed it to her but Alice shook her head, refusing to accept it. 'It's from that bloody Jack Shaw. What does he mean about the key he gave you and your promise to take him what was inside the locker?'

Alice trembled inside; she'd never known Bob to be angry with her, but he was now. 'I didn't know where Jack was until he sent me a key to a locker at Euston Station. He wanted me to fetch the stuff inside and take it to him. When I didn't do as he asked, he came here,' she said. 'He turned up at the back door because Lee's men were watching the front.' Alice raised her head and looked at her husband. 'He wanted me to go away to America with him.'

'And now he's angry with you for not keeping your word. He says he's leaving for America tomorrow and if you don't meet him with the stuff he's going alone.'

'Good,' Alice said defiantly. 'I don't want stolen stuff – and I don't want Jack Shaw. I'm finished with him. I told him I'd take him the stuff to get rid of him, but I never intended to do it.'

'Is that the truth?'

Alice nodded. 'I gave the key to the police.'

'You did what?' Bob stared at her. 'Blimey, Alice, that's torn it! You may be called to give evidence – you could even be accused of being involved with criminals if that stuff was stolen.'

'I gave it to Constable Sallis. He said I was in the clear, but his boss might want to speak to me . . .' Alice's hands trembled. 'I didn't know what else to do, Bob. Butcher Lee's men follow me sometimes. I daren't fetch that stuff – if I did, they would take it from me. Jack said I should ask Michelle, but I wasn't going to get her into trouble.'

'Why didn't you tell me?'

'I thought you would be angry that Jack came here – you are angry, aren't you?'

'Yes,' Bob looked at her coldly. 'You shouldn't have let him in, Alice, and you shouldn't have taken the key. You didn't go to him, so I believe you when you say it's over, but I'm going to the police. I want to know what's happening – if you're in any trouble.'

'Oh, Bob,' Alice's eyes filled with tears. 'Please don't be angry with me. We've been so happy . . .'

'I have to know I can trust you while I'm away. What kind of a marriage do we have if you have other men here – make them promises?'

'I swear, nothing happened between us. I don't want him – you can trust me, it's over.'

'I hope so,' he said and reached for the jacket he'd taken off earlier.

'Where are you going?' Alice caught at his arm in fright. 'Please don't go – stay and have your tea.'

'This has to be sorted,' Bob said, his mouth set in a grim line.

'You're not leaving me?'

Bob looked at her for a moment, but he didn't smile. 'No, I shan't leave you, Alice, but I wish you'd told me. If you'd trusted me, you would've told me – and there's no love without trust.'

Bob walked out of the door, leaving Alice to stare after him. She felt shattered. If Bob turned against her, it would all be spoiled. When she'd married him, she hadn't realised what a good man she'd got, but she did now and she loved him. She'd discovered how much on holiday and believed she'd managed to put the past behind her, but Jack's letter had ruined all that – and now she wasn't sure what the future held . . .

'May I have a word, Mrs Manning?'

Alice stared at the police constable standing outside her door the next morning and moved back as her heart began to race, allowing him to enter without speaking a word. Her husband came into the hall and saw who it was; he hesitated and then said, 'Ask him through to the kitchen, Alice. I'll put the kettle on – unless this is an official visit?'

'Well, sort of, but no one here is in trouble,' Constable Sallis said, taking off his helmet as he followed Alice into the warm kitchen, with its yellow and white flowery curtains and the scrubbed pine table, which was covered with signs of baking. 'Something smells good. Rock cakes I think?'

Alice laughed. 'Coconut buns and a lemon drizzle cake,' she said. 'Sit down and Bob will make a cup of tea – you can try the cake or the buns, but the cake is an experiment. I've never made it before.'

'Take no notice of Alice,' Bob said as he set the kettle on the gas ring and lit it. 'She's a real good cook. What is it then, Constable?'

'I had a word with my boss after we spoke last night. I've been told to ask Alice if she'll do something to help us bring them villains to book,' Constable Sallis said and cleared his throat. 'It's not something I like to ask – it might be dangerous. But it would be helpful if she agreed.'

Bob frowned at him. 'I don't want my wife in any danger.'

'Listen to him, Bob. I'm not afraid of that lot, even though they are rogues.'

'It's like this,' Constable Sallis said. 'We opened that locker, Mrs Manning, and we've found a lot of evidence as well as stolen goods. I reckon whoever put that stuff there was using it as insurance against the rogues who were after him.'

'You mean Jack Shaw?'

'Yes, though there's no evidence it was him, mind – but there's a lot of stuff that will put his friends inside for a few years. The thing is, my boss wants to catch them red-handed. He says the things we've got — photos, papers – are all right, but he wants something concrete afore he goes ahead with the arrests. We'll only get the one chance at these villains and we've nothing to connect them to the pinched stuff in that locker. It could make all the difference . . .'

'Spit it out then, man,' Bob said. 'What do you want Alice to do?'

Constable Sallis placed the key on the kitchen table. 'We want Alice to fetch that stuff from the locker. The evidence has been taken out, but the jewels are still there. We want to catch the villains with that stuff in their possession.'

Bob glared at him. 'You want Alice to be the bait so they snatch the stuff and then you nab them – is that right?'

'Not quite. We think they'll grab it away from Alice and take it back to Mr Lee, and then we'll pounce. We'll have men in plain clothes in the club and uniformed men nearby. As soon as they take the stuff to Lee, we've got him.'

'No,' Bob said firmly. 'They might hurt Alice when they grab it. I'm not risking it. I'll fetch the stuff.'

'That wouldn't work. They would know you'd make a fight of it and probably just follow you to see where you took it – besides, it's Alice they suspect. She's the only one that can make it work. But I don't blame you. I told my boss you wouldn't agree.'

'I'll do it,' Alice said quickly, then, as Bob protested, 'They'll never leave us alone, Bob. Even when we went to the pub the other week, they followed us. The only way is to see them put away – you know it is.'

'Alice will be safe – we'll be following you. If at any time you seem in danger, one of my men will step in.'

'No, leave that to me,' Bob said, looking at Alice. 'I'll make sure she's all right but I shan't attempt to stop them getting away – if it's a copper they'll smell a rat, but if it's Alice's husband they won't suspect anything.'

'Bob, I don't want you to get hurt!'

'I'm not happy about you placing yourself in danger,

Alice, but you're right. These people are evil and it's time they were stopped. If you want to go through with it, I'll follow and watch out for you – the cops can keep under cover until they spring their surprise. That's my terms, otherwise you're not doing it.'

'I agree with your husband, Alice,' Constable Sallis told her. 'I wouldn't want my sister or wife running the risk, but if your husband knows what he's doing, then we're all right – but make sure you let go when they grab the bag from you. Don't fight it or they might hurt you.'

'All right, I'll remember,' Alice said. 'When do you want me to do it?'

'Tomorrow morning at ten o'clock, please. Leave your baby with a neighbour you can trust; we don't want any slip-ups.'

'I'll take her to St Saviour's and leave her with Nan for a while.'

'Yes, the child will be safe there,' Constable Sallis agreed, and stood up. 'I'll tell my boss you've consented, Mrs Manning. I know he will be grateful – and, whatever happens, your name will be kept out of it.'

'Thank you, I'll see you out . . .' Bob went to the door with him and Alice heard them talking in low tones. She frowned as she heard the baby whimpering and went through to her, picking her up and taking her back to the kitchen. Susie was ready for her bottle.

'It's all arranged,' Bob said when he returned. 'I hope you know what you've agreed to, Alice. These men are dangerous and they may be armed with knives or even a gun.'

'Oh, Bob,' Alice shivered as she looked at him. 'I

know all they will want from me is the bag – but if you get involved, they might hurt you. Please don't do anything unless you have to, for my sake.'

'I'm not a coward and I can take care of myself,' Bob growled. 'It's you I'm anxious about, Alice. I don't want you getting hurt.'

'And I care about you,' she said, going to him and putting her arms about his waist. 'Believe me, Bob, I do care. I should hate it if anything happened to you.'

'It won't,' he said, and he was looking at her in the old way, with care and concern. ' Remember what the constable said and let them take the bag.'

'I will,' she said and looked up at him. 'You're not angry with me now, are you?'

'No, I'm not angry. I love you, Alice. But I want you to trust me. Whatever happens in future, tell me.'

'I promise,' she said. 'But Jack won't come back again. His letter said he was leaving for America. All I meant to him was someone he could use. He seduced me with pretty words and a few drinks – and then he thought he could use me to fetch that stuff, but I refused. I've finished with him, and I'm only doing this so that they can put those evil men away and give us some peace.'

Bob closed his arms about her, holding her tight. 'I never want to lose you, Alice love. You and Susie mean too much to me . . .'

'You won't lose me,' she promised. 'I didn't know what a good man I'd got, but I do now. Michelle told me I should grab you quick and marry you. She was right, but then, Michelle usually is!'

THIRTY-EIGHT

'Nearly finished?' Mark asked, entering Angela's office as she took a sheet of paper from her typewriter. 'I'm taking you out for a meal this evening – but first we're going to talk about us.' He took out a small leather diary from his pocket and opened it. Now, I've provisionally booked a flight for the seventh of January – that will give us ten days in France at a skiing resort in the Alps.'

'Oh, Mark . . .' Angela said, hesitating as she pulled her diary out. 'I've got an appointment on the eighth of January with one of our sponsors.'

'If we postpone again, we could wait for ever. Do you want to spend some time with me?'

'Yes, very much.' Angela saw the quizzical look in his eyes and laughed. 'You know I do. Very well, I will postpone that appointment. Just after Christmas is as good a time as any to take a holiday. I'm sure I can square it with Sister Beatrice.'

'Excellent.' Mark bent to take the book from her hand. He pulled her to her feet and into his arms. 'I've been fretting at the bit to get back to you, Angela. You do know that I adore you?'

'Yes, I know.' Angela covered her typewriter. 'Where are we going this evening?'

'Somewhere special. It's a surprise. I want to spoil you, my love.'

'Yes, I'd like to be spoiled,' Angela said, and then as they left her office and walked to the lift: 'I've been working on my Christmas Orphans' campaign, Mark – and I've come up with something that might be a big—'

Mark pressed his fingers to her lips. 'Not tonight, my darling. We've got the rest of our lives to plan this splendid campaign of yours. For this evening at least, I want you all to myself . . .'

Sister Beatrice saw them getting into the lift and smiled. They looked happy together and that was a good thing. She was aware of Mark's plans to take Angela off on a skiing trip after Christmas, and of his hopes for the future, because he'd called in to have a talk to her earlier. He'd known how disturbed she'd been by that wretched board meeting when it looked as if a move to the country had been contemplated.

'I do not think I could consider taking on the position of Warden at such a place,' she'd told him frankly. 'I am London born and I understand the children here and their needs. I lived in the same streets when I was a child, and though my family wasn't as poor as some, I was familiar with poverty. My usefulness is here, Mr Adderbury.'

'Yes, I do understand that.' Mark had smiled with the easy charm that won him so many friends. 'It was never my intention to ask you to move, Sister. I think we always envisaged that St Saviour's would stay where

368

it is in Halfpenny Street – but many of the bigger homes are moving out into the country, where I think the children have the chance of a better life – do you not agree? I believe that we may build in the future, when the time is right for such a move.'

'Some children will benefit from it, no doubt. Yet there are others who will rebel and even run away. If you study the statistics given in various reports, you will know that the percentage of children running away from their orphanage has been increasing. Some of that may be down to bad management and even ill-treatment, but I think some is undoubtedly because they do not want to be torn from the world they know.'

'Yes, you may well be right,' Mark said. 'We all of us want to do the best for our children, but too often they are not consulted. It may be best to let them choose in as far as that is practical.'

'Well, that will be for you and others . . .'

'No doubt,' Mark said. 'But if I am ever able to raise the funds for the kind of complex I envisage, it will be a vast step forward. Think of the children you have here enjoying access to sports facilities on site as well as an indoor pool . . .'

Beatrice smiled inwardly. She thought his dream impractical and unlikely ever to be more than that, because it would surely cost too much to build. Mark Adderbury was a man of vision, but this time she believed he would discover he was hoping for too much – a swimming pool indeed!

As she approached the sick ward the door opened and Nan came out, looking pleased with something. She saw Beatrice and smiled, moving towards her.

'I was on my way to see you,' she said. 'Have you time for a quick chat? There's something I need to talk over with you.'

'Something wrong?'

'A few doubts I have, concerning one of my carers . . .'

Beatrice frowned. Nan didn't often come to her with her troubles, so it must be something unpleasant. 'It's Tilly again,' Nan said, looking over her shoulder to make sure none of the other staff were passing and could overhear. 'She seemed more cheerful when Angela moved her into the Nurses' Home, but recently she's been looking very unhappy. I suspect something is upsetting her but she won't tell me anything. I wondered if she might talk to you.'

'She isn't a Catholic, is she?'

'Not to my knowledge.'

'Then I doubt she will have much to tell me,' Beatrice said. 'Angela took the girl on. Perhaps you should ask her to talk to Tilly.'

'Yes, perhaps. She's had a lot to do recently, what with one thing and another. I didn't like to bother her. I think she's up to her neck with arrangements for Christmas. She and Father Joe are putting on a concert for us, as well as the carols – and we're having sponsors and friends of St Saviour's to the carol service on Christmas Eve.'

'Yes, Mark told me about all the plans for Christmas.' Beatrice shook her head. 'He spoils these children, Nan. It worries me that they will leave here expecting too much – it is a hard world out there and they will have to face reality.'

'So many of them have tragedy in their lives,' Nan

said thoughtfully. 'Surely it can't hurt for them to have some fun?'

'Perhaps. Well, if you're truly concerned about Tilly, perhaps I should talk to her,' Beatrice said. 'Send her to me tomorrow morning and I'll see if I can discover what is troubling her.'

Tilly had a good idea why she was being summoned to Sister Beatrice's office that morning. Nan had been cross with her on three separate occasions, because she'd made mistakes. Each time she'd apologised and Nan had told her to get on with her work and be more careful in future.

'When you drop a tray of glasses it costs money to replace them, and broken glass is dangerous. Make sure you sweep it up properly and don't leave it lying on the dining room floor.'

'I'm sorry. I thought I'd got it all,' Tilly said, on the verge of tears. The problem was that she'd been so worried that day she hadn't known what to do with herself. When she'd left home she'd thought her stepfather would leave her alone, but three times in the last week he'd been waiting for her as she left St Saviour's and walked through the gardens to the Nurses' Home.

'I thought I'd catch you, Tilly love,' he'd said in a soft persuasive tone. 'Your ma wants you to come home and so do I.'

'I'm never coming back while you live there,' Tilly had retorted fiercely, and she'd been made to regret it when he grabbed her and twisted her arm. 'Leave me alone, you brute!'

'You watch your mouth, girl,' he said. 'Your mother

has done nothing but nag me since you left and I shan't put up with it – if you don't come back I'll leave her and then she'll starve or end up on the streets.'

Tilly had pulled away from him and Michelle's father had come into the garden to fetch something from the shed. When her stepfather saw him looking curiously at them, he shrugged and walked off, but not before he'd warned her again what would happen to her mother if she didn't oblige him.

She tapped softly at Sister Beatrice's door and was invited to enter. Opening it reluctantly, she went in and stood in front of the nun. Due to her illness, Tilly hadn't seen a great deal of her since she'd come to work at the children's home and she was still in awe of her.

'You wanted to see me, Sister?'

'Yes, Tilly, I do.' Beatrice looked up and nodded. 'You may sit down. I asked you to come to my office so that we can talk in private. Nan tells me that you have been making mistakes. While everyone has accidents sometimes, when too many things happen it makes us wonder why. Are you happy with us? Do you enjoy your work – or is it simply that you find it boring?'

'Oh no, Sister,' Tilly said instantly. 'I do like it here. Everyone is friendly and I'm sorry I dropped those glasses the other day . . . and for all the other things I've done. I do try not to make mistakes, but . . .' her words tailed off. How could she explain that she was tired due to lack of sleep and worry?

'Are you upset about something?'

Tilly gulped and hung her head; then she brought her gaze up. 'Yes, I am – but you can't help me, Sister. No one can.'

'We can't help you if you don't tell us, but I am not easily shocked, Tilly. Even though I have taken the veil, I understand the problems a young girl may face. Are you in trouble?'

'Not that sort!' Tilly's face flamed. 'But I might be, if he has his way – he's always after me and makin' threats. He says if I don't go home, he'll leave me ma. But if I do he'll keep at me until he gets his way . . . And there's me little sister Mags. What if he starts on her?'

Sister Beatrice frowned. 'Are you saying this man – your stepfather – has been here bothering you?'

'Yes, Sister, he has. I thought I'd be safe here when Mrs Morton got me the room, but he was waiting in the garden the other night and he grabbed me – and threatened me. He said if I didn't go home he would make Ma suffer. I know she won't cope if he leaves her. She never has since my father died – and she'll be back to her old ways . . .'

'And what were they?'

'Drinkin' and pickin' up any man that looks at her,' Tilly said and a tear slid down her cheek. 'She brought them home most nights when I was a kid – but then she found someone who was prepared to marry her and look after us both. He was all right, like a father to me and his own kids until I was seventeen, and then he started lookin' at me . . . well, you know. I've been fightin' him off for the past year. I had to get away, but he still won't leave me alone.'

'I am very sorry, Tilly,' Beatrice said. 'One thing I can do immediately is to have a bigger gate put on the garden and make sure it is locked. It means the nurses will have to enter through St Saviour's or carry their key, but I will not have men climbing into our garden and upsetting our staff.' She looked at Tilly thoughtfully. 'I'm not sure what more I can do, Tilly. I do see you are worried about your mother's welfare, but if he is such an unpleasant character, your mother might be better off without him. And if you're worried about your young sister, you should speak to the Welfare department about him.'

'He hasn't touched her, as far as I know. And Ma would kill me if I fetched the Welfare on her, but I can't help thinkin' that he might . . . He's such a pig!'

'Perhaps your mother should be made aware of what sort of man her husband is. She might tell him to leave herself.'

'She wouldn't manage,' Tilly said. 'I know no one can help, but thank you for listening – and I'll try to do better, if you'll give me another chance.'

'I do not wish to sack you,' Beatrice said. 'I feel that your life has been hard enough, Tilly. Is there no one, no male relative, that could help you?'

'No.' Tilly forced a smile. 'I can take care of myself, Sister – but unless I give him what he wants, he'll make Ma suffer.'

'If you will take my advice, I should ignore his threats. Bullies seldom carry them out, you know. Believe me, I have had personal experience of these things. Have you considered that he may be settled and satisfied being looked after by your mother? Why do you not call his bluff and let him do his worst – if he does go off and leave her, you could return home then and help her to manage.' Sister Beatrice rose and walked round the desk, taking hold of Tilly's shoulder. 'Be brave, my dear. The worst is often much less than you fear.'

Tilly thanked her and left the office. She knew she was lucky that Sister Beatrice was giving her another chance, and she must try harder to make sure she did her work properly – but it hadn't solved her problem. Tilly knew that her mother cared for the man she'd married; she would put up with anything rather than lose him – even if it meant that he was creeping into her daughter's bedroom to force himself on her.

Tilly blinked back her tears. She wasn't going to give in to him. She would rather die than let him rape her, but her decision was going to make things difficult for her mother. Yet if Tilly gave in . . . No, she couldn't, she wouldn't let the brute touch her because it would strip away all her self-esteem and she'd rather throw herself in the canal.

THIRTY-NINE

Alice resisted the urge to look over her shoulder. Bob had told her that she wouldn't be able to spot him following her and she wasn't to try. If she did she would betray her nerves to the other men following her, and she knew there had been two of them: she was used to it happening. One of them had been loitering across the street when she left her home, and the other one had hopped on a bus when she did, sitting right behind her. So if she'd tried to avoid the first tail she'd still have had the second after her. She'd often wondered why they bothered to follow her, but now that she knew what had been in that locker, she understood. They'd suspected that Jack might try to use her to fetch the stuff and they wanted it – they wanted it badly.

It all made sense now. Alice knew that Jack had never loved her, despite all his fine words. He'd been using her all the time, laughing at her for being fool enough to give him her heart. Oh, he might have fancied her, but he'd never loved her – not the way Bob did. She wondered where Bob was. She knew he'd probably be at Euston already, because it was only when she had that bag that Lee's men would go for her.

She tried not to be afraid; Bob was good at protecting people, it was what he did for a living, and Susie was with Nan at St Saviour's. Bob had taken her there himself; they didn't want anyone to know she was there and the gang only followed Alice.

Getting off the bus as it reached the station, Alice was aware that her shadow had jumped off at the last minute. She tried to think clearly, stopping at a newspaper kiosk, loitering as if she were uncertain, because that's how she would have felt if she hadn't known there were plain clothes policemen mixing with the crowds. Making her way to the lockers, Alice searched for the number that matched hers and saw it. Her heart was racing now and she clenched her hands, the nails pricking her palms as she felt the dryness in her mouth. She almost wished she hadn't said she would do it, but if she hadn't her shadows would never leave her.

Lifting her head proudly, she walked to the locker and then took the key from her pocket. The bag inside was an old leather portmanteau. She reached for it, heart pounding as she extracted it and left the key hanging. Turning, she walked quickly towards the entrance. It was as she reached the newspaper stand that she felt the touch on her hand and realised that someone was near. Glancing to her left, she saw a man she recognised, the scar on his face as deep as ever. Perhaps it was because she'd seen him and disliked him many times that Alice reacted so fiercely. As he tried to take the bag from her, she snatched it back.

'You're not having it,' she said, glaring at him.

'Give it here, you little bitch,' Big Harry muttered and pulled on the bag sharply. 'It will be the worse for you if you don't.'

Remembering her instructions, she let go of it suddenly and Big Harry's eyes narrowed. 'I'll be back for you, bitch,' he muttered. 'You're going to get what you deserve.' He raised his hand to strike at her, landing a blow on the side of her head. Alice staggered and would have fallen but the next moment the other man who had followed her earlier came up and grabbed her arm.

'We'll take her with us,' he muttered. 'I don't trust this one.'

Alice pulled away from him desperately, but he held on to her arm, propelling her forward. She could smell the stink of beer on his breath and an underlying stench that she associated with stale sweat. 'Let me go or I'll scream,' Alice muttered. 'I shan't come quietly!'

'Let the bitch go, Ned. We'll deal with her later,' Big Harry said and strode off ahead of them, ignoring his colleague. Clearly, he was more interested in getting the stolen goods back to his boss, but Ned was determined to hang on to her.

Alice opened her mouth to scream, but the man clamped his large hand over it, muttering threats. She bit him as hard as she could, and he took his hand from her mouth, swearing at her furiously. Then the knife was in his hand, pressing into her side as she was dragged along in Big Harry's wake, though it was hard to see him through the crowds. Alice felt the despair wash over her, but then someone grabbed her by the arm and she was wrenched away from her captor.

'Get out of here, Alice,' Bob warned and pushed her behind him.

She gave a cry of alarm as the thug turned on him, knife in hand. Terrified that Bob would be injured, instead of running as he'd told her, she stood, feet glued to the ground as the two men struggled for the knife. It was a desperate struggle; Ned was strong and determined. The knife flashed out twice and Alice was sure it had struck Bob. Screaming, she watched in horror as they struggled, uncertain which way it would go, and then she saw the knife go flying through the air and fall skittering across the ground. Watching in stunned silence, Alice saw Bob stagger and she thought he would go down, but he rallied, twisting the rogue's arm back behind him until she heard a crack and a scream and the man who had attacked her went limp and sank to his knees.

'You've broke me arm, yer bastard,' he muttered, seconds before three uniformed policemen surrounded him and he was carted away. The whole thing had taken a few seconds but for Alice it had seemed an eternity.

'Bob,' she whispered. 'I thought you weren't coming.'

'I had to let Big Harry get away,' Bob said. 'He isn't the one the police want . . .'

Before he could finish the sentence his eyes rolled back and he swayed towards her. She tried to catch him in her arms, but he was too heavy and brought her down to her knees as he collapsed.

'He's hurt – he's been knifed!' Alice cried, and one of the uniformed officers came to look. Blood was running from a wound in the side of Bob's chest. 'That man had a knife and he hurt Bob. Oh, God, he's hurt bad . . .' Tears were running down her cheeks. Bob was hurt and it was all her fault. He hadn't wanted her to do this and now he was injured – he might even be dying . . . and she couldn't bear that, because she loved him. Until this moment she hadn't realised how much she cared for the man she'd married. It had grown slowly without her really understanding the shift in her feelings, but now, suddenly, she knew that she loved him and her life would never be the same if he died.

'Don't worry, Mrs Manning,' the officer said. 'We'll phone for an ambulance. We'll look after him. Are you all right?'

'It doesn't matter about me,' Alice said, kneeling by her husband and looking at his white face. 'I've got a few bruises but Bob is hurt bad . . .' She bent over him, running her fingers over his face as the tears fell. She could see the blood staining his shirt and it terrified her. Oh, why had she ever agreed to this madness? Alice had done her bit, handing the key in, she shouldn't have taken part in this stupid plot. If Bob died because of it, she would never forgive herself . . .

Alice was sitting on a hard seat in the hospital corridor when Michelle found her later that afternoon. She was carrying Susie's carrycot and looking anxious as she sat down next to her.

'I came as soon as I could, love,' she said. 'When Sister got the message that Bob had been hurt, she told me to bring Susie to you and said she would take over in the sick ward. She said if you needed me I should stay with you all night and not bother about coming in tomorrow.'

'I'm glad you're here,' Alice said. She looked down at her sleeping child and caught back a sob. 'We were so happy, Michelle. Bob loves me and Susie. He didn't want me to do it, but I insisted. Oh God, I wish I hadn't. If anything happens, it'll be all my fault!'

'Have they told you how he is?' Michelle touched her hand in sympathy. 'Bob's a strong man. He's got a good chance of pulling through.'

Alice nodded, wiping her tears with the back of her hand. 'I'm such a fool, Michelle. I didn't know what a good man I'd got . . . And now it's too late!'

'It isn't too late.' Michelle squeezed her hand comfortingly. 'They haven't told you he's dead, have they?'

'No.' Alice gulped back the sob. 'No, but it's been ages. I'm so scared, Michelle. I keep thinking of Sally when her boyfriend was killed. She's so brave, but I don't think I could be brave like her. I don't know what I'll do without Bob . . . I love him. I didn't know it until Bob was hurt bad, but now I do . . . and it's all my fault.'

Michelle gave her hand another squeeze. 'It looks as if the doctor is coming . . .'

Alice could scarcely breathe as the man in the white coat and horn-rimmed spectacles came up to her. He had a kind, sympathetic face but his grave look only made her more terrified.

'Well, Mrs Manning, I'm glad to tell you that we've managed to stabilise your husband. It was touch and go for a while – unfortunately the knife has damaged his lung . . .' Alice caught her breath sharply, her fingers digging into Michelle's hand where she was gripping so hard. 'However, he's through the worst.

He's going to have to stay in hospital for a while – and we're not sure yet what the consequences of this attack will be . . .'

'What does that mean?' Alice asked breathlessly.

'Your husband is in the Army – military police, I believe?' She nodded, unable to speak, and he went on, 'His injury may mean that the Army will have to discharge him – he may not be able to carry on with the work he was doing, Mrs Manning.'

'No!' Alice could barely speak, her voice was choked with tears. 'Bob loved his job. He was so proud of what he'd achieved . . .' The tears overflowed. 'This is all my fault.'

Michelle wrapped an arm around her. 'No, it isn't. You mustn't blame yourself, Alice . . .'

But of course Alice did. She would always feel that it was her fault.

'A nurse will fetch you in about half an hour,' the doctor said. 'You may sit with your husband for a while, but then you should go home.'

Alice nodded, wiping her face with the back of her hand as he walked away. 'Bob will hate me for this,' she said miserably. 'That job meant so much to him.'

'It wasn't your fault,' Michelle insisted. 'The bloody cops should never have put either of you in this position!'

'How do you know what happened?' Alice stared at her.

'I saw the early evening paper on my way here,' Michelle told her. 'The police have arrested Butcher Lee, Big Harry and a couple of others. The whole gang is behind bars this evening, bar Jack Shaw – and if he's still in the country they'll get him too – and it's all down to you. The paper doesn't name you; it actually says a brave woman and her husband helped them to bring the criminals to justice, but it doesn't take a professor to work out it was you and Bob. At any rate, I put two and two together because I saw Constable Sallis when he came to tell Sister. I didn't hear much, but her voice was raised when I went to her office, and he came out looking like a scalded cat!'

Alice smiled slightly at the picture this conjured up. 'Bob said he didn't want me to do it, but I thought I ought – and he insisted on being there to protect me. I wish I hadn't agreed now. I was a fool!'

'Yes, perhaps it was foolish, but it was also very brave,' Michelle said. 'Bob won't blame you, why should he?'

Alice didn't answer. She knew that her husband had been proud of his work, proud of what he'd achieved – and now he was going to lose it all, thanks to her. He hadn't wanted her to do what the police asked, and she should have listened to him instead of thinking she knew better. She bitterly regretted her decision and wished she could undo it, but that was impossible. You could never turn back the clock.

Susie had begun to grizzle. Michelle bent down to rock the cot.

'I think she's hungry,' she said. 'Give me your key, Alice. I'll take her home, feed her a bottle and put her to bed. I'm going to stay with you tonight.'

'Thanks,' Alice said. 'You're a good friend. I shall come home on the bus when they tell me I've got to leave. There's food in the larder, make yourself a meal.'

'I'll look after Susie and have a cup of tea. We'll eat when you get back, Alice.' Michelle kissed her cheek. 'Stop worrying about what you can't change, love. Bob is alive – that's all that really matters, isn't it?' Michelle picked up Susie's carrycot and walked off, leaving Alice to wait alone.

'Yes . . .' Alice looked after her gratefully. Michelle was right: it was the only thing that truly mattered. She still had Bob and that made her lucky – luckier than Sally, who had lost the man she loved. Bob might be angry with her because he'd warned her against doing what the police asked, but he wouldn't hate her. Please God he wouldn't hate her for what had happened to him!

'Mrs Manning, you can visit your husband now.'

Alice stood up and went with the nurse. She was shaking inside, but she kept her head high. The nurse was telling her that Bob was still under the anaesthetic and wouldn't wake for a while.

'You can see him for a few minutes and then you have to leave. Your husband is being cared for, Mrs Manning. Tomorrow afternoon you can visit and I'm sure he will be much better then . . .'

'He looked so pale and fragile,' Alice said with a sob in her voice when she sat over her Spam and chips with mushy peas, and a cup of strong sweet tea. 'Much younger; it almost wrenched my heart out, Michelle. I honestly didn't realise how much I loved him until I saw him lying there like that.'

'You're very lucky,' Michelle said and reached out to touch her hand. 'You weren't in love with him when you married, were you?'

'No. I was fond of him; I liked him and I knew he loved me – and he was there when I needed him – but I wasn't in love with him. I think that happened on our holiday. I'd known for a while that I cared for him, and I'd decided I never wanted to see Jack Shaw again – but I still didn't know for sure. Bob was lovely in bed . . .' Alice's cheeks were pink and she felt shy. 'Jack dazzled me with his talk, Michelle. He was good at kissing and teasing, but making love . . . well, it was more a case of taking what he wanted. Bob was careful to give me pleasure. I didn't know it could be like that – and he's so lovely with Susie. He says he's her father and I don't think he could love her more if he was her real dad.'

'You've been luckier than you know,' Michelle said slowly. 'Eric wants to marry me. I've been talking to him on the phone, and I think he wants to adopt Matty – that child adores him. As important as my nursing is to me, I want a family one day. Eric understands that and I'm sure he would be good to me – the way Bob is to you.'

'But there's someone else?'

'I thought there was, but now . . . No, there isn't,' Michelle shook her head decisively; she'd decided that Richard Kent was not for her. He hadn't bothered to get in touch since that trip to the museum, even though she knew he'd been to St Saviour's to see Sister Beatrice. But the deciding factor had been his evident boredom in the café when he was supposed to help look after the kids. That was when she'd realised that he wasn't the kind of man she wished to spend the rest of her life with. Michelle wanted children and she didn't think Richard was interested, which meant he wasn't the one for her, even if he was very attractive. Eric on the other hand would be a wonderful dad and a devoted husband. 'I think Eric may be the one – the one I can trust . . . but how do I know for sure?'

'You should be certain,' Alice said. 'I didn't have much choice. Bob offered me all the things Jack didn't and I took them, but I didn't expect to be happy – and I have been . . . I shall be, if Bob comes through this . . .' her voice trembled and she had to blink hard to keep back the tears.

'He will,' Michelle assured her. 'The doctors told you he'll pull through. He might not be quite as strong as he was though.'

'I'll always be there for him, whatever happens,' Alice said and looked at her friend. 'Be certain what you want, Michelle. I've been lucky, but you owe it to yourself to be sure of how you feel. You shouldn't marry for Matty's sake alone . . .'

'Yes, I know you're right,' Michelle said. 'Now, I think we should get some sleep.'

'You must go into work tomorrow,' Alice said. 'I'm glad you're here now, but I'll be all right tomorrow.'

'What about Susie, when you go to the hospital?'

'Nan told me I could take her to St Saviour's whenever I need to. I'm going back to work soon – only for a few hours at a time – and Susie's coming with me so that I can feed her. Nancy will keep an eye on her while I'm working.'

Michelle nodded. 'You're lucky, Alice. I don't think Sister would have agreed to that a few months ago, but she seems to have eased her restrictions a bit. Perhaps her illness has softened her up.'

'Nan says I'm a good worker and they need girls like me. Some of the new ones haven't worked out.'

Michelle nodded. 'Yes, you were one of the best. It hasn't seemed the same without you and Sally. Tilly means well and she's trying hard, but she needs more experience.'

'I haven't met her yet, but she sounds all right,' Alice said. 'I might not be able to start back for a while – it all depends how Bob is when he comes out of hospital.'

'Your husband comes first,' Michelle agreed. 'Stop worrying, love. People are more resilient than you think. Bob is a decent man; he'll come out of this and find his way, you'll see.'

Alice sighed with relief as she saw Bob sitting up against the pillows. He had a hospital pyjama jacket on over the thick bandages she'd seen the previous evening and was in the end bed of a ward with ten patients instead of the small room she'd sat in. All the wires that had been attached to his body had gone, and he was awake, looking eagerly towards the door as she entered.

'Bob, love!' she said and gave him the newspaper and a small bunch of grapes. 'I wasn't sure what to bring. I thought you might still be asleep.'

'I'm a lot better this morning,' Bob said. 'Don't look so worried, Alice. I shan't die on you just yet.'

'Oh, Bob, don't be so daft,' she said, giving a giggle of relief. 'I thought you might last night.'

Bob's smile vanished. 'Are you all right – and Susie?'

'We're fine. Nan is looking after her this afternoon. She has a few hours off and she's taking her out in the pram. She says she wants to be Susie's nanna and I think she means it.'

'Good. My mother died years ago, and your mother isn't interested. It will be good for Susie to have Mrs Burrows as her nanna . . .' Bob hesitated, then, 'The doctor came to see me earlier, Alice. It seems that the knife blade went in at an angle and one of my lungs was slightly damaged – and that means the army probably won't want me. I'll be invalided out on a small pension.'

'I'm so sorry, Bob,' Alice said, her throat tight. 'I know how you felt about that job – and it's my fault you've been hurt.'

'Don't talk rubbish, love. I knew what I was doing and I should have been more careful. I could have broken his arm immediately, but I hesitated and that was my mistake – they tell us to act decisively, but you were there and I was more concerned about . . .' he broke off, then, 'It comes down to this: if I can't continue in the Army I'll have to go back to what I was before I joined. I'm a fully trained mechanic, like Eric. I've got a bit saved up, and I don't want to work for a boss, so I'm going to get me own small garage and do repairs. There are more cars about now, or there will be once the factories really get going. I've got enough to set up, but that won't leave us much over so I'll probably ask Eric if he wants to come in with me as a partner.'

'You can trust Eric, but I'm not sure he wants to leave the Army.'

'He can't until the end of next year, but I think he will then, especially if Michelle says she'll marry him and they go ahead and adopt that boy.'

'What if he doesn't want to come in with you? I can go back to work – Nan says they'll look after Susie for me, so I'll be able to feed the baby and do a few hours' cleaning and caring – but it won't be enough to pay our rent and food.'

'I'll find a way,' Bob said. 'If this had happened in the line of duty I'd have got compensation, but it was in my own time so I'll only get a few shillings' pension. But we'll manage somehow, Alice.'

Alice nodded, knowing that he was putting a brave face on it for her sake. 'I know we shall, love,' she said. 'I wish I'd said no now, but—'

Bob shook his head. 'We don't look back, Alice, and we don't feel sorry for ourselves – there's a lot worse off than us. We'll manage. I shall be able to work, but I'd prefer to have my own business . . .'

Alice reached for his hand. 'You'll get it one day, love. Perhaps Eric will come in with you, but if not we'll have to wait a bit, that's all.'

'What really matters to me is you, Alice. Have I got you?'

Tears choked her and she couldn't stop them falling as she bent down to kiss him softly on the lips. 'I love you very much. I didn't know how much until I realised that I might lose you, Bob, but now I know. And there won't ever be anyone else for me, I promise you that.'

'Then nothing else matters,' Bob said and squeezed her hand. 'Get off home and look after our Susie. Before you know it, I'll be home again.'

Walking back from the hospital, Alice noticed that some of the shops had hung coloured lights up and there were festive displays in their windows. Christmas was only a couple of weeks away. During the long war they'd all endured, the shops had struggled to come up with a Christmas display that made people want to stop and look, but gradually things were getting back to the way they'd been pre-war. Some things were still in short supply, but there were more goods in the shops and more food. Alice had ordered a nice chicken from her regular butcher for their Christmas dinner, but she wondered now if Bob would be home in time to share it.. If he had to stay in, it would be nice if the hospital would let her spend the day with Bob, but knowing how strict they were about visiting hours, she didn't think that would happen. She would visit him after lunch and stay until the nurses threw her out. It was Susie's first Christmas and she ought to have her daddy with her. Tears filled Alice's eyes as she blamed herself once more, because no matter how much Bob denied it, it was her fault that he was injured and she couldn't forgive herself.

FORTY

Looking at the children's drawings had given Angela a marvellous idea for the Christmas campaign. If she took photographs of the best and had them printed on cardboard with a greeting from the children, Sister Beatrice and the other staff, they would make lovely greetings cards. They could send them to their supporters and friends – and, if they had some made with blank insides or a seasonal greeting, they could sell them at the fair she'd decided to hold that weekend. She could even design a calendar and have fifty or so printed up to sell. She knew someone who would do a small job like that quickly for her.

Angela felt like clapping her hands and shouting for sheer joy. She'd been struggling to come up with an original idea and there it was, staring her in the face. If the cards and calendar were a success she might be able to find a firm that would be interested in turning some of the pictures into wooden jigsaw puzzles, with a share of the profits going to St Saviour's.

'Nancy,' she said, calling the girl to her with a smile.

'Do you think you could get the children to draw some Christmas pictures for me, please?'

'Of course, Mrs Morton,' Nancy said. 'In fact I've got some here, if you would like to look at them now.'

'Please. I have an idea, and the sooner I get it started the better.' Angela went through the pictures, taking some out of the pile and setting them to one side. 'Perfect! Please take these ones I've picked out, and write the name of the child that drew each one on the back. The pictures I choose for my project will earn several stars for the children who drew them and their teams – and if they do any more, I'd like to see them.'

'They will love that,' Nancy said and smiled. 'Drawing is a favourite with them all, and I know they will love the idea of doing some pictures of Christmassy things.'

'Good, I'm really pleased,' Angela said and left her to get on. She had one more call to make this morning and then she could leave to do some last-minute shopping for Christmas presents.

Angela frowned as she wondered about a gift for her mother. She couldn't leave her out, even though she was angry with her. No, she would buy something that would go through the post easily, and a card. Since leaving the clinic, Angela's mother had written to her only once. The letter had been full of her own plans for the future, including her divorce, with not one word of remorse or concern for the pain she'd caused her husband – though she had apologised if Angela was upset. In anger, Angela had thrown it into the fire without more than a cursory glance at the apology, but she knew she had to contact her mother. She couldn't let things slide . . . especially if she married Mark quite soon.

Mark had spoken of marriage more than once when he rang her but as yet they hadn't got round to discussing details. She thought that he might be saving that for Christmas, when they should be able to spend some time together at last. A smile touched her mouth at the prospect of seeing Mark this evening – she had some good news to convey. But in the meantime there was work to do.

Kelly was peeling potatoes when Angela entered the scullery. She looked up and smiled at her, wiping her hands on a towel.

'Is there something I can do for you, Mrs Morton?'

'I wanted to tell you my good news.' Angela laughed as she saw the girl's look of apprehension. 'I did say *good* news, Kelly. Your family has been awarded one of the charity's houses, and you can all view it this Saturday. I've written down the details for you to take home.'

'Oh, Mrs Morton!' Kelly said, her face lighting up. 'I can't believe it – how did you manage it?'

'The committee decided that your case was the most deserving. I did no more than put your name on the list, I assure you,' Angela told her. 'We have twelve houses for renovation, but yours was one of the first to be completed by the charity. I hope you'll be happy there, all of you.'

'I don't know how to thank you. It's so wonderful!'

'You have already thanked me.' Angela nodded. 'I've got some more news for you, Kelly. I've spoken to Sister Beatrice and to Nan, and they have agreed that you can become a carer. Nan will explain your duties and show you what she needs from you. You'll be working nights,

393

but you will have to wait a week until you can start your new duties. We've hired a girl to replace you here in the kitchen, but she can't start immediately.'

'Oh, Miss Angela,' Kelly said and rushed to hug her, planting a kiss on her cheek. 'You're an angel. I knew you were sent by God so I did!'

'Well, we shall expect you to be on time and do your job properly, but I'm sure you will.'

'I'll never let you down,' Kelly vowed. 'I shan't forget this, miss. It's the best Christmas present my family ever had!'

'It will be a help to us if we have someone who doesn't mind being on nights most of the time, though you will work the day shift now and then. If you're happy with that arrangement, then it's settled.'

'I am, Mrs Morton – very happy,' Kelly said shyly. 'I can't thank you enough – and Mammy will be in heaven!'

'Angela . . .' Mark said as she opened the door to him that evening. He put the bottle of French wine he was carrying on the small table in the hall and took her into his arms; she went willingly and he kissed her, feeling her response and closing his eyes as the longing he'd kept in check for so long rose up in him like a great tide. 'My darling girl, I've been looking forward to this all day, being alone with you . . .'

'Not as much as I have,' Angela said. 'It's been a good day – but a long one.'

'Are you tired, would you rather stay in this evening?'

'I think I might – but I don't want to spoil the evening for you, Mark. I know you've booked a table, but I do

394

have some food in the fridge, I could rustle something up . . .'

'It won't take a moment to cancel.'

Mark used the telephone in the hall to make the call, apologising and rebooking for another night. She looked up at him with a welcoming smile as came through into the pleasant living room. The apartment she'd made her home was at the top of what had been a warehouse before the war. An enterprising builder had restored the fire-damaged building, turning it into a light and spacious block of flats with skylights overhead. Angela had furnished hers with antiques and comfortable seating and made it her own with quirky twists that gave it a unique character. They sat down together but Mark kept hold of her hand, looking into her eyes. 'You do know that I love you and want to marry you, don't you, my darling?' he said and knelt down by her side, taking her hand in his and carrying it to his lips to kiss it.

'Mark, I've been so afraid that I'd lost you – I thought I'd kept you at a distance too long . . . and I've been angry over things that weren't your fault. How can you put up with me?'

'I told you after John died that I would always be there for you, dearest,' he said and traced the line of her cheek with his fingertips. 'What I haven't dared to tell you before is how much I love and want you, Angela. I knew you weren't ready and I thought there might be someone else in your life – and then . . .' He drew a deep sigh. 'Well, we don't need to go into all that again. I can only hope you care for me enough to marry me?'

Angela felt like her heart would burst as he said these

words. 'I care for you deeply,' she said, her eyes shining as she smiled up at him. 'For a long time I couldn't think of you as anything but a friend – but then, when I thought I'd lost you . . .' She shook her head, her hair soft and silky, and its perfume rose like a cloud to inflame his senses. 'We've both been fools, Mark – but we shan't be any more, shall we?'

'Not if I have anything to say about it,' Mark said and bent his head. His kiss was tender and sweet with a hint of the underlying passion that filled him. 'I want you, Angela. I love you and I want you – to make love to you – for the rest of my life.'

'Are you asking—' Angela got no further because he took her in his arms and kissed her again. She responded, melting into him until it felt as if they'd become one. 'I love you, Mark, and the answer is yes, whatever you were asking . . .'

'Are you very hungry?' Mark asked and rose to his feet, pulling her up with him. 'Or could that salad wait for a while?'

'It can wait,' she whispered in a husky, sexy voice that made him ache with need. 'But I can't.'

'Angela darling . . .'

She laughed as Mark's strong arms swept her off her feet, holding her close to him. Angela let her hands stray up into his hair at the nape of his neck. Her fingers began to stroke the tender spot there and he growled low in his throat as the heat spread through him, his breath quickening as he looked down at her. Those azure eyes seemed to entice and tease; this was the woman he'd dreamed of so often, all the sadness gone and only love left – love for him.

Angela's bed looked freshly made and, as he gently placed her down on the edge and sat beside her, he could smell the sweetness of laundered sheets and lavender. Somehow between them, though afterwards he could never recall how, the covers were thrown back to reveal crisp white sheets and both his and her clothes were discarded over the floor and chairs close to the bed. Achieved with giggles, moans, teasing kisses and clumsy fingers, he was aware of buttons popping and a fragile blouse being torn, probably beyond repair, but nothing mattered. They were eager and needy and they came together with frantic haste, as the restraint and loneliness of years boiled over into heated passion.

She was so damned beautiful! Mark lost his head, because in all the dreams he'd had of making love to her nothing had come close to seeing the soft pearly whiteness of her skin and the gentle curve of generous breasts and a slim waist, and the gentle swell of her belly that made him want to bury his face in its softness. Her long legs were smooth and shapely as he ran his finger down them, between her thighs. Kissing each part he touched, right to the tips of her toes, he felt her tremble with her own need. He breathed her in, kissing and caressing her with his tongue and stroking fingers, exploring each new exciting place with tenderness and pleasure in the treasure he'd longed for. Touching her, kissing her, holding her naked body close to his was all heady excitement, his hands stroking down the arch of her back, her silken flesh quivering at his touch as she moaned and pressed herself against him.

She was so hot and wet when he sought out that intimate core of her sexuality and stroked, his fingers moving with a delicate touch that made her gasp and arch beneath him. It was like playing a priceless violin, as he paid her homage, the sweetness of her breath on his face and her perfume enveloping him, as they came together in the beautiful rhythm of love. As they lay together afterwards in the sweet aftermath of perfect loving, he felt drained of everything, as if all the pain and wanting and weeping had all gone out of him, swept away on a tide of desire and sweet fulfilment.

'Mark,' she whispered, and he pulled her into his side. 'Oh, Mark, I feel so wonderful – happy . . .' She looked up at him as he raised himself on his elbow and gazed down at her searchingly. 'I wasn't sure if – but it was so right – so good between us . . . I feel . . .' she laughed and reached up to touch his face. 'I feel different – new . . .'

Mark smiled and bent to kiss her. 'I'm exhausted, hungry and – don't ask me to explain, because I couldn't: I've never felt like this before, I don't think there are words to describe it. I suppose utter contentment might come close.'

Angela laughed, shaking her hair out as she sat up. He liked the slightly shorter bouncy style that made her look exactly as she had when she was twenty-two and he had first set eyes on her at a party. 'I think earth-shattering might be nearer the mark,' she said, and then slid her long slim legs over the bed, reaching for a pale blue silken robe, which she tied loosely at the waist. She still had the best ankles Mark had ever seen on a woman.

'As you're so exhausted and hungry, stay there while I cook the steak. The salad is waiting in the cool box.'

Mark made a grab at her as she passed him on her way through to the kitchen, but she avoided him and laughed. He got out of bed and followed her, finding her about to place the steaks in a pan. Still naked, he put his arms about her and nuzzled her neck.

Angela turned and kissed him, her eyes bright with laughter. 'Please behave yourself, Mark. I'm trying to show you what a good wife I shall be.'

'And when was that decided?' he asked with mock severity. 'I'm not sure I quite recall.'

'Who said it had to be the man who asked?' Angela said, throwing her challenge at him with eyes as bright as a cheeky robin's. 'I've decided that's what I want – are you going to deny me?'

'I wouldn't dare,' he murmured. 'Come back to bed, darling – and then I'll cook the damned steaks.'

Angela sat with a sheet of paper in her typewriter, staring into space. She hadn't typed a word yet – she was too ridiculously happy to think about a mundane report. After John's death she hadn't expected to feel like this again. It wasn't the same as she'd felt when John had swept her off her feet and married her before she had time to touch earth again. No, this time she knew exactly where she was and what she was doing. Mark's love seemed to close the circle of her life, completing what she already had and making it whole.

Her work had given her a great deal, but she'd known something extra was needed. Mark's loving; his presence in her bed when they woke up, made love yet again and then rushed madly from the bathroom to the kitchen, time only for a cup of tea and a slice of buttered toast that they finished eating in the lift, because they were both late for work, were a joy to her.

And it could be the same every night and morning from now on . . . A sigh left her lips; she hadn't thought it was possible to feel this content. Not that it would all be plain sailing. They would need to decide where to live, and Angela didn't want to give up her apartment. Mark said he could sell his and they would live in hers until they bought something in the suburbs. She knew he meant when children came along, and that might be sooner than Angela wanted, given their passion for each other.

'I shan't ask you to give up work when it happens,' Mark had told her as they lay in bed discussing the future. 'I'll share the child care and we'll have a nanny for the times that neither of us can be there. I know that's what you want. I would never ask you to give up the work you love so much.'

No one else but Mark – no other man – would ever have made that promise; he was ahead of his time, a special, caring man. Angela knew it, just as she knew he would keep his word and enjoy doing it. Mark wanted children, as she did, but he didn't believe a woman's place was necessarily in the home. What she wasn't sure of was how she would feel when the babies did come along – would she want to continue working? She smiled to herself. Was it possible to have it all? To have a husband she loved, children, and hold down a job she knew was vitally important? She would certainly have a damned good try!

Smiling to herself, Angela started typing. Everything was well under way with the Christmas campaign. She'd had her cards printed to sell at the bazaar she was holding that evening, then on Saturday they were taking the children to the pantomime, and she was keeping her fingers crossed that for once the sick wards would be empty so that none of her children need miss out on the treat this year. She'd even managed to persuade Sister Beatrice to come along, as well as Mark and her father.

Angela's father was coming up to town for a few days that weekend. He would be there for the pantomime and the carols, and then she would go home on Christmas Eve. Mark wanted a quiet wedding in the local church before they went on their holiday, which was now to be a honeymoon.

'Angela, could I have a word?' Nan said, breaking Angela's happy train of thought. 'I know you're busy with all the preparations for the concert on Sunday afternoon and the bazaar this evening, but could you come and have a word with Tilly please?'

'Of course, Nan. What is the problem?'

'She arrived at work this morning with her stockings torn and blood on her hands and knees. It seems she had an accident on her way in.'

'On her way in to work?' Angela was surprised. 'I thought she was living in the Nurses' Home?'

'Yes, she is, but last night her mother came to meet her from work and begged her to go home. It seems that one of the children was ill and her husband – Tilly's stepfather – didn't come home last night or the previous one. She was in a bit of a state, so Tilly went home with her. Now she's in floods of tears and she wants to talk to you.'

Angela smothered a sigh and left her desk. It was too much to hope that everything would run smoothly for the whole of the day . . .

'Ma was in such a state she couldn't do anything,' Tilly said, wiping her cheeks on the hanky Angela gave her. 'I had to get Mags and Roddy off to school and then I ran all the way to catch my bus . . . but I had to cross the road and a bike came round the corner and knocked me off my feet. I missed the bus and so I walked in, but my knee hurts and I know I'm late and you'll be fed up with me and my problems—'

'We're not so hard-hearted,' Angela said, smiling as Muriel offered the trembling girl a cup of tea. 'When you've had your tea, I want you to go up to the ward and let Michelle look at your knee. First of all, what happened when you were knocked over by this bike – was it deliberate?'

'No. It was the apprentice from the butcher's on the corner. He's not long started work there and he couldn't have been more apologetic about running into me, but it was my fault – I was in such a hurry to get here, I stepped into the road without looking.'

'Tilly, we don't want you to kill yourself getting here,' Angela teased. 'All I ask is that you do your work properly when you're here.'

Tilly threw her a watery smile, then, 'Ma is certain my stepfather has left her,' she said, 'but he hasn't taken anything. I think he might have had an accident. I was wonderin' whether I should telephone the hospitals. What do you think, Mrs Morton?'

'I think you should get yourself up to Michelle

and ask her to look at your knee. I'll ring round for you – now what is your stepfather's full name?'

'Arthur Mallens,' Tilly said and blew her nose on Angela's handkerchief. 'I'll wash this for you and return it. Thanks ever so much for helpin' me, Mrs Morton.'

'No promises, but I'll do what I can. Off you go now . . . can you manage to walk by yourself?' Angela asked as Tilly hobbled a few steps.

'I'll help Tilly,' Nancy said, entering the kitchen. 'Jean is with the infants while I have a cup of tea. Take hold of my arm, Tilly.'

'You're all so good,' Tilly said, eyes watering once more.

'Well, I should think you could do with a cup of tea yourself after that, Angela,' Muriel said when they had gone, but Angela shook her head.

'I won't stop now, if you don't mind. I've a lot on this morning – and I must ring round the hospitals and the police station first, for Tilly's sake . . .'

FORTY-ONE

Michelle patched Tilly up and gave her an aspirin to help with the pain in her knee. She listened while the girl told her tale of woe and then hobbled off to do what she could. Nan would put her on light jobs until her knee was better, but Tilly was determined to work and refused to take the day off.

'I couldn't do that after all Miss Angela and Nan have done for me,' she said. 'I should've looked what I was doin', but everything's been topsy-turvy all night.'

Michelle got on with her duties in the ward. Fortunately, they hadn't had any serious illness recently and she was keeping her fingers crossed that none of the children would go down with the flu or a bad tummy bug before the weekend. All the children were excited about the pantomime on Saturday and the concert in the church hall on Sunday. Several of the children had been rehearsing their parts for weeks and it would be a shame if any of them had to miss it.

'Why, it doesn't look as if you've missed me at all,' Wendy said cheerily as she came into the ward. 'I've only this minute got back, but I thought I'd best come straight over in case you were rushed off your feet.'

'We've been lucky these past few days, it's not been busy at all,' Michelle said, looking at her bright face. 'It seems the trip did you good – how are the twins settling?'

'Really well,' Wendy said and smiled happily. 'They love being on the farm with their aunt and uncle. Samantha's spending her days learning to cook with her auntie, because she won't start school until she's learned a bit of French. Henri Bernard is as pleasant as his wife, and he absolutely dotes on the twins, especially Sarah. He takes her everywhere on his shoulders. He's teaching her to ride the pony – and she loves it. You should hear her chatter away in French! She's picking it up much faster than her sister, and she never stops talking to Monsieur Bertrand – it's almost as if something has unlocked inside her and she's a different child.'

'I'm so pleased,' Michelle said. 'I know Angela will be too. Have you seen her yet?'

'Not yet. Nan said she's very busy so I thought I would come here first and see if you need help.'

'Well, since you're back, I think we'll do a hair inspection – make sure none of them have nits. It doesn't seem to matter how many times I scrub them clean, back they come.'

'That's because a lot of kids don't get their hair washed often enough at home, so our children catch them at school,' Wendy said. 'When are you going to fit it in? It's the pantomime on Saturday . . .'

'We'll do the little ones in the morning and then bring the others in in batches once they've had their tea.'

'There will be some long faces then,' Wendy said, but the smile didn't leave her eyes.

'You look so happy,' Michelle said. 'I thought you would be miserable, having to leave the twins in France.'

'I'm going back next time I have a holiday.' Wendy laughed huskily. 'The twins want me to – and Henri and Françoise have invited me to stay whenever I wish . . . and I think I shall!'

Wendy obviously had a secret. Michelle suspected it was more than just her affection for the twins drawing her back to France, but she clearly wasn't ready to talk about it yet. Perhaps she'd met someone out there and fallen in love, or at least been attracted to someone.

The thought of Wendy finding love reminded Michelle that she needed to make up her mind what she was going to do about Eric, especially with Sister Norton waiting for an answer on Matty's future. Eric had told her when she rang him that he was coming home this weekend, and she'd managed to get him a ticket for the St Saviour's concert, though she couldn't get one for the pantomime.

She was going to have to decide once and for all, because although Matty was still in the wheelchair he would be coming back to St Saviour's for Christmas – and Michelle didn't want to raise his hopes of a family life unless she was sure . . .

'I hope you don't mind me popping in?' Wendy said later that afternoon. 'Nan said you were busy earlier, but I knew you would want to hear about the twins . . .'

'I do indeed,' Angela said. 'Are they happy there?'

'Yes, very content,' Wendy told her. 'It is a lovely big

old farmhouse with whitewashed walls and a thatched roof, and they have a huge old-fashioned bread oven where Françoise bakes gorgeous fresh loaves and croissants every morning. She gives the girls lots of butter and honey, eggs and soft white cheese, and thick slices of ham – and she is teaching Samantha to cook her special stews. Sarah didn't want me to leave, but I've been told I can visit whenever I like.'

'It sounds perfect, I almost envy them,' Angela said. 'I know much of France was devastated by the war, but it sounds as if the Bernards escaped without much damage.'

'I wouldn't say that.' Wendy frowned. 'André – that's Henri Bernard's brother – was in the Resistance and he has lost one hand and his face is scarred. He isn't bitter though. He can do most things he needs – he drives the tractor and can dress himself, though it isn't easy for him to cut meat on the plate.'

'Does he live with Françoise and Henri?'

'No, he has his own cottage on the estate, but he works on the farm and he has his meals with them.' A faint colour had touched Wendy's cheeks. 'He's really nice, Angela – and he likes the British. Some of the French don't, but André and his family made me very welcome.'

'And did you like André?' Angela asked with a teasing look.

'Yes, very much,' Wendy said and blushed. 'Oh, I hardly know him as yet, I realise that, but I enjoyed my stay. I'm going back in the spring to see them all again.'

'That sounds wonderful – you can tell me more over

a cup of tea later,' Angela said. 'Meanwhile, could you find Tilly and send her to me, please? I've got some news for her and it isn't good so I think I need to tell her in private.'

'Yes, certainly,' Wendy said and smiled shyly. 'I didn't ever think I could feel love again, but I think I might . . .'

Angela smiled in return as the nurse left. She was glad Wendy had enjoyed her stay, though she would be missed if one day she decided to go and live in France. But what was occupying Angela's thoughts right now was young Tilly. What she had to tell her was not pleasant . . . not pleasant at all.

'Arrested for attempted rape?' Tilly blanched as Angela told her what she'd discovered. 'Oh no, Mum is going to be so upset when I tell her – and she'll have to know, because the police will be round and—'

'Yes, your mother will have to know,' Angela said. 'I'm sorry, Tilly. I tried the hospitals first, and there was no news there so I rang Constable Sallis. He told me your stepfather got drunk and then followed and attacked a young woman on her way home from her shift serving behind the bar at the pub.'

'Is she all right?' Tilly was white and shaking.

'The police say she is in hospital, but they wouldn't tell me anything more. I'm afraid there are witnesses who will testify to his having harassed her at the pub earlier that night – and she has named him as her attacker.'

'It could've been me,' Tilly said. 'It could have been me he attacked. I shall have to go home, Mrs Morton. I can't keep the room at the Nurses' Home – Ma will be in a terrible state when she finds out and she'll need me.'

'Well, don't get yourself knocked down again,' Angela said. 'I'm not sure what I can do to help you, Tilly, but I'm here – along with Nan and Sister Beatrice. We shall do our best to help, whatever your problems.'

'Thank you,' Tilly said and her eyes were moist. 'I'll work hard when I'm here, Mrs Morton – but I might be a bit late some mornings. If Ma starts her drinking, it will be me that has to get the kids off to school. Roddy and Mags are old enough to wash and dress themselves. Roddy could help with breakfast, but he's often lazy.'

'I expect they think you'll do it for them, Tilly. You might have to put your foot down and make them do their share. Talk to Nan about coming in later, ask her if you can change your hours,' Angela said. 'Nan is the head carer so the decision is hers – if she is prepared to adjust your shift, I will have no objection.'

'Thank you,' Tilly said. 'I was about to leave when Wendy caught me. I'd better go and tell Ma – I know she'll go to pieces, but it's my day off tomorrow, so perhaps she will have calmed down by the following day.'

'Off you go then, Tilly,' Angela said. 'I'm sorry it wasn't better news.'

'As far as I'm concerned it wasn't bad news: if he's in prison, he'll leave me alone,' Tilly said. 'It's me ma I'm worried about . . .'

Angela sighed as the girl closed the door behind her. She'd hoped Tilly would be all right once she was settled in her room at the Nurses' Home, but now she would have to return home to help her mother get over the shock. She could only pray that Tilly's mother wouldn't go to pieces as the girl feared and take to drinking and behaving wildly. What hope did Tilly have of having a life of her own if that happened?

Tilly caught her bus easily and found a seat near the front. Her knee was throbbing and painful, but she'd managed to do most of her chores at work. She was dreading walking into the house and seeing her mother's eyes. Even though Tilly had learned to fear and hate her stepfather, she knew that he brought home decent wages, and it was due to him that her mother stayed sober. It would ruin everything if Ma started drinking again; Tilly knew she would be both the breadwinner and the main carer for her family then.

She couldn't abandon her family, but if she somehow arranged her hours to look after the younger ones, it wouldn't leave her any time at all for a life of her own. Getting stiffly off the bus at the stop near her house, Tilly's steps lagged as she walked to the door and opened it.

She could hear the kids yelling and knew that already the mayhem had begun. When she entered the kitchen her brother was fighting with her younger sister while her mother sat staring at them, a bottle of beer in her hand.

'Stop that if you want any tea,' Tilly said, and they turned to stare at her. 'Have you washed your hands?'

'Ma's drunk,' Roddy told her, his eyes dark with anger. 'The bloody old man has gone off and got himself arrested!'

'I know,' Tilly said. 'I've been told, but I'm here now and I don't want any fightin' – do you hear me?'

'Mags wants her tea,' he said as he went over to the kitchen sink. 'She was screechin' at me and I told her to shut up, that's all. What we got for tea then?'

'I've got a tin of spam and you can run down and get some chips from the corner shop if you like.'

Roddy's eyes lit up and he took the money she held out. 'I'll bring plenty. I'm starvin'!'

Tilly nodded. She took hold of Mags' arm and marched her to the sink, washing her hands and face with a cloth rinsed out under the tap. The water was nearly cold, which meant her mother hadn't made up the stove all day.

Mags looked at her and then stuck her tongue out. 'I 'ate you, Tilly,' she said rudely. 'An' I 'ates 'er an' all.'

'Well, I don't much like you at the moment either,' Tilly responded cheerfully, knowing of old that her half-sister's tantrum would cease once she was over her temper and tears.

'I don't like Ma bein' like that,' Mags wailed, but Tilly gave her a shake.

'Ma is upset,' she said. 'Look, love, be a good girl and I'll take you to the concert on Sunday afternoon. There will be jelly and cakes afterwards, I shouldn't wonder.'

Mags stopped crying and stared at her. 'Promise?' she demanded and Tilly nodded, drying her face. 'What about Roddy, will you take him too?'

'If he wants to come and he's good,' Tilly said. 'Now, be good for me, love. Ma is ill and we have to help her – all of us.'

'Why did me da go away?'

'I don't know, Mags,' Tilly lied; the child was too young to understand what kind of a man her father was. 'I know you love him—' She broke off as the child shook her head. 'You don't love him?'

'He keeps touchin' me rude places,' Mags said. 'I'm glad he's gone, Tilly. You won't let him come back 'ere, will yer?'

'No,' Tilly promised and her expression was harsh as she looked at her mother silently holding her empty beer bottle. How could she have let that happen? She must have been aware of what he was doing. Tilly was old enough to look out for herself, but Mags was only a kid. 'I promise you, I won't let him come back here.'

She'd kill him if he dared to step over the threshold after what Mags had told her! It was bad enough that he'd been after her, but the knowledge that he'd touched her young sister made her spitting mad. If Arthur Mallens had walked in that minute, she'd have stuck a knife in him. It was then Tilly realised she wasn't afraid of her stepfather any more. And she wasn't going to let her mother get away with her sluttish behaviour either. It was time Tilly told her some home truths and once the children were safely tucked up in bed, she would make sure that her mother understood she had to do her share if she wanted Tilly to support her in future . . .

Michelle saw Eric waiting for her when she left work that evening. He was standing under a lamppost smoking a cigarette, but he dropped it on the ground and stamped on it as she walked up to him.

412

'You must be frozen,' she said as she joined him. 'It's really cold now – cold enough for snow.'

'Well, it's nearly Christmas,' Eric said and put his arm round her waist. 'Shall we go and have a coffee to warm us up – or do you want to go straight to the hospital?'

'Let's have a warm drink first,' Michelle said. 'I didn't explain very well on the phone, but it's to do with Matty . . .'

'Yes, I gathered that,' Eric said and looked puzzled. 'Sister Norton had a word with you about his future. What's the problem?'

'Did you tell Matty that you were willing to adopt him?'

Eric laughed and looked pleased. 'Well, sort of. He said he liked you and asked me if I was going to marry you. I told him yes, if you would have me, and he asked if he could come and live with us if you said yes . . .'

'So I suppose you agreed . . .' Michelle frowned and Eric looked at her. 'He told Sister Norton we were getting married and she wanted to know if we would adopt him.'

Eric was silent for a moment, then, 'Well, why don't we? Get married and adopt the lad. I'm sure we could work it out somehow. He'll be at school during the day, so that won't stop you working shifts – and as soon as I've finished with the Army I'll be around to give you a hand.'

'Do you really want to marry me and adopt him?'

Eric looked into her eyes. 'I think it's more whether you want to take us both on, Michelle. You know how I feel about you – I'll marry you as soon as you say the word.'

413

Michelle smiled. 'Mum was asking me when you were coming round for tea again – shall we make it supper after the concert on Sunday?'

'A St Saviour's concert?' Eric laughed. 'That's a rare treat to offer me, Michelle – so what do you want me to say?'

'Yes to both questions,' she said. 'We'd better have that drink and then go and talk to Sister Norton.'

'What's the answer to my question, Michelle – are you going to marry me or not?'

'Of course I am, you daft thing,' she said and hugged his arm. 'Come on, you can buy me sixpence worth of crackles from the chippie – I'm starving!'

FORTY-TWO

'Blimey, that were lovely,' Billy said when he and Mary Ellen sat on the back stairs and shared the remainder of the bag of sherbet lemons they'd bought on their way to the pantomime that afternoon. 'I never thought it would be as good as that, did you?'

'Rose took me last year,' Mary Ellen said and sucked on her sweet. 'When Sister Beatrice wouldn't let me go 'cos you were hiding in the attics, but Miss Angela took me to see *Bambi*. I liked that even better than *Mother Goose*, but it was your first time.'

'Yeah, well I thought it was funny,' Billy said. 'I'm glad Timmy got to see it. It was thanks to him being in a wheelchair that we got to sit down the front. It was brilliant when we got thrown them toffees – and that funny bloke dressed up as Mother Goose winked at us and threw us balloons and things.'

'Yeah, it was lovely, being at the front. The others had to sit much further back, so it was nice that Timmy said we were his special friends and they let us sit with him.'

'He's a good lad, Timmy. And he's started getting

better since he moved into St Saviour's,' Billy said. 'Me and Nurse Wendy had him walking in the ward yesterday. He walked all the way down and back, but he said his leg ached afterwards.'

'That's wonderful. It can't be nice for him, having to go everywhere in a wheelchair,' Mary Ellen said. 'Did I tell you that Rose is going to take us both to the pictures the day before Christmas Eve, and then she's having dinner with us at St Saviour's on Christmas Day. Last year she had to work, but this year we'll all be together. She's got nowhere else to go and, if she helps out, Jean can leave early to have tea with her family.'

Billy nodded, but didn't show much enthusiasm. Rose might have made a concession and included him in the outing to the pictures, but he knew she wasn't doing it because she liked him. Knowing Mary Ellen, she'd told her sister she wouldn't go without him.

'Have you got Marion and Timmy a present for Christmas?' Billy asked. 'I thought we ought to get Nipper and Jim something as well . . . we could put together, if you like?'

'I've got one and sixpence left,' Mary Ellen told him. 'Rose usually gives me something when she comes, but it will be too late to go shopping then.'

'Well, I've got three bob,' Billy said. 'I won five bob for running at the club – but I've spent some of it. I reckon we can get a few presents between us.'

'Yes, we'll put together, and if you spend more than me, I'll make up my half when Rose gives me some pocket money,' Mary Ellen smiled at him. 'We'd better go before it's lights out or Sister will be on the warpath.'

Billy chuckled. 'Nah, she ain't so bad as she used to

be, Mary Ellen. This morning, she came up to me and congratulated me on being the best runner in the county.'

'She didn't see you kicking that football in the hall, though, did she?' Mary Ellen said. 'I've almost finished making my cards, have you?'

'Not yet,' Billy said. 'Do you know what I heard this afternoon?'

'How can I know, daftie?' Mary Ellen said as she got to her feet.

'I heard Staff Nurse Michelle tell Miss Angela she was getting married after Christmas – and Miss Angela sort of smiled funny. I think she's getting married too – to Mr Adderbury.'

'That will be lovely,' Mary Ellen said and giggled. 'Do you think they'll have a big iced cake and bring us some?'

'Michelle, I'm glad you've come!' Alice greeted her with a huge smile as she opened her front door. 'Constable Sallis is leaving now. I visited Bob this afternoon and he said not to come again this evening, but I'm not sure I can wait to tell him the news!'

Michelle followed her inside, nodding to the police officer as he passed her on his way through the hall. Alice already had the kettle on when she reached the kitchen. She could see the excitement in her face and sat down, watching as her friend set out the tea tray.

'Are you going to tell me what's happened?'

'You'll never believe it,' Alice said and laughed with the excitement she could not contain. 'I can't myself and I've just been told . . .'

'Told what?'

'It seems there was a reward for the return of some of those jewels that Jack Shaw stole. Some of them were worth thousands and thousands of pounds – and Constable Sallis says that I'm going to get half the reward. One of the coppers was hurt bad in the raid on Mr Lee's club and they've decided that half of it will go to his wife.'

'He was only doing his job. You handed that key in and you took the risk – your husband's been injured too!' Michelle objected. 'I think any reward should be yours, Alice.'

'I'm not greedy and I'm sure that policeman's wife can do with some of it too,' Alice said, looking like the cat that got the cream. 'Besides, the reward was for five hundred pounds – five hundred, Michelle! We'll get two hundred and fifty pounds – and that means Bob will have enough to open a business and we'll still have a few quid left to live on until he starts to earn money!'

'Does that mean he won't need Eric as his partner?'

'No, I'm sure he'll still ask him,' Alice said, grinning like a Cheshire cat. 'Bob and Eric are mates, exactly like you and me, Michelle. It will be perfect.'

'Yes, especially as I've decided I'm going to marry Eric!'

Alice stared, her mouth open. 'You're never . . .' She gave a scream of delight and flung her arms around her friend. 'That's lovely – if you're sure?'

'I am,' Michelle smiled, unable to contain the happiness she felt inside. 'I took him home for supper after the pantomime and Mum really likes him. We're going to have a quiet wedding after Christmas – Eric already has his eye on a nice house with a garden – and we shall adopt Matty soon as we can. Sister Norton will let us foster him at first and then we can apply to adopt him. I'm still going to keep on nursing until I have a baby, Alice, but Matty will be at school all day and I'll fetch him back to St Saviour's until it's time to go home . . . Besides, once Eric is out of the Army, he'll be his own boss and we can work out our hours, so there'll always someone around for him.'

'That's wonderful,' Alice said. 'I know Eric is in love with you – but are you certain? What about Dr Kent? I thought you might care for him?'

'I did like him for a while, and I know he's a good doctor, but he isn't very patient with children when they're fit and well and making a noise.' Michelle smiled. 'Eric is lovely with kids. I wondered if it was only his sister's children and Matty – but he was every bit as good at the concert. He had them all in fits of giggles.'

'As long as you like him enough – you know . . .'

'We kissed last night – really kissed – for the first time,' Michelle said. 'I wasn't sure until then, but now I know Eric is the one. He loves me and . . . well, I love him too.'

'It was the same with me and Bob,' Alice said, 'except that I almost had to lose him to know how much I love him.'

'It's such a pity he won't be home for Christmas,' Michelle said. 'I hope he's out of hospital in time for our wedding. Eric wants him to be our best man.'

'I'll tell Bob when I visit next.' She gave a sigh. 'I still feel bad about him losing the job he loves on account of what happened, but it means he'll be here all the time, and that's what I want, Michelle. I think things will work out all right, him and Eric together – and us as best friends. We'll be able to mind each other's children as they grow up and swap clothes they've grown out of . . .'

'Hang on a bit; we're not married yet!'

'You will be soon,' Alice said. 'Look, why don't we take Susie and go round the hospital? I can go up and tell Bob the good news while you look after Susie for me.'

Michelle glanced at her watch. 'Have we got time?'

'Visiting is from six until eight – we'll be all right if we go by bus – and I think this deserves the fare, don't you?'

Michelle agreed, and Alice scurried round, collecting her jacket and the baby. The girls looked at each other in excitement as they left the house and ran for the bus.

'They've got those bad men,' Billy said to Mary Ellen as they sat in their usual place on the back stairs. He offered her his bag of liquorice cuttings and told her to take a handful. 'Constable Sallis told me this morning. I reckon he got an earful from Sister, but he said he wanted me to know that the men who paid to have that factory set on fire were going down for a long time. I think they might hang that Big Harry, though I bet his boss gets away with it.'

'Why should he?' Mary Ellen said, sucking on the liquorice, her mouth and tongue black with the stain. 'He's as guilty as the rest of them, isn't he?'

'Yeah, I reckon he's guiltier, but men like him usually get away with it – unless they've got good evidence to convict him.'

'I think it was our Alice and her husband that helped the police get them,' Mary Ellen said. 'She's very brave – do you remember the way she stood over Arthur with a rolling pin when he tried to steal our Christmas food?'

Billy shouted with laughter and chewed loudly. 'Yeah, that was so funny. I almost wished Arthur would wake up so that she could whack him! I miss Alice and Sally, don't you?'

'Yes, it's different now. Tilly is all right though.' Mary Ellen sighed. 'Rose talks to Sally Rush sometimes at the London, and she likes her. I asked Rose when she was going to get us a house of our own, but she said she can't work and look after me. I reckon I'm stuck here for good.'

'It ain't so bad,' Billy said. 'We've got a lot of mates now: Marion, Jimmy and Nipper, and Tim – and young Ernie an' all; we got ter look after them, Mary Ellen. I don't reckon they'd manage without us, 'specially Tim. He's beginning to walk better, but it's goin' to be ages before he gets rid of that rotten iron on his leg. I'll have him watching the football this winter, and he loves the athletics, even though all he could do was sit in his wheelchair and watch. He was there when I won all my medals for runnin'.'

'Yes . . .' Mary Ellen smiled. 'I was with Rose that day so I couldn't come and watch. I asked her to bring me to the Athletics club, but she dragged me up West to buy some shoes and a winter coat for best. I didn't want to go but there was a sale on at Peter Robinson's and she said if we didn't get them now they would cost a lot more after the sale.'

'Sisters!' Billy scowled. 'Who needs them? Your Rose

421

only thinks about her nursing and what she wants. You stick with me and our mates, Mary Ellen. One day we'll have a home of our own – and it won't be in no rotten slum, believe me. I'm going to work hard and I'll make decent money and look after you.' He put his hand in his pocket and brought out a handful of pennies and a couple of sixpences. 'Constable Sallis gave me five bob. He's getting a promotion over them arrests and he reckons I did him a favour tipping them the wink about seein' Jack Shaw at the zoo. It means I can put more towards the presents for Jim and Nipper. You'll see, Mary Ellen, I'll be earnin' enough to take you on holiday before you know it and then we'll get married.'

'Don't forget I'm going to college to be a teacher,' Mary Ellen said. 'Nan says I'll be good at it, and I like looking after the tiny tots.' She smiled at him. 'Rose promised we can go to Lyons for our tea, Billy – and she says I can take you and one other friend, so I'll ask Marion to come with us, shall I? I suppose Rose tries to make up for what she can't give me – and I'd rather be here than live in that awful house that made my mum ill.'

'Yeah, we're all right here,' Billy agreed. 'I'm running in two more races next month, and Artie Martin is goin' in for the high jump. You want to go in for the long jump, Mary Ellen. I've seen the girls jumping in the sand pit and I reckon you could do better than any of those sissies.'

'Billy, you shouldn't call them that,' Mary Ellen reproved. 'I'm looking forward to Christmas now, aren't you?'

'I still reckon me and you would've been a better

Mary and Joseph, but Marion was chuffed that they chose her, and Jimmy's a bit sweet on her so I reckon he'll be all right as Joseph, don't you?'

'Yeah, he'll be OK, and Nipper is one of the shepherds, so is Ernie. They asked me to be the second angel, but the costume was too small so they gave it to one of the infants instead. I don't mind; it will be fun with the carols and the tree again. Tilly and Jean were dressing it with Wendy before we went to the concert. Shall we go and have a look?'

'Yeah, let's,' Billy agreed.

'I love Christmas!' Mary Ellen said and started humming a carol under her breath. It was her second Christmas at St Saviour's and she wondered how long it would be before she had a home of her own. Still, at least here, she was with Billy and the others. If Rose got them a house she wouldn't want all Mary Ellen's friends round there when she got home. So maybe she was better off where she was. 'Yeah, what do you think we ought to get for Nipper then, Billy?'

FORTY-THREE

'Those cards and the calendar were an inspiration,' Sister Beatrice said, spotting a pile of them on Angela's desk that afternoon. 'Have you sent them to all our sponsors?'

'Yes, I felt they deserve something to thank them for all they do for us,' Angela replied. 'We charged for the concert tickets this year, which brought in quite a nice sum. I've also raised some money from selling the cards – more than I anticipated. And those envelopes with pictures of the orphans, taken off-focus, so that you can't recognise any child in particular, have brought in a great many small donations. We've only managed to distribute them in London thus far, but I'm hoping to send them out further afield next year.'

'You work hard for us,' Sister Beatrice said. 'I wouldn't have any idea what to do to raise money for the charity.' She frowned then, 'I am glad we were on the same side regarding the new home in the country.'

'Naturally, I'm on your side, Sister. I know you care for these children, as I do.'

'Yes, you do,' Sister Beatrice smiled. 'I had my doubts

when you first came to us, Angela, but you've done a good job – and I have to thank you for taking care of everything while I was ill.'

'I did my best, but this is a two-woman job, Sister. It needs both of us.'

'It certainly does,' Beatrice said and nodded decisively. 'I've been visiting Timmy this morning. He seems to be settling in well and is a great pal of Billy Baggins. It appears that Billy has been taking him out in his chair and looking after him very well.'

'Yes, Billy decided to take Timmy under his wing from the first, and everyone follows his lead so all the children have made him welcome.'

'I believe I seriously misjudged Billy when he first came to us.'

'Oh no, Sister, he was a complete tearaway, but between us, we've performed a tiny miracle. I'm amazed when I see the difference in him these days.'

'It shows us what patience and a bit of discipline can do.' Beatrice nodded her satisfaction. 'I believe the children are excited about the tree and presents . . . and the Christmas play went down very well yesterday at the church hall.'

'One of the angels looked rather an imp, but Joseph and Mary did very well.' Angela laughed. 'We've all put small gifts on the tree, but Mark has filled a huge sack with presents. He wraps them all himself, you know. I think he is almost as excited about Christmas as the children are!'

'Yes, well, that brings me to the reason I came to see you, Angela. You haven't said much to anyone, and I know you've been having a collection for Staff Nurse

Michelle's wedding gift, but somehow everyone knows that you will be getting married in the New Year – and the children and staff have some small gifts for you. There will be a bottle of sherry and a sponge cake in the dining room this evening – so please let us raise a glass to you and Mark.'

'That's so kind. We didn't expect . . .' Angela was surprised; they hadn't told anyone about the wedding and she'd thought it was a secret. 'I'll ring Mark, shall I?'

'I think you'll discover that he knows,' Beatrice said, and looked pleased with herself. 'Well, I shan't keep you – I am sure you have a great deal to do.'

Angela stared as the door closed behind the nun. It must have been she who had told the staff and instigated the party and the gifts; Sister Beatrice was the only one Mark had told and Angela hadn't said a word to anyone at St Saviour's yet. Her father and Sister Beatrice were the only two that knew, although she was in the process of sending out wedding invitations to a few close friends. Sally Rush would be busy with her nursing exams, but Angela was going to invite her and Michelle, as well as a handful of friends from home – but they'd planned on a small celebration party at Angela's apartment after their return for their London friends.

How surprising that the woman who seldom cared for parties of any kind had chosen to take the time and trouble to arrange this for her. Angela felt warmed and pleased by the gesture. It made her feel that the future looked bright for them all at St Saviour's and she felt a surge of excitement at the coming festivities.

However, it was time she got down to work. She still had several more cards to write for people at home who had supported her campaign for 'Angela's orphans', as people spoke of them in the village, and with each one went a letter of gratitude for past support and a few lines explaining her future plans for fundraising.

Angela set to with a will and she was finishing her last letter when the door opened and Kelly Mason walked in. She was smiling and looking happy and she placed an envelope on the desk.

'This is from my family, Mrs Morton,' she said. 'We've moved into our new house in time for Christmas, and even though I'll be working extra shifts on the day, Dad has wangled us a big goose as well as a joint of pork, with all the trimmings and a tree. He said we'll celebrate as usual on the day, and we'll have the cold pork on Boxing Day, but I've been invited to a friend's house for tea.' Kelly blushed. 'I've got a new friend – he's like me, got a big family to help out, so he understands I can't always go out, but he doesn't mind.'

'That's lovely for you, Kelly.' Angela opened the very pretty card and thanked the girl. 'I'm so glad the charity approved your family for the new house,' she said. 'I only had a small say in the matter, Kelly, but if it helped I am so pleased.'

'My dad said I was to thank you 'specially, Mrs Morton; he says until you brought that doctor round we didn't stand a chance of being moved. We know how lucky we've been.'

Angela smiled and nodded and Kelly left her, humming a Christmas carol to herself as she went off to get ready for the evening shift. Covering her typewriter for the evening, Angela was about to leave her office when the door opened again and Mark walked in.

'Perfect timing,' he said, giving her one of his special smiles that made her heart leap. 'I suppose you know about the surprise party by now? Sister Beatrice said she was going to warn you.'

'How did they know? I haven't told anyone.'

'You can't keep a secret in a place like this,' Mark teased. 'Perhaps you've been walking around with a soppy smile on your face?'

'Yes, perhaps I have,' Angela said as he picked up her suit jacket and held it for her. 'It was lovely of Sister Beatrice to arrange this for us, wasn't it?'

'She isn't a bad old stick, if you keep on the right side of her,' Mark said, that wicked look in his eyes. 'If we're being toasted for our engagement, I suppose I'd better give you this. I was planning on saving it until Christmas Eve when we left for the country, but . . . give me your hand, darling.'

Angela held out her left hand as she saw that Mark had produced a dark blue leather ring box. He took out a square-cut emerald, which was surrounded by beautiful white diamonds, and slipped it on to her third finger. It was a perfect fit and took Angela's breath away.

'It's gorgeous, Mark! How did you know that I love emeralds?'

'It was a guess. Besides, I didn't want to give you a sapphire.'

John's ring had been a sapphire and diamond cluster. For a moment Angela's throat tightened, but she dismissed the memory. Memories were best tucked away, out of harm. She had a whole new wonderful life to look forward to and she felt a surge of pleasure as she looked into the eyes of the man she loved.

'Thank you, darling,' she said and reached up to kiss him softly. Mark's arms went round her, pulling her closer, deepening the kiss until she was breathless and melting in his arms. 'Oh, Mark, I feel so lucky . . .'

'I'm the lucky one,' he murmured huskily. 'Now, my love, we'd better go and meet these good people. I for one cannot wait to see what the children have made for us.'

FORTY-FOUR

Tilly joined Nan and the others who were toasting Angela and Mark Adderbury. She stopped long enough to admire Angela's ring, sip her glass of wine and nibble a chocolate biscuit, then decided she'd better head off. She would have liked to stay to the end of the party, but she was needed at home. As she turned to leave, Muriel touched her arm.

'Pop into the kitchen on your way out. I've got something in my pantry for you, Tilly.'

'I'm not sure what you mean,' Tilly said. 'I'm working most of Christmas, Cook – and Sister said I could tell my brother and sister to have their tea with us and listen to the carols on Christmas Eve. So they'll have a few treats here . . .'

'Well, I might have a few bits for your family as well,' Muriel said, 'but this isn't from me. That new butcher from the corner shop brought in a parcel of meat for you – lamb chops and some sausage meat, and a pork pie, I think he said. He said it was to say sorry for knocking you over. I reckon he was disappointed not to see you, but you were on an errand for Nan.'

'Oh!' Tilly was surprised. A gift of extra meat would be useful for her family, especially with her being the only breadwinner now. She couldn't afford a goose or a joint of pork, so chops and sausages would be a quick and easy meal, and her mother wasn't likely to bother herself with preparing anything special for Christmas, even though Tilly had sorted her out a bit and she'd promised to stop her drinking. It probably wouldn't last, but Tilly would manage somehow. Even if Ma was sober, Tilly knew she'd be the one cooking dinner at Christmas and every night. If she didn't do it, all they would get was a bit of bread and dripping. 'I've got some stewing meat for a pie for Christmas day, if my brother puts it in the oven for them; if not we'll have it when I get home, but the chops will be lovely for Boxing Day. I wonder what made him bring them?'

'I think he felt bad about knocking you over, Tilly,' Muriel said. 'Thought he'd make it up with a few bits from under the counter – you know what these butchers are; they always have a bit extra for their favourite customers.'

Tilly laughed and agreed, but she was thoughtful as she went to fetch her coat. The accident had been her fault, not the butcher's. It was nice of him to send her some meat for Christmas – and she didn't even know his name.

Perhaps she'd drop in the shop on her way home and say thank you. Tilly had been shocked and upset when the accident happened, but now she thought about it the young man on the bike had had a nice smile . . . and he'd cared enough to bring round that meat for her. Tilly's life had been pretty awful for a long time, but things were looking better now her stepfather had been locked up and wouldn't be around to cause trouble. There was nothing to stop her going out now and then, or having a friend.

Tilly smiled as she turned in the direction of the butcher's shop. It was only right to say thank you; he couldn't think she was being forward after he'd been round to see how she was. The shop window was blazing with light and a few turkeys were still hanging there. She wondered what the butcher did with them when he closed the shop for Christmas, but as she lingered outside, deciding whether she dare ask if any of them were going cheap, the door opened and the young man came out, minus the bike.

He stopped in surprise as he saw her. 'You didn't mind me bringing that meat round?' he asked, looking tentative.

'Nah, 'course not,' Tilly said. 'I came to say thank you. You needn't have done that . . . sorry, I don't know your name?'

'It's Terry – Terry Bates,' he said. 'They told me your name was Tilly Tegg – is that right?'

'Yeah, it is,' she replied and laughed. 'I was in a right state when you knocked me over. I thought if I was late for work I'd be in trouble. I've been warned a few times and I can't afford to lose my job.'

'Do you help your family out?' Terry fell into step beside her as they walked to the nearest bus stop. 'I was thinking you might like to go out one night?'

'I might,' Tilly said. 'I'd have to get the kids' tea first – there's my sister Mags and brother Roddy, and they rely on me to look after things when me ma ain't right . . .' She hesitated and then fixed him with a straight look. 'You may as well know for a start – me stepfather is in prison for assaulting a young girl and me ma drinks sometimes.'

'Sounds as if you've had a rough time,' Terry said and looked sympathetic. 'My father likes his drink a bit too much at times and Ma swears by her Bible, so you can imagine what it's like in our house when Dad gets a bit tipsy. Shall I walk you home then? What are you doin' for Christmas?'

Tilly linked her arm in his. 'Cookin' dinner, I expect, but they can get their own tea . . . if you fancied goin' for a walk or somethin'?'

'Ma cooks a huge dinner and expects me and Dad to eat the lot. I like a nice walk in the afternoon on Christmas Day.'

Tilly gave a sigh of contentment. She'd got the job she wanted, her stepfather was no longer a danger to her and now perhaps she'd found a boyfriend for herself. Life was looking very much better than it had a few weeks previously . . . maybe she'd even get married one day and the kids at St Saviour's would make her a present like they had for Angela . . . She smiled as she thought of the woman who'd helped her and hoped she was enjoying her special evening as much as Tilly was enjoying hers.

Mark popped the champagne cork, letting the fizzy drink bubble over into the napkin before he filled their glasses. He handed Angela her glass with a smile, seeing that she was bending over the gift the children had made for them. It was a collage of different pictures drawn and painted by the small children and signed by all of them, each adding a message with a picture of some sort, and it had been framed behind glass so that it would keep bright.

'Look at this one from Mary Ellen and Billy Baggins,' Angela said. 'They hope we shall be happy forever and ever and have lots of babies!'

'Good idea,' Mark said.

'And this one is from Timmy – he's the young lad with polio. He says he loves being at St Saviour's and thanks me for bringing him here . . . and here's one from Archie, Nipper, Jimmy . . . and Matty too. Michelle must have taken it to the hospital for him to sign – oh, they're all so lovely!'

'You deserve it, Angela,' Mark said and raised his glass. 'Here's to you, my darling and to the future . . . May we have many wonderful years together.'

'Oh, Mark,' Angela's throat was tight with tears as she touched her glass to his. 'I'm so happy. I can't wait for our wedding day . . .'

Mark put down his glass and kissed her softly on the lips. He smiled into her eyes, his fingertips caressing the curve of her cheek. 'We have Christmas presents to deliver on Christmas Eve and then we can go home to your father's house and get ready for the wedding. I've got the special licence in my pocket and everything is arranged.'

'I haven't done anything, except choose a dress,' Angela said. 'You and my father have done it all.'

'Well, it gave us both a lot of pleasure to do it,' Mark said. 'You've been busy, Angela – but you did make time to write and tell your mother about the wedding I hope?'

'Yes, I did. I don't think she will come, but I knew I must ask – and I have, but don't hold your breath.' Angela grimaced. 'I'm not sure I really want her to come, in the circumstances, but she is my mother.'

'Yes, she is,' Mark said. 'If you let the breach widen you would never forgive yourself, Angela.'

'No, I suppose not,' Angela said. 'That is such a pretty cut-glass vase the staff bought for us, Mark. It will look lovely on that table in the hall. The one I used to have there was broken, so I think I'll stand it on the table.'

'You can do that later,' Mark said and put his arms around her. 'Come to bed, Angela. I've wanted to be alone with you all night . . .'

Angela stood listening to the choir of staff and children singing carols. The sound of their voices raised in praise to God was beautiful and brought tears to her eyes. Mark had finished giving out the presents and gone off to change out of his Santa suit, though apart from a few of the very small children they all knew it was him dressed up to give out their gifts.

Excitement had reigned for the past hour, but now they were all standing quietly listening to the carols before everyone trooped into the dining room for sausage rolls, mince pies, fairy cakes, orange juice, lemonade and sherry or wine for the adults. Some of their supporters had been invited to listen to the carols and so Mark had decided they'd better have wine as well as sherry.

She turned to him as he came to join her with a smile of welcome. 'Feel better to get out of that thing?'

'The beard tickles a bit,' Mark admitted, 'but I

wouldn't miss this for the world, Angela. To see those kids' faces when they tear the paper off . . . it's priceless.'

'It's heartbreaking to think that, for some of them, this is the only proper Christmas they've known. Before they came here many of them had never been given a present or a toy; they had poor diets and second-hand clothes. You've transformed their lives, Mark.'

'I didn't do it alone,' he said. 'I'll admit it was my idea to get something started when I saw how badly a place like this was needed – but there were many others who helped, like my colleagues on the Board who contributed, and above all you and Sister Beatrice.'

'But you're the one who cared enough to drive it forward,' Angela said, squeezing his arm. 'And we shall get that holiday home you want, if not next summer then the one after.'

'Yes, with you by my side, I'll make sure of it,' Mark said. 'I love kids, darling – all sorts of kids, regardless of colour, creed, pretty or ugly, it's all the same to me. I simply want to make them happy . . .'

'Good,' Angela turned to kiss him on the lips as the lights went up, signalling the end of the carol concert. Angela's kiss was plain for everyone to see, and the sight was greeted by some giggling and then a cheer and then clapping from the children. Angela laughed and would have moved away, but Mark held her tight and kissed her thoroughly and everyone laughed.

'And now that we've proved how much we love each other to all and sundry, I think we'd better go and feed them all,' Mark said and led the way into the dining room where a table laden with as much festive food as could be managed, with some rationing still in place even now, was waiting for them.

Mark filled wineglasses and sherry glasses, smiling as everyone came up to him, remarking how well things had gone.

'Yes, we're very pleased,' he said and raised his glass. 'First of all I want to thank all the staff for their efforts, today and every day of the year – and in particular Sister Beatrice, whom we are very glad to have back with us after her illness. I would also like to thank Angela for all her efforts and, indeed, each of you, our supporters and friends, for caring that our children have the kind of life all children should be entitled to but sadly aren't.'

'Hear, hear!' several voices chorused.

'And so it only remains for me to wish all of you – our guests, our staff and most of all the children in our care – a very happy Christmas and may 1949 be a wonderful year for all of us here at Halfpenny Street!'

'To St Saviour's and all associated with her,' Father Joe said and sipped the good Irish whisky Mark had provided for his benefit. 'May God and Christ be with us now and always . . .'

St Saviour's
will give them hope…

When there is nowhere to turn…

One place will give them hope.

The **Orphans** of **Halfpenny Street**

CATHY SHARP

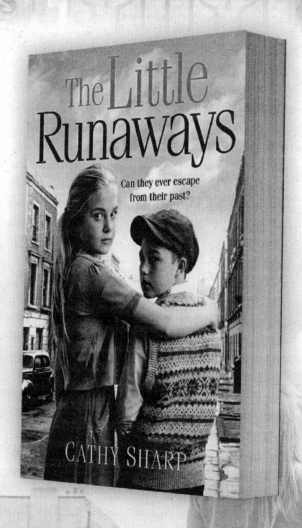

Don't miss the first two books
in the Halfpenny Street series,
both AVAILABLE TO BUY NOW